SOMEONE TO WALTZ WITH

BARBARA BRYANT

'In every parting there is an image of death'
– George Eliot: Scenes of Clerical Life (1858)

PROLOGUE

CHRISTMAS EVE 1970

Through the leaded panes of the kitchen window the light faded as the early dusk deepened and turned to midwinter dark. She moved across the room and rested against the warmth of the Aga.

The silence was intense, tangible, in the empty house.

The old dog pushed his head against her trousers, nudging for attention. She reached down and ran her hand along the length of his backbone. 'Now, old friend, let's tackle the vegetables.'

She dropped the supermarket's ready-washed potatoes and leeks onto the draining board. What a blessing after the mud-ridden ones of years ago.

She eased her shoulders back, resting one hand on the white draining board. The sanitised vegetables lay there, temporarily forgotten, as she gazed out beyond the blackening window, seeing back into the past, on a journey of erratically connected memories.

Arriving home for that magic childhood Christmas, when wicked Long John made them laugh so. Listening to the first litter of pigs squealing with new life in the old brick shed beside the river. The river flooded brown and swollen, lapping at the gate during the bad, black days. Watching the dawn with Nancy and Philip that September morning. Nancy, and then Nancy and Philip together again at home, little Angela swamped in a child's bed in their second spare room.

'So long ago.' The dog reacted to her voice, and heaved himself up to come across to her. She patted him. 'Shall we have a cup of tea to cheer us up?'

She pulled the old Parker Knoll chair closer to the kitchen table and nibbled at one of the mince pies. She'd been so looking forward to the ease of just the two of them, to a simple, cosy, undemanding Christmas. Then, during this afternoon, the sense of aloneness had crept up on her, until now she felt hollow-tummied, sad inside.

She passed the end of the mince pie to the dog, who made a mess of eating it, dropping crumbs on the tiled floor. She leaned down to retrieve the bits and thought it was just as well Tess wasn't there because she'd be sure to disapprove. The other two wouldn't have minded, not noticed even. The children were good friends, no sibling rivalries. When she had told them the truth about Angie's mother, she'd left the bit about her father blank, mirroring what was on the child's birth certificate.

'Better that way. Much better, to let some of our secrets die with us.'

She patted the dog. 'This, old dog, will not do.' She reached up to the radio kept on the top of the fridge, switched it on. 'I love Christmas and I'm going to enjoy it.'

The crystalline voices of the King's College choirboys rang out. She stood up, took a deep breath and sang with the choir: '*It came upon the midnight clear, that glorious song of old, from angels bending near the earth…*'

She didn't hear the car pull onto the gravelled drive, nor the back door open.

CHAPTER 1
NOVEMBER 1918

THE COALS CRACKLED, hissed and flared up. The hem of the starched petticoat itched against the back of her knees. She fidgeted and hooked her blue patent-leather shoes round the chair legs, and fingered the coarse brown wool. 'Won't the soldiers find these blankets scratchy, Mummy?'

'Soldiers have rough skin, Katherine. And the trenches are cold and muddy.'

She slid out of the chair and began to sort the knitted squares into neat piles of grey and brown on the soft carpet.

'I've done masses – enough to make a blanket. Can I go back upstairs?'

'When Nanny is ready. Finish one more square before bedtime.'

'This wool feels horrid and it's horrid colours. Anyway, Nanny said the war is nearly over.'

But she sat back down and picked up a skein of mud-coloured wool. She tied the end into a knotted circle round one needle and pushed the other one through the loop. Short lines of uneven plain stitches began to grow into a lopsided square.

The sound of footsteps in the corridor outside, then the double rap on the door before Nanny stepped into the room. Her crisp white uniform matched the white in her hair.

'Is everything all right?' Mummy's voice was sharp, suddenly sharper.

'Yes, madam. He's taken the medicine.'

'Nanny, remember you said I can practise reading to Peter tonight.'

'Yes, Kitty dear, I know.' Nanny held out her hand. 'Up we go.'

Once the drawing room door closed behind them she asked, 'Why does Peter have medicine?'

There was a slight pause. 'To keep him well, dear.'

'I don't have medicine.'

'Peter has a weak chest.'

At teatime last Sunday, Mummy and Granny had been talking, whispering, about Peter having to go to another doctor.

'But Nanny, last… '

'Come along now. Up those stairs or Peter will be asleep before you get there.'

He was not asleep. He was sitting up in bed, flaxen curls bright against the white linen.

'Look!' He held up his sketchpad. 'I drew a horse.' He focused two violet-blue eyes on Nanny. 'This is what I want – a proper rocking horse. Will you tell Mummy and Daddy, please?'

Nanny was straightening the sheets. She stood up. 'Young man, you know very well your mother said rocking horses are dangerous.'

When Nanny was safely out of the room, Peter giggled.

'You dared me, and I did it. They won't say no. If they do, I shall spit out my horrid medicine.'

'Oh, Peterkin, don't. It's to keep you well.' Although he looked well enough already, his cheeks pink. 'I hope they give in, then you can be St George and I can be the dragon chasing you.'

She climbed onto the side of the bed. 'Shall I try to read or shall we talk?'

'Talk. Just pretend to be reading when Nanny comes back.'

. . .

Every day Peter drew another horse. Then he began to paint in the colours – shiny black coats and red reins – and wrote *This is the horse we want*, and gave the pictures to Mummy.

Until one morning, Pa came up to the nursery. He was in his lawyer's black jacket and high starched collar, the things he wore when he went to court.

'Mummy's right. No rocking horse.'

'Why can't we have a rocking horse, Pa?' She was disappointed and surprised. Often Pa allowed her to do things that Mummy disapproved of, like putting a sugar lump in an orange and sucking the juice through the sweetness or playing croquet with a tennis ball on the lawn and roaring with laughter when the ball rocketed into the flowerbeds.

'Because they are big and heavy. You, or worse, Peter, might fall off and get hurt.'

Peter hurt?

'We won't. We will be careful. Pa, please.'

'No, my little Kitten. I'm sorry, but no. Now, I must go to work.'

Next Sunday Pa's brother came up to the nursery. Uncle Bertie lived with Granny because he wasn't married. He was a lawyer, like Pa. He sat down and listened carefully while they told him about the rocking horse.

'I expect your mother's worried. I am sure I can persuade my daredevil brother easily enough. I'll see what I can do.'

Kitty crept downstairs after him, and hid outside the drawing room doorway.

'They are children. They must have some fun.' Uncle's voice was quite clear.

'They are too young. They'll have an accident.' Mummy sounded cross.

'Kitty is eight now, and Peter's very mature – way beyond his ten years, sometimes I wonder... well, never mind that. You can't wrap him in cotton wool. It won't work. I shall give them a rocking horse, Dorothy.'

She ran back up to the nursery. 'We're going to get a horse, Peterkin. Uncle said so.'

Three weeks later a dark green Harrods van edged up the driveway, its roof just scraping under the branches of the cedar tree. Beside her Peter leaned forward, pressing up against the glass of the nursery windows.

'Now, children, you must not let me down.' Uncle's hand was firm on her shoulder. 'I've said you'll be sensible.'

'We will. We promise. Don't we, Kitty?'

'Yes. Oh, yes. Please, can we unpack it now, before you go?' She pulled at Uncle's hand, drew him back from the window. 'It's going to live in the corner, away from the fire, Nanny said.'

'Not *it*,' Peter reprimanded. 'He'll be our proper horse, with a name.'

It took two men, caps under their arms, to carry the massive box up the two flights of stairs to the nursery.

'Let's meet your new friend. Decide whether he's a Ned or a Black Beauty.'

The horse was definitely not a Black Beauty.

'Oh, look, he's brown, all except for his ears.' The pitch-black ears were large and pricked forward. 'They're soft inside. Just like a real horse. Look, Peterkin, he's excited, he likes it here.'

Peter gazed for a moment. 'His coat is shiny, like a new conker.'

'Ladies first.' Uncle lifted her onto the saddle. 'Now lean forward a little, and then back.'

'Ooh!' she cried as the horse moved on its rockers. She clutched the soft brown locks of the mane, and tried again.

'Remember, only the rider is allowed to make the horse move.'

Uncle turned to Peter, bent down to lift him up. 'Your turn.'

'I can manage on my own, thank you.' Peter clutched the saddle, and levered himself up. He rocked the horse and then leaned forward, patting between the ears.

'Good boy!' Peter looked towards the door. 'Mummy, look! This is Conker.'

Mummy was standing in the doorway. She crossed the room, coming to stand beside the horse, and smiled up at Peter sitting astride it.

'I can make him trot.' Peter bounced and the horse rocked forward bringing the outsized ears level with Mummy's face.

She took a step back. 'The ears are sharp – they're very pointed.'

Uncle Bertie leaned against the bookcase and watched as they took turns riding. When they unsaddled the horse and started brushing its long tail with an old hairbrush, he gathered up his jacket and said, 'I must go. Be good and careful now.'

Conker helped Robin Hood rescue Maid Marian; he went into battle with a banner (an old mop) held high; he carried Peter across the plains of America, outrunning the cowboys; and sometimes he stood still, watching them while they talked. Of course, he needed feeding and grooming for hours at a time.

All was well until one afternoon when Nanny was downstairs making nursery tea. Peter wanted Conker to win the Grand National.

'Faster Kitty! Push him.' Peter waved his arms at her. 'Properly! Not like a little girl. Do it properly!'

Stung, Kitty jumped onto the front of the rocker. The horse's head lurched downwards and Peter shot over it, falling with a thump.

'You silly girl! Why didn't you wait till I'd got his reins?' And then as she started to cry, he added. 'It doesn't matter. All jockeys fall off.'

He was rubbing his arm, and there was a gash on his cheek oozing blood.

Feet, lots of them, running along the passageway. Nanny and Mummy appeared at the same time.

'Whatever has happened?' Mummy ran to Peter.

White-faced and bleeding, Peter took command. 'Kitty, help me up. Now, Mummy, don't panic. My horse shied, he was frightened.'

Later, after Peter had been patched up and calm restored in the nursery, Nanny said Kitty should go downstairs to say goodnight.

She was about to knock on the drawing room door.

'That horse must go.' Mummy's voice was shrill through the heavy polished wood. 'Peter says the horse shied. He won't say anything else. I expect Kitty pushed him. He went right over the horse's head and the ears cut his cheek. I wish your brother had never bought the thing.'

Pa's voice, quiet, but easy to hear. 'I am sure it was a shock, but fortunately no real harm is done.'

'No harm! How can you say that? He's frail. Something like this could kill Peter in his condition. That horse must go.'

Kill Peter? Peter die? Conker go?

No.

She pushed the door open.

'It was my fault. I won't do it again. I promise. We love Conker.' Gulping back tears now. 'I don't want Peter to die.'

'Kitten!' Pa scooped her up into his arms, holding her so tight that his heart beat against her ribs. 'Don't cry. Mummy has had a shock, and you, too. Now, let's dry those tears.'

Over her head, he said, 'Dorothy, I'm sure they have learned their lesson. We'll say no more about it. I'll pour you a sherry and take Kitty back up to Nanny.'

Upstairs, she snuggled down between the sheets, warm and safe. Nanny's soft hands smoothed the hair back from her face.

'You won't go will you, Nanny? You won't let Peter die, will you?'

'Ah, dearie, whatever makes you ask that? Of course I won't go. Now, what shall we do tomorrow?'

'Go for a walk up on the Downs.'

Next afternoon they arrived home tired and windswept after walking along the chalk ridgeway, taking turns to push Peter's heavy chair.

Upstairs the coal fire was burning brightly and the table was set for nursery tea, near to Conker's corner.

'Conker!' She ran across the room.

Nanny, puffing from carrying Peter up the stairs, set him down and stood catching her breath.

'What's the matter?' Peter asked.

'His ears! They've sawn off his ears.'

He ran across, clutching out at her hand.

'Don't cry, Kitty.'

Then his face puckered. Nanny remained in the doorway, momentarily transfixed.

Peter was inconsolable. And angry. He refused to eat his tea or even to sit at the table.

'You must, dear. You will be ill if you don't eat.'

'I will be sick if you make me.'

Ill? He mustn't get ill. But he'd never give in. And Kitty's own tummy was rumbling. How to make him change his mind, eat something. And then the idea came.

'If we eat our tea, we could… ' She stood on tiptoe, whispered.

'Shh! All right.' Peter turned to Nanny. 'Will you go downstairs now, please Nanny. I'll eat my tea.'

Nanny hesitated but then she nodded and left the room.

'I'll get the things, you eat this.' Kitty stuffed two sardine sandwiches into her mouth, put two more on Peter's plate, and got his brushes and some pots of poster paint from the toy cupboard.

He chose the biggest brush, opened the red paint, and slapped it on the raw stumps where the beautiful soft black ears had been.

'It's going on the carpet.'

'Serves them right. I hate Mummy. He's our horse. I hope her horrid carpet is ruined.'

Using his foot, he rubbed more red paint into the soft blue rug.

'Quick, she's coming back. More, Kitty. More on that ear, and down his face.'

They scuttled back and were sitting at the table, sandwiches in hand, when Nanny opened the door.

'Children! What have you done? Whatever will your mother say?'

The paint covered the sawn-off stumps and was running down

the horse's face, dripping off its nose, making a spreading patch on the rug.

'I am very angry with Mummy. Poor Conker is hurt. He is bleeding. We have used all my red paint, and the brown.'

'Peter's eaten his tea.'

That evening Pa came up to the nursery to inspect the damage. Tall above Kitty, he stood beside the horse, his face expressionless.

He looked from her, to the carpet, to the horse, and back.

Pa was never angry.

'I'm sorry, Pa. Please don't be cross with us, Peter did eat his tea.'

'Cross? I'm not cross, Kitten.'

Then she saw his eyes were twinkling. His moustache twitched and the familiar smile appeared. 'You have been busy. It's very realistic.'

Later Pa came up to read her bedtime story. He turned the page only once before he put the book to one side. 'I don't want you worrying. It's my job to look after Peter. Mummy's too, and Nanny's, but not yours.'

CHAPTER 2
AUGUST 1922

UNCLE BERTIE PROPOSED A PICNIC LUNCH, with brass-tray racing down the slopes of the Downs, at Chanctonbury Ring, as a treat on her twelfth birthday.

'Like when we were boys.' Uncle grinned at Pa.

'The weather is too hot; it is not good for Peter.' Mummy looked cross.

'Please, Mummy.'

'I should like to watch,' Peter said. 'It's Kitty's day, she must choose.'

'My dear, we shall be fine,' Pa said. 'With us out of the house you'll be able to get ready for Kitty's tea party.'

So they set off in Pa's big car, with Peter's chair in the boot. Her presents had to wait until teatime, with the birthday cake.

They ate the picnic in the shade of the trees at the bottom of the slope.

'Come on, Kitty.' Uncle picked up one of the old brass butler trays, handed her the other and together they walked up the steep slope of soft downland turf.

They squatted down onto the trays, anchoring themselves with feet and hands firmly on the chalky ground.

'Off we go!' Bertie lifted his feet in the air, then tucked them onto the tray, and began to slide downhill bumping over the short dry grass. He cheered and held up his thumb as they gathered speed.

Her tray sped down the hill towards Pa and Peter at the bottom of the slope.

Peter clapped. 'Come on, Kitty! You're winning.'

Pa waved his cane in the air, cheering.

Halfway down, Uncle swept past her, feet in the air, racing away until his tray hit a ridge and bucketed over. She slid past swishing on down to the bottom.

'Well done!' Peter was bouncing around in his chair. 'Uncle, she won.'

'Those damn stones.' Rubbing his backside, he turned to Pa. 'This is a wild game. The stones hurt a good deal more than they used to!'

'The best of three – that's what you said, Uncle.' Peter stood up, unbalancing the chair so Pa had to grab at it. 'Go on. Do it again.'

She and Uncle climbed back up to the top of the ridge. The sun was burning hot on her head.

'You look hot, and I'm parched.' He squeezed his knees up to his chest, fitting on the tray. 'Ready! Steady! Go!'

Her tray hit the lumpy ground ahead, pitching her onto the grass. She sat up, gingerly touching her stinging knee.

Uncle was already at the bottom.

What was happening?

Uncle and Pa were bending over Peter's chair.

She scrambled upright, grazes forgotten, and ran on down.

'Steady, old man.' Pa's voice was sharp. 'Where's that bloody phial?'

Peter's face was blue. He wasn't breathing properly, an awful rattling sound coming out instead. Pa sprinkled something onto a handkerchief and pressed it to Peter's face.

Uncle put an arm round her shoulders.

'Your father's used the stuff. He'll be all right now.'

The rattling stopped, the blue faded, but Peter's face was grey and dripping with sweat.

'God almighty! Let's get into the shade,' Pa ordered.

'What's happened, Uncle?'

'Shh. Peter can hear.'

Pa wiped Peter's face with his handkerchief and then his hands.

'Well done, old boy. Very brave.' Pa straightened up, and mopped his own forehead. 'Must have been the heat, and the excitement.' He held out a hand. 'Come here. Your Peterkin needs a kiss.'

She stepped forward, holding tightly onto Pa's hand, and planted a cautious kiss on Peter's clammy cheek. Silent and subdued, the four of them set off for home.

Mummy was waiting at the foot of the front steps.

Pa lifted Peter from the car and her welcoming smile turned into grim, cold lines as she looked at Peter. She didn't speak, didn't even say hello, but silently followed Pa as he carried Peter upstairs.

'Let's ask your cook for a drink.' Uncle led the way towards the kitchen.

Cold and queasy, she started to tremble, so much she had to sit down in Mrs Bird's chair by the range. Peter's repeated visits to doctors, his days in bed, and the outings when he was confined to his chair had become more frequent recently. But when she asked if he felt ill he invariably replied no, not at all, just tired.

'There, there, miss.' Mrs Bird was red in the face from the cooking and smelt faintly of raw onions but her ample arms felt solid, warm and comforting as they tightened around her shoulders. 'You have a good cry, let it out.'

The birthday tea party was abandoned. The cake left for another day, her presents stacked on the corner table in the dining room.

In the early cool of the evening Pa suggested they go to see Granny. They walked past the stern stonework of St John's church, where they went every Sunday morning with Mummy, and then along the wide pavements with the houses hidden from the road by cedar trees and banks of rhododendrons.

As they walked, Pa talked.

Sometimes they paused, stopped walking, because what Pa was saying was difficult to take in, and once because he had to get out his handkerchief.

Granny opened the front door herself.

'My dears!' She hugged Kitty, and looked directly at Pa. 'Edgie, your brother's waiting for you in his study with tea or something stronger.'

Granny's snug was her inner sanctum, crammed with books and needlework. The room was warm in winter, with thick red velvet curtains and a coal fire. In summer the windows, framed now with curtains of cornflower-blue chintz, were thrown open, and the coals in the fireplace replaced by pots of geraniums.

Photographs of her family were everywhere. The large silver-framed one of her husband and their two sons had pride of place on her writing desk. And beside it was the one of a very young-looking Granny and Grandpa on their wedding day. Kitty couldn't really remember Grandpa who had died when she was little.

'Bertie told me what happened.' Granny pushed a wisp of grey hair back into place. She sat forward in the wing chair. 'I've known for some time and thought you were owed the truth.'

No words came. She looked directly into the familiar face with its watery eyes.

'Darling, don't try to be brave.'

'Pa cried a bit.' Kitty swallowed. 'Oh, Granny, I knew… you know… sort of knew. Peter's so brave, he never complains. Not even today. Pa told me everything. He said Peter will get iller, worse. No one can do anything, they can't mend the hole in his heart. One day it will just stop.'

She struggled on, sniffing, fiddling with her hankie. 'Pa said he and Mummy think I should go away to school. Granny, I want to stay with Peter, until… '

The tears engulfed her. Granny pulled her into her arms.

'Supposing he dies when I'm away.'

By the time they crossed the hallway in search of Pa and Uncle Bertie, Granny's silk blouse was sodden, but the talking had helped. The lonely, long-pent-up, unspoken fears and emotion inside eased a little.

There was a strong smell of Pa's favourite tobacco, despite the windows left open to catch the warm summer breeze. A blue and white cloud of delphiniums and gypsophila filled the wide hearth.

Pa and Uncle Bertie stood propping up the mantelpiece, one on each side. Like two bookends. Only Pa was taller, and was wearing his new white and tan shoes. And that yellow silk cravat.

Uncle Bertie, tapping out his pipe into the big green ashtray, glanced across at her and immediately went back to work on his pipe, using his silver penknife to scrape around the barrel.

She went towards Pa. He reached out for her hand. His face, looking downwards into hers, was lined, older. No one spoke. She must break the silence.

'I'll go away to school, Pa, if it helps. Granny's right, it will be nice to make friends. She said if I go this term I will be back for Christmas.' She pulled her hand away from Pa's, twisted her fingers around her wrists. 'Please may I be the one who tells Peter?'

And so it was. Mummy insisted on hiring a car to take her to school at the start of term but came by train to collect her for the four weeks of the Christmas holidays. It was a crisp afternoon, and a watery sun was still just slanting through the big trees on the drive beside the house as they arrived home after the long journey.

'You do look grown up.' Peter kissed her on both cheeks, kept hold of her hands, but stepped back, scrutinising her.

'It's the uniform, and these horrid woollen stockings.'

'You are happy there, aren't you? Not covering things up in the postcards you write?'

'Really, really happy. After the first couple of nights. My best friends are Liz – her mother's an actress, and Emma, who lives in St Peter Port, you know, in the Channel Islands.'

'Come on upstairs. Nanny and I've decorated the nursery.'

They had transformed it into a grotto of holly, ivy and paper chains.

A strange voice shrieked, 'Shan't.'

'He won't finish the words.' Peter went over to a huge birdcage. 'Now Long John, be a good boy, say "happy" for Kitty.'

The bird strutted along his perch, tapping his beak on a metal bell suspended from the bars of the cage.

'He looks haughty.' She bent down to look more closely. The

vivid green feathers fluffed up. She stepped back quickly. 'How did you persuade Mummy to let you have one?'

'I asked Pa.'

'They always said no before.'

'I know. But it's different since my attack at Chanctonbury. Now they know I know.'

A grin spread across his face, and he lowered his voice. 'I'm trying to teach Long John to say things I'm not allowed. Like when Reverend Trott is here when I'm supposed to pray. I'm teaching him to say "It's time to go".'

'You wouldn't dare!'

'I do. It'll make me laugh and help me forget Trott's shammy words. It won't hurt anyone, they won't realise.'

'Oh, Peterkin.' She put her arms around him.

'Now, Kitty!' He pulled away from her. 'I'm going to have fun. I will enjoy every moment, everything that happens.'

Peter kept on trying to persuade Long John to say 'happy' but the bird steadfastly refused; each time it articulated clearly: 'Shan't, shan't, shan't'.

A week later Reverend Trott and his wife came to have nursery tea. Mrs Trott was a dull, untalkative woman whom Peter described as a bit of a woolly pear. All afternoon Long John was unusually silent, perching with his beak sunk into his bright green chest feathers.

'We should be going.' Both Trotts stood up.

Then Long John flapped his wings, strutted along the perch and in piercing falsetto tones shrieked, 'Time to go! Time to go!' Followed at once by 'Haaappeeee! Haaappeeee'. Not a glimmer of a smile on Peter's face. Kitty held back the giggles until the door closed, and then, bent double, they laughed and laughed, the tears running down both their faces.

In every way, it was a perfect Christmas. Snow fell on the Downs and Peter was well enough to go with them all to Granny's for Christmas lunch.

On her last day before going back to school, there was just enough daylight to have tea without turning on the electric lights.

'Oh, Peterkin, I'm longing to go back.' She reached across the table to squeeze his hand. 'I'll miss you horribly. But I do love school.'

CHAPTER 3

MARCH 1926

THE TRAIN PUFFED along in the valley at the foot of the South Downs. Ma hadn't insisted on coming on the long journeys to and from school since her fifteenth birthday. The first time she made the journey alone, she'd been nervous, worried lest she missed the right station to change trains. Nowadays she relished the time alone, enjoyed discreetly studying the other passengers and watching the countryside as it softened from the bleaker Midlands landscape towards home.

She filled the hours by doing some of her holiday prep, and then by dozing off towards the end of the journey. Up until the moment when the engine chugged onto the viaduct across the estuary at Shoreham. The sound of the wheels rattling over the steelwork heralded home. School was forgotten, home beckoned.

Now she looked down through the girders at the low-tide expanse of mud below, where curlews, and even a heron, were mining for lugworms.

The train wound its way below the great rounded hills. The sun, sharp and bright in the spring sky, lit the trunks of the birch trees so they shone silver under crinolines of twiggy branches. In the crisp light of the cloudless March morning, the bursting buds on the boughs glowed red.

The train slowed, the rhythm of its wheels lengthening. She stood up, pulled on her hat, checked in the compartment's mirror and adjusted it – at school it must be straight, here she could put it as Liz had shown her, at a slight angle. She gathered up her gloves and dressing case. With a final jolt the train stopped. The nice old porter, the one who had been gassed in the war and who wheezed alarmingly when he pushed the trolley, was walking along the platform opening compartment doors.

They were both there.

'Mummy! Peterkin!'

'Katherine, how tall you've grown!' It was true; she needed to bend slightly to kiss Ma.

Peter, abandoning his chair, looked slighter than ever but mature, even rakish, sporting a red silk cravat, his hair parted in the middle.

'I like your hat,' he said. 'Mummy's arranged a proper supper party for us. Granny and Uncle Bertie are coming.'

It was indeed a proper party. Candles flickered on the glass and silver. A long low arrangement of hothouse flowers stretched along the middle of the table. Cold cucumber soup, some sort of white fish folded into a box-shape, and then their very favourite, roast pork.

Even before he picked up his knife and fork Peter took the crisp crackling in his fingers and crunched it loudly. Ma saw, frowned disapprovingly across the table.

Peter gave one of his wide smiles, but muttered under his breath, 'It's my treat, my crackling, I'll eat it first if I want – before I die.'

No one else had heard. She began to talk quickly. 'We've started dancing lessons at school.'

After the pudding, the two of them left the grown-ups to port and peppermint teas.

Once they were upstairs, she stretched her legs out, wriggling off first one shoe, then the other.

'You're wicked, suppose Mummy had heard.'

'I whispered it, and they were all talking. Only you heard.'

'Just as well. She'd have had hysterics, ruined the party.'

'It was my crackling. I shall eat it first if I want,' he said, and then added, 'I don't have to pretend with you. It is true, Kitty, it may happen that way – that I just die halfway through doing something.'

'I know, but because it's true you must be careful about saying it.'

'All right. Sorry. Now tell me everything.'

She did. About how they were going to do a Gilbert and Sullivan opera as the school summer play, how poor Liz felt ill, really ill, every month when she got the curse, and how Emma had a boyfriend at home in Guernsey but her mother didn't know, and about the dancing.

'We partner each other, it seems odd dancing with another girl. Waltzing is my favourite.'

'Show me!'

'Not now – we need music, and they'd hear. We'll do it properly one day before I go back next term.'

They talked until they heard Uncle Bertie cranking up his car, Pa wishing Granny goodnight and the bolts pushed to on the front door.

'Quick, Peterkin. Pretend you're asleep. When they've gone to bed, I'll come back.'

The next morning she felt horribly tired but Peter said he wasn't, even though they had talked until there were streaks of pink in the eastern sky.

'I don't need much sleep, Kitty. I often read all night. Or sketch, and paint it in as the daylight comes.'

The weather turned warmer. The countryside developed a mist of green and the daffodils in the garden nodded in the soft southerly breeze.

Kitty and Peter set off for a picnic near the big windmill, Peter's chair, doubling as a cart, loaded up with a packed lunch, his easel and paints and, at Ma's insistence, a waterproof picnic rug.

Sitting in his chair, Peter sketched out the shape of the mill, the squat body of the building dwarfed by the four blades. Kitty watched, idly making a daisy chain, as the picture on the easel took shape, the clump of trees on the top of the Down easily identifiable. Peter dipped the brushes in and out of the colours on his palette, screwing up his eyes against the sunlight as he studied the windmill.

'I'm tired.' He began to pack up his paints. 'I want to see if there are bluebells. Do you mind pushing me through the woods?'

The first bluebells misted the ground on both sides of the deep pathway, the faint haze of blue stretching up the slopes and into the thicker woodland. The sweet delicate scent wafted towards them.

'Will you pick some, Kitty?'

She knelt, feeling down into the grass, snapping off the stems. She left the chair perched on the uneven track and stepped towards a tall clump with one white flower in its midst. She trod onto the young bracken, its new fronds still brown and curled up. Like a snake. Snakes? Adders were drawn out of hibernation by the warm spring sun. Clutching the bluebells she jumped back onto the path.

'Remember those scabious you picked for me from the Downs last summer?' Peter held out his hand for the flowers. 'Thank you. I can smell a bonfire.'

As she pushed the chair on along the rutted path, she too smelt the woodsmoke strong above the scent of the bluebells. The path widened and levelled off to a flat grassy clearing.

She stopped, ready to turn back. 'Oh, it's travellers.'

'No, they are Romany people.'

On the far side of the clearing there was a gypsy caravan, a painted one, with the wooden shafts resting on the grass. The smoke from a campfire spiralled above the trees. A shaggy-coated brown and white horse cropped at the grass and hens were scratching at the rough ground.

Kitty hesitated, about to turn the chair back, when a woman with a black shawl round her shoulders, her grey skirt brushing on the ground, appeared from behind the caravan. Her face was weathered, deeply tanned.

She smiled. Peter stood up out of the chair.

'Good afternoon. May I stroke your horse?'

The woman smiled, nodded, muttered some words Kitty couldn't understand, and nodded again.

The horse lifted its head as they approached, but then stood, impassive and unresponsive while they stroked its neck.

The woman came over, holding out two carrots and pointed to the horse.

'Oh, thank you!' As Kitty took the carrots the horse pushed towards her. She held out her hand, carefully flat, and felt the hairy muzzle gather in the carrot.

She handed the second one to Peter. He reached up, patted the horse, let it nose into his jacket and watched as the creature smelt out the carrot.

Peter coughed, wheezed, and reached out to Kitty who helped him back to his chair. He said, 'Give her the bluebells. Go on.'

She wiped her hands on the sides of her skirt and took the flowers from the basket.

'Would you like these for your caravan?'

The woman looked directly at Peter. She took the flowers, stepped close, split the bunch and handed half to him. In English, she said, 'For your journey.'

It was long past teatime when Kitty finally turned the chair into the driveway at home. The gravel was thick, newly topped up while they were out, too thick to push the chair, so Kitty walked backwards up the drive, hauling the chair.

'Ma's standing by the front door.'

'On the lookout for us!' Peter muttered.

'What a long time you've been.' Ma bent close to Peter. 'Did you have a nice time, dear? You weren't cold, were you?'

'The sun is hot.' Peter screwed up his face. 'Don't fuss. Anyway, I'm going to… '

'Peterkin!' She looked hard at him. 'Show Mummy your picture of the windmill.'

He caught her look, hesitated, and then said, 'This evening I shall finish the picture to give to Kitty. Please arrange to have it framed.'

. . .

22

It was the sound of a car on the thick gravel drive below that woke her next morning. Through her bedroom window she saw the car going away from the house, rounding the bend of the drive. So early?

She put on the cotton frock from yesterday, didn't wash, just ran a comb through her hair and went downstairs. Pa was at the breakfast table, alone.

'What's happened?'

'Peter wasn't well in the night. Your mother is with him. The doctor's just left.'

She ran back upstairs, hesitated outside Peter's bedroom. No sound. She eased the door open and peeped round it.

Peter, his eyes closed, was propped high on pillows.

'Shh!' Ma put a finger to her lips.

'I'm not asleep.' Two violet-blue orbs, huge in the white and wizened face, opened wide for a second. 'Come back later Kitty, so we can talk.'

She stayed with Pa in the drawing room. They read the paper, tried to do the crossword and played silly, pointless games of cards.

They could hear the nurse moving around, going up and down the stairs with hot water, but by lunchtime there was still no sign of Ma.

'Pa, I want to be with Peter.'

'No, Kitten.' It seemed years since he had called her that. 'No, your mother doesn't want you – or me, for that matter – to go in, for fear we disturb him.'

She watched as he cut his omelette into tiny pieces, pushing the squares of cold deflated egg around his plate.

'I can't eat anything either. Let's go in the garden.'

The fresh air helped. She felt less queasy.

Pa stood, silent and still, his face turned towards the trees at the bottom of the garden. She reached for his hand.

'Peter and I have talked about it. He knows, and honestly he's not afraid.'

With a moan, a guttural, animal moan, he hugged her to him. She felt the tears, warm and wet, falling on her forehead, trickling down and joining the ones on her cheeks.

They went back into the drawing room at teatime. She poured the tea for Pa, and a cup for herself too, but she couldn't drink it. They sat, unspeaking, in the gathering dusk. The house was silent. She heard a door upstairs open, close.

Footsteps on the stairs. Not Ma's pattering but a man's feet, stopping in the hall.

No knock before the door opened.

The doctor came in. Without a jacket, his shirt sleeves rolled up.

She pushed past him to run up the stairs.

She turned the handle on the door to Peter's room.

The door wouldn't open. It was locked.

She stood for a moment, looking at the polished brown wood, at the round enamel doorknob.

'Peterkin!' she whispered, holding her face close to the door. 'I wanted to come back. So we could say goodbye. Talk properly.'

The tears coursed down her face.

Ma was there, on the other side of the thick door, crying.

'Let me in, Mummy!'

The sobbing got louder.

She lifted her hands, thinking to bang on the door to get Ma's attention.

Wrong! Wrong to disturb the dead.

She dropped them to her side.

The dead.

She clamped her hands over her mouth to stop the howl. She turned and stumbled back along the corridor.

In the safety of her own room she fell onto the floor and knelt against her bed.

'Dear God, keep him safe and happy.' She buried her head in the bedding.

Heavy shoes, a man's footsteps, up the stairs, along the corridor.

Pa's voice. 'Dorothy, let me in.' The words were softly spoken but clear enough to hear through her door. Louder, sharper, 'That's enough, let us in.'

Her mother's crescendo of wails stabbed at Kitty. She pulled the pillow down, held it over her ears. Still the scene went on unabated, with Ma's coarsened voice screeching strings of terrible words.

'Be quiet, woman. Think of Kitty, of the servants.' Another stream of abuse at Pa.

Pa shouting too, now. 'Be quiet!'

Banging echoed down the corridor. Someone was hitting Peter's door.

'Christ almighty! He is my son!'

Footsteps moving fast down the stairs. The front door banged.

Acid churned into her throat. She grabbed a towel and lurched across the passage to the lavatory before the vomit welled up into her mouth. She knelt on the floor, hands resting on the cold porcelain, sweating, shaking with cold.

She stood up and reached to pull the chain. She crept along to Peter's room and put her hands flat against the polished face of the door.

Is he still here? Is he dead? Suppose he isn't?

'I won't go.' Whispered louder now. 'I'm here. So we can talk if... ' Slowly she let her hands slide down the wood. She curled herself into a tight ball on the rough coconut mat.

Which was where Mrs Bird found her. 'Glory be! It's six o'clock! Wherever is your mother? You are as cold as ice. Tea, hot sweet tea, for you, my girl.'

Outside the rain drove down, steady and solid, out of a still, grey sky. Tears running down the panes of the nursery windows.

Inside, the room was bleakly empty. Immediately, brutally, this room, the heart of their years together, had been stripped of their past. Sanitised. Made cold. Conker's corner, which had become Long John's until the poor bird was jettisoned for fear its feathers carried disease, stood empty and bare.

His bedroom too, where the hospital bed and nursing paraphernalia had been, taken away so soon, too soon.

She stood back from the window – the hearse was coming up

the drive. She turned away, tried not to see the undertakers walking beside as it crept towards the house.

Black frock coats, black hats, black vehicle – don't look inside it.

Her own clothes black, too. Anything else was unthinkable.

Except that underneath her tightly buttoned coat she had put on her brightest jersey, the electric-blue cashmere one.

She pulled the nursery door closed behind her. Rested her hand on the banister rail, pulled her shoulders back and set off down the stairs to join the cortège waiting on the gravel outside.

Once in the church, the awful walk through endless rows of black in the pews beside the aisle completed, she sat between Ma and Pa.

Close, too close – yet so far – a lifetime away – the small white coffin. Alone. Surrounded by the cold stone of the pillars. The organ dirged on, pulling nasty chords in her gut. Reverend Trott intoned, endlessly, the sort of words Peter so hated. Beside her Ma wept noisily, though without the awful screamed abuse of the past few days.

'Let us pray.'

Again.

She knelt, but talked in her head. 'Peterkin, if it were me in that box, what would you do now? Undo your coat, show off the blue jersey, and insist they all sing a marching song? Sorry, I'm not as brave as you.'

The tears rolled down her cheeks. No noise, no gulping. Just water, running.

At the graveside, while all the heads were bent, eyes closed in the final prayers, she pulled the bunch of bluebells, kept in water in her room until today, from her coat pocket and dropped them onto the coffin.

'Good night, Peterkin, sleep tight.'

When they got back to the house, Ma ignored everyone, shut herself, wailing, in her bedroom.

In the dining room, purple rhododendrons decorated the

sideboard. Platters of sandwiches, sherry glasses and the slices of Madeira cake were set out on a purple tablecloth.

'Granny! I must go up to my room. Please come up with me.'

Upstairs, they sat on the bed. Granny's arm was warm around her shoulders.

'Talk to your father later, my dear. He's going to suggest you move after you finish school. Right away from the memories here.'

'We wouldn't be near you.'

'Darling, no, but you'd come to stay whenever you want. Think about it.' There was a catch in Granny's voice. 'Your father needs someone to do something for. Someone he can make happy.'

After the last of the lowered voices faded up the driveway, she washed her face, put a comb through her hair and crept through the silent house.

Where was Pa? In the drawing room? She peeped round the open door.

Alone. Silent. Staring out of the window. He turned.

'Have a glass of sherry.' He pushed the window open. 'At least the sun's come out, lifts the gloom a little. Thank you for being here and for being so sensible.'

Kitty sipped at the sherry. Its warmth hit her empty tummy.

'It's dreadful for your mother. She never ceases telling me it has been years of hell. He was my baby too. So much hope, so much love. Now nothing.'

'No, that's wrong. Not nothing.' She sat on the stool beside his chair. 'Don't listen to Mummy. Peter loved life, made it fun – like you do.'

Which was true, but mostly it was his confident honesty that had made his company so precious. And his wicked, irrepressible sense of humour.

'When we were in the church, I thought how he'd have hated the pompous solemnity – all grey and black. Peter was bright colours. You and I, we won't let them fade.'

CHAPTER 4

JUNE 1930

THE SOFT HILLS of the South Downs, etched clear in the early-morning sunshine of midsummer, gave way to the well-farmed fields and white-painted picket fences of Surrey. Their hired car had driven away from Worthing early, before breakfast, leaving Pa to lock up the emptied house, all the tangibles of their lives carefully wrapped in endless off-white paper and loaded into the Pantechnicon for the journey north. Except for the few boxes that would fit into the boot of the car, two overnight cases, and the packet propped beside her on the seat.

The journey into London was beastly, hot and fume-filled. They drove through Pimlico into the centre. As the motor car manoeuvred through the traffic, she felt her eyelids dropping, and abandoned any attempt at staying awake.

Something woke her. The crick in her neck hurt. Her mouth was parched dry in the heat of the car, and she had pins and needles in her right arm. She shifted her shoulders, eased her head up and peeped at Ma, who was fast asleep on the seat beside her, her smaller body allowing her head to rest on the leather upholstery, and looking a good deal more comfortable.

She wound down the window, letting fresh-smelling air blow over her face. The sun still shone, merciless, on the black metal of the car.

Flat fields reached away to the horizon. The road ran straight ahead with wide verges from which the drifts of cow parsley toppled onto the sticky tarmac. Not at all like the winding, sunken roads at home. No, not home. Not any longer.

Away across the fields, a touch of familiarity materialised in this alien landscape: a windmill. Its sturdy arms, white against the sharp blue of the open sky, dwarfing the stubby body.

Their overnight cases and the boxes from the boot of the car stood heaped on the edge of the gravel driveway by the steps leading up to the bright red front door.

She picked up her mother's dressing case and her own, and walked along the path through the shrubbery round to the back of the house.

'Where's my case?'

Catching the querulous tone in Ma's voice, she dumped her own case to free up a hand to turn the knob on the door into the scullery and walked along the passage by the kitchen with its new Formica cupboards and linoleum floor, past the boiler room with its faint, acrid smell of burning coke, and into the airy hallway.

Upstairs, Ma was already in the big bedroom. 'I don't know where to start. You'll have to help, not go wandering off round that garden. In Ceylon my mother had servants.'

How best to handle her? Sometimes charming and fun, occasionally loving, she so quickly became bitter when things didn't go her way.

'You look tired, Mummy. Why don't you take one of your powders?'

'I can't think why your father isn't here yet.'

'Oh, well, we left first.' She pulled the door shut firmly, not quite quietly, and went across the landing to her own room.

Sunshine poured through the window. There was a faint smell of new paint. Already a bluebottle had got itself the wrong side of the glass. She eased the fussing thing towards the open casement and pushed it on its way.

The garden had the full-blown look of late June, plants and

leaves billowing in the breeze. Beyond the lawns, the rose beds and the vegetable plot, a belt of trees stood tall against the sky.

Somewhere distant a church clock struck three.

Sorting through the tea chests stacked in the bedrooms, she found sheets and blankets. She opened her overnight case and put her nightie and washing things on the bed. Then she took the corrugated cardboard wrapping off the square packet. She rubbed the tarnished gilt of the frame. The windmill's white sails against a sapphire sky – she smelt again the smoke from the gypsy's fire. *Show Mummy the painting*. Their last day together. *Come back later*. But there hadn't been a later.

She propped the windmill painting on her dressing table.

A series of blasts on a klaxon-horn sounded from the drive below.

Pa's here…

She dashed down the stairs, opening the front door as the car crunched to a halt. She was lifting the handle on the driver's door even before he had switched off the ignition. He swung his long legs over the running board and stepped down onto the gravel. Kitty stretched up to put her arms round his neck.

'Well done Pa! Was the drive difficult?'

'No. This old girl went like a bird – fifty miles an hour after I cleared the outskirts of London. She topped seventy back there on the flat stretch. How's our new home?'

'Awfully nice. And modern, all white paint. Mrs Richards, she's our new cook, is here already making lunch. My room looks over the garden.'

The car's bodywork was covered in dust. There was a steady spiral of steam emerging from the radiator. 'Did she boil?'

'Of course not!' Pa sounded offended. He lifted up one side of the bonnet. 'Only what you'd expect after a long drive.'

He pointed into the greasy innards of the engine.

Kitty bent down, peered in.

A cough behind them.

'Dorothy, my dear! How hot it is. Is the house cool inside?' In two strides, Pa was leaning down to put an arm around Ma's waist. 'How clever you were to find this place.'

Kitty wandered off to explore. The path in the vegetable garden led through a latched gate into the wood. The wood was cool, the shaded ground still damp. She leant against the smooth trunk of a giant beech tree. In the sultry heat only the bees kept working. She stretched out her arms, turning her hands upwards to catch the dappled sunlight.

Her mood lifted in relief that Worthing with its neat streets, and their house with its brown woodwork and the memories of nurses and the pervasive smell of Dettol, were gone. No shadows of death loomed over this place. The idea of starting new, somewhere different, had been exciting – a bit like going away to school. Once Pa had found that Dobneys, solicitors near here, wanted a new partner to do the court work, Ma had begun looking for a house.

She dozed. Snapped awake at the sound of an expensive motor car coming up the driveway. She worked her way around to the back of the house, ran fingers through her curls in front of the mirror in the scullery and went along to the drawing room.

Ma was perched on the sofa beside a tall, unfashionably dressed woman with greying hair piled high in a wispy chignon.

Pa rose to his feet. 'Mrs Dutton, this is Kitty.'

'Welcome to Norfolk. I like everyone to call me Elma. My husband is rector here. The vicarage garden backs onto your wood. There's a gate through. Tennis isn't my thing but I don't like our court wasted so Kitty, do come across and use it.'

'Oh, I'd love to, thank you.'

'No young of our own, I'm afraid, but I do like to have the future around me.' Elma Dutton stood up, her long grey skirt almost touching the floor. 'I should let you all get on.'

Pa gazed as the engine revved and the Lagonda swept away. 'I can't imagine the Reverend's stipend pays for that expensive machine.'

'Pa, you're jealous!'

'She's not what I expect of a vicar's wife.' Ma's voice had lost its social tone, sounding petulant now.

Elma Dutton seemed a good deal more interesting, and

interested, than Reverend Trott's mouse of a wife. Don't say it, don't rock the boat. Change the subject.

'I'll pick a bunch of rhododendrons for the house.'

Avoiding the bees, she snapped the thick woody branches, choosing some pale apricot blossoms, their petals like soft tissue paper, and mixing them with a few of the harsher, brighter red ones.

A week later all the packing cases had been emptied and the pictures and books arranged so the house felt like home. The weather had held dry, hot too, but Ma had thrived, saying how her childhood in Ceylon taught her how to manage in the heat as she bustled around colonising Copse End.

'I'm going to explore the vicarage tennis court, Mummy. Everything here looks perfect now.'

She changed into her white linen tennis dress, slipped a navy cardigan over her shoulders and set off.

The gentle breeze ruffling the trees earlier had dropped. The afternoon sun, high in the sky, was hotter than she expected. The path wound through the trees, and opened out of the wood onto a stretch of uncut grass. The mown oblong of a tennis court lay a few yards away.

A cluster of people, their white tennis clothes vivid in the sun, were sitting on the veranda of an old summerhouse on the far side of the court.

'Come on over.' One of the girls stood up and waved. Kitty walked over to the building and gingerly went up the six wooden steps. The faded woodwork held the warmth of the sun. A stack of rackets, tennis balls, some cricket stumps and two bats stood in one corner.

'I'm Jo. Elma Dutton told us you'd moved in next door. We're practising for the Hunstanton tournament.'

Jo's handshake was firm. Freckles just showed on her un-made-up face. 'Will you join in a doubles game?' She called across to the two men who were perched on the balustrade: 'Come and meet Kitty.'

'This is Christopher Brownlow. He lives on a farm miles away, beyond Castle Rising.'

Christopher shook her hand, smiled. He looked too sophisticated to fit Jo's description. His clothes, expensively simple, well worn, were beautifully cut.

'And this is Alistair. I've known him for ever, he almost lives with us.'

Alistair, keen faced, with crinkly red hair, jumped down, offered a sweeping bow. 'At your service, m'lady.'

'Come, on, Kitty, let's beat these chaps! Best of ten games.'

Jo and Alistair, the two extroverts, sparred about while Christopher, calmer, less chatty, acted as a foil to their exuberance.

At five games all, Jo said, 'Come on, decider game.' They got to deuce three times before the girls won with a sneaky drop shot from Jo.

The victors and the vanquished sat in the shade finishing lemonade from the big china jug that stood with an odd assortment of tumblers on the felt-less card table in one corner of the summerhouse.

Jo bounced her racket on the end of her plimsolled feet. 'How about the four of us going in for the mixed doubles at Hunstanton? Alistair, you and I together. Kitty with Christopher.'

'Don't let Jo bully you. She's bossy.' Alistair tapped his racket on Jo's head. 'Known you too long, old girl.'

'If that's okay with you?' Christopher looked hot, his face flushed red, and his very English hair, mousy and straight, was flopping forward.

'Oh, yes, of course.'

'Jolly good.' Jo was standing up, brushing dried grass off her skirt. 'First, you must come over to my place. Meet my mama and things. Would your mother come, drive you over?'

'She doesn't drive, but I can borrow Pa's car I expect. Anyway, when… ' Too complicated. Not now, not to people I don't know. 'When we moved up here, to the country, my parents promised me a little car of my own, not wait till I'm twenty-one, so I'll soon be driving myself around.'

CHAPTER 5

JULY 1930

SHE SPENT some time checking her appearance in the full-length mirror beside her dressing table. The boiler suit fitted well, skimming her figure. She rolled the sleeves back a couple of turns, exposing neat, slightly tanned forearms. She undid the top two buttons at the neck so the blue of her jumper just showed.

'Now let's have a look at you!' Pa folded the newspaper and placed it on the breakfast table, scrutinising her. 'My word, that's very fetching.'

'Don't be sarcastic, Pa.'

'I'm not.' He winked. 'You look workmanlike and seductive.'

'Don't be coarse.' Ma didn't approve. 'When we promised you a car of your own I hadn't expected this sort of thing.'

Pa had organised with Mr Pither, who ran the garage in the High Street, to show her how to look after a car.

'But Mummy, we'll be able to take the car to Norwich, shop in Bonds.' Ma frequently bemoaned the lack of shops in Dereham but she liked the department store in the city.

'Yes, dear, but you must be careful.'

'She's had plenty of practice in the Ford,' Pa said. He had encouraged her to practise up and down the drive in Worthing, and then let her drive to tennis tournaments or friends, picked her up later. She had treasured those drives – alone, they talked freely, two grown-ups together.

'Won't take her long to get used to a modern car. Though you're right, of course – one day the government will introduce some sort of test before youngsters are allowed to drive.'

'I am not going to wear a skirt, not in the workshop.' Soften it for Ma. 'Don't worry, Mummy. It's only for a couple of weeks.'

Mr Pither's garage was in the old forge, converted into his workshop when the blacksmith moved away from the High Street. Rusting horseshoes still adorned the big double doors and the walls in one corner that were blackened from the furnace.

Inside Kitty sniffed at the fumy smell, a mixture of oil, paraffin and petrol. She tapped on the door of the cubbyhole where Mr Pither had his paperwork and the clumpy metal cash till.

'Here I am!'

Mr Pither, tweed jacket on top of neatly ironed overalls, stood up and pushed the stool under the paper-littered wooden shelf.

She felt his glance and thought his face lightened as if he were surprised, or maybe relieved, at her clothes. She said, 'I'll try not to hinder you. Try to be a bit helpful. Pass you the tools or something.'

'I've a big job on today. De-coking Dr Glaser's Ford. Had it for years, he has. Still it'll be handy for you, miss – you can see how the engine fits together as I take it down. Very precise your father was, said you've got to know how an engine works before he'll give you your own motor.' He riffled around in a cardboard box and pulled out a pair of gloves. 'You'll need these.'

She followed him through to the workshop. Puddles of thick oil lay on the dusty floor. Heavens! Oh, well, nothing for it now, and she stepped forward, placing well-polished leather lace-ups onto the sludge.

Mr Pither took the greasy black metal engine apart. He handed her the larger pieces, explaining what they were, but he laid the nuts and screws on the bench beside him.

The gloves were too big, long flapping tags on the end of her fingers, and she pulled them off.

He worked quickly but without hurrying and it surprised her how soon the innards of the engine were laid around the floor. He didn't stop for tea or anything but a couple of times he had to put down the tools, wipe the worst off his hands and go to serve petrol at the white Esso pump outside.

'We'll have broken the back of this by lunchtime.' He was lying flat on his back under the car, draining the sump.

From outside the sound of a throaty engine speeding along the road grew louder. The engine changed down into a lower gear and the car drew onto the forecourt outside.

There was a sudden and immediately suppressed mutter from Mr Pither. The legs sticking out from beneath Dr Glaser's Ford started to shift.

'Don't you stop,' Kitty said. 'Let me, I can work the petrol pump.'

'If you're sure, miss.'

Emerging into the bright sunlight, she blinked. A sports car, canopy down, was waiting at the pump. Too late she spotted the wiry red hair.

Oh Lord. Alistair. And his passenger. Straight brown hair, blown about, flopping over the broad face.

'Good God!' Alistair gasped and sat, mouth ajar, staring at her.

'Can that be my tennis partner?' Christopher Brownlow smiled and got out of the car, brushing the strands of hair back. 'Forgive Alistair. He has no manners at all. Didn't go to the right school.'

'Nothing wrong with admiring a pretty woman, old boy.' Alistair eased himself out of the driver's seat. 'You'll set a fashion in that thing, Kitty. What the devil are you doing here?'

'I'm learning a bit about how a motor car works. Helping out too.' She smiled and lifted the nozzle off the pump. 'How many gallons?'

'What?' Alistair remained rooted to the spot.

'Come on, old man, we're in a hurry, remember?' Christopher nudged Alistair.

'Ah, yes. Just a couple of gallons.'

She took the money, offered him a receipt and walked back into the workshop.

. . .

Mr Pither said it was a real help when she served petrol. She enjoyed the passing conversations with the drivers, watching as the pump registered the gallons.

Alistair's car appeared to need frequent, and rather small, amounts of fuel to keep it going.

By the end of two weeks at the garage, she could identify warning noises from engines, change spark plugs and fan belts and mend punctures on inner tubes.

'Thank you. I've enjoyed being here. I hope I wasn't too much trouble.'

'I'll give you a job any time, miss. Except young ladies don't work as mechanics!'

Why shouldn't women be mechanics, do this sort of thing?

'I'll be buying petrol when I get my car. Pa's promised me a Morris Minor.'

Curtains drawn back, the sun shone through the open window onto her face. By the date of her birthday, nearly two months after the longest day, the early morning sun was noticeably lower in the sky.

The coffee smelt good as she pushed the dining room door open. Ma's half-grapefruit, scraped empty, was pushed to one side. Pa was tackling his egg and bacon. They must have started early.

'Sorry. I didn't think I was late.' Two envelopes, cards of course, rested against her cup.

They chorused, 'Happy birthday!'

Pa handed her a package wrapped in expensive paper and tied with blue ribbon.

'This is our present.'

No car then!

She tried to cover the frisson of surprised disappointment with a wide smile and, to show enthusiasm, tore at the blue ribbon.

Pa returned to his egg. Ma was dabbing bits of butter onto one corner of her toast, eating that piece and then repeating the process.

Kitty lifted lumps of wadding out of the box. A single key fell on the table with a clatter.

Pa clapped his hands, roared with laughter. 'Fooled you! Look outside.'

Not a Morris Minor. A two-seater coupé! Its soft roof rolled back. Sleek lines. No cumbersome running board.

'Come on, both of you.' She led them, Ma's tiny soft hand and Pa's so large she held it only by the fingers, down the front steps.

The car's glossy navy paintwork gleamed in the sun. Beckoning her to independence. She was free to drive where she wanted, when she wanted. Able to give Jo a lift and to run errands for Ma, be a bit useful.

She reached down to put her arms around Ma's narrow shoulders and kissed the softly powdered cheeks, first one then the other.

'Not out here, in public!'

'Sorry, Mummy.'

Pa winked. She reached up and planted a kiss on his bristly cheek.

He leaned forward to open the driver's door, stood back. 'Your chariot awaits, ma'am!'

Soft new leather, warm from the sunshine. The polished wood on the dashboard.

Her body slid back onto the driver's seat.

She held the steering wheel in both hands, running them around it, and looked up at their smiling faces.

'Golly! Thank you so, so much. She's so sporty. And smart.'

'Dear, we like having you to spoil,' Ma said.

'We're expecting you to chauffeur us around.' Pa winked. 'She drives well, quite speedy, plenty of push in that little engine. I thought you'd like the colour.'

'Driving her will be exciting. I can go on my own to the Hunstanton tennis tomorrow, not need a lift from the others.'

At once Ma frowned. 'Kitty dear, it's a long way on your first drive.'

'Your mother's right. I'll come along as co-driver.'

· · ·

Next evening, Kitty was turning into the main road out of Hunstanton. This route home was a bit longer, but it was a straighter, faster road.

'I'm going to put my foot down, Pa. Put Speedy through her paces. Pretend I'm driving in the Monte Carlo rally.' She was surprised how quickly the arm on the speedometer touched fifty.

Pa sat placid, pipe in hand, in the passenger seat.

'You've always managed the old Ford well. This is more highly tuned, lighter built. You'll get a lot of fun out of her.' He puffed on the pipe, and she caught a wisp of the musky scent from the tobacco. 'Can't say I'm surprised Jo and that red-haired chap won – she's good, and he's competitive. You can see it from his face, determined chin, firm features.'

'Alistair's a bit of a devil. On my first day at Pither's he pulled in for petrol when I was serving at the pump. Christopher was with him.'

'Hell's bells! Your mama would have had a fit. She tells me Christopher has a big place, hundreds of acres.' Pa chuckled. 'I suppose Alistair's car needed petrol every day?'

'How did you know?' A moment's thought. 'That's what you'd have done! Don't tell Mummy, or I'll never hear the end of it.'

'She's in good form. Thinks you're meeting the right sort of people. Approves of Brownlow.'

'Jo says his father died so he didn't go to Oxford or anything, just left school to run the estate. He's nice, easy to be with. We spend time together talking, about his farm, and the animals. He's got a lovely dog, Snudge. He's asked me to a dance, a proper ball, next week.'

'Will that be fun, dancing with him?'

'Oh, yes. He's sophisticated in an un-showy way. He's a good dancer – one hot evening after we finished playing Elma lent us her gramophone and we all danced around the tennis court, in bare feet on the dry grass.'

...

On the day of the dance, Ma fussed.

'You must rest, dear, so you sparkle. Your first ball here, you must look your best.'

Kitty didn't rest, but knew she sparkled that evening.

Christopher, always good company, proved to be a quietly efficient escort.

On the perfectly French-chalked floor, they tangoed, fox-trotted and waltzed the evening away, the champagne flowed and the heady scent of the flowers mingled with Parisian perfumes.

Christopher knew everybody, introducing her as they moved from dance floor to buffet and the cool of the conservatory. Jo had warned her about this, saying Christopher was the most eligible bachelor in Norfolk and she must expect other girls, and their mothers, to regard her with suspicion.

She loved every minute of the evening and was mildly ashamed when she realised she had fallen asleep in the car as Christopher drove her home.

He didn't seem put out. 'A sort of Cinderella. Only your coach here hasn't turned into a pumpkin.' He leaned towards her, touched her cheek. 'Thank you for your company.'

She pushed the front door closed, took off her silver shoes and crept upstairs.

The weather turned wet in September, putting an end to long afternoons of tennis and chatter with the other three on the vicarage tennis court. Instead, she and Jo spent the afternoons together, mostly at Jo's home. Then, in October, she drove them both to lunch on the opening day of pheasant shooting at Christopher's farm.

It was all very jolly, a huge spread set up in what had once been, apparently, a Tudor cart-shed and everyone, guests and shooters, dressed for the outdoors. Christopher's mother, grey haired and elegant, constantly shadowed by the two black Labradors, gently made sure everyone had enough to eat and drink. Afterwards Alistair gave Jo a lift home, and Kitty drove back in the dusk alone.

CHAPTER 6

DECEMBER 1930

SOCIAL ACTIVITIES PAUSED as the December days shortened and the weather became cold and grey. One day not long before Christmas, she came away from one of her long chats in the kitchen with the news that Mrs Richards' son Jim, a pig man at the local farm, reared turkeys to earn a few extra coppers.

'I do wish you wouldn't gossip in the kitchen,' Ma said.

'We weren't. We were talking about farming.' Talking normally, like two human beings.

Pa intervened. 'I think we should have one of the boy's birds. Help the lad earn a bit. I'll give you the cash, you go and choose one.'

She walked the couple of miles to the farm, pleased to get out of the house and have some exercise, though the wind was a biting north-easterly – straight off the Russian steppe, she'd heard. The countryside looked bleak, brown earth stretching away in all directions.

As she came close to the cluster of barns, a racket of squealing broke out, rolling across the silent fields.

She picked her way through the mud. A youth, leaning over the side of a brick sty, lifted his cap.

'I've come to choose one of your turkeys for our Christmas lunch.'

'Yes, miss. Mother said.'

She looked over the waist-high wall. 'That poor sow! However many piglets are there? Was it her squealing?'

'No, she's happy enough. You have to watch they don't smother the little ones when there's that many. It was fatteners, the older ones, shouting for their dinner.'

The baby mounds of life were nestled up to the sow, suckling, the little tails twitching around in excitement.

'Those look like puppies. Cosy, not at all dirty.'

'People think they're dirty because they feed by digging in the mud. That's wrong, and they're intelligent – give me a pig over a cow any day.'

Walking home, her coat wrapped tight, her head bent against the wind, she breathed in the air, her mind full of the sow and the heaving mass of tiny trotters and wiggly tails. Farmers mostly looked happy, busy doing something useful – why not accept Christopher's offer to show her round his farm?

A week before Christmas she drove Ma into Norwich for Christmas shopping. She nudged the car into a parking spot. Speedy was a dream to park, with a good lock and lighter steering than on Pa's Ford.

The town bustled with a vibrant mixture of country life – gunsmiths, saddlers, and the county set shopping in Bonds department store. The cathedral spire dominated the gentle gradients of the streets so the place felt worthy of being called a city, and much nicer, more interesting, more real, than flat, straight, suburban Worthing.

'Don't be late for lunch, Katherine. I've booked a table for one o'clock.' Ma straightened her hat, pulled on leather gloves. But she waved cheerily as she walked away.

People crowded along the pavements, making it difficult to get a good look into the shop windows crammed with Christmas goodies, and she had to wait ages to pay in the china shop.

The wicker basket got heavy and her tummy had begun to rumble.

Golly, almost one o'clock! She started to hurry, cutting back towards the restaurant via a side street. A black Ford, just like Pa's, was tucked into an unkempt backyard.

Like Pa's?

She gasped. TM5 was Pa's number plate.

She stepped closer, stood on the edge of the rubble and looked around. Wherever was he? Why park here? At dinner last night she and Ma talked about coming to Norwich today, about where to lunch – Pa hadn't said a word, not about being here in court, or anything. Being secretive. Another of his unexplained absences. Damn. A puff of grey cloud cast a shadow on the easy happiness of the day.

She stepped back onto the street. Better hurry on.

Ma, already settled at a corner table, her hat and coat hooked on the rack behind her, had a glass of Dubonnet in her hand. She was often more fun, more relaxed perhaps, when she was away from home, eating in a restaurant or having a cup of coffee in a tea shop.

'Have a sherry, dear. A Tio Pepe? I've done so well and found just what I wanted. Look at these, I couldn't resist them.' She eased open the shop paper revealing a snow-white tablecloth, with napkins to match, embroidered with a wide border of dark green holly and red berries.

The midwinter dusk was already settling in as they loaded things into Speedy, and it was dark as she swung the car into the drive at Copse End. Tea was waiting, set in front of the drawing room fire. Pa arrived home with parcels, presents he said, when she asked. No point in mentioning she'd seen the car.

All morning on Christmas Eve the gamey smell of turkey giblets boiling down into stock escaped from the kitchen and up the stairs and even into her bedroom.

She peeped into the kitchen, easing the door open, and a cacophony of other smells burst forth. Mrs Richards, using her hands to reduce cubes of stale bread into crumbs for the stuffing, looked up, smiled. 'Come on in, miss.'

'Will I be in the way?' Mince pies cooling on racks and several mixing bowls covered the kitchen table.

'What a thing to say. You could never be in the way.' Mrs Richards pointed to the only unoccupied corner of the table. 'Sit there, miss.'

'There's a lot of work for you with Pa home for lunch today. What can I do?'

Kitty stayed in the kitchen until lunchtime, chatting and washing up the pans as Mrs Richards moved from one task to the next.

'I'm starving. The cheese topping on your fish pie smells awfully good. I hope Pa is back soon.'

But by half past one there was no sign of Pa, and Ma told Mrs Richards to serve lunch.

Later, while she was listening to the carols from King's College, converting her purchases into presents with ribbon and tissue paper, his Ford rumbled onto the gravel outside. As he came up the stairs, she opened her door to say hello, but he'd gone straight into the spare bedroom. He didn't appear for supper.

The only forerunner of daylight on Christmas morning was a grey streak in the sky over the wood when she edged the curtains, closed on long winter nights, apart. She touched the glass on the window but it was quite dry, no sign of condensation: no frost outside, no white Christmas this year. She pulled the curtains back together again, switched on the bedside lamp and began to dress for church.

The church was packed. The carols, all the old favourites, were sung with gusto and the sermon was brief, a mere gesture to convention. The bonhomie of the day was tangible as the final chorus of 'O Come, All Ye Faithful' rang out and the congregation crowded out into the aisle, pausing to exchange Merry Christmases.

Back home Pa insisted on pre-lunch sherries all round, taking one to Mrs Richards in the kitchen.

When Mrs Richards brought in the plum pudding before she

went home for her own meal, Pa stood up. 'The turkey was delicious – pass on our thanks to your son.'

Ma dished out small portions, just a tablespoon full, of the rich pudding.

'Traditional, but too much.' Pa pushed his plate aside and got up from the table.

Something changed – without a word Ma got up. As she led the way into the drawing room her smiles faded into set lines around her mouth.

Do something. 'Shall I make some coffee before we open presents?'

Through the open door, the murmur of their talk changed. Ma's voice rose, going up several tones. 'I can't help there being an empty chair.'

'Dorothy! I only said it was odd just the three of us, not seeing Mother or Bertie at Christmas. Don't, please, spoil the day.'

Kitty closed the dining room door. She didn't want to hear any more because she dreaded what was coming next. She heard it anyway, bits of it. Always the same. 'You've ruined my life. You and your brother. He made Peter worse.'

Oh, God! Oh, God! Why does she do it, and today of all days?

The front door slammed, and then the Ford's engine started up, roared away up the drive.

She sank down at the debris-littered table. Tears of wet disappointment dribbled down her cheeks, tears for the happiness of the day now shattered.

Peterkin! Why did you go? Where are you? What if you hadn't died? Was it the day at the windmill? Did you get cold?

The grandfather clock struck six, loud and echoing through the silent house.

She crept into the warm kitchen and turned on the light. Desperate not to attract attention, hating the thought of facing Ma, she took off her shoes. She padded around. She boiled some milk, found the big tin of Lyles golden syrup and put two tablespoons of it into the hot milk. She leaned against the sink, sipping the toffee-tasting comfort. The sense of aloneness eased a little. There were things away from here to look forward to – going to see the foxhounds meet, stroking the dogs, the horses, meeting Jo, and Alistair and Christopher: they'd be there too. Then Jo's party on New Year's Eve, staying the night after. And Christopher's promised tour of his farm in January.

Crockery and glasses littered the kitchen table, and the dining room was as they had left it. This lot must be tidy before poor Mrs Richards arrived in the morning. Plate by plate, glass by glass, methodically Kitty worked her way through the piles. She laid drying-up cloths on the kitchen table to deaden the sound of the cutlery and afterwards scrubbed it down. She wiped the polished dining table with a warm wet cloth, and polished it off with a clean dry one. It looked neat and tidy. That was better. She boiled the kettle for a hot-water bottle, collected her pile of presents to open in her room and crept through the silent house up to bed.

At breakfast next morning, there was no sign of either Ma or Pa.

'Madam's unwell, miss.' Mrs Richards brought in the coffee. 'She will be staying in her room all day.'

Pa finally arrived home at teatime. He was carrying a brace of pheasants. She went to meet him in the hall. He hardly paused, headed towards the kitchen.

'Must get these to Mrs Richards. They came from the Boxing Day shoot.'

Better to let it go at that. He clearly didn't want to talk. Nor was he dressed for a day's shooting. Take it as an attempt to restore an appearance of domestic normality.

On New Year's Eve, before the dusk started to settle, she put her party dress and overnight case into Speedy's boot and set off for Jo's party. They danced in the galleried hall, with its furniture and rugs cleared away, until someone suggested a game of sardines. The house, its handsome medieval heart added to by successive generations, lent itself to the game, offering countless hiding places.

She headed down to the basement and opened a wooden door

beside the laundry room. Inside, before her eyes adjusted to the dark, someone chuckled. It was Alistair, comfortably seated on a large wicker basket. At his suggestion they relocated everything, including the ironing table, making a substantial barrage, ensuring it was ages before any of the others joined them.

At half past eleven Jo's mother appeared in the hall blowing a whistle and called out, 'Time to Conga.' She put her hands on the waist of the man nearest to her and propelled him forwards, up the staircase.

A straggly line of dresses and trousers followed, snaking along the galleried landing, down the back stairs to the kitchen, out into the stables, round through the sunken garden, until somehow they arrived back in the hall exactly as the clock struck twelve.

Bottles of champagne stood ready on the long oak sideboard. Beside the glasses were plates of cut squares of Christmas cake, stacked into pyramids. Jo's father popped the champagne and they drained their glasses to link hands for 'Auld Lang Syne'.

Later, upstairs, Jo stifled a yawn, and looked down at the makeshift bed on the floor. 'Will you be all right on that thing?'

'It's fine. I learnt to like hard beds at school.' And scratchy blankets and flannelette sheets. 'School seems a different world. My friend Emma did a season in London, was a proper debutante, the year after we left school. Liz – she's the one who wants to be an actress, like her mother – Liz and I had lunch with Emma a couple of times that summer. I hope you'll meet them both at my twenty-first dance.'

She slipped her feet between the crisp linen sheets, turned the pillows lengthways and propped herself up. 'Alistair and I chatted for ages in the broom cupboard. He wasn't fooling about. He's nice, Jo.'

'He's been around ever since I can remember. He had a fearful temper when we were little. All that red hair. His father's very strict, red-headed too. Mummy says Alistair came here to escape the regime at home. He was flirting with you.'

'He's fun. I don't think the flirting's serious. I don't want to get married.' Not exactly true. 'Well, maybe I do. Have a house of my own to look after, lots of babies, a garden and dogs.'

'Christopher has the big house and dogs.'

'He's good company, but a bit proper.'

'He's shy. Underneath those public-school manners he's unsure of himself.'

'He's going to give me a tour of the farm, tell me about the pigs.'

'Pigs! Whatever for?'

'They interest me.'

Snudge, his coat standing out black against the whitened ground, nosed around in the hedgerows.

'Jolly cold today,' Christopher said. 'Are you sure you want to do this, Kitty?'

'Oh, yes. I've been looking forward to it.'

They spent the morning inspecting the milking parlour and the grain store. A dozen calves were being hand-reared, fed warm milk from metal buckets.

'Golly, there's no smell. They look so clean and warm on all that straw.'

Outside again an icy wind buffeted her face. She had to keep pulling at her headscarf as it flapped up over her nose and mouth.

Christopher leaned towards her, shouting above the noise of the wind. 'That chap's been with us ever since I can remember. He knows his job is here for life, but the younger workers are worried. Our cook's son may lose his job. Elma is going to set up a help-group for unemployed farm workers. Things are dreadful around here – it's a combination of the new machines and the slump. Pray for a mild winter, we can't cope with too many of these Arctic days.'

Christopher pushed at one half of a solid wooden door. 'We keep these closed, try to maintain the warmth inside.'

There were two concrete pens on each side of the passageway. Tiny mounds of pink flesh were attached to the belly of the sow in the nearest sty.

'How old are they?'

'Just days. These over here, they're a month old.'

'Puppies,' she thought again. She gazed, taking in the oaty warmth, resting her elbows on the wall. She felt Christopher restless beside her.

Walking back, she quizzed him about how much it would cost to buy a sow, to feed her, and how much the piglets might fetch at market.

'Let's find Mother and that bowl of soup she promised.'

CHAPTER 7

AUGUST 1931

A MARQUEE MUSHROOMED on the lawn. Inside the white cavern, tables and flimsy gold chairs set on blue carpet edged the circular parquet dance floor. The two tent poles, the size of telegraph posts, grew into columns of greenery as garlands of hops and honeysuckle were wound around them.

'Pa calls it a shindig to annoy Mummy, so she insists on saying it is a ball.'

'She told me she wants to make your twenty-first birthday perfect for you.' Jo stretched, perching her sun-bleached hat on her neat little bob hairstyle.

'Perfect for my only child is the usual phrase. I shouldn't grumble. Liz and Emma – you know, from school – are staying.'

Next morning the tension in the household was palpable. Pa left before breakfast for a busy day in court.

It was a relief to climb into Speedy for the drive to Norwich railway station to meet Liz and Emma.

The train pulled in, all huff and smuts. Carriage doors swung open, and the porters moved forward with their trolleys.

Shingled black hair, tall, and – yes, smaller bouncing blond curls. Waving frantically she wound through the throngs of people to greet her friends.

· · ·

Just after midnight, the band softened the music and led into 'The Last Waltz'. As the final notes fell away, the lights came up. A brief and raucous verse of 'Happy Birthday' followed and then people began to drift away, white ties askew and hair no longer neatly coiffed.

In the warmth of the night, she stood between Ma and Pa on the edge of the driveway as the last car drove away. She reached out for Ma's hand. 'It was a wonderful party.' After all the tension of the preparations, the evening had been just that. 'Thank you for all your hard work, Mummy.'

'You looked lovely, dear, dancing with Christopher. Now, don't stay up too long with those other three, chatting.'

Pa smiled. 'Come along, Dorothy. Time for us to hit the sack.'

For once Ma didn't pull away as he put his arm around her waist.

The others were in the drawing room, curled up on the sofas, kicked-off shoes lying on the floor.

'I feel sick,' Emma said.

'You do look a bit the worse for wear. Did you have a lot to drink?' said Liz.

'It was the cocktails. You're meant to drink them quickly, while they're still laughing at you.'

Liz looked disapproving. 'Only one, not as many as you had. They were almost neat gin. Here, have some milk and tell us about Alistair and that tall man you were with for the last waltz.'

Emma giggled. 'I had to find someone who was big enough to keep me upright – the floor kept coming up to hit me.'

'You were dancing with Alistair before,' Liz said.

Jo looked pensive, not her usual bouncy self.

Emma frowned at Liz. Then she said, 'We agreed, at dinner, that we'd do that. It was an act. I told him about Jean-Pierre.'

'Jean-Pierre?' Liz was gushing suddenly. 'Oh, darling, tell! Are you going to get married?'

'Yes. We've – well, you know – pre-empted that.'

Silence.

Inadequately, Liz said, 'Gosh!'

'No one knows. It just sort of happened the first time. Now we make love in French. In the woods. On the flat rock on our little beach. Anyway, Daddy's talked Mummy round, says why shouldn't I marry a local.'

Kitty knew he'd been her boyfriend for ages. 'Be happy, Emma.'

'What about Christopher, Kitty? You danced with him a lot. He's very nice,' Emma said.

'I can't imagine being married to him, being like you and Jean-Pierre are, with him. I thought when the right man came along it would just happen, be all right. Ma's never talked to me about it. She's a dreadful prude, or a hypocrite, sex is taboo.' She changed the subject. 'Liz, tell us about your acting.'

'Every time I do an audition they say I'm not quite right for the part,' Liz said. 'I've got a job. Your mother'd be horrified. It's at Fortnum and Mason, in ladies' fashions.'

Emma recovered herself first. 'Do you meet lots of rich women?'

'Not often. There's a grand old dowager duchess but she lives alone in a flat near Marble Arch. She tries on lots of dresses but never buys anything.'

'Perhaps she can't afford them,' Emma said. 'Wouldn't it be awful to end up like that? Alone, eating stale bread and cheese in a cold flat. I'd rather die young.' A slight pause. 'With Jean-Pierre's arms wrapped around me.'

'You incurable romantic!' Kitty chuckled.

Within days of the happiness of her birthday party the atmosphere in the house deteriorated, getting worse all through the autumn until now it was horrid.

Outside, heavy and low, the November clouds drizzled. Inside, the house lacked life and light.

The tension and discord between Ma and Pa were obvious whenever they were together, although Pa mostly gritted his teeth, not responding to her jibes about money. All this last week Ma had been at her worst, alternately nasty and then in floods of tears before shutting herself away.

Now, as Kitty walked through to the kitchen to talk to Mrs Richards about next week's menus and the orders from the tradesmen, she switched on the hall lights to lift the gloom. A bacon joint bubbled away on the cooker. Mrs Richards was chopping parsley.

'It's my turn to help with the orders and things. I'm afraid Mummy's ill in her room.' Be straight with her. 'Well – not really ill, just miserable.'

'Miss Kitty, it's sad for you all. Your mother so distressed again.'

'She punishes herself by thinking about Peter dead.'

Mrs Richards used the knife to gather the parsley together, turned the pile around and chopped at it with renewed vigour so the noise of the knife on the wooden board almost masked her muttered 'More a case of punishing you and your pa.'

'Peter was intelligent enough to be a happy person. I wish Ma would try to remember the good things instead of these ghastly histrionics. All we've got is memories so we must keep them happy.'

Mrs Richards stopped chopping.

'Now, miss, lets sort out the orders, keep the household going.'

There was a strange tense feeling at the breakfast table. After the two days closeted in her room last week Ma had seemed back to normal, until this morning.

She pushed aside her half-grapefruit and gave an artificial little cough. 'This house is too large. We need somewhere smaller.'

Pa stayed silent.

What? Why? Smaller?

'I love it here. You used to like it.' Damn! It was silly, a mistake to challenge Ma in this mean mood.

'Your father treats this house like a hotel.'

Pa erupted, knocking his half-drunk coffee over the white cloth as he threw the newspaper onto the table and walked out of the room without bothering to close the door.

The front door slammed. The car, at full throttle, spun away up the gravel.

Try to make peace. 'My napkin will soak up the spill.'

Poor Pa, life is miserable here for him. He's not the fun person he used to be. No wonder he stays out. There is no need to move. She just said that to hurt him.

Ma didn't look up. Exaggeratedly she stirred the sugar into her coffee, the sound of metal on porcelain loud in the silence of the room.

The weather turned wet and cold. For three weeks, things seemed normal – it was not exactly happy in the house, but life carried on. Kitty took Ma shopping a couple of times and spent a good deal of time over at Jo's.

One evening, Mrs Richards had stewed oxtail, one of Pa's favourites. Ma ladled the rich gravy onto Pa's plate. Then, with a provocative jerk of her chin, she said, 'Our new home is nearer the town, it is called Otters.'

What?

Eyes focused on the plate, Pa kept on taking meat off the bone.

'What do you mean? New home?'

'Kitty dear, you will like it.'

'Will I? Where is it? Pa, do you like it?'

Ma's face set, solid and cold.

'Pa, where is it?'

'Ask your mother, Kitten. It's her decision.' Pa folded his napkin, stood up, rested one firm hand on her shoulder as he paused behind her chair. 'I hope you like the place.'

Cold fingers of fear crept up as she lay in bed that night. She tossed around until the sheet had tangled up in her legs.

She climbed out of bed and pushed her feet into her sheepskin slippers. She buttoned up her housecoat and padded downstairs. The light was on in the drawing room.

'Hello, Pa.'

He jumped slightly. His feet were resting on the coffee table.

'Can't sleep, Kitty?' He eased back into the chair. 'Share a glass of port with me.'

He filled a glass with the deep-coloured wine from the decanter and passed it to her. 'It's when one's alone... that's when I find things most difficult to cope with.'

He tapped away at his pipe, puffing life into it. Topped up his glass and raised it to her.

The embers of the fire flickered brighter.

'Don't be alone, Pa. She enjoys home-making, she's good at it. I expect it will be okay.'

'House-making... yes, she can be.' Tap, tap, tap. Straggling threads of tobacco dropped into the ashtray. 'She does want to do the best for you, wants you to have the right sort of life.'

'She'll enjoy walking into the shops, seeing people. You and I can drive out, go off on our own.'

'On our own – yes, in one way.' He hesitated, as though he might say something more. Instead, he turned off the table lamp, laid his pipe into the ashtray and led the way out of the room. 'Time for your beauty sleep. Night-night, my Kitten.'

Ma's moods improved as she began to organise the move, yet whenever she talked about the new house and the practicalities there was a complete absence of discussion with Pa as if he wasn't in the room. He often stayed overnight in London because he was representing clients in court.

On 11th November, Kitty set out alone for the Armistice Day service. It was already raining and worse was forecast. With an eye on the weather she dressed carefully, decided not to risk the camel coat and chose the green herringbone tweed. She tilted the matching felt hat slightly to the left.

The market square was crowded with the lines of uniforms giving an order to the front rows. The flags, the British Legion's and the regimental standards, hung limp, too wet to flutter, sagging in the forlorn wind.

After the final prayers and the blessing, Kitty hurried away along with the rest of the drenched crowd when a familiar voice hailed her.

'My dear, I haven't seen you for ages. Where have you been?' Elma Dutton, hatless, her hair escaping from the chignon, long coat flapping open above the knee, was beside her in two long strides. 'Come back for sherry to warm up. This weather is just too dreadful. We're having a little luncheon party!'

Once welcomed into the haphazard warmth of the vicarage, Kitty took off the sodden hat and stuffed it into the pocket of her coat, which she added to the pile in the hall.

The drawing room was buzzing with chatter. The few uniforms, dark greens and reds, stood out against the mass of respectful black civilian suits and ties.

Two men sat in wheelchairs pushed into the bay window. Their neatly shaven faces were pale and drawn. Rugs, suspiciously flat, covered their laps and no shoes showed below the rugs. Kitty perched on the arm of the sofa, introduced herself and talked about the downpour beating against the windows.

Elma came across.

'Kitty, my dear. Sweet or dry sherry?' She gestured. 'This is Nigel Gifford. He's acting as my waiter.'

Vivid blue eyes crinkled into a smile. Crisply creased trousers, shoes that shone so you could powder your nose in them. Not in uniform, but a military man, too young to be retired – not a sign of grey in the neat black hair, yet somehow he seemed mature, quietly self-assured perhaps.

He looked down at his overloaded tray of glasses with brown liquid shimmering at the rims. 'May we do away with the formalities? If I drop this lot it'll make a fearful mess.'

His obviously regimental tie, wide stripes of black and red, matched those of the veterans in wheelchairs.

'Oh, yes, definitely.' Kitty motioned towards the men beside her. 'Let me take the sherry round. George and Henry here would much prefer to chat with you.'

'Good. Then I can introduce Kitty to people.' Elma sailed off into the throng.

'You'd best keep up with her.' Nigel Gifford smiled. 'She's a bit of a tempest, but her heart is solid gold.'

At lunch, Kitty sat at Elma's end of the table between Nigel Gifford and William's curate, the new one who was rather sweet but very boring.

'What a dreadful day for Armistice.' Nigel twisted his chair round slightly to face her. 'Whereabouts do you live, Kitty?'

'We're going to move a bit away, a couple of miles, so as to be closer to Dereham.'

Elma's face shifted, switching into the conversation.

'My dear, how very convenient.' Elma helped herself to more mashed potato before passing the dish round. 'But you must keep using the tennis court, and come to my meetings.'

'Oh, I'd like that. I want to do something useful. Or get a job. But with so many unemployed that would be unfair. I've been talking to people about breeding pigs.'

'Pigs!' Elma, not normally surprised by anything, sounded taken aback. 'Whatever does your mother think of that? Would she like you to have a farm?'

'Well, it's only an idea.' It felt uncomfortable to be the centre of attention. 'Mummy doesn't know, she wouldn't understand.'

'My grandparents used to keep pigs,' Nigel said, leaning forward in his chair. 'I think there's a future in farming. I joined the local farmers' visit to the Ministry of Agriculture to talk about the agricultural unemployment. We're campaigning for unemployment insurance.'

After pudding, everyone gathered up coats and drifted away.

Kitty skipped down the vicarage steps with the still sodden hat crunched up in one hand. Elma's enthusiasm was like a tonic, evaporating problems or perhaps just putting them into perspective. The move might not be such a disaster, and maybe Ma was right about money – Pa could sell the Ford, share Speedy.

She stepped off the footpath, out of the damp shelter of the wood, onto their gravel drive.

Pa's car! Parked by the front steps. But why wasn't he at the office, or in court?

Running up the steps, she pushed open the front door.

'Pa!'

He was sitting in the hall chair, wearing his Harris tweed sports jacket and red silk cravat.

Suitcases and boxes lined up along the wall.

'Kitten, I've been waiting for you.'

'After the service, Elma invited me to lunch. Mummy was in bed again – it's a weekday. I didn't think you'd be here.'

'It doesn't matter. I must talk to you.'

Her stomach lurched, sank, twisting downwards.

'I don't think you'll be entirely surprised. You know how things have been between your mother and me. We are to separate. I am going to live in London. I've got a flat. It's for the best. She isn't happy and blames me for that.'

Dear God.

Not surprised. Had half-expected this.

No, not exactly this. The fact perhaps, but not the happening.

Suitcases and all his stuff going away.

No Pa at supper tonight, or breakfast in the morning. No Pa.

'Don't go. Please.' She flung herself at him. 'I know she's horrid to you and very difficult. But that's how she is. Please stay for me. If you stay, I won't get married. I won't leave you alone with her.'

'Kitten! Poppet! Come in here.'

In the drawing room, Pa sat down on the sofa and pulled her down beside him. 'Forgive me. I should have talked to you earlier but I didn't, don't, want to upset you.'

His face was furrowed. He looked a very old man suddenly.

'Since, since… ' He took a deep breath. 'Since poor Peter died the only thing I've wanted, worked for, is for you to be happy and safe. I realised soon after the move here that Mummy and I were finished. It's been hard keeping up the pretence, socially, and being stuck in that dreadful little office all day.'

'Pa, I didn't realise. I thought you were happy here too.'

As if he didn't hear her he carried on talking.

'It was worth it. Seeing you blossom, enjoying Speedy. No one can put the clock back. The whole of your life is before you. Your mother and I don't matter any more. I have friends in London. Your mother has friends here, and the church. She can play her cards and manage her own social life, won't have to worry I'll embarrass her. And you must make your own life.'

She opened her mouth to protest but the words, her breath even, gagged in her throat.

He stood up. 'I'm going now. Help me with my stuff.'

'No!'

'Yes. No point in prolonging the agony.'

Stop him. Hold him here long enough to talk. She took his hand.

'Stay! Pa, please.'

He took his hand away.

Then he came closer, the safety of his arms went tight around her shoulders.

'Come on, brave girl. It will be better. Don't deny me some happiness.'

They aren't happy. Ma is more real, less artificial, softer, when he's not here.

She clung on, her face pressed into the rough surface of his jacket. Now her nose was dribbling. He smoothed her hair as if she were a child again.

'I'll write. Talk in letters. The same as you and Peter did in postcards.'

Peterkin died. But it was she who'd gone away first, moved on, made new friends, happy at school. Left Peter alone in the aseptic cotton wool Ma had wrapped him in, with ghastly Reverend Trott and constant, miserable, stressing care. Peter was never sloppy, he made himself happy – always. He hadn't tried to stop her going away, he didn't begrudge her new friends, her separate happiness. He started the postcards so they could share the good bits of life.

Pa ran his finger under her eyes. Reached into his top pocket and passed her his red silk hankie. 'Let me see a smile, just a little one, before I go.'

Before he goes?

'Will you come back for Christmas?'

'No, it wouldn't work. Must be a clean break.' He opened his black leather bag. 'I am working for these people. Use that address, Kitten. Help me now. Bring this out for me.'

She stuffed the thick embossed paper into her pocket, took the briefcase from him.

Down the steps. Onto the gravel.

To the car.

He put the briefcase on the passenger seat, piling the other luggage in the boot.

Reached out, held both her hands for a moment. 'Goodbye, Poppet.' He pulled the door closed, starting the engine at the same time.

Salty tears trickled onto her lips as the noise of the engine faded away. She stuffed the hankie into her mouth to silence her howl as she ran upstairs to hide under the bedclothes in her room.

Sometime in the dusky afternoon as she huddled under the counterpane, still burying her head in the pillow now wet with tears, the telephone bell shrilled through the house.

Steady footsteps on the stairs. Three gentle taps on the bedroom door.

'Jo's on the telephone.' None of the usual hard edges to Ma's tone.

Held her breath, tried not to sniffle, burrowed deeper.

Ma's footsteps receded down the stairs.

'She'll ring you back, Jo, dear.'

Jo, dear? Where had that come from?

She sat up. Hiding, shutting herself away? Like someone else.

She tidied up, used more make-up than usual to disguise the red and soggy face, and went downstairs.

Ma was knitting by the fireside.

'Hello, dear. Don't forget to ring Jo.'

So, despite the cataclysm which had just struck the house, life was to go on, no discussion. Yet there was a softness about Ma and her concentration on the knitting. Trying to make the best of the mess.

CHAPTER 8

DECEMBER 1931

SHE DIDN'T WRITE a postcard to Pa, she wrote a proper newsy letter, in an envelope. She told him about the colours she'd chosen for her room in the new house, and the film she'd gone to see with Jo.

She searched the post every day, hanging around for the postman to pedal up the drive, until a picture postcard of the tigers at London Zoo arrived. Only a few simple lines. He didn't pick up on her news, wrote he was busy in court, and London was getting ready for Christmas.

For the first time in her life, she wasn't enjoying the preparations for Christmas. The darkening days stretched ahead and she dreaded Christmas lunch – alone with Ma, both of them dwarfed by the turkey on the table.

In the afternoon on Christmas Eve the postman delivered a handful of cards and a bulky envelope with a London postmark. She ran upstairs to open it.

'Happy Christmas, I hope the enclosed is your colour. With best love, Pa.'

She unfolded the sheets of wrapping and had to catch at the shimmering fabric as it slid out of the tissue paper. A headscarf in a pattern of flowing, soft greens. She held the silk to her cheek, as relief, if not happiness, flickered inside her.

Somehow, Christmas Day had to be got through before she went with Jo and Alistair to the Boxing Day meet in the square, and on to lunch at Christopher's afterwards.

Make the best of things. She changed into a favourite skirt and cashmere jumper, lit the drawing room fire early, and got out the bezique playing cards.

They left Copse End on a bitterly cold January day. The move to Otters went smoothly. It was mercifully dry, though snow was forecast.

Ma was quietly in control. When the removal men left at the end of the long day Ma poured two glasses of sherry. They shared a picnic supper at the kitchen table.

Exhausted, they went upstairs.

'Goodnight. Well done.' She kissed Ma on the cheek and closed her bedroom door.

There was *The Windmill*, already hung over her bed.

She straightened the picture, and whispered, 'Goodnight, Peterkin.'

The smell of coffee and toast woke her next morning. Mrs Richards said she liked working for Kitty and her ma and that she'd be pleased to work shorter hours, so it had been agreed that she would come for the mornings, leaving them to cook and serve the evening meals.

Together they spent the next few days unpacking and within the week everything was neat and tidy.

'I shall go to my cards tomorrow,' Ma announced, 'while you go to see Jo.'

The flickering flames threw patterns into the darkening room. Sitting beside Jo on the old sofa, their feet resting on the fender, they watched the snowflakes tumble against the window.

'Ma is easier, happier I suppose. She's got friends, has canasta afternoons,' Kitty said. 'The only time she gets pompous is when Christopher's around. Then she reverts! The other day she said he'd be ideal as son-in-law.'

'Queen Victoria was empress of half the world when she was growing up. No one questioned the status quo. Daddy says that the last war changed things for ever and that the empire won't last long now,' said Jo.

'Ma's *Daily Express* has a piece about the Imperial Scheme helping our economy with trade from the empire, but I think your father's right. One of the women at Elma's meeting last week shocked us all by saying the empire is finished and that England will never get back to where we were before the war. Elma's meetings are interesting – will you come to the next one?'

'Maybe,' Jo said.

Outside the flakes melted as they hit the window. A log on the fire snapped as it burnt through and the clock struck the half-hour.

'What's up?'

Jo fiddled with her fingernails, looked up. 'We haven't told anyone yet, but Alistair and I are going to get engaged.'

'Wonderful!' Kitty said. 'You're lovely together! A proper pair.'

The ground had been blown dry by a steady wind from the east and the clouds were unthreateningly high in the sky, so Kitty walked the couple of miles back to the vicarage. The changes in Ma didn't extend to approval of the vicar's wife meddling in left-wing politics so Kitty hadn't said she was going to Elma's meeting.

At the vicarage, William was winter-pruning the roses in the flowerbed at the front of the house.

He straightened up, rubbing his back. 'Elma's inside, getting the teas ready.'

'I'm early. It didn't take as long to walk as I expected.'

'She'll be pleased with a bit of help.'

Shedding her coat in the hall, she went in search of Elma and found her in the kitchen, furiously buttering scones.

'I'll do that. And be waitress.' She liked handing things round.

The drawing room, large by most standards, was packed. Wherever would they all find to sit?

Her last tray was empty, just a couple of misshapen scones left, so she turned to go back to the kitchen.

A hand touched her elbow.

'Those two look lonely.'

Sapphire eyes. Nigel Gifford!

The rest of that dreadful day had obliterated the memory of Elma's Armistice Day do. Pa in the hall, waiting to go away.

'Remember, we talked about pigs at lunch?'

'Yes – it was just an awful day.'

'Torrential rain. Now, suppose I take both scones and find us somewhere to sit?'

She dumped the tray in a corner, went straight back.

He'd got a stool for her and placed it alongside the arm of a sofa.

Bits of her scone crumbled down on the carpet as she bit into it. 'Oh dear.'

'Don't worry. Best to ignore it, you won't be the only one.'

'You're managing much better.'

'Years of practice!' Grinning. 'My father's a vicar. I was weaned on vicarage scones. How are you getting on with your pigs?'

'As if I'm taking tea with them!' Fancy him remembering. 'They fascinate me. The pig man, our cook's son, is out of a job. He's joining the army.'

'He'll do okay, so long as there isn't another war.'

Of course, that regimental tie on Armistice Day.

'Were you in the war?'

'Hang on – I'm not that old!'

Just then, Elma took control, rattling cutlery on crockery. She called for silence and introduced the speaker.

By the time the meeting finished the clouds had lowered, threatening rain and bringing the dusk early.

She went to retrieve her coat. Nigel was beside her, held it for her. She straightened the belt, knotted it over one hip.

'Let me give you a lift home.' Shafts of blue directed from his eyes to hers.

'It's no distance. But, yes! Please.'

His car, an elderly Austin 7, stuttered to a start, but bundled along well enough on the main road.

'Don't bother to go down the drive. Drop me here.'

Obediently he pulled up on the verge. 'Will you have lunch with me? I could find a pig farm. Or better, maybe we'll go to the livestock market at Thetford next Thursday?'

She woke with the birds on the Thursday morning. Sat up in bed, saw the milky blue of a post-dawn clear sky and looked at the clothes waiting on her chair.

Last night, after a good deal of thought and uncharacteristic indecision, she'd decided to wear the softly pleated tweed skirt, its heather brown and sky-blue dog-tooth check lightened by the pale blue cashmere twin set.

'You're very dressed up, dear.' Ma poured the coffee. 'I bought that outfit for you to meet Christopher's mother. It's not till tonight that you're dining with him. You said you were going shopping this morning.'

She had said that because it seemed more plausible than going to watch pigs, cows and probably poultry change hands.

'It's comfy. It's a shame to leave it hanging up, kept for special.'

'What time is this young man arriving?'

Ma knew the name. She'd told her, and that his father was a vicar.

'Nigel! About half past nine.'

Ma persisted in hovering in the hall.

The old Austin 7's engine rasped as it turned into the drive.

'Bye, Mummy. I'm off.' She pulled the front door shut.

He held the car door for her. His duffel coat was open and a long woollen scarf was wrapped around his neck. He looked more solid, broader shouldered, than she remembered.

Settling himself behind the wheel, he turned, lowered his chin a fraction, and asked, 'Still happy to go to the market? We'll find somewhere for a bite of lunch afterwards.' A lopsided grin crinkled up to his eyes. 'I've never taken a girl to a livestock market.'

'I told Mummy we were going shopping!'

'Well, we are. We're just not going to buy anything.' Then, 'For God's sake keep your hands in your pockets. I don't want to have to find a home for a herd of pigs.'

'I could keep one in the garden.'

'I'm not at all sure this trip is a good idea. You are not – not, I repeat – to take pity on any creature you see today.'

At the market, Nigel elbowed a path through crowds of men dressed in market-day-best jackets and plus fours to find a ringside vantage point.

The concrete floor was swept clean, but the strong odour of farmyard mingled incongruously with the smells of shaving soap, hair oil and mothballs emanating from the crush of farmers.

Hands? One in each coat pocket. Definitely.

In the ring, a large bull, held safely by a rigid pole fixed to the ring on his nose, pawed at the ground.

The auctioneer stood on steps on the opposite side of the selling ring, shouting out figures in quick succession as the bids came fast from all around him. How did he know who was trying to buy the handsome, muscular, straight-backed creature?

A succession of dairy cows followed, the black and white Friesians all bones, the Guernsey heifers smaller, with soft brown eyes.

'That's the last of the cattle.' Nigel's hand was warm on her arm. 'Pigs next.'

She forgot the jostling aromas, ceased to hear the background chatter.

The sow was low slung and round nosed, her ears half-pricked like a puppy's when it's not yet able to make the muscles work all the way to the tip. Neat, flimsy ankles above the hooves and a long, solid, course-haired body. The snout snuffled around the cold floor, found nothing. Across the ring the auctioneer's assistant rattled pignuts in a metal pan. The head came up sharply and the little tail uncurled to stand upright in excitement as the sow ran towards the sound of food.

Next into the ring was a boar, easily twice the size of the sow, and then several lots of young fatteners, squealing around the ring.

The auctioneer climbed down off his platform.

Nigel put his hand on her shoulder. 'Back to earth, Kitty. Sales over!'

What? That's all? In so little time?

The crush of people eased, turned away from the ring to break into chatting groups.

'Let's find somewhere for lunch.'

Nigel drove, steadily, confidently but not fast, for a few miles before he turned left into an unmarked narrow lane. The road, set between deep banks, twisted down a steep hill.

He swung the car onto a rough patch of grass in front of a whitewashed building.

A cottage? One latticed window peeping out from under the thatched roof.

A movement beside the car caught her eye. She looked up.

An inn-sign attached to a telegraph pole swung in the breeze. The Shire Horse. A pub.

'It's simple – rustic – inside. Spotlessly clean. They do simple food.'

He lifted the latch on the front door, stood back for her to go into a low-ceilinged bar with huge old beams. A log fire blazed in the inglenook fireplace.

A man leaned against the corner of the bar. Leather spats covered the bottom halves of his woollen trousers. Two muddy spaniels lay at his feet.

The man banged his tankard on the wood. 'Landlord! Customers!'

'Am I all right in here?' Normally there was a saloon bar for visitors and women whilst the public bar was the territory of the locals.

Both dogs were wagging their tails. She bent to stroke the silky heads.

''Tis the only bar, ma'am. So long as the dogs like you, it's all right with me.'

'Good day to you.' The publican appeared behind the counter. 'Pint, sir? A half for the lady?'

'And two bowls of your Irish stew, please.'

Kitty settled on the bench under the window. She inhaled the heady wood-laden air. Nigel brought the beers over and sat down on the other side of the table.

Low sunlight shone through the window and lit up his face. Well etched. Fine featured but not bony. He lifted his glass to her. 'Cheers.'

She sipped the amber liquid. The warmth of the room, the smoky atmosphere, the images from the morning and Nigel's presence crept over her, enveloping her in a gentle euphoria.

'Now tell me about this interest in swine.'

'Pigs – swine doesn't sound right! They're intelligent, clean animals. And I love roast pork.'

His raised his eyebrows. 'No hypocritical sentimentality then!' he said. Smiling, he added, 'I ordered lamb to be safe.'

'As children we used to have Irish stew for lunch.'

'Do you have brothers or sisters?'

'No.' Then she added, 'Not now.'

His face registered the significance. 'Something happened? What?'

'My older brother. Peter. He was an invalid, he was born with a bad heart. It never worked properly. Then he died.'

'Does it hurt to talk about him?'

'Not to talk about Peter, no. I like to do that.' Now, here with this man, she wanted to go on, to say the hurtful truth. 'I wasn't allowed to see him the day he died. I never said goodbye.'

'But you were friends, shared things?'

'Yes, that he was going to die. Go to sleep forever. That's why I wanted to talk to him one last time.'

He reached across the table, squeezed her hands. 'Remember it's easier for the one who goes away.'

Just then the publican came over with two steaming plates, which he set directly onto the surface of the bare wooden table with the cutlery and two squared-off glass cloths, starched and pristine, for napkins.

Onion, turnip, and the thick grassy smell of boiled mutton.

Smoothing the makeshift table napkin onto her lap, she said, 'Now, you talk – tell me about the army.'

'I went to Sandhurst straight from school. There were plenty of opportunities for young officers in the aftermath of the war.'

The broth smelt good but it was scalding hot. He was spooning it around the plate.

'I had ten years in the regiment before being invalided out. I had a weak chest.' He abandoned the spoon, helped himself to a chunk of bread. 'I want to try my hand at farming. Did you guess?'

'No. Really, not.' Had he thought she was pretending an interest in pigs? 'What sort of farming?'

'Start small, something my army pension will stretch to. Then build it up.' He was concentrating on the broth using the knife and fork to separate the meat from the bone.

'The sow this morning went for thirty-two guineas. In a few months her piglets would sell as weaners. You could soon get your money back, couldn't you?'

'One could.'

The farmer and his dogs left. The publican took away their empty plates, and began washing down the bar top.

'Time to go,' Nigel said. 'I'll settle up.'

They strolled back to his car. He drove away up the narrow lane and turned onto the main road. He didn't talk but she felt no need to break the comfortable silence – she was storing away things he'd said.

They reached the outskirts of Dereham.

'We're nearly back. I'm sorry if I've been quiet.'

'Don't be.' He took his left hand off the steering wheel and let it rest on her arm. 'It's nice not making conversation for the sake of it. Let's go to a movie. Have you seen *The Scarlet Pimpernel*?'

Let's. Let us. There was an ease about the gentle presumption of his invitation, no artificial social courtesies.

On the edge of the small gravel turning area beside the front of the house, he turned off the ignition and came round to hold the door for her.

'I'll check out the films, telephone to confirm. Look after yourself till then.'

He raised his hat in farewell. The engine stuttered, got going and pottered away up the little drive.

She pushed the front door closed as the hall clock chimed, slung her coat over her shoulder and started up the stairs.

Half past three. Thursday. Oh God, dinner with Christopher – this evening.

Change, have a bath, make an effort to be excited. She sighed and went on up the stairs.

The evening was not a success. The hotel dining room was so quiet that their conversation carried round the formal room to the handful of other diners. The food tasted as dull as the surroundings, she wasn't hungry and the beef was overcooked. She tried to liven things up by making artificial conversation. Christopher withdrew into stolid conformity.

When the journey home, full of stilted attempts to be polite, was over, she closed the front door and went to draw herself another bath. Shamelessly, she used all the hot water to make it deep enough to wash away the evening.

CHAPTER 9

FEBRUARY 1932

THERE WAS TIME, and it was tactful, to have tea with Ma before going upstairs to change before Nigel arrived to take her to the cinema.

'You and Jo could go together.'

'Jo's been. With Alistair.'

'They are engaged. You already have Christopher as a boyfriend.'

'No, Mummy. Christopher's just a friend, one of the set you think so much of.' Unwise and not necessary, that.

'If you're not careful you'll get a reputation.'

A reputation? Going to the cinema? 'Don't fuss, Mummy. I must get ready.'

Nigel shepherded her into the darkened auditorium just as *The Scarlet Pimpernel* flickered up on the screen.

'My friend Jo says the film's a real swashbuckler.' She failed to mention that Jo had also given her a searching look and asked whether it was Leslie Howard, or Merle Oberon, or adventure films that Christopher didn't like.

She tucked her coat under the seat and settled back.

When the lights came up, Nigel grinned. 'I thought I'd lost you, you didn't move.'

'I've been in Paris, in velvet and lace, defying the French Revolution. I need a minute to come back here.'

The air struck cold outside. As she tightened the belt on her coat, Nigel's arm came round her shoulders.

She let herself lean against him. His hand slipped down on the inside of her arm, against the side of her chest. It wandered forward.

'Let's keep each other warm.'

They walked in step back to the car.

He put a hand under her chin, kissed one cheek and then the other before letting his lips drop down onto her mouth. His tongue eased between her teeth.

Eventually, he drew away from her, tracing her face with his finger.

'Home, girl. How about lunch in Norwich next week?'

The following Tuesday, on the way down to breakfast, she hesitated, let her foot outline the pattern on the stair carpet. Because of Ma's disdainful comments before the cinema trip, she hadn't talked about the film. Nor had Ma asked, or shown any interest in her evening out. So there had been no need to stir things up by mentioning today's outing. Now, that seemed feeble, dishonest too.

She settled into her chair, poured her coffee.

'Nigel Gifford and I are going into Norwich for lunch today.'

Ma pushed her grapefruit to one side, frowning. 'He doesn't seem to be a very suitable companion for you. I gather his father is a vicar somewhere.'

Not suitable? Because his father is a vicar?

'What's wrong with his father being a vicar?'

As soon as the words were out, she knew it was a mistake.

'Don't imagine Christopher Brownlow will accept tarnished goods, my girl.'

'Mother!' Damn her! Tarnished goods. Loving, being loved, makes you tarnished? No wonder poor Pa went. 'I don't want any breakfast.'

She rushed from the room, almost bumping into Mrs Richards.

'I'll bring something up to your room, miss.'

In her room, Kitty took the tray, and rested it on the side table. 'I'm sorry to put you to this trouble.'

'We can't have you getting any thinner.'

'I'm going to Norwich with a friend.'

'With Miss Jo?'

'No. Nigel Gifford.'

'That'd be Reverend Gifford's son, who joined the army.' Mrs Richards frowned. 'There was talk. Did he leave?'

'Yes. Do you think I can wear my new slacks, the ones I had on the other day?'

'They suit you very well.'

At the first stuttering sounds of the Austin 7, Kitty ran down the stairs and out of the door. Doubtless Ma was at one of the windows. It was a huge relief that Nigel's greeting was purely social.

In Norwich they ambled along, arm in arm, window shopping. They gazed at the wickedly expensive antiques in Frasers. After lunch, they spent ages browsing in a bookshop eventually leaving with a trophy each, *Blind Corner* by Dornford Yates, and *War and Peace* for him.

'I tried to read this great tome once before.'

She studied the frontispiece and then closed the cover. 'I don't think I could try, even though it's such a classic. Look at all those endless names, strings of letters in strange combinations. I couldn't concentrate, despite having endless hours to fill.'

Abruptly he changed the subject. 'If you enjoy that one, I'll build up a collection for you. He's written lots more – the Berry books. Let's get back to the car now, head for home.' Once they had cleared the outskirts of the city, Nigel reached over and laid one hand on her knee.

'You're not in a hurry to go home, are you?'

No. His gaze was very direct. He did not look like a man who was about to suggest more shopping.

He swung the car off the main road into a narrow country lane, and pulled into a gateway surrounded by trees.

The heat of his body warmed her through her clothes.

'I feel safe, as if you're just another bit of me.'

The finger tracing her face stopped. The other hand, fingering the bone on her shoulder, slipped down a few inches.

'Safe?'

She put her arms under his, tightening them around his body.

'Yes – as if whatever we do together will be right.'

His eyes were bluer than ever, the pupils tiny pinpricks. She moved herself into the curves of his body, aware, but unbothered, that she was in precisely the sort of situation that no young lady should ever, ever allow to develop.

His fingers were exploring her and she pushed her hips towards his. He pulled away from her, placed one hand on each of her shoulders and said, 'Arm's length, for the rest of today, my pet.'

The world smiled. All of it – the massed spring flowers in the garden, the cows in the field, the stolid roadman, even Ma smiled. The sky was blue – or would be any moment despite the grey clouds and pouring rain. The grass was green. Her hair curled softly just as she liked. Whichever garment she pulled from the wardrobe fitted perfectly, felt right and looked good.

And then, she answered the telephone one morning.

It was Christopher's mother, as sweet and gently charming as ever. 'Will you come to lunch on Easter Monday? Then we can all go on to the point-to-point.'

Christopher! Out of sight and out of mind since that dismal evening.

Taken by surprise. 'Oh, thank you. Well, yes.'

What to do? How to tell Christopher? Indeed what to tell him, and when?

. . .

On Easter Monday, Ma, her feathers all puffed up, waited in the hall, stood at the front door, waving, as Christopher drove them off to Hunstanton.

At the point-to-point, she was lucky.

'That's the fourth time your horse has won.' Christopher screwed up his betting slip. 'Obviously not my day!'

'Oh, Christo!' He didn't look as if he minded very much, but she needed to soften things for him. 'There's still the last race. I'll choose for you.'

When neither of her choices came in, one fell and the other was pulled up, they laughed together.

On the drive home, she touched him on the arm and said, 'I need to tell you something. Not while you're driving. Will you pull over so we can talk?'

Without any enquiry, he changed down, and pulled off the road.

Liquid-chocolate eyes. His face reddened by the sunshine. He ran his hands through the blown-about hair.

Say it now. Be frank!

'I've met someone. I love him. I can't come out with you any more.' It sounded so bald, unkind.

'I guessed something was up.'

'I'm sorry – I shall miss our friendship. And your mother and Snudge.'

She had to run a finger under her eyes. Silly tears.

'None of that, Kitty. Be happy. Make your nest with all those babies you want so much.' He put his hands on her shoulders, leaned across and kissed her, directly on the lips. 'For friendship's sake.'

Ma was hoeing around the roses next day. As good a moment as any to tell her.

'I shan't be seeing Christopher any more.'

'I think that's a shame, dear.' The hoe kept on scratching through the earth. 'The weeds are bad this year.'

Was that it? Not even a why not, let alone any angry criticism?

'Nigel's coming to pick me up later. Can I do any shopping for you?'

'No, dear. Will you bring Nigel in for a glass of sherry when you get home?'

When they arrived back home Ma, changed into soft clothes, was definitely in charming-hostess mode. The decanter, glasses and a silver dish of salted almonds stood ready.

Nigel, solicitous in his gentle, unintrusive style got Ma talking about Ceylon and her banyan-tree-sheltered schooling.

Refusing a second drink, he stood up. 'I mustn't keep you.'

He shook Ma's hand, put on his hat, raised it, and left.

Bubbling with relieved happiness, she drove over to see Jo that afternoon.

'I've lemonade and something a bit stronger by the hammocks in the orchard.'

'You look well, bouncing in fact, Jo.'

'I've never been so happy. It's all such fun.' Jo lifted her glass. 'You look pretty good yourself. Blossoming, I'd say. Tell!'

She did. All of it. A huge outpouring of pent-up happiness.

'You should tell Elma. Let's find Mummy.'

'How exciting!' Jo's mother hugged her. 'Do bring him to lunch one day.'

Afterwards Kitty drove on to the vicarage.

William opened the door. 'How well you look. I think Elma's in the kitchen.'

She was.

'I've missed you lately. What's kept you away?'

'In a way it's your fault – I'm going out with Nigel Gifford.'

'Thrilling! He's just right for you, so stable, and that bit older. I worried for you after your father left.'

William appeared, loaded with books and papers.

'Isn't it wonderful? Kitty and Nigel have fallen for each other.'

'Nigel?'

'Yes, dear, you know, Nigel Gifford,' Elma said.

His smiling face set. In disapproval? Then he said, 'He's a kind man. I must get on.'

Spending time with Nigel became a glorious habit. The Nigel-less days were brief intermissions during which she caught up with her own things.

The day she went to meet his parents, his mother, Mary, was waiting to welcome them – with the front door already open as the car pulled up. Small-framed and trim, her hair grey but curly still and framing her smiling face. From her Nigel had inherited the vivid blue eyes.

His father was tall, thin and a little stooped across the shoulders, and definitely not a snappy dresser. He had served as a chaplain in the trenches. The gentle humour and warmth of affection between the three of them relaxed and charmed her.

June became July. In the sunshine they walked, they picnicked, they shopped, and they laughed, kissed and cuddled.

One day when they were eating scotch eggs in Thetford Forest, she told him about the South Downs, the bluebells and the last picnic with Peter. 'We used to talk about everything – like you and I do now.' He leaned over, kissed her neck.

In Norwich, they wandered off the main streets. And came across the yard where Pa's car had been tucked away. Not even quite two years ago.

'I can see now what was happening, or not, between Ma and Pa. No wonder he left.'

'Is that why she never had more babies?'

'I never thought about it. Perhaps. I do miss him, but less now you and I are together.'

The hot sunny July weather broke into thundery downpours. Even here, on the eastern edges of Britain, August was notoriously damp.

She was in the hall, sifting through her post, neatly stacked by Ma. Birthday cards. But nothing from Pa. Surely he hadn't forgotten her birthday?

Nothing from Nigel either. Doubts gnawed in her guts. This time last year life was normal: Copse End dressed overall, for her birthday dance. Pa, the perfect host, opening the dancing.

She left the envelopes unopened – something to look forward to on her birthday morning. Outside the clouds had blown away, leaving a blue sky.

She wandered out into the garden with her knitting. She'd hardly knitted a row before the telephone rang.

'Telephone!'

In the hall, Ma hovered with the receiver. 'It's for you. Nigel.'

She took the receiver, stretched the curly chord to its limit to get out of earshot.

'Shall we celebrate your birthday with a picnic at Cley?'

Perfect. Wonderful. Alone with him under the wide open skies.

'He's giving me a birthday picnic lunch.'

'A picnic lunch on your birthday?' Ma hadn't moved. 'Don't be late. I've a special dinner organised for us here.'

The roads, straight and flat, were clear of traffic with just the occasional farm cart, and once a farmer driving a flock of sheep from one field to another. The church clock at Cley struck midday as Nigel pulled the Austin to a stop alongside The Three Swallows.

'This chauffeur deserves a kiss.'

A soft hand on each of her cheeks as he kissed her lips. 'Let's walk first, then eat.'

As they strolled north towards the marshes, the ethereal beauty of the place caught at her, carving out a pit in her guts. Even the windmill, made into some sort of a house, was nostalgic.

'There's been a windmill wherever I've lived. They look clumsy until the sails turn and then the power and the purpose make them elegant.'

'Cervantes' crazy knight thought they were giants. Didn't he attack them?'

'I hadn't heard that. They're sort of stoic friends to me.' Peter loved them, drew lots before that last painting. Pa used to call them turbines in the air. Used to. Does he still? No windmills in London. Is he still there? Does Ma know? Granny and Uncle Bertie, they must know. Surely.

'You're miles away.' He was smiling, not put out.

'Sorry. Yes.'

'Is it a good place?'

'This is a much better one.' She reached out and his hand clasped hers tight, almost hurting as her finger joints crushed into each other.

He let go her hand. 'Come on, race you to the beach.'

It wasn't very far. She sprinted off, and reached the shingle before him.

'Here, Kitty.' Out of breath, he pulled her down beside him onto the warm shingle.

'I love here. The vast sand dunes and the sea stretching to the edge of the earth. The sea looks flatter than it does in Sussex because the land leading up to it is so flat. Standing on the Sussex cliffs gives you a sense of separateness from the sea. Here the land merges into sea.'

The tide came in fast over the flat sand until soon it lapped near their feet.

Once back in the car, he drove to a copse where they had picnicked before. He got an immense wicker box out of the boot. Carefully he squared up a proper white damask cloth in the centre of the picnic rug on the ground.

He picked out a bottle of champagne, let the cooling wet towel drop onto the grass by the basket as he eased around the cork with his thumb until it burst off, sending up a frothing fountain of shaken-up liquid.

He lifted his glass to her, drank deeply.

'Happy birthday.'

The cool dry bubbles bounced off her tongue, zinged down into her tummy. A fizz of relaxed happiness – but Nigel was watchful, watching her. Not relaxed.

He put down his glass, took her in his arms.

'I love you, Kitty, but... '

'Oh, Nigel, I... '

'Shh. I have to tell you something.'

Her heart rattled against the inside of her chest. Something unknown and huge loomed between them now.

He was rubbing his thumb along her wrist, holding her tight, tautly. He shifted to face away from her.

He kept her facing away from him.

'It isn't the truth that I was invalided out of the regiment with a weak chest.'

The acidity of the champagne came back up into her throat.

Had he been court-martialled? Run off with his commanding officer's wife? Embezzled the mess funds? These were ridiculous ideas, quite out of keeping with the Nigel she knew.

Then again, perhaps she didn't know him so well.

He drew a deep breath. His body tensed. She reached for his hand, held it tight.

'I was very ill.' His hand was hurting hers. Gripping it, scrunching her finger joints together. 'I had TB.'

Pulmonary tuberculosis. Feared, deadly, a contagion. Never spoken about. Shut away.

Coughing up blood.

But Nigel didn't cough. He looked normal, wasn't shut away, wasn't infectious.

She stayed as he had shifted her, facing away from him.

Why should this make any difference?

He was the same man, no different, the same person; his body was the same; he was still the broad-minded, wise person.

There it is then.

'I love you. Nothing's changed.' Twisting in his arms, she turned to face him. And realised that the balance of the relationship between them had altered. 'Tell me what happened.'

Hesitantly he started. The bald facts – his illness started with a cough – the quack picked it up.

'I've never talked about it. I couldn't have told Mother this sort of thing.'

As he described the horrors, clammy cold crept up her spine.

Despite the sun on her back and the warmth of his body, she shivered. The vicious pain and discomfort. The medieval treatments when he wished he were dead and was surrounded by men dying. Living with the humiliation of an illness so feared by society it couldn't be spoken about.

'I'm so sorry not to have told you before. So sorry you have to know about it. So sorry. Forgive me.'

'Let me hold you.' She pulled him round to face her. Saw the streaks on his cheeks. Touched the lines of tears with her fingers, kissed each of his eyes in turn.

'Kitty, will you marry me? Now, knowing this?'

'Yes! You won't ever be alone again. I promise. We'll be together, always.'

She kept hold of his face. Saw the blue eyes glistening still and wondered how to help, how to make him realise it didn't alter how she felt.

'We'll have a pig farm and a houseful of children.'

'Do you mean that?'

'Of course. I want to marry you.'

His face relaxed a fraction. A glimmer of a twinkle. 'Not that. The pig farm.'

'Beast!' She managed to get her hand under his left armpit before he realised what she was about and had him squirming in exquisite agony.

She moved slightly to let him roll over on top of her and ran one hand down his back to feel his buttocks, used the other to put fingers in the hair on the nape of his neck. His body moved on hers. One hand seeking into her blouse. The other on her hip. She shifted, letting her blouse open.

He lifted himself on straightened arms, so his eyes looked down, directly into hers. 'This won't do. You're supposed to come over all proper, pulling your clothes back together.'

'That would be a lie. I want us. Please.'

His hands moved down.

Stopped. Went up to her shoulders.

'No, love. We are going to do this properly. After we're married. Not in a field, getting you pregnant, having a shotgun wedding.'

'I like the field. And the sun.'

'I promise we'll find a field, just like this, when we're married. How do I ask your father for your hand in marriage when I haven't met him?'

'I'll write to Pa.'

Again.

CHAPTER 10
AUGUST 1932

WHEN SHE GOT HOME she went in through the back door and crept upstairs. She threw off her clothes and lay on top of her bed.

Without Nigel beside her things became real – his illness… But that was all right because she understood now that having TB didn't make someone a monster; they'd have a farm, and he'd promised they'd try breeding pigs; he wanted lots of children too, and didn't mind she hated the idea of a nanny for them.

How to get hold of Pa?

Downstairs she peeped into the dining room. The table was laid, candles already flickering beside a dish of aspic-glossed duck decorated with cucumber and cherries, the clear jelly catching the light; a cut-glass bowl of raspberries, and the slim brown neck of a bottle of wine resting in the cooler.

So much effort for two people. Why? For what? To make a happy occasion? To do the right thing?

And then, something twisted in her tummy – Ma would be on her own, alone here when she married Nigel. Ma, left with memories of one child long dead, and deserted by Pa. She was often difficult, manipulative and sometimes even cruel, but she could be good company, fun and loving.

Standing by the table, fingering the shining silver cutlery, she knew that against her instinct to be open, for tonight she must leave Ma with the idea that nothing special had happened today.

Ma sparkled during the evening, at her best. Kitty tried to join in, to pretend. It didn't work.

At last, having forced the rich food down, she said the day in the sun and fresh air had been too much. 'I must go up to bed.'

Alone in her room nausea rose in her throat. She got to the bathroom just in time and pulled the chain to cover the noise of her retching. Back in bed she tossed and turned, alternately shaky cold and then sweaty hot.

She woke early, unrested and still on edge. She telephoned Jo, climbed into Speedy and left the house before breakfast.

Jo was waiting by the front door.

'I'm dying to hear whatever it is.' Jo went over to open the casement window. 'Gosh, it's hot! How was your birthday picnic?'

'The picnic? I'd almost forgotten about that. We're going to get married!'

'What! Why ever didn't you say? Come here. I'm thrilled for you.' Jo took a step back. 'What did your mother say?'

'I didn't tell her. I couldn't face it last night. I had muddled-up dreams about Peter and Nigel in the night. There's something else. Promise you won't tell anyone.'

'Not if you don't want me to. Is it so dreadful? You're not...?'

'What? Oh, no, but that wouldn't matter.'

Still she hesitated. Words spoken aloud could not be retrieved.

'Come on – spit it out.'

'We all thought... Nigel told me... he'd resigned his commission just because of his weak chest.' Another long pause. 'He didn't have pneumonia. He had TB. Tuberculosis.'

'Good God.' Jo's intake of breath was audible.

'He's quite well now. He was lucky, or perhaps they caught it early. The awful, medieval treatment worked. Fresh air and exercise are important. He's looking for somewhere to start a farm. I am so happy when I'm with him. Even yesterday. We talked and talked. He said how it helped to tell me about it. I love him and I need him and he loves me and now I know he needs me.'

'Whatever will your mother say? Or your father. Will he approve?'

'Pa doesn't reply to my letters. I haven't told you – I suppose I'm ashamed, but I think he must be cross with me after all for staying with Mummy.'

'That doesn't sound like your pa.' Jo looked lost in thought, studying her fingernails. 'Sorry to say this, but I find your ma hard to be with, all buttoned-up emotionally and old-fashioned as if she's still living in a Victorian colony. None of this will be easy.'

'Are you saying I shouldn't marry Nigel?'

'No, just warning you. Go home now and tell her. It'll only get more difficult the longer you put it off. I'll give you a start and then come over, and be a little bit of a diversion. You can tell me your news and I'll be all excited and say nice things about Nigel so she realises other people approve.'

Ma was sitting in the shade of the lime tree at the end of the garden, busy crocheting.

'Hello, dear. The weather's too nice to stay inside. Sit here beside me.'

'Thank you for my supper last night. Sorry if I was a bit quiet.'

Say it. Now. Jo's right. It will only get more difficult. Now.

'Nigel asked me to marry him.'

The crochet hook stopped moving but Ma didn't look up.

'Well, dear, that's your first proposal. There will be plenty more. He can't have thought you'd accept, so I shouldn't think any more about it.'

'I did accept. I love him, Mummy. We love each other.'

There was hardly a pause. It was as if Ma had prepared for this. 'He hasn't any prospects. He resigned his commission, abandoned his army career, and his father is only a vicar. It is flattering, of course, when a man says he loves you, but you don't know anything about marriage. And he's not one of your set, dear.'

Kitty bit her lips together. Be patient. Don't rise to it. Explain. Make her understand, feel sympathy for Nigel.

'There's something else, Mummy. Something you'll understand. Nigel was very ill. A bit like Peter.'

Ma's head jerked up as two staccato words shot out. 'Like Peter?'

'Well, not quite, because Peter... ' Oh, God, this was not helping. 'No, not really like Peter. Nigel was invalided out of the army. He didn't resign. He had tuberculosis.'

The crochet thread and hook shot onto the grass as Ma leaped up, shaking, visibly angry. 'How dare you? Like Peter? A grown man with that disease! Waste your life on an invalid? You shall not marry him. I will not let you throw yourself away.'

They both turned at the sound of a car on the gravel.

'I don't want that woman in my house. Tell her to leave.'

Ma's small, increasingly broad frame quivered as she walked off towards the back of the house.

Jo wasn't surprised. 'I'm sorry. Come home and have a game of tennis. Give her time to cool down.'

When Jo dropped her back home, she stopped on the road. 'No need to stir up a hornets' nest. Good luck.' She held both thumbs in the air and drove away.

In the heat the dry gravel scuffed up dust onto Kitty's open-toed sandals – they hadn't played tennis, just sat and talked. She rounded the corner, swinging the unused cardigan. The driveway opened up to the circle by the front door.

Someone here.

Crikey – an Austin 7 neatly parked by the open front door.

Nigel. Definitely his car.

Where was Ma? Where was Nigel?

She jumped up the steps in two strides, into the cooler hallway. Voices from the drawing room.

Nigel's back, the square shoulders. He was on the sofa with his back to the doorway, facing Ma, who was in her usual chair by the open window. He turned and stood up.

Ma smiled her perfect-hostess smile. 'Nigel and I have just had a cup of coffee.'

Taken aback at the volte-face from earlier, and at Nigel's

physical presence in the room, she couldn't think what to say. Hello? Smile, just smile.

'I thought I might as well drop by.' The sapphire eyes held hers, deliberately, directly. 'Your mother kindly invited me in despite my not being expected. She told me about your saying we should wait a few months before we announce our plans to anyone else. I think that's very wise of you, darling.'

She returned his look, reading a message in the unblinking sapphires.

Wait a few months! The manipulative old cat!

Nigel spoke. 'It'll give me time to get the farm going and your mother is right, the New Year is a much better time to announce a wedding.'

Rebellion and righteous indignation bubbled up inside.

Nigel went on quickly. 'Now, let's drive into Norwich, look at the shops and the auctioneers' windows.'

With ruthlessly determined speed, Nigel took her by the arm, said a courteous goodbye to Ma and shepherded her into the car.

'I never said that, never said anything about waiting. Ma made that up... I'm so sorry.' Then, 'I don't want to wait.'

He reached across, laid his hand on hers and squeezed it gently.

'Cheer up, love. I guessed she was twisting things. Listen, it isn't a bad idea, for now anyway, if it gives her a chance to get used to the idea. She was actually very sweet when I turned up unannounced.'

He slowed the car, pulled off the road. 'I need a kiss. Several.'

It took ages to write the letter to Pa that evening. When could he give her away? In the New Year? It would be in the church here... Nigel's father is a vicar... So far, so good, but what to say about where Pa could stay, and what about paying for it all? She crossed out those paragraphs, re-wrote the rest.

Once she'd safely sealed up the envelope, she wrote shorter ones to Granny, Liz and Emma. Now late for pre-supper sherry with Ma, she left the envelopes on the hall table for posting the next day.

. . .

The heat of August faded into a gentle September, dry enough to let the blackberries ripen sweet and warm and the leaves to flutter off the trees at their own pace.

The absence of any reply from Pa was a nagging fret, which became a welter of alternating fear and anger as the weeks went by. She wrote again, suggesting she and Nigel meet him for lunch. Jo, immersed in plans for her December wedding, when consulted, was lost for words, and then suggested writing to Granny.

But Granny hadn't replied either. Neither of them. Cutting her off because of Ma? She kept her worries about this from Nigel.

She spent endless days with Nigel. They drove miles looking for somewhere to live. Farm hunting, she called it, because the house was less important than fields and farm buildings. They broadened their searches going further and further afield.

One lunchtime, they were sitting together on the wooden bench against the front wall of The Shire Horse, two halves of bitter and the local paper lying on the table.

'I want to get a place sorted.' Nigel touched her hand and let it rest there. 'I didn't mention that your mother was pretty firm that I must be settled, have a proper home for you, before we announce our engagement.'

So that explained Ma's volte-face and seemingly placid acquiescence.

'We will, Nigel. As soon as Christmas is over we'll find the perfect house. With fields and barns.'

Jo and Alistair married on a bitterly cold December day. Jo, in a low-cut white satin dress, kept warm with a white fox stole around her shoulders. The diamond necklace inherited from Alistair's mother glittered, matching the frosted world outside the church. They glowed happiness and Jo's mother showed none of the conventional tears as they all waved the happy couple off on their honeymoon in Vienna.

. . .

On Christmas Day Ma was in one of her making-it-special moods. Together they went to church, roasted a chicken for lunch.

'We must listen to the king – history being made!' Kitty prodded the coals into life and turned on the wireless.

Ma had been sceptical; she thought the monarchy needed to stay remote. As the broadcast began, she half-rose from her chair.

'I know – it seems wrong, sitting, but I don't think he can see us, Mummy.'

In silence they listened to George V's gravelly voice speak about the marvels of modern science and how all the peoples of his empire, 'so cut off that only voices from the air can reach them', were now linked by wireless.

'I wonder whether my old ayah in Trincomalee is listening,' Ma mused, and reminisced about her childhood, the gloriously coloured flowers, the elephants... 'Ayah gave me my set of teak elephants. You have to keep them facing the door, to safeguard you if there's an earthquake.'

CHAPTER 11

JANUARY 1933

KITTY'S SENSE of isolation lessened as the worst of the icy snow thawed away, though she missed the old easy popping over to see Jo.

She was packing away the Christmas decorations, all carefully taken down before Twelfth Night, when Nigel telephoned.

'There's a small farm advertised, but it's out in Essex. At Flimstour.'

'That doesn't matter, does it? If you're worried about the Austin 7 making it, I can take Speedy, while you navigate.'

She left early next morning to pick up Nigel. It was a long way but she enjoyed driving with Nigel beside her.

'Flimstour – this is it. We're looking for Mill House.' The road ran through the centre of the village, shops on the right-hand side with a triangular green and a duck-pond on the other. 'Turn left, here.'

The road ran downhill for a couple of hundred yards. She changed into second gear to negotiate a right-angled bend at the bottom of the hill alongside a river. A tall, red-brick building with a mill-race dwarfed the river.

'Opposite the mill.' Nigel pointed. 'Here, on the left. My word, look at those outbuildings.'

The house was built of soft red brick, its big-paned Georgian windows closed against the January cold. A wide set of shallow steps curved up to the front door.

It was better by far than she had dared hope – a study to use as a farm office, a drawing room with a huge open fire and floor to ceiling windows. The kitchen looked out over the back garden down towards the river.

Back in the car, ready to leave, she reached across to him. 'We've found our home. The room next to our bedroom is a perfect nursery.' She kissed him, rubbing warmth into his hands as she did so.

'I'll move in right away.' Nigel ran his fingers along her forearm as she reached down to change gear. 'How long do you need to organise our wedding?'

For Pa to reply? Damn him! Will Ma want to outshine Jo's wedding? Cope with that later. 'Will your father take the service?'

'Yes. Come in, tell Mother about the house.'

Nigel dropped his coat on the kitchen table and went in search of his parents, leaving her standing by the stove. The kitchen was warm and smelt of vanilla and baking cake.

Mary burst through the door from the hallway, followed by Bernard in the oldest of his favourite green jumpers.

Mary came across, hugged her close.

'Can we fix a date for the wedding?' Nigel said. 'In April, after Easter, so the church can be decorated.'

It was pitch dark by the time Kitty, awash with love, left for home.

She drove along the familiar road, relishing the womb-like comfort of the darkness surrounding her with the headlights beaming along the road ahead. A gentle, euphoric calm enveloped her.

A home to make her own – going to sleep in Nigel's arms, waking up beside him, long evenings together, ironing his shirts. Babies – becoming little people, to read to, talk with. A farm. With pigs.

Then reality began to intrude. Anxiety twisted in her tummy.

How will Ma react? What about Pa?

'I don't want Pa spoiling things.' Disloyal words. No one else had heard. But the words had been spoken, were out there in the world. 'There, I've said it. Okay, so who does give me away?'

Next morning Ma was in the conservatory, nipping brownish leaves from the plants, the ones she kept inside during the winter. A faint lemony smell came off the bruised leaves.

'I'll just finish trimming these before breakfast.'

'Mummy, the house we saw yesterday is perfect. Nigel's going to move in straightaway. We need to fix a date for the wedding.'

Ma's neat little fingers continued to work away at the plants, the sound of the scissors snipping loud in the silence.

'I don't think any of this is wise.' She turned, laid the scissors with her gardening gloves in the wooden trug. 'A rented house.'

'Mummy! This is rented. Copse End was. We have waited, as you asked, until we have somewhere to live before announcing our engagement. It is a lovely house. And garden. Come and see it, we'll drive over this afternoon.'

'I'm playing cards this afternoon.' The words were clipped.

'We checked with Nigel's parents about dates – after Easter so the church can be decorated.'

'What do you mean going behind my back and arranging things?' The round charm of Ma's face distorted. 'Katherine, you are not to waste yourself on this man. I've let you play around because I thought you'd realise he has no future.'

Play around? No future?

'Mother!'

He's a human being, not a ruddy commodity.

Careful, Kitty. Humour her. Bring her round. Take a deep breath. Smile.

'You don't know Nigel as well as I do. He is loving and kind and we'll be happy running a little farm. When I have babies, you can come to help with your grandchildren. We want to be married here, with Nigel's father taking the service.'

'Grandchildren? Babies? I suppose you think I want to be like your father's mother. Interfering. Like she did in my marriage, siding with your father.'

Pa's mother? Granny?

'She didn't interfere.' Did she? 'She helped with Peter – all those days when you were ill.'

'I did everything for Peter. Your father, his family, they blamed me for his illness.'

'That's not true. No one blamed you.'

'Yes, they did. You, too. No one was there. When he died. They all left me alone.'

Images of that day, carefully buried, flashed before her.

'That's a lie. Pa and I were there. And the nurses.'

Anger, frustration and years of pent-up grief burst through her control. 'You sent Pa away – you told him to get out of the house. I've never told anyone, *anyone*, that you shut me out, left me to howl on the cold floor, I've kept your cruelty secret, embarrassed for you, trying to make allowances for you. Why should I? You shut Peter's door. You left me outside, which was where Mrs Bird found me. She took care of me. You are selfish, and cruel. And vile and… '

She ran from the conservatory through to the hall and grabbed the keys to Speedy.

She didn't drive carefully, her eyes blinded by tears. But it was a short distance and the road was clear.

She hardly parked the car, fell against the vicarage front door, leaned on the bell.

The door was opened by William, who took one look and called, 'Elma! Elma!'

'Yes, yes. I'm coming. Whatever is the matter…?' Elma's voice trailed off. 'William, put the kettle on, please. We'll be in your study.'

Gulping back the tears, she began to talk.

Her final revelation about Nigel's TB, imparted only after a promise of absolute secrecy, made Elma gasp.

'What a tangle! I feel responsible.'

She went over to the mantelpiece, and started absent-mindedly shuffling the collection of onyx Buddhas along the shelf.

'My dear, I know how much you love each other. Nigel is a dear and a deliciously good-looking man. I know your mother. She is difficult and a snob.'

Another long pause, while she moved the little Buddhas back to their original position. 'I don't like your mother but I understand her fears for your happiness. I am sure she wants what is best for you, though you may not see it like that. She means well even if she's making a mess of it. Some of this may be her own fault, but she is alone and that can't be easy. Give her time. Come over here when you need to let off steam. Now, drink this tea.' Elma ladled sugar into the cup. 'Too early for a gin, I fear, but this'll shore you up.'

Back home, there was an unreal feel to the place, as if it was a stage-set – Mrs Richards preparing lunch in the kitchen, Ma arranging flowers in the drawing room.

They ate lunch in artificial calm, though Ma was evidently trying to make peace.

'This is very good macaroni cheese. Have some more, Kitty dear.'

As ever, Ma wasn't going to say sorry, admit, recognise perhaps, her wrongdoing. But Elma was right. Ma may have meant well.

'No, thank you.' Don't be contrary. Take the olive branch. 'Well, just a little, please.'

The appearance of normality restored once again. That afternoon Kitty wrote a long letter to Pa, begging him to help, and one to Liz.

Ma, off to the hairdresser, offered to post the letters. She came back with cake for tea.

For the next three weeks, Kitty managed to keep her patience, sustained by Nigel's calm affection and by frequent visits to Elma. An uneasy peace reigned at home with Ma acting as if Nigel and their engagement did not exist, freezing out any conversation on the subject.

As one interminable day passed into another, Kitty lost her usual bounce, no longer getting pleasure from the daily trivia. Jo said she looked tired, Elma insisted on stiff gins.

Nigel moved into Mill House, bought a sow, and found an elderly farm worker called Mason to help with the heavy work.

Together they spent hours talking round and round about how and when they might persuade Ma to accept their marriage, and then ended up spending the rest of their time together in increasingly passionate embraces, which did nothing for either of them.

She chose not to say that Pa still had not replied, that she was no further towards knowing who might walk her up the aisle, stand beside her at the altar, give her away.

One day it got too much. At lunch in the pub, she left half her drink and said the Irish stew was tasteless.

Outside, he stood between the cars, and tried to kiss her. 'Let's meet tomorrow, then.'

'Oh, for God's sake, Nigel, don't be so nice. What's the point?'

She pulled away from him, drove off without glancing behind her. By the time Speedy was coasting along the main road tears were pouring down her face. She pulled up, considered turning back. Nigel would have gone, and there was no point. No point at all.

Eyes dried, nose blown several times, she started up the car and drove on. Stupid, selfish to have been cross. He'd been trying to help, had been endlessly patient. And Ma. Acting in her own mistaken way, without anyone to help. Perhaps the Pa she had known wasn't the real man, was a front put on for her benefit. Why else hadn't he kept in touch?

The sun, absent behind clouds all morning, broke through spotlighting the spring-green grass along the verge to a sharp emerald. Along the straight mile, she pressed hard on the accelerator, watched the needle on the speedometer swing round.

On impulse, she went to the little florist's shop and bought a dozen yellow tulips.

Ma was out at her regular Mothers' Union meeting. Kitty used her key to open the front door, clutching the tulips in one hand.

A pile of letters lay on the mat. The relief postman delivered late, and sometimes muddled up the addresses. She scooped the envelopes up together, and began to sort the higgledy-piggledy pile.

A brown envelope for Ma, the butcher's bill probably; a postcard invitation for Ma to play cards.

Goody, Liz had replied and another, with a London postmark… At last! Pa!

Pa's spidery thick-nibbed script. Keys and the tulips fell to the floor. She tore at the envelope, pulled the sheets of thick paper out.

Dearest Kitty,
It's nearly a month now, and still no letter from you…

Her heart thumped against her ribs. The backs of her knees went watery. She reached for the table, sat on the hard hall chair.

… and I had hoped you could find the time to come up to have lunch with me one day.

Lunch?

No letter from you?

No letter from you.

Ma always sorted the post when it arrived.

Ma posted my letters.

In the safety of her bedroom, she locked the door. The horrors, for so long dark shadows hidden away, reawakened. Peterkin. She reached up, touched the brushstrokes defining the windmill, the solid sails against the sky.

'Peterkin, you were brave, wilful too. You'd have managed her, made her see things your way. I can't. I'm going to live with Nigel. Unmarried. Live in sin.'

She stuffed clothes into a case. Reached up, took the painting in one hand, the case in the other, and went down to Speedy.

'Good God. Kitty.'

He was beside her in an instant as she ran in through the kitchen door at Mill House. He held her tight, let her sob. 'I'm here. You're safe. Don't talk yet.'

His calm stilled her tears. She stuttered out half-sentences, spilled out about Pa and the night of Peter's death. 'The cook found me. I never told anyone.'

'Unforgivable.' His face was set, hard. He pulled her down beside him on the wooden settle under the window. 'I will not let her drive you to disgrace yourself by living with me before we're married.'

'I don't care about that. It's only words, and social convention. A way of showing off to other people. A chance for the Trotts of this world to be centre stage. I couldn't face all that pretence now. It serves Ma right.'

'Ah, love, your tears have turned to anger. Listen, some conventions matter, they are useful.' He dropped down on one knee. Smiled up, took hold of her left hand. 'And some are nice.'

He unclenched his palm. Blue stone, tiny pearls. Gold. He slipped the metal, warm from his hand, onto her finger. It fitted exactly. A shaft of sunlight caught the sapphire.

'We will be legally man and wife before we live together. I want you to be Mrs Gifford.'

He stood up, pulled on his sports jacket.

'I'll organise a register office wedding. That won't take long – about three weeks.'

'Three weeks!'

'Go home now. Don't tell your mother. Keep it our secret. I won't tell anyone either. We'll still meet. Bring a few things with you each time, I'll bring them back here. Chin up, pet.'

She twisted the ring off her finger. 'I'll try.' And wiped the salty deposits off her eyelashes. Made an effort to smile. 'I'll keep this on my long gold chain and wear it where no one can see it. I won't tell anyone either, not Jo, nor Pa when I write.'

Thank God there was no sign of Ma at home – a cards afternoon with after-the-games sherry before they all went home for their suppers.

Upstairs, locked in her room, she tried to write to Pa. Tore up the first two attempts into tiny pieces that she pushed to the bottom of her handbag. The words about Ma looked harsh and disloyal. She started again, must get the letter in the post. Finally, with lots of crossings out, she finished. She read it through.

Dearest Pa,

I got your last letter today. I've never got any others, not since your card the Christmas before last. This is difficult, I am ashamed for her, but Mummy must have been keeping them, and she can't have posted the one I wrote to you when I told you about Nigel Gifford, and our wanting to get married. We still do…

Don't tell him we are definitely going to…

… but Mummy does not approve. I am a bit busy for a few weeks but I'd love to meet for lunch.

She signed it, put some hugs and kisses, and then added a PS.

I am sorry for all the crossings out, but this was a dreadful letter to have to write. I never really THOUGHT that you wouldn't write, but then I didn't know what to think. Please write to me c/o a friend at Mill House, Flimstour.

For two weeks she managed, somehow, to keep courteous social calm with Ma. She read late into the nights, unable to sleep, and made a pretence that everything was normal. She took a few clothes and a handful of treasures, books, and Peter's postcards, each time she crept out to meet Nigel.

One day Ma was out for lunch so she met Nigel at The Shire Horse. He pushed the plates to the far side of the table, wiped it dry. He spread out two sets of long sheets of paper.

The register office forms.

'Sign here, and here, where I've pencilled in crosses.'

They agreed to meet four days later. In the railway station car park and then not again until she drove herself over to the register office.

The Austin 7 was parked, unmissably, at the entrance. She handed the last of her packaged-up belongings.

'Which one of these do I bring with me for our honeymoon?' Nigel asked.

'I marked it. Where we are going?'

'Bad luck to tell you. It's only for a couple of days, while Mason looks after the farm.' Nigel smiled but the lines on his face showed deeply etched. 'This came for you.'

'Pa's written!'

On her last night at Otters she poured herself an extra sherry, drank it quickly while Ma dished up. Her hands quivered and her stomach was in turmoil. Ma, in utter ignorance, insisted on two games of rummy.

'Goodnight, Kitty dear.'

Tomorrow night she wouldn't be here. Ma would be on her own.

Without even a goodbye. Cruel to deceive her, to abandon her.

'Ma… '

The hard corners of Pa's envelope, tucked deep in her skirt pocket, rubbed against her waist. *Try to forgive her, but it is better to keep her at a distance for now, so she cannot make trouble.*

'Goodnight, Mummy.'

CHAPTER 12

APRIL 1933

'Mrs Gifford.' He kissed her hard on the lips. She moved forward in the passenger seat and turned towards him, and pressed her lips against his.

She leaned across, ran her index finger round his lips. He took her hand away, kissed each finger.

'No more cars for us.' He held her eyes. Her tummy turned over.

'I don't suppose we either of us got much sleep last night. We'll stop at the first café and hope it's decent.'

'I'm starving. That old couple at the register office were sweet when you roped them in as witnesses. She kissed me and wished me luck. We'll never meet them again yet their names are on this certificate. Our children will think they were our friends.' She folded up the certificate and lifted the map book from between the seats. 'Where are we going?'

'You have to guess.'

They drove south, through London, out towards the west, dropped down through Surrey. As Nigel negotiated the high street in Winchester, she looked again at the map.

'The New Forest. That's it!'

When they arrived at the hotel, built in soft-coloured stone, he led the way up the steps, through the glass-paned front door, over the thick carpet, to the reception desk.

The porter carried the two suitcases, both Nigel's, up the wide shallow staircase, unlocked the bedroom door and put the cases on the luggage racks. He handed Nigel the room key.

'Thank you, sir.' The porter accepted the coin Nigel handed him, and closed the bedroom door.

Nigel pushed the bolt across the door.

She froze. The bed behind her was huge, a proper four-poster. Evening sunlight, low in the sky now, flooded into the room, silhouetting him.

She couldn't see the expression on his face. He stepped towards her.

Lifted her up in his arms, dropped her on the bed. She could see his eyes now, bluer than ever she remembered. Felt the warmth of his body, his hands moving over her stomach. Stopped thinking.

Next morning they walked along the lawned verges of the forest, past a cluster of ponies, mares with foals nibbling at the short grass, on their way to the village post office to send telegrams.

'What will happen when Ma reads this? I've written *Nigel Gifford and I married in Bishop's Stortford yesterday. Love, Kitty.*'

He didn't reply at once. His face was impassive. Then he smiled, said, 'That's nice, to end with your love.'

Duty done, they strolled towards the river. Ducks, full of morning verve, were plunging into the estuary, churning up the water as they splashed down.

Half a dozen cattle grazed on the village green, a long, wide stretch of closely cropped grass. They paused by the bow-fronted window of a teashop.

'Good smell of coffee,' Nigel said.

'Look, that big cup, the one decorated with the pigs. It's for sale, there's a price tag.'

They had a pot of coffee, and shared a toasted teacake. Nigel went to pay, and she saw the waitress taking the breakfast cup and saucer from the window.

'For you, love,' said Nigel.

'You must have one too. One each.'

'The blue and white willow pattern, the one with a windmill.'

They strolled away from the village, along a track, the coconutty scent of the gorse, full in its yellow blooms, blown into their faces by the breeze. They turned off the track. The grass path wound through a spinney of silver birch trees.

Disturbed, a lark trilled its warning, and spiralled up into the sky, higher and higher, until it was no more than a dot against the blue.

She reached for his hand. 'I'm so happy. Thank you.'

She moved her hands into his jacket, reaching around his back, feeling the muscles. He was taller, but her legs were long. Her hips met his.

'You promised. That day at Cley, you said we'd find a corner of a field.' She knelt on the grass, pulled him down, knowing now what she wanted.

She felt the strong spring sun on her bare back. Lifted herself to watch his face, saw his eyes darken, felt him pull her tight onto him.

Afterwards, sated, she dropped fast asleep.

She woke, smelt the gorse, heard the lark. He was wide awake, smiling at her surprise.

They went home to Flimstour via Bishop's Stortford to collect Speedy. Nigel beat her back to Mill House. As she stepped out of the car, he scooped her up in his arms and carried her into the hallway.

'My bride! Over the threshold. Now, let's walk round our grounds, beat the boundaries as they say.'

Holding hands, they went out through the kitchen door and walked across the lawn towards the river. The low sun shone through the tall willows, dappling the water.

'Look. Swallows.' Kitty pointed. A handful of the birds darted along the line of the water. 'Catching the flies, midges. Summer's on its way.'

. . .

She hadn't wanted to tell Pa in a telegram, a few bald words, no explanation, so she had waited till they got home and then wrote a proper letter.

Pa replied by the return of post.

I found this little book of Brooke's poems in Foyles. I am sorry the cheque is not bigger but I hope you both enjoy spending it. Come for lunch soon. Good luck, Kitty.

She burst into tears. Nigel put his arms around her, held her close.

'Ah, my love.' He used his handkerchief to dry her cheeks. 'Suppose we go into Stortford, buy something special with some of his money. Something you can keep.'

She sniffed. 'That's a nice idea.' Blew her nose, gave him back his hankie. 'We could have lunch out.'

She chose a Royal Worcester flower vase, white porcelain decorated with dusky pink tulips.

A letter came from Ma. She wrote that as a mother she could do nothing more. Signed '*Mother*'. No love.

Liz came to stay for a weekend, bringing her increasingly brittle London ways with her. She adored Nigel, said she was dreadfully jealous and would never find anyone half so dashing in town.

On Sunday afternoon, after tea, Nigel drove Liz to the station in Stortford in time to catch her London train. Kitty was still tidying up the kitchen when he got home.

'I can't think how we made so much washing up. This has taken me ages.'

He leaned against the dresser. 'The car was a devil to start again. I think we should see what we can get for it. Cut our losses.'

'We can manage with Speedy. What will the Seven fetch?'

'Enough to invest in a new, younger sow.'

The garage man in Stortford said the Seven was in good condition for its age.

Nigel banked the money ready for when they went sow shopping at the livestock markets.

The next week they left Mason to finish off the morning round of feeding and mucking out and drove over to Stortford. The ringside was less crowded than when they went to Fakenham on their first date.

'The next few are gilts, mostly in pig.' Nigel grinned at her. 'You decide – you've a natural eye for livestock. And bid!'

A pig, clean enough, padded into the ring. She snuffled around, without much enthusiasm. Two farmers competed, briefly, in the bidding. Kitty checked – hands firmly in her pockets.

'Not for us, eh?' Nigel smiled. 'We don't have to buy one today. It can wait a week or two.'

The next animal looked thin, its coat lacklustre.

'No, I'd like to get on with it. Besides, the carter can deliver if we buy today.' Another pig was ushered into the ring.

Head in the air, snout raised, eyes bright under the canopy of ears. A long straight back. The white streak stark on the sow's shoulder contrasted with the shiny black withers and rump.

Kitty's right hand was in the air almost before the auctioneer opened the bidding. She raised it again as a farmer on the opposite side of the ring raised his shooting stick in a bid. Her heart was thumping away. The farmer shook his head.

'She's yours,' Nigel said. 'Congratulations.' He went to the desk to pay while she found the carter, a crumpled, uncommunicative man, but he seemed competent enough with the animals.

Kitty drove home fast to be sure of arriving before the sow. In anticipation of a purchase they had left a sty ready, clean straw, fresh water.

The carter let down the ramp, opened the wooden gate at the top. They stood, one on each side of the ramp, ready to steer the animal into her sty.

With considerable caution, the sow placed her two front trotters on the ramp. The curly tail twitched. The snout lifted.

'Come on, Flossie!' Kitty called. The pig, responding to her voice, looked up, pointed her snout and walked decorously down the ramp, straight into the sty.

'Where did that name come from?' Nigel asked. The sow was snuffling around to retrieve the last of the barley mash, a welcome-home meal to settle her.

'I've no idea. She answered to it, though.'

'Ah, well, Flossie you are, my pig.' Nigel bent down, tickled the sow behind her ears.

In September, Jo and Alistair came to stay for the weekend. Jo was pregnant, large and due in a few weeks' time, so the four of them spent a gentle two days, making the most of the Indian summer, eating lunches outside and chatting under the shade of the tree during the afternoon. The pigs, especially Flossie, were inspected and admired.

As they left, Jo stood on tiptoe to kiss Nigel. 'You've fulfilled Kitty's dreams. I've never seen her look so well. Bless you.'

Alone again, Nigel took her arm. They walked to their spot on the edge of the lawn where it sloped sharply down towards the river. The day was warm and sunny, the air crisp, a film of mist and bonfire smoke hovering over the water.

'Idyllic, wistful September afternoon.' Nigel took her hand.

'Autumn makes me sad.'

'It shouldn't, you know. Harvest, nature sowing her seeds of spring. No spring or summer without autumn and winter, my love.'

'Teach me to like it.'

'Come here.' He pulled her close. 'The best thing about people staying is having the house to ourselves after they go. I miss my morning glories when you're up doing breakfast.'

'Me, too.' She touched his face. She almost preferred the mornings. Or the evenings on the rug in front of the drawing room fire.

Just a few idyllic months since Dereham and Ma – a forgotten world.

Not quite.

'Jo saw Ma out shopping. Ma avoided her, crossed over to the other pavement. It'll soon be Christmas. I must try to mend things between us. Do you think Elma would help?'

'Of course, my dear,' Elma said when telephoned. 'William has kept in touch with your mother, and we give her a lift to church on wet days. I'll do a little lunch for the four of us. Leave it to me.'

Kitty arrived first. Her hand shook, threatening to spill the stiff gin and French, as Elma answered the door to Ma.

'Come in, Dorothy.' Elma's voice carried, louder than usual. 'Kitty's here already so it's a quick gin and Dubonnet for you before lunch.'

Elma swept Ma into the room.

'Hello, Mummy. I brought you something from a rather nice shop in Stortford.'

And that was that. Nothing more was said, Ma unable, as ever, to face up to the reality of her behaviour or to apologise. The lunch party was civilised, repairing the worst of the quarrel.

Nigel was delighted. 'Would you like to ask her here for Christmas?'

'That's noble, but no, I don't think so. She can be very difficult. It'd be easier to stay friends with her at a distance.'

She felt for his hand. 'Anyway, I want you to myself on Christmas Day. I'll help with the mucking out and morning feeds, and on Boxing Day before we go over to your parents.'

Late in the afternoon on Christmas Eve, she was perched on a chair, reaching up to hammer the holly into the beams in the big kitchen and singing along with the carols from King's College on the wireless.

Wherever was Nigel? He shouldn't have taken so long to collect the capon from the farm on the other side of the river.

The curtains were undrawn, the light reflecting on the black glass of the windows.

She jumped when she saw the kitchen door start to open.

Nosed open. By shaggy brown and white fur. A pair of bright beady eyes stared up, met her eyes. Advanced. The furry creature, cat-size but bigger boned, shouldered its way into the room. It seemed bothered by something round its neck.

'Hey, leave that alone, fella!' Nigel appeared on the other end of a smart black lead. 'This, my love, is your Christmas present.'

She was off the chair, holly and hammer abandoned, and on her knees beside the dog. 'Where did you get him? He's got a goatee tuft for a beard.' Stroking the dog, she said to it, 'That's a very smart ribbon you have on, it makes you look like a pirate. I don't think you like it, or the envelope!'

Standing up she flung her arms around Nigel. 'He's lovely.'

'He's been remarkably good, till I tried to tie the bow on with your Christmas card.'

'Does he have a name?'

'He's yours, you christen him. He's feisty. He came from that farm where we get hay. He's only a few months old.'

She found newspaper and an old saucer and gave the dog some milk. 'You nurse him on your lap. The vegetables are about to catch in the pans.'

He finished his gin and tonic. 'I need another gin. I should have bought a basket. Sorry, didn't think.'

'We must have something that'll do.' She stopped spooning out the mashed potatoes, gestured with the enamel ladle. 'What about that old chair, the one we found at the back of the stables?'

'Good idea. Leave those plates, hold this chap.'

The muscular little body stayed still in her arms, warm against her.

'He's gone a long while again, little dog.'

She was about to go out, through the front door towards the barns, when something thumped against the back door. The dog growled.

Nigel was propping the chair against the top step.

'Sorry, I slipped. Too much gin. Damn thing has a mind of its own.'

She giggled. Opening the larder door, she pushed the dog inside and closed the door again.

'I'll pull it in.'

The short square back of the chair jammed in the doorframe.

Nigel, upright now, tried to lift it. The cushion fell out, oozing clumps of horsehair. Eventually they pushed and pulled it in, shut the back door.

There was a loud scrabbling from inside the larder. The little dog came out, dwarfed by a muddy leek held proudly in his mouth. They doubled up with laughter.

'God, it's filthy.' She used the floor cloth to wash the chair, wiping off the worst of the grime and revealing shiny chestnut leather. They moved it to beside the range. Horsehair bulged out through the holes on the box-like narrow arms.

'What a chair. Someone must've cut two sides out of a wooden box – the back's no higher than the arms.' Kitty giggled again.

'Mock not. It's low, stumps for legs – easy for the puppy to climb into it.'

He picked the dog up, settled him in the chair. The exhausted creature fell fast asleep.

On Christmas morning, they took the dog round the fields. The black and tan bundle of wiry fur nosed out an unsuspecting rat in the food bins and dispatched it with alarming speed. Then he turned his attention to the big Tamworth sow. Two front paws planted forward, muscular little body taut, the dog faced up to the old pig, growled, and then as she flicked her ears and turned away, he began to bark.

'You ferocious little mite.' She bent down, picked up the quivering volcano. 'Barney. That's his name.'

In the short January days, Nigel went outside at first light, before breakfast, to see to the pigs. Mason arrived later, after he'd attended to his own hens and milking cow, to do the mucking out and other chores.

For weekday lunches, she made soup, or sometimes they had the odd slice of leftover cold meat, which they ate at the kitchen table. She lit the drawing room fire before Nigel finished outside and they settled in for the evening. They played cards, mostly bezique but racing demon if they were feeling frivolous, and listened to plays or concerts on the wireless, and planned the days ahead.

'There's a piece here about the new television service that the BBC is starting.' Nigel was reading the newspaper.

'I can't imagine. I like making my own pictures, watching the fire too.' She changed the subject. 'I ought to see Mummy again. Maybe take her out to lunch, do a bit of shopping together. I'll be back for tea, keep the time with her short.'

'You'll feel better for doing it. Barney here and I will have the fire alight, and drop scones ready.'

The day started well, Ma smiley and happy browsing round the shops.

'You look well, Katherine.' Followed by a searching look. 'Bonny.'

'I'm getting fat, Mummy. This shirt is tight, and I need a bigger bra.'

'It suits you, dear. Let me buy you that pretty cardigan.'

Kitty arrived home tired. The fire was alight, the drop scones ready, and Barney insisted on jumping onto her knee when she sank into the sofa.

'Ma was fine. I remember she was always better out, even when I was small.' The flickering firelight threw shadows on Nigel's face. 'Thank you – knowing you were here to come back to made it easier to cope with. Do you know she even mentioned Peter, quite normally – she said Peter always liked me in blue. Neither of us mentioned Pa.'

'Why don't you meet in London? Easier for him to find the time. I'll drop you at the station.'

'Sometime soon. Yes.' She felt her eyelids dropping. 'I'm sleepy, Nigel. Must be the warmth.'

'More likely exhaustion, all that anticipation and tension. Early bed, tonight, my love.'

She slept well, but woke still feeling tired and queasy. Up and about, cooking up the mash for Flossie's tribe, she began to feel better.

The following morning, she turned over in the bed. Nigel was awake.

'Kitty?' He left the question hanging, his hands not finding their way into her nightdress as usual. 'It's market day. I'll make us tea, bring it back up here.'

The sweet tea warmed down into her stomach.

She felt under the sheet for the cord on Nigel's pyjamas.

Later he bagged the bathroom first. 'I'll miss the first few lots if I don't hurry.' He pulled on corduroys and a jacket. He came round to her side of the bed. 'Thank you.'

He ran down the stairs, the front door slammed shut.

She lay, luxuriating in the warmth of the bed and dozed off. She woke when Barney barked at the postman and was surprised to see the time. Downstairs she fed the dog, and began to sort some washing. A wave of nausea hit her as she bent over the sink.

Sick? In the morning? She looked at the kitchen calendar, the one from the seed merchants.

'I've missed two months without realising... but give it another month before I go to the doctor... Not say anything till I'm sure... Maybe I'm not... '

'But I bet I am!' She darted up the stairs, into the smallest bedroom. The one they had ear-marked for a nursery when they first saw the house.

'Now, Barney, not a word to your master until I am sure about this.' The dog had raced up the stairs ahead of her. His ears pricked up and he set his head on one side. 'I shall tell him he's going to be a father later, in my own way.' She pulled the door closed on the little room and skipped down the stairs.

She stuck to her plan. Nigel came in one day when she was cleaning out all the kitchen cupboards.

'Good Lord, does that need doing?'

'A bit of spring cleaning. And I've written to Pa, suggesting we meet next week.'

She dressed carefully. Would Pa be very smart? He had suggested they lunch in the Great Eastern Hotel at Liverpool Street, writing,

'Easier for you, and convenient for me. The food is quite nice and we'll be able to talk.'

The train was a few minutes late. She hurried through into the restaurant. He was there waiting. Lawyer's jacket. Tall as ever as he stood up. Yet somehow different.

'Kitten!' He kissed her cheek. 'How well you look. Smart.'

'You too, Pa.' But it wasn't true. The clothes, yes, but he looked so much older.

Although the food was nice, she talked so much that it took a while to make respectable inroads into the roast lamb.

Pa didn't seem hungry. And he led the conversation, drawing her out about Nigel, the farm, Barney, Jo even. Using all his lawyer's skills. He didn't want to talk about himself. Each time she asked about him and what he was doing, he distracted her. Once she came close to blurting out that he might be going to be a grandfather. But she held back, stuck to her plan.

Nigel was waiting on the platform when her train pulled in. Wrapped in his arms, the odd and un-Pa-like superficiality of the lunch faded.

'It was lovely to see him. He had to get back to court. He didn't want to talk about himself. It didn't seem quite like the old days. He looked older.' Less real. But somehow it seemed to matter less now, wrapped in Nigel's arms. 'But I'm different too, with us, the pigs, and... ' Don't tell him – not till the doctor's confirmed it. 'Other things.'

She managed to be patient, and waited another four weeks before she made an appointment, one morning when Nigel would be out at market, to see the doctor.

He examined her on the couch, and then waited while she pulled her clothes back together and sat in the chair by his desk.

'Now, Mrs Gifford, you are quite right. You are definitely expecting. Let me see, according to your dates your confinement will be at the end of August. Plenty of time for you to make all the arrangements, accommodation and so forth.'

'That's all organised. We have a lovely room almost ready as a nursery. Beside our bedroom.'

The doctor, male, middle-aged and unexciting, looked over his glasses, his face impassive.

Whatever is the matter with the man, why doesn't he smile?

'Is something wrong with the baby?'

'No, I'm sure the baby is healthy. You're big for your dates but that's nothing to worry about.'

The doctor's face, heavy-featured, set into a frown.

He lifted his stethoscope, put it down, back on the desk, coiled it around on itself, used his hand to sweep non-existent dust off the leather desktop.

'I am your husband's doctor. I am aware of his condition, of his tuberculosis.' The doctor took off his spectacles. 'I expect you know a newborn baby must be kept apart from anyone with TB. It's contagious. Your husband will infect the child. Your baby will have to live quite separately from your husband.'

The room swam around.

The doctor caught her seconds before she hit the floor.

She struggled, shaky, back into the house. Nigel was at the market, wouldn't be home for hours.

Barney raced around, welcoming her.

She shoved the dog away. Stumbled up the stairs, into the lavatory.

Not live with Nigel.

Her life here, all the things she treasured, destroyed.

What about Nigel? To tell him he's got to go because of his TB? Not allowed to touch his baby, his child?

The bile rose in her throat and she retched away again, on nothing. Waves of heat swept over her, then the sweat turned cold.

Her legs dissolved into jelly. She sat on the floor. Tried to stand up. Vomited again.

Being sick? Straining? Women lose babies that way. Only the doctor knew she was pregnant, no one else. Women often miscarried. There were back-street abortions in towns. Using knitting needles.

She pulled the bath towel round her shoulders, leaned against the bath.

Suppose she lost the baby?

Perhaps one day there'd be a cure for TB, there was talk about new treatments. She could wait, have a baby then.

She stood up. Shaky still, she hung onto the door handle, paused at the top of the stairs. Decided.

CHAPTER 13

FEBRUARY 1934

BURNING pokers tore her tummy apart. Sour taste in her mouth. Someone screamed.

'I can't give her any more morphine, sister.' A man's voice. 'Mrs Gifford, the pain will ease.'

Firm hands on her shoulders. The light hurt.

She tried to lift her head. Everything spun round.

'Don't try to sit up. The doctor's given you something to ease the pain.'

White. White sheets. Sharp light. White apron. Navy dress. White cap. Grey hair. A nurse? The cap turned away. Wood sounded on wood as the nurse pulled up a chair.

'Your husband is waiting outside. You're called Kitty, he says. He found you of course, and called the ambulance, but we have not told him what we found.'

Slowly she formed the question. 'The baby, will it be all right?'

'No. You have lost them. Dead. You are badly ruptured inside. What did you do?'

'I was at home. I… ' Kitty started to cry.

'Well, I dare say you had your reasons. Though he seems a lovely man to me. Anyway, you've made yourself very ill. No more babies for you for a while. Now, we're going to get you into a private room and then perhaps you'd like to see your husband. We will tell him the bare facts, that you are badly ruptured, that you have lost twin foetuses and will take a long time to get better. What else you tell him is up to you.'

The room went hazy and the sick came up again. Damp warmth on her legs. Voices, not just the nurse, another woman.

'Doctor gave her more morphine, sister.'

'Kitty, we're getting you into bed.' This voice, the new one, was more solid. 'Breathe deeply, through your nose.'

The knives sliced through her tummy again.

'There, well done. That's you tidied up.'

She stirred in the sheets. Hands on her hands. Squeezing them. Pressing on her wedding ring.

'Smile, show me you're awake.'

Nigel.

'That's better. Sister said I mustn't stay long. Don't talk. Thank God you're all right. I'll come back this evening.' He kept hold of her hands. His hair looked blacker than ever in the white room. 'Go to sleep. Dream about home, and Barney, and me feeding the pigs, and lighting the fire. The house will be horrid without you. I love you, Kitty. Now rest.'

His lips brushed her cheek. He squeezed her hands.

The door clicked shut.

The next few hours floated past. She lay in a morphine-induced stupor, hardly aware as the nurse lifted her arm from the bed, wrapping the cloth tight, counting her heartbeats.

The ward sister bustled in, carefully helped her get into a propped-up sitting position, and washed her face and hands.

'It's almost six o'clock and your husband will be here shortly.'

The woman had curly brown hair, rosy cheeks. Starched white apron. White cuffs. Clean, bleached fingers.

'I'm sorry. I've made a lot of work for everyone. Thank you.'

She was rewarded with a warm hand on her shoulder. 'That's what we're here for. Don't apologise, just help us get you better. I'll send your husband in now.'

Nigel manoeuvred in, encumbered with his hat in one hand and a vast bunch of hothouse flowers in the other. He dropped the flowers on the end of the bed, and cupped her shoulder bones in his hands, bent his head close to her face.

'My God, you gave me a fright.'

His lips were soft, warm on her cracked ones. He ran his thumb round her cheekbone.

'Sister says you're a tiny bit better. Does it hurt dreadfully?'

'Not so much now. They gave me a lot of morphine.'

He was perched on the edge of the bed, his hands back on her shoulders.

'I'm sorry, so sorry.' She tried to take a deep breath, felt the pain sharp in her ribs. He saw that, squeezed her shoulder.

'Don't try to talk, Kitty.'

'I must! I don't know what they've told you... ' Then she whispered, 'I didn't fall down the stairs. I did it deliberately.'

Their eyes met, unblinking, opening a door into each other's souls.

'I wanted to be sure, then to surprise you, that's why I went to the doctor before I told you. But the doctor said... '

She stopped. Her eyes like lead, dropping. Bile churning in her chest. What about his humiliation, his tears when he'd told her about his TB? She had to find a way to tell him what the doctor had said without destroying him.

She took a sip of water.

'I need you, it's not only love, and those things. I feel safe with you, like there are two of me. That sounds silly, I mean we feel the same things, I don't need to tell you things, you... '

He put his hand softly over her mouth.

'Shh. I need you too, much more than you realise. Having you has blotted out the horrors of the hospitals and treatments, given me a purpose, made me a whole person again. I can guess what the doctor said. Not everyone would agree, but I've heard it before. Not many men have a wife who loves them as much as you showed your love this morning.' He knelt down beside the bed, rested his head against her body. 'We won't tell anyone, we'll keep it secret to ourselves. You slipped down the stairs, and lost your babies. The only thing I want is you back home, with me.'

She clung onto him, felt their tears mingling, dampening the crisp sheet.

'This won't do. I was told not to upset you.' Nigel pulled away, still holding her hands. 'Barney wants you home, too. He's in the car. Tomorrow you can see him through the window.'

She caught his lighter mood.

'Get him a bone from the butcher. And I don't think nurse would approve of those lovely flowers on my bed. Far too extravagant, but lovely. I feel tired, will you come tomorrow? I'll ask the doctor about coming home.'

His face set for a moment, but she was too tired to work out why.

'Tomorrow I'll bring books and playing cards. We can play racing demon – well, perhaps not, but you could play sevens, or something.' He kissed her, pulled the sheet up around her shoulders and crept out.

When the nice ward sister was changing the sheets on the bed next morning, cleverly without moving her, Kitty asked, 'How soon will I be able to go home?'

'The internal rupturing is severe. Any exertion, movement even, and you will start to haemorrhage again. We shall have to see how you get on, but two or three weeks.'

For three weeks they insisted she stay in hospital until, at last, she was allowed to go, on the strictest instructions to rest and not to lift anything, not even a teapot, for three months.

When they got home, Nigel wanted her to go straight up to bed. She refused, said that she would be just as safe on the sofa in the drawing room, that she couldn't bear to be shut away from life going on in the house. He relented, put more logs on the fire, brought pillows and blankets downstairs, and put tea and books beside her.

'Nigel, you're very good at this!'

He grinned, kissed her eyes. 'It's self-interest. I want you back to normal.' He pulled the door shut. Opened it again. Smiling broadly, said, 'Anyhow, I had plenty of time to see how it's done.'

She lifted the newspaper, ready to throw it at him. 'Don't!'

She put her head back onto the pillows. Warm and comfortable, the pains all gone several days ago, she dozed.

They ate supper, fish pie prepared by Mason's wife, on their laps in front of the fire. He sat on the floor at her feet, his head resting against her on the sofa, while they listened to the dance band programme and afterwards the nine o'clock news, and then he helped her upstairs to bed.

'How wonderful, my own bed, my dog, no antiseptic. You and me together again'

Reading her thoughts, he took both her hands. 'Soon. The doctor gave me very strict instructions, you know. I'll be up in a minute, when I've tidied up, put Barney out and things.'

To keep the farm going Nigel asked Mason to work longer hours, and Mrs Mason came to do in the house, cooking as well as cleaning.

Jo motored over for lunch one day. Nigel left them alone, saying he must get on with the farm work. She hugged Kitty, and said, 'Don't worry, there's plenty of time, you'll have other babies.'

After a moment's hesitation, Kitty replied with only, 'Everyone's been so good to us. I treasure all the kindness and help.'

She meant it, yet would have been happy if she and Nigel were an island, cut off from the rest of the world. There was a subdued ecstasy between them, heightened she supposed by the recent horrors, and they loved as she had never dreamed two people could. They found ecstatic happiness in the most mundane moments, shared jokes, Barney's escapades, and the wonders of the fire not smoking despite the south-westerly gale. And in bed they managed, between them, to ensure that Nigel had his morning glories and her too.

Her body was back to normal. No sharp snagging aches as she bent or twisted. Although Nigel continued to worry, tried to stop her, she insisted they work together during the midsummer hours of daylight, fencing the big field into four smaller paddocks.

She held the posts straight while Nigel used the sledgehammer to settle them in place, then they took one handle each of the heavy metal post tool and thumped each post deep down into the ground.

Kneeling to tap in the staple to hold the bottom of the pig wire, Nigel grinned up at her. 'This is the last of several hundred bits of bent steel. Thank God!'

Healthily exhausted, they sank onto the garden chairs as the long summer evening turned to dusk, drinking Pimm's, listening to the nightingales, watching the reflections from the sky turn the river silver.

Nigel broke the still calm, slapping at a mosquito on his bare arm. 'Ruddy things. It's the only problem with this spot. Still, it has to be better than being inside, listening to the news. Hitler and his Nazis stomping in well-regimented hordes at rallies, hounding the Jews. Just the tip of an iceberg, I fear. We may have won the last war, but I don't think the Germans accept they lost it.'

'Will it come to that? To war? Another war?' All those dead men, hundreds and thousands shot to bits, dying in the mud. In that rich earth, a richer dust concealed. A poet's softening of the reality. What about the others, the ones who have to relive the horrors every day, every morning as they wake?

'Maybe.' He said. 'These pacifists, calling for disarmament, have got it wrong. Inviting trouble.'

The days were shortening. The low-slung sun shone warm on her face as Kitty sat by the open back door, slicing the last of the runner beans.

The branches of the fig tree dipped towards the ground with the weight of the fruit.

Barney lay on the grass, stretched out.

She gave up on the last few tough over-grown runners, pushed them to one side. Barney stirred, watchful of the change in activity. Her first proper Christmas present from Nigel.

Their second Christmas less than three months away. The sparkle of Christmas to break the midwinter gloom. Lunch with Pa again – he'd promised not in a station hotel this time, but at Simpson's in the Strand, with saddle of lamb carved at the table.

The cosy safety of log fires and long evenings of autumn. Ah, so Nigel had managed to teach her to enjoy the end of the year.

He was shifting the straw in the barn, stacking it up to make space. A dusty job, which was making him cough. She took their special breakfast cups, minus the saucers, over to the barn. Nigel was on the top rung of the wooden ladder as it rested against the tower of straw, and turned at the sound of her voice.

'Tea!' She sat on a convenient bale, rested the cups on the surprisingly solid surface of compacted straw. 'Why don't you leave this for a bit? The sun's hot, our Indian summer.' The straw scratched on the back of her stocking-less legs.

'It's not going to last. We're past the equinox. More dark hours than light ones from now on.'

He was right. Overnight the late swallows and sunny days disappeared and were replaced by wind and rain blowing cold across the flat landscape, blowing leaves from the trees into the first soggy heaps by the back door, and keeping them both inside.

The wet weather went on, day after day of driving rain. The fields became a quagmire. The mud stuck to their boots, and Barney's undercarriage. It got trodden into the barns, and the sties. Dried mud appeared in unlikely places throughout the house. They both got colds. After ten days, she was better, but Nigel's hung around. He developed a chesty cough.

Worrying that he was doing too much, Kitty suggested he go to bed early. He wouldn't hear of it. He poured them a drink, but didn't finish his and picked at his food. During the night, he coughed a lot, a deep rasping cough, until, eventually, she got up, made tea, and rearranged his pillows, so he was propped upright in the bed. His skin felt hot, clammy hot under her fingers. Unsure what else to do she got back into bed.

Woke guiltily. Not quite light outside – her usual time to go downstairs, stoke up the range and make their tea.

Nigel moved beside her. Started to cough.

He couldn't stop. She pulled him up, patted his back, fetched more water. 'Sip this.'

He spluttered on the water, but it helped.

'Sorry about that!' He wiped his face, blew his nose. 'I'm not sure I can get up yet.'

Not yet – no, not at all today. but she didn't say that, just, 'I'll ring the doctor. You stay here, keep warm.'

And he did. He drank his tea but when she went back up with a boiled egg and bread and butter soldiers he had dozed off. The doctor came in on his way to morning surgery. 'Plenty of fluids, and rest, and keep the room warm. I'll come in again tomorrow.'

By the evening Nigel seemed more himself, his colour looked better too. She took his temperature.

'Just over a hundred. Stay here.' With sharp twists of her hand, she shook the mercury in the thermometer down.

'No, I'm coming down for supper with you. A proper evening.'

So they played cards in the drawing room in front of the fire. He started to cough and his face was flushed again.

'Let's go to bed. I'll do the hot-water bottles.'

He was asleep by the time she got upstairs, so she crept in without turning the light on, and snuggled down into her side of the bed. She slept solidly, undisturbed.

Sunlight, shafting through the curtains, woke her. Nigel, evidently wide awake, the cobalt eyes watching her, was lying still beside her.

'Cuddle, please. Don't get up yet.'

She smoothed the lock of black hair off his face.

'I must, it's late. Mason'll be here soon. And you need your hot drink.' She couldn't read the expression in his eyes. 'I'll be back in a minute.' She kissed each eye, and slipped quickly out from the warmth of the bed.

Downstairs, Barney bounced out of his chair, back up into it, then raced to the back door, barking. She turned the key in the door, opened it and pushed the dog outside.

It was Sunday, of course, but Mason was there already.

The kettle took ages to boil, the range not drawing properly in the strong winds.

She made the tea. Poured two cups, added milk, put the cups, on their saucers, onto the tray, and started to go upstairs.

Remembered Barney, shut in the garden. Turned back into the kitchen, dumped the tray, and called the dog. The air was cold and she shivered in her dressing gown.

'Barney!' She whistled again. The dog appeared. 'Oh, you're filthy. Again!'

She shooed him into his chair, closed the kitchen door behind her. Picked up the tray again, went on up the stairs, pushing their bedroom door open with her foot.

The tea tray crashed to the floor.

'Nigel!'

He was half out of bed, his head lolling down; blood had trickled out of his open mouth making a red pool on the carpet.

She knew.

She tried to lift his head and shoulders back towards the bed. He was still warm, but like a sack of potatoes.

'Nigel! Nigel!'

She knelt beside the bed, her arms around him, tried to keep him warm.

Until the warmth left his body.

CHAPTER 14

NOVEMBER 1934

THE WHITE ROSES AND TULIPS, the ones she'd asked for, rested on the coffin.

'*Love divine, all loves excelling…* '

The words swirled around from the congregation behind her and from the choir in the stalls beyond Nigel.

Nigel.

No. Not Nigel. He isn't there. He has gone away. Already. Gone on before I got upstairs with the tea.

Mary Gifford was weeping, silently, the tears gushing down her face.

Prayers led by the canon from the cathedral.

Nigel's father, silent, unmoving. Will his faith help him through this?

'*The king of love, my shepherd is.*' Love, love.

She had chosen the hymns. She had implored that the service be kept short, just two hymns, and a psalm. No sermon.

The canon stood in front of the coffin. The pall-bearers lifted it, and shuffled forward past her pew, and then stopped.

Waiting. For her to step in behind it.

His last journey.

Polished wood. A bit of cheap brass.

The black-jacketed shoulders of the pall-bearers.

She stood by the raw earth, not hearing the words of the prayers.

The pall-bearers loosened the wide welts of cord to lower the coffin, with her flowers and Nigel's cap badge where she had pinned it amongst them, into the pit.

The canon touched her elbow, intoned '*Earth to earth, ashes to ashes, dust to dust.*'

Amen.

She felt them all step back, leaving her alone on the edge.

Safe journey. Sleep tight.

She turned. Mary Gifford was on one side, his father on the other. Together they stumbled away back to the rectory.

She got through the door, into the hall. Then she let out an animal howl. Someone took her upstairs, stayed beside her.

Nigel gone. Gone. I killed our babies. Nigel knew, understood. Nigel's children.

Come back, Nigel.

People came and went. *Have a cup of tea, dear, please.*

Finally, his father.

'Kitty, dear, Nigel would hate to see you like this.'

Somehow she stopped. Lifted her head from the bed cover, turned to him.

'Sorry, I know, I know, and you and Mary, it's worse for you.' She gulped, sniffed. 'Is the tea still here?'

It grew dark outside, the dawn came, she didn't sleep, didn't even undress.

One morning she heard the church bell tolling, not the muffled single toll when the coffin was lowered but a normal Sunday morning sound.

Sunday morning. She found her mother-in-law in the kitchen.

'I can't stay here for ever, Mary. Poor Mason, he's abandoned with everything to look after.'

'My dear, do whatever you think is best. Come back any time. You don't have to ask, just appear.' She held out her hands. 'You're my link with Nigel.' The shadow of a smile lightened the lines of grief on the older woman's face. 'If you're sure you want to go, Bernard will drive you home, open up the house with you, light the fire and things. Promise to telephone me every day or I shall worry terribly about you there, alone.'

Bernard drove her back to Flimstour the next morning. The leaden skies matched their mood. She was grateful to her father-in-law for not filling the silences with small talk.

He helped her out of the car, stood beside her as she unlocked her front door. She turned to him.

'I'd like to go in on my own.'

'Yes, I can understand that.' He kissed her, and put an envelope into her hands. 'Here's a few pounds to tide you over, my dear. The last thing we want is for you to worry about money.'

He left quickly, fearful no doubt that either or both of them would break down.

She did, as soon as the door closed behind him. Utter desolation overwhelmed her. She sank onto the bottom stair and let go.

Daylight. The hairy warmth of the dog snuggled up in the bed.

'Barney, whatever time is it? You loyal thing.' He lifted his head, ears perking up. 'Do you know, boy, I finally slept.'

Last night as she climbed into the empty bed, the tears had begun yet again. For a while, Barney had licked at her face and then scrabbled at her shaking shoulders, until he'd given up and settled on the floor with a huge sigh.

The dog's action had pulled her together a bit. She had turned on the light, and made an effort to minimise the awful emptiness on Nigel's side of the bed.

She used the bedspread from the spare room to cover half the bed, put a pile of books where his pillows would have been, made a nest for the dog using an old blanket. She had folded up yesterday's clothes, and laid out a new set for today – the first change since she'd got back from Nigel's parents. When was that? God, it must be three days ago. Not ten days since... she had stopped herself: she had to manage this by not thinking back, not yet.

In the morning light, she caught Barney's beady eyes watching her.

'All right, boy. Let's get your breakfast.'

She was putting the kettle on when the bell sounded from the front door, setting Barney barking.

'Good morning, vicar.' She could never remember the rector's name. He didn't seem a very memorable sort of person but he had been there, and kind, the day of Nigel's death and helped to arrange things for the funeral at the Giffords' church. 'Will you come in?'

'No, my dear, I won't. It's just a quick call to see how you are. I was talking to a fellow rector yesterday. He has a young friend who knows a bit about pigs and has a farm. We thought he might be able to help you. Here's his telephone number.' The face above the white rim of the dog collar looked troubled. He frowned and said, 'Let me know if I can do anything, anything at all.' His eyes kept going to her face, then he averted them, but they went straight back.

'That's kind, thank you.'

Closing the door, she stuffed the slip of paper by the telephone.

Long past the poor dog's breakfast time.

As she went back into the kitchen, the dog slunk under the table, ears down. The half-prepared dog-dish of meat and baked bread on the kitchen table was empty, licked clean.

'Oh!' She took the bowl, rinsed it under the tap and put it away on its shelf under the sink. The little dog emerged, ears up again, nuzzled at her shin. 'It doesn't matter. Nothing matters. Well, you do.'

She reached down and lifted the muscular body close. 'I'll keep you safe, won't forget you. Don't go away, little chap. Please.'

Mason tapped on the back door, shuffled in, cap in hand. The hall clock struck – and went on for ages – God, eleven o'clock. Ten was the time for his morning tea.

'All fed, and mucked out ma'am.'

Fed! The feed was expensive, used up big chunks of Nigel's army pension. He waited until the pension cheque arrived before he ordered from the seed merchant and had stocked up for the winter – nuts and the straw. A barn full of straw. Dusty straw. Coughing.

Mason's wrinkled face swam away. She grabbed the side of the sink. Bent down, pretended to rinse her hands.

Mason waited. 'I'll be in this afternoon, then. Tidy things up for the night.'

Nigel did all the afternoon feeds, the bedding down in the evenings. Not any longer. Never again.

Mason pulled the back door closed behind him. Poor embarrassed man!

It was grey outside, had never really got light all day, when she heard Mason outside in the afternoon. She put Barney on a lead, imagining him running off in the dusk, and went outside. Flossie whined in pleasure.

'The sow's pleased to see you. It's chilly, now, you go back inside, keep warm.'

She closed the door, and heard the cold silence of the empty house.

She sank into Barney's chair by the range in the kitchen. The dog jumped onto her lap, and she dozed off.

A sharp knocking on the front door woke them both, and set Barney barking, his hackles bristling up. Kitty stumbled out to the hallway. Shivered in the cold. Opened the door.

Jo, her face cocooned by the turned-up collar of her fur coat, stood in the dusk.

'I did ring the bell. Forgive, but it seemed simpler just to appear.'

'It's lovely to see you. Do you mind sitting in the kitchen?'

In the brighter light of the kitchen, Jo held out her arms.

'Come here, let me give you a hug. Oh, Kitty, forgive me, but you look dreadful. Whatever can I do?'

The human comfort was nearly too much.

'Jo, dear, you being here is enough. Careful, though, or the dam will burst again.'

'This house is freezing. I'm chilly and I bet you didn't have a proper lunch. I shall make us a hot chocolate for starters.' Jo was delving into her wicker shopping basket, turfing out gloves and handbag. 'I brought us brandy and some Gentleman's Relish. Have you got bread for toast?'

Jo chattered on while she found a pan and boiled the milk.

'Loads of sugar, good for you,' she said, and poured brandy into the cups.

She buttered the toast, spreading the anchovy paste right up to the crusts.

'I hate the idea of you being here all alone. My mama says you'd be welcome to stay with her. She always liked having you around and she says the house feels empty now I've gone.'

'I feel safe here. Closer to him. And there are things I have to do. People are very good.' The warmth in her tummy spread upwards, making the words come more easily. 'Granny asked me to spend Christmas with her and Uncle Bertie, in Worthing. I don't want to, I want to be here, hang onto the things that were us for as long as possible. After Peter… '

'Here.' Jo passed a hankie across.

'Sorry. Peter's room, all his stuff, they'd cleared it away. Washed out with Dettol. Nothing left of him, not even the smell of him, his paints and things.'

Jo shifted on her chair.

'It's all right. I know that Nigel's gone away, dead. Not coming back. But there's bits of him, and us, here still. For a while yet. We only had one Christmas together. This year I want to remember that, feel it again. On my own.' She looked at her watch. 'Jo, I'm selfish. It's nine o'clock. You must go, Alistair will think you've been abducted or something.'

'No, he knows I'm here, he won't worry. He's good with baby Tavish.' Jo pulled on her gloves. 'I hate to leave you alone again.'

Elma, told of her determination to spend Christmas on her own, did not hesitate. 'I won't hear of it. Christmas Day if you must, but you shall spend Boxing Day here. And stay. Bring the dog. Leave your Mr Mason to cope with the livestock.'

On Boxing Day, she woke with the faintest lifting of the dark outside and pushed her feet onto the bedside rug, straightened upright. Barney emerged from between the sheets.

Christmas Eve had been bad, the worst. She had sat in the kitchen and wept. For endless hours. During the day. Until going upstairs, she noticed Peter's windmill, all blue sky and hopeless hope. Reprimanded, she went outside and cut an armful of holly, full-berried still, and came back in and put two big jugs of it in the kitchen.

She broke down again listening to the carols. Emotion spent, she'd made an effort on Christmas day itself – lit the drawing room fire, and roasted a couple of potatoes around a tiny bit of pork shoulder, which Barney helped her to eat. The two of them had been in bed, with a hot-water bottle, by seven o'clock.

The drive to Dereham was an effort, but also an occupation. There was a satisfaction in achieving it.

Elma wrapped her long arms around her. She let her head drop onto Elma's shoulder. Smelt the exotic, expensively discreet Chanel perfume, and wondered at the contrasts of this woman. No dress sense, looking, so often, like a monk who had found his clothes in a dressing-up box. With a mind as sharp as any, but kind. Always aware. Taking gentle care of William.

'Dearest Elma, it's wonderful to be here.'

Elma's welcome, the strong gin and tonic and Boxing Day cold turkey all helped, in some way, to right the uneven keel of her emotions – Christmas was past, the annual rhythm of new life and Elma's confident care alleviated the dreadful depression of the last few days.

Two days later she got back to Flimstour at dusk. Barney raced around the driveway while she pulled her bag from the car, and opened the front door.

'My God, Barney, this house is cold.'

She dumped her handbag, scarf and gloves on the kitchen table. There was a strong smell of bleach, a sure sign Mrs Mason had been in.

She bent down, spun the range's draught vent round to its maximum and topped up the fire with the scuttle of coke.

Propped against an enamel plate was a note from Mrs Mason. In neat capitals: '*Welcome Home. I baked the steak and kidney pie this morning.*' She eased open the careful folds of the greaseproof paper parcel, touched the egg-glossed golden pastry.

The stack of post on the table had grown. As a way of limiting the hurt, she had left the Christmas cards and the envelopes that, no doubt, carried well-meant words of condolence in a growing stack of unopened mail. In the first couple of weeks after the funeral, she had made the mistake of opening these and had been horrified at Ma's wicked words – *if only you had listened to me.* Disappointed, too, in Pa's shakily written letter in rather formal language about their pre-Christmas lunch postponed *until we both feel more up to it* – not that she would have gone, but what did he mean? *We both?*

Liz, dear caring Liz, had written too much, too many words. There were no words, they simply diminished the reality.

Her eyes went back to the pie. Her tummy felt empty, used to Elma's pre-supper cocktail and casual comfort food. She put the pie in the oven, and poured a gin and tonic.

She and Barney slept the clock around that night, waking as the hall clock struck ten.

She was just about to do Barney's belated breakfast when the telephone rang. It was Jo. 'I thought you'd be back. I'm going shopping in Colchester today. Come and meet me for lunch.'

Surely, Jo normally shopped in Norwich, or even Ipswich?

Jo was pregnant again, but still her usual bubbly self and they giggled together over a couple of dreadfully old-fashioned maternity dresses she tried on, and at Barney who barked furiously when he caught sight of himself in the full-length mirror.

Before they parted, Jo made her promise that she would come to stay for a couple of nights, nothing social, she promised.

Tired after what seemed like a busy day, Kitty sank into Barney's chair. The pile of post remained to nag at her. She dreaded it; there would be letters of condolence, well meant of course, but needing a reply. Replies she couldn't begin to think about constructing. The telephone rang.

Mary Gifford's gentle voice. 'Come over for lunch at the weekend, and stay the night to break the journey. Please dear, if you feel up to it.'

She went to lunch and spent the afternoon with them but insisted on going home rather than staying the night. The vicarage was too full of memories of the funeral and dark days after. She could manage her raw grief in very small doses.

She talked, even conversed one-sidedly, to the dog. It helped to break the silence in the house, and she could guarantee a response if food or an outing played a part in what she was saying. 'Barney, I've hardly had a day to myself. Everyone has been so good.'

Unimaginably, unexpectedly kind.

Mason kept appearing, chopping wood, tidying round outside, sweeping the front steps after he had seen to the pigs.

The pile of post still loomed. She leafed through it, shuffling the obvious Christmas cards unopened into a drawer.

'Today, I shall do nothing until I've opened all of it, and put it into separate piles.' She pulled up a hard chair to the table, pointed Barney towards his chair. 'Your walk must wait, so you sit there and look at me and make me get on with it.'

She tried not to read the sympathy letters, knowing they'd start her crying, so she slit them open and left them waiting for a reply when she felt stronger.

The bills were mostly small and expected and nothing she couldn't handle.

Until she opened the one from the seed merchants for pig feed: it was overdue but she'd forgotten it. Nigel would have anticipated the bill, sold an animal to pay it.

Hating it, she sat down and wrote to Uncle Bertie asking for help.

She stood up, letting the dog jump down.

'Let's walk into the village, post this blessed letter, buy you a bone and something for supper.'

The air was fresh, dry, an easterly wind. Barney scavenged around in the frozen undergrowth, bouncing over the solid tufts of grass. She caught the dog's excitement and felt a bit better. When they arrived at the shop, she tried to make him wait outside.

'He's all right,' the butcher called out. 'Come for a bone.'

She shortened Barney's lead as he snuffled through the sawdust on the floor. A whole side of beef hung, reaching to the floor.

'I've a nice lamb carcass.' It did look nice, neat and clean-skinned beside the beef. 'The kidneys have sold, but the heart is a nice one.'

'Yes, please.' It was a good idea – unexpectedly she looked forward to standing at the range, chopping onion and parsley, putting the casserole in the oven, waiting for the cooking smells to meld as the meat softened.

As she walked home the bare hedges, skeletal trees, the fields and the distant wood on the hill looked real again, three-dimensional, instead of like a backcloth to a stage on which she had no part to play.

There were good days when she felt able to think about where she could live and what she could do when she had moved from Flimstour and sold the pigs. She'd realised she would have to leave Mill House, to cut the umbilical cord with the life she and Nigel had only just begun to make.

Elma, and more quietly William too, had encouraged her to talk about her future. Liz enjoyed working at Fortnum and Mason, but Kitty couldn't imagine living in the grime, smog and tarmac of London. Her other friends were married, running homes and families. Even Emma in Guernsey. Emma wrote often, happily devoted to Jean-Pierre, but without any babies.

Then there were the grim days. These were the ones when she stayed inside, sat in Barney's chair, watched the rain on the windows, wasn't hungry, didn't eat, cried in a limp sort of way, didn't bother with the wireless; on these days the present was even less real than the future.

Uncle Bertie replied at once enclosing two cheques, one made out to the seed merchants and one to herself, which was unexpected and lovely.

Each week she bought *The Lady*, scouring the columns of situations vacant. Should she train as a nanny, try to be a substitute mother?

Companion wanted for elderly lady. Live as family. At Jo's she showed them the advertisement.

'But it might be awful. Not your home. Suppose it didn't work out, you'd be penniless and homeless.' Jo nudged Alistair. 'What do you think?'

'Ghastly idea. Some evil-tempered old trout, hated by her own family. Don't touch it with a barge-pole.' The flickering germ of optimism died. He must have seen it on her face, because quickly he said, 'Barney might bite her.'

Jo said, 'It's very early days still. Give yourself time to think straight, Kitty.'

CHAPTER 15
FEBRUARY 1935

STILL EARLY DAYS it might be but she needed to make a start on thinking straight. She listened to the birds busying themselves – territorial birdsong, ready for a new season. Starting afresh.

Watched two yellow-beaked blackbirds skirmishing on the grass.

She could stay on here for a bit – the lease on Mill House had been for five years – at least until she worked out a plan, got a job, trained for something. But the pigs could go, must go. No more feed bills she couldn't pay, had to ask Uncle Bertie to pay. Once the animals were gone she wouldn't need Mason, whose wages, tiny as they were, she couldn't afford either.

In the barn she lifted the lid on the metal bin of pignuts, waited a moment for Barney to pounce if a rat shot out, and then peered in – half-empty already.

Where was that bit of paper the vicar had given her? With the name of the farmer who might take the pigs?

Otherwise, they'd have to go to market.

Not that. No.

She found the vicar's note tucked behind the bread bin.

'*Iain Chester, Five Oaks Farm, Dennington*', and a telephone number.

It felt awkward telephoning a total stranger for help. The

farmer might not answer. Might have forgotten, might not want the animals any more. Might never have wanted them.

Do it now. Don't put it off.

'Uncle James said you might telephone. Shall I come over this afternoon? You can show me the pigs and we'll see what can be done.'

It was another grey afternoon. There wasn't a lot of daylight left. She opened the road gate, waited ready in rubber boots.

No sign of any sort of farmer. A red motor car roared past. Reversed back, swung into the drive. Lord, where was the farmer, and who on earth was this?

'Mrs Gifford, I'm Iain.'

Mrs Gifford?

Not any longer. Mason says ma'am. The others say Kitty.

The man looked uncertain, uncomfortable. 'The farmer, about the pigs.'

She showed him the sows, tickling Flossie as she whinnied a welcome, and then the weaners rooting about in the orchard.

'They're in good condition. You're selling them?'

'Well, yes, I suppose so.'

'I've got pigs myself. Large Whites. I'm going to turn the farm into a modern enterprise. I'd look after them well.'

Look after them well?

Where, where is his farm? Will he just flog them at market, turn Flossie into pounds of sausages?

'Look, why don't you come over, to see for yourself? I could drive you over, tomorrow morning say.'

What? Why?

She must say something. Make a decision. He was looking at her, waiting. She loved them. Nigel would hate it if they weren't well looked after.

'Yes, all right.' Then, 'Thank you.'

After he had gone, she fed Barney, sat by the range in his chair, staring at nothing. Somehow, she had to be ready in the morning. Why ever had she said she would go?

She stood up. 'Barney, make me pull myself together. Hot-water bottle. Bed. You must come with me, keep me company, boy.'

Next morning she waited in the drive, Barney at her side. She had slept a little better and the winter sun, risen well above the bare trees, warmed her back.

The red car swept up the gravel.

'I hope you don't mind if my dog comes.' She had hold of Barney's lead.

'He's welcome – we'll squeeze him in. My place is north of Woodbridge. It shouldn't take too long.' He held the door for her, adding, 'This old girl does a fair speed.'

As they sped off, Kitty made an effort at conversation.

'I used to live in Dereham.'

'Nice town. I stayed near there while I was buying the farm last September. Now I've got livestock I'm living in the farmhouse. My mother has stayed on with her friends the rector and his wife. We've lived with them ever since my father died.'

This was a good deal more information than she had the energy to handle, so she lapsed into silence.

He drove fast but he handled the car skilfully, making the gears work hard, accelerating out of the corners. Even so, it seemed a long while before they left Ipswich behind and he turned off the road to Diss.

'Almost there.' The road was narrow, bending through a hamlet. He changed down into third, and looked at Barney, happily cuddled up on her lap. 'He'll be pleased to have a run around the fields.'

She didn't know what to say. All much too difficult. They were in wide open countryside, further north of Woodbridge than she had expected from his description, almost in Norfolk in fact.

The car slowed again, turned into a single-track lane and then sharply right onto a driveway, bumping over a sort of bridge.

'This is it.' The car came to a stop alongside a brick building. Barney sniffed at the window, whimpered. There was a house a bit further up the drive. Barney jumped out of the car.

'We walk through here,' the man said. 'This moat goes all

round the house. It was a Saxon farmstead. Round the back, it spreads out into a fair-sized pond.'

He strode off along a wide track through the trees. Barney raced ahead.

Across the moat, the track opened out into a traditional farmyard. In the cluster of buildings, half a dozen sows snuffled around in the bedding. The pigsties were spacious, and immaculately clean.

The farmer, Iain, was talking again.

'I'm going to develop the farm, model it on the way the Danes are producing pork. Get modern rearing units from there. Expensive but an investment.'

Her head was hurting, aching, and her eyes too. There was a harsh muscular pain between her shoulder blades. In fact she ached all over.

'I don't want any money for our pigs. I'd like you to have them, so long as you don't sell them. Perhaps we could go back now, I need to be home.'

In the car she was too tired to talk, too tired to bother about it. Clutched Barney on her lap. The farmer glanced at her a couple of times as he sped the sports car along but didn't attempt to break her silence.

She must say something. 'This is good of you. I don't know how I could have coped otherwise.'

'That's okay. I'll collect the pigs in a day or so.'

When Iain, as good as his word, came three days later to collect the pigs she stayed in the kitchen, leaving Mason to cope. She sat in Barney's chair, cuddling the dog close to her, couldn't bear to look out of the window, tried not to hear the animals squealing.

If she were honest, it was a relief when the pigs were gone, despite the emptiness around the house, the silence, the lack of life in the sheds and fields.

Mason stayed on for two weeks cleaning up the barns and sties and tidying around. She paid his last week's wage, and wished him well, not expecting to see him again. But he continued to appear two or three times a week and took it upon himself to chop logs and sweep the paths. She tried to offer him money, but he replied, 'No thank you ma'am. You can't be doing the outside work, and it gets me out from under Mrs Mason's feet.' So she made him coffee and sat down to chat while he drank it.

Without animals to draw her outside, she took Barney out less until the little dog became restless and started to chew the edges of the drawing room carpet. So each morning she walked up to the shop in the village. The days were longer, the sun a little higher in the sky.

The farmer sent a brief letter saying that the pigs were well, and that *'the sow you called Flossie has just produced a fine litter. Feel free to call in and see them any time you are nearby. Regards, Iain Chester.'*

At the end of the month the weather turned.

'In like a lamb and out like a lion this year it is,' Mason said, putting the basket of logs by the kitchen door.

'March is a strange month.' Picking the very first bluebells, the sun warm on their backs, while Peter painted. A lifetime ago. Two lifetimes ago. Stop it. 'Thank you for your help.'

She closed the door. She fumbled for her hankie, blew her nose. 'Right, boy, I must sort myself out.' She went into the hallway, telephoned Elma.

Elma, well-informed as always, chatted about news. 'Mussolini throwing his weight about, Germany re-arming, menacing in the Saarland. I quake for the future. Still, my dear, that's enough. I met your mother in the butcher's shop last week. She looked well.'

'I've decided to ask myself for lunch at Otters with Ma – the anniversary of Peter's death is coming up. It's a rotten time of year.'

Ma, waiting on the steps, did look well and sweetly welcoming.

'I bought you these, Mummy.' A bunch of hothouse yellow roses.

'Come in, Katherine. Let's have a Dubonnet.'

Clearly in polite social-hostess mood.

'Yes, please, Mummy. While we talk.' Tensed up, she diverted the conversation when it veered anywhere near to Nigel, marriage, Flimstour, or the future. As ever, there was no mention of Pa.

Elma had been right. Ma was relaxed and much more comfortable being in control of her social life. Not cut out to be a mother. She chatted happily about last night's canasta game, and some tea party for the church.

Kitty got away as soon as the pudding, spicy apple pie with clotted cream, was finished.

Thankful that a pretence of normality was restored between them, that Ma had behaved, no mention of Nigel, she pushed Speedy along the straight road.

Had Ma heard that she'd seen Pa?

Poor Pa. On his own. In London. He'd looked so old, and thin. Why hadn't she pulled herself together, kept their promised lunch date before Christmas?

She blinked away tears as they prickled into her eyes.

Because she'd been absorbed in her grief. Self-indulgent grief. Hadn't thought about Pa. Why in God's name had she gone to see Ma today, and not bothered to see Pa? The tears began to stream, so she couldn't really see. She pulled the car onto the roadside verge at the next crossroads.

Beady black eyes studied her. The dog heaved a huge sigh and curled himself into a tight ball on the seat.

The white-painted signpost was missing one of its wooden arms, the one pointing right. The left-hand one read 'Dennington'. Dennington?

The pig-farmer, of course. She had forgotten, never replied. Flossie. And her piglets. Newly alive creatures. Hope. Unsullied by time or tribulation, miniature heaps of uninhibited enthusiasms.

'Shall we go to see Flossie? Anything rather than go back to our empty house.' She tickled behind the dog's ears.

Ran her fingers under her eyes. Pulled a hankie from her bag, blew away the worst snuffles, moved the gear lever into neutral and pressed the self-starter.

She followed the signposts and found herself driving along a typical East Anglian lane, curves, not bends, and with verges, no steep banks.

The countryside was flat, the trees, skeletal without their summer flesh of foliage, prominent in the landscape. Oak trees. Five Oaks, of course.

She found the entrance to the farm, turned in, carefully negotiating the bridge over the moat.

For a couple of minutes she stayed sitting in the car, partly to look around, and partly to announce her arrival, and realised she'd hardly noticed the place when she came before.

The sporty red car was there – a Riley Lynx, parked alongside the brick barn. It wasn't really a barn, too small, and it had an upper storey, but no window, under a gabled roof. Once a cart-shed, perhaps.

On the far side of the lawn, water lapped at the banks of the moat. A dingy bobbed around, a rope tethering it to one of the bigger trees.

The house looked plain at the front, three tiers of leaded casement windows, with tall chimneys at each end of the building. A farmhouse, not stone, just colour washed, creamy yellow in the sunshine.

Barney was resting his front feet on the dashboard beside her. He bristled as someone came out of the thick belt of trees to the right of the house. The farmer, Iain.

Kitty opened the car door. Too late, she realised she wasn't dressed for a farm visit – neat black court shoes, silk stockings, grey overcoat. She stood on the driest piece of ground she could reach, and waved. 'Hello. I was passing by, so I took up your invitation to call in.'

'I'm sorry, I nearly didn't recognise you. In your Sunday best, I mean.'

He looked uncomfortable, turned his eyes away from her.

'I'm afraid I'm not dressed to visit a farm.' She must explain. 'I've had a dismal morning, and saw a signpost to Dennington, and thought about Flossie, and the others.'

'Don't worry. Let me find a pair of boots. I expect if we put in lots of socks you'll be able to waddle round. You'd better come into the kitchen, if you don't mind, while I sort something out.'

The kitchen was warm, a kettle humming on the range. Through the panes of the window, she caught a glimpse of the moat flowing into a large pond.

The farmer returned, proffering cleanish rubber boots and several pairs of socks. Sitting on a chair, she discarded the polished shoes and layered on the socks.

'That's you booted and spurred, though the wet clay gets on everything. You'll need to be careful of your coat.'

'I'll want to stroke Flossie. The coat can go to the cleaners.'

Flossie recognised her, whinnying with pleasure. Kitty leaned over the sty wall and tickled the sow behind her ears. The farmer stood back, a bit behind her.

'She looks well and happy,' Kitty said, and turned to face him. 'How quickly the piglets grow!'

'Would you like to see the rest of the stock? Now you're here?'

They toured the farm, the farmer navigating onto the least muddy paths, finishing at the gate to the big fields across the lane from the farm. Barney appeared beside them from time to time, only to dash off again.

'What huge oaks.' She counted the trees. 'Five.'

'It's said they've been here about four hundred years – planted in Henry VIII's time, for his 'hearts of oak', I suppose. The pigs enjoy rooting around for the acorns.'

She bundled Barney back in the car. 'I must go, but thank you. Flossie looks very well.'

He stood watching as she turned the car, waved as she drove off.

It was late when she got home. The drive had gone well, no flats, which she dreaded in the dark; she was well able to deal with the tyres and inner tubes in the daylight, but at night, in the dark, she hated having to juggle the torch and then search for the nuts.

Barney bounced ahead of her into the kitchen, pushing at his empty dinner bowl.

'In a minute, boy. I'm hungry too.'

She shed her coat, hanging it over the kitchen door. She bent, picked the dog up.

'Home, Barney, our home.' She tickled him under his chin. He wriggled. 'Let's light the drawing room fire first.'

The wood, dry in the long-laid fire, caught quickly, flamed up. She went into the drinks cupboard, poured a stiff gin and tonic and carried it through to the kitchen.

'Cheers, Barney!'

The dog ignored her, his eyes remaining fixed on his bowl.

There was cold lamb, rather a lot of it left over from a half-shoulder she'd cooked. Nursery supper – so she fried an onion, minced up the meat, boiled macaroni and mixed it all together, popping it in the oven to heat through. She cut some of the meat for the dog who sat up on his haunches, begging.

She went upstairs, changed into a pair of slacks. The sweet smell of fried onions and cooking lamb spread up the stairs.

She laid a tray for herself with a crocheted tray cloth, and carried her supper through to eat beside the fire.

Replete, she put her empty plate on the floor where Barney discreetly licked it clean. She watched the shapes made by the flickering flames. The nine o'clock news on the Home Service was full of Hitler, and Germany's ambitions, and the Italians eyeing up parts of Africa. She turned the wireless off, all too depressing, and far away.

Tired, but not tired enough to sleep. She tossed in bed, half-awake. Ma, Pa, Peter. Ma on her own, behind her glass walls of social mores. Did Ma know where Pa was living? Poor Pa. He had been distant, unreal, not like he used to be. Was that why she hadn't made the effort to see him again since that one time?

The hall clock chimed – twice.

Restlessly awake she went downstairs, wandered around the kitchen, made a milky drink. Opened the back door for Barney. The weather had changed, there was a wind and rain blowing in the air. The night-time cold got to her, goose-pimples spotted on her legs.

She snuggled up to the hot-water bottle.

· · ·

The next day was foul, and one of her worst. Her body ached with tiredness after yesterday and the sleepless night. The rain poured down all day. Eventually she made some supper, listened to the wireless. She put the dog out before going up to bed. Still only nine o'clock. The dog came bounding out of the darkness, shaking wet off his fur.

She got a towel, was rubbing him dry, when the telephone bell shrilled. Whoever would ring at this time? She dropped the towel and went into the hall.

She lifted the receiver.

'Uncle Bertie here.'

At this time of night!

'My dear. I have some very sad news.'

Granny?

'I am afraid this will be a great shock. I don't like to have to tell you on the telephone. Will you sit down, please.'

'What's happened?' She did sit on the hard hall chair. 'Is Granny all right?'

CHAPTER 16

MARCH 1935

'He must have known he was ill. He kept it from all of us, not just you. The funeral will be here, next week. But we'd like you to come and stay. As soon as you can get here. Don't be alone.'

Pa! On his own. Dead. Alone. Cold.

She dropped the receiver back on its stand, and stumbled up the stairs to the bed where she lay as the grief welled up in a great gulping wave of hysteria. The raw physical pain below her ribs was sharp again.

Knew he was ill. Yes – he'd looked ill, not old like she'd thought. He did know – he'd deliberately headed her off when she asked where he was living, how he was, didn't let her talk about him at all. Just wanted to hear her news. Before he went. Come back later. She hadn't, wasn't allowed. She could, should, have gone to lunch with Pa, had been too selfish, self-absorbed. Like Ma. All daughters get like their mothers. She should be a mother by now, two children in the house here. She killed them – selfishly to keep Nigel to herself. But Nigel went away. He hadn't been alone, only for a few minutes. Peter hadn't been totally alone.

Pa had been alone.

And so it went on. Lying on top of the counterpane, in her clothes.

She woke icy cold, her mind muddled in the dark. Remembered and the pit of her stomach dropped out.

She went to look for Barney, found him asleep in his chair. She boiled water for a hot-water bottle, and took the dog back up with her.

She lay, warmer but sleepless until dawn, when she got up, packed a case and bundled Barney into the car.

As she drove into the suburbs of London, she stopped at a Shell garage to fill up with petrol. Later, needing to spend a penny, she found a lay-by with a tall hedge on the A23 as London became Surrey.

Speedy laboured up the steep hill of the Downs by Findon; the last of the light shadowed the curves of the hills. Round, understated hills with their carpets of short grass. Warm, south-facing slopes.

Almost there, the exhaustion, physical and mental, set in.

Uncle Bertie was waiting for her in the garden, apparently weeding his mountainous rockery in the gathering dusk.

'Thank you for coming – your being here will help Mother. Me, too, my dear. Come in.'

As they walked up the steps into the hall, the gracious calm of the old house enveloped her. Her childhood sanctuary from the stressed atmosphere at home.

'Stop, Uncle. I need to cry.'

He held her close.

'Sorry.' She blew her nose. 'Okay now. I won't upset Granny.'

Poor Granny! She had shrunk, withered, looked grey and bent, leaning on a stick.

'I'm so sorry – I can't find the right words.' She clasped the cold bony hands.

'There are no words. Don't try to find them. Just remember the good things, the love you received and gave.' Tears rolled down the drawn, sagging cheeks. 'Don't worry about me, I'm too old to need hope. You are young still, younger than you realise. Try to hope, to look forward, to enjoy and help others enjoy.'

On the morning of the funeral she woke unrested after confused black dreams. She held Granny's arm as they followed the coffin into the church. The wet trickled out of her eyes. Her throat tightened.

She pushed her thumb into her mouth, bit on it.

For the next unending forty-five minutes, she struggled to control tears. Did not sing because she had to concentrate on not doing anything. She knelt and stood up along with the rest of the congregation, gripping Granny's hand. She bit into her bottom lip as she felt the hysteria bubbling up in her chest.

She followed the cortège back down the aisle, swallowed the bile in her throat. Gasped the fresh air with relief.

Afterwards, back at the house, Granny welcomed each of the mourners as they came up the steps. Composed, she found something to say to each of them. She was an old lady, had just buried her son. What a stark contrast to Ma's histrionics after Peter died.

Uncle Bertie, overseeing the drinks, pressed a glass into her hand. 'Gin and French, my dear. More your style than the sweet sherries.'

When they were alone Granny produced an album packed full of photos and bits of memorabilia of Pa. 'Take a photo, Kitty. This is when he won a tennis cup. Or this one – with you and Peter.'

She took that one – a young Kitty and Peter, for once not in his wheelchair, playing croquet with Pa.

She left for home next morning, straight after breakfast. Kissed Granny goodbye, promised to write with her news and plans.

She broke the journey just on the edge of London by which time she badly needed to spend a penny. Barney was fidgeting too.

'There's a pub. It looks a bit of a road-house, but maybe that's what we need.'

A chain-link fence surrounded the car park. There wasn't any grass so the fence posts had to satisfy the dog's needs. She wound the leather lead over her arm.

Together they found the bar. There was no menu, nor any sign of food, but she persuaded the barmaid to make a ham sandwich, shop-bread and margarine. She gave the crusts to Barney.

The kitchen at Mill House was warm, the range stoked up by Mason. She made tea and sank into Barney's chair.

The telephone bell shrilled.

'Darling! I couldn't go to bed without ringing. Are you all right? Was it all quite awful? I went into church this morning, the one near work, and said some prayers for you, and your poor pa.' Liz's fruity tones ran on. 'I'd have telephoned earlier, only I went to the first night of Mummy's play at the Apollo. How you are, really?'

'Back here, alone – well, with Barney. Poor Granny. I don't think I can talk about it, not just now.'

'I want to see you, but I'm so sorry – I can't get time off work,' Liz said. 'Will you come and stay here? The change will be good for you. Mummy could get us seats for the show.'

Travel to London. Go to a theatre. Dress up. 'I'm not sure – I get so tired.'

'Well, you go to bed now. Good night.'

Liz telephoned again the next evening. 'I do think you should come up. Don't stay there all alone. I'll meet you at Liverpool Street and we'll take a cab home. Mummy says she'll treat us to supper after the play. At Sheekey's, where the cast go. Guy Rodgers, you know, the heart-throb, stars in the play. It won't cost you anything, just the train fare. I'll ring you tomorrow evening and we'll fix a date.'

The next morning, in daylight, after a decent night's sleep, the idea of the trip was less daunting. 'Barney, remind me when Liz rings I am to say yes.'

But what about the dog? He couldn't go to the theatre, to Liz's flat.

'Whatever shall we do?'

The dog wagged his tail, jumped off the bed.

'No, not now. I'll have to think of something.'

A week later, and still she had no solution to what to do about Barney. She lay late in bed worrying. Would Mason come in and let the dog out, feed him? No, the poor man had managed to get another job, she couldn't ask him. Jo? No, she had much too much of her own to cope with. Calling off the London visit was out of the question because Liz had rung several times, and two seats were reserved in the front row of the stalls.

The little dog fidgeted around, jumping on and off the bed, standing by the door. Clearly in need of the garden. She didn't bother with washing and make-up, just pulled on the old tweed slacks and went outside.

The days were lengthening. The sun was warm and the primroses showed creamy white under the tree.

Back in the warmth of the kitchen, she spooned coffee into the percolator and slid it onto the hotplate. Barney, his two front paws resting on the low back of his chair, watched her, waiting for his breakfast. The front doorbell jangled in the hall. The dog shot out of the chair at the sound.

She unlatched the front door, opened it.

The farmer.

'I collected a side of bacon from the smokery yesterday. I'm taking a gammon joint over to mother. I wondered whether you'd like this one.'

He was clutching a large muslin packet. Barney was jumping up, trying to grab the package and barking. The poor man looked distinctly awkward and Barney was not helping.

'Stop it, Barney.'

'He can smell the bacon.'

'He's waiting for his breakfast, sorry about this.' Remembering her manners. 'Do come in. I've just made coffee. Would you like a cup?'

'Well, yes, please. It was jolly cold when I left home.' He went on, the words rushing out. 'It was colder than here, and the sun wasn't up at all. Took me an age to de-ice the windscreen, I used two potatoes and a mug of glycerine.'

She led the way through the hall and down the two steps into the kitchen. Barney was still snapping at the muslin round the meat.

'Where shall I put this out of harm's way?'

'On the dresser – at the back. That chair is the warmest spot, so long as you don't mind Barney's hairs.'

'They'll brush off. I'd like a dog. We never had one at home. I've got to do something about the rats at the farm.'

The farmer sat down. Immediately Barney jumped onto his lap.

'Sorry, he's used to having his own way.'

'I wasn't sure how you'd like the bacon, but I expect your butcher will slice off some rashers.'

'Oh, yes, thank you.' She put her big, pig-decorated cup on the table, hesitated at the dresser: there were the proper tea-service cups, and the other breakfast cup, the blue and white windmill one. Nigel's. The teacups looked prim and small. She took the windmill one. Filled it to the brim, handed it to him. Sat down at the kitchen table.

'Does your mother come over to the farm?'

'No, my uncle does. She doesn't get on with him. Different sorts of people, those two. It's all a bit complicated.'

The air of diffidence in him was at odds with the racy car, the expensive, if understated, country clothes and the ambitious plans for his farm.

'Families often are. Mine is anyway.' She stopped. Nigel's hadn't been. They were kind, normal people. He had brought that with him to her.

'Uncle Harry's a bit of a character, made a lot of money in the Yukon prospecting for gold and then came home to East Anglia and married the lady of the manor. He had the money, she had the land. He was my guardian after Father died. I was only a kid. My parents were old when they got married. I think my arrival was a surprise.'

He sipped his coffee. Then the talking started again. 'I expect you miss having stock around the place. The fields will need grazing.'

'I suppose so, but I shan't stay on here, not for long,' she replied.

'Sorry, none of my business.' The callow youth was back. He stroked the dog, and said, 'This chap will miss the freedom of the fields.'

'He's happy in the car and I'm sure he'll settle wherever I go, so long as it's not London. He'd hate that... I'm supposed to be going up to London, to a show and things. I can't think what to do with him.'

The man wasn't looking at her, just stroking the dog. He didn't say anything, the talking seemed to have come to an abrupt end, so she went on.

'A friend from school days is taking me – well, her mother really. She's on the stage and has a part in the play.'

'How glamorous.' He glanced up, then looked away, stroked the dog again. 'Look, would it help if I had this chap while you're away? If you'd trust me with him. He could come to the farm for a couple of days. Help with the rats.'

Barney go to the farm? Leave him with a stranger? Send the little dog away so she could go off to London? Would he run away, get lost? For the sake of seeing Liz? Who'd rung again. Jo had told her she must go, not to let Liz down.

Into the silence he added, 'Flossie'd be pleased to see him.'

She pushed her cup away, stood up, walked over to the sink.

'Now I've said yes I simply have to go, but I have no idea what to do about Barney.' She looked at the wiry-haired dog, curled up into a tight little ball on the farmer's lap. Decided. 'Could you? If you're sure, it would help.'

'That's settled then.'

'He'd be no trouble.'

'Don't worry, we'll manage. Look, shall I pick him up on my way home tomorrow? An extra day won't matter. Save you driving.'

The farmer's car, with a nicely tuned deep-throated hum, turned away out of the drive. She picked Barney up, held the stocky body close. 'Well, my friend, that's you organised. It's only till Friday. I'll have been to London and be back here by then.'

She felt a quiver of what might be anticipation. 'Let's find clothes fit for London.'

Barney raced upstairs, jumped straight onto the bed. Oh, God! Let's hope your new friend doesn't mind the muddy paw prints all over his house.

. . .

The red car reappeared just as the dusk was settling the next day. The farmer left the engine turning over and bundled the dog and his baggage into the car without any ceremony.

That evening, rattling around in the empty house, she took a hot-water bottle to bed early.

The next morning she went to the hairdresser. As she stepped out into the fresh air, her natural curls, newly trimmed and washed, bounced in the breeze. She crossed over the road to the draper's shop opposite and bought a cream silk blouse. Neat and new, to lift the dull navy of the soft woollen suit retrieved from the back of the wardrobe where it had hung, unworn, for months.

She packed the smallest of her suitcases, tucking spare underwear, her black patent high heels and an evening bag into the bottom before laying the petrol-blue velvet cocktail dress and jacket, folded over tissue paper, at the top of the case to save them from creasing.

Two days of black cabs, the new neon lights in Piccadilly Circus, a theatre, and for company, Liz – interested in everyone, and optimistic in a theatrical sort of way, but underneath it all a caring person.

She pulled the front door to, turned the key, put it safely in her bag and walked down the steps.

CHAPTER 17

APRIL 1935

THE SMOKE and steam from the engine cleared. Liz, still in her shop-girl uniform, was in the crowd waiting behind the tall ironwork of the ticket barrier.

'Darling, you look stunningly smart. The cabs are over here. We'll go straight back to my place. It's rather ordinary, I'm afraid.' Characteristically Liz didn't draw breath. 'I can't believe you're here. I'm thrilled. This is going to be the greatest fun.'

And it was.

London was not Kitty's favourite place, too much noise and dirt and not enough grass, but the bustling excitement of the metropolis was infectious. Liz's father treated the two of them to dinner at Simpson's in the Strand that evening because he wouldn't be going to the play tomorrow; he'd done duty at the opening night, and once was enough. The next evening Kitty enjoyed the play, not least because sitting in the front row of the stalls made her feel part of the performance. And Guy Rodgers was a good actor as well as being stunningly handsome.

After the curtain came down Liz eased their way to the aisle, and led them round to the stage door, past the autograph hunters. They waited in the communal dressing room, inhaling greasepaint and perfume, while Liz's mother scraped off her stage face. They joined a disorganised gaggle of the cast to stroll to the restaurant tucked away in a side alley, and settled at a long table covered in a red and white gingham-patterned oilcloth.

She sipped the champagne, which appeared to be the only drink on offer. There were a couple of empty seats, one on her left. Everyone was talking. Somehow, when the actors and actresses were together, and, she supposed, relaxed after the performance, the cast seemed more like ordinary people. Kitchen-sized bowls of crabmeat and prawns with brown bread and butter were placed, without any ceremony, on the table, and people began to help themselves.

'May I sit here?' The unmistakable tones of the leading man distracted her private speculations about the cast. Modestly, he said, 'Hello, I'm Guy Rodgers.'

Hot plates of lobster thermidor followed the cold shellfish. With exquisite good manners, Guy made her feel part of the group. The champagne flowed as he became the focus of the party, telling outrageous jokes with immaculate timing. His repartee moved across the table, obviously aimed now at Robert who on the stage took the part of the butler. She suspected the relationship between these two was well established and went beyond the theatre. Not that anyone, even in this Bohemian company, would risk saying so. Howsoever it might be, she enjoyed their humour and guessed that they in turn enjoyed having a new audience for their banter.

Someone called time on the party, saying, 'One o'clock in the morning. That's past my bedtime.'

Safely in a cab, bound for Liz's rooms, she leaned back into the seat and wiggled her feet out of the high heels. 'That was wonderful fun. I daren't think how much supper cost, all those bottles of champagne, but I loved it all.'

'Guy stands the drinks at supper if he's there. He's rich as well as famous. I think he was taken with you, Kitty.' As soon as the words were out, Liz sucked in her breath. 'Sorry, silly of me.'

'Don't worry, it's okay.' Poor Liz, embarrassed, hadn't meant to be tactless. It was okay, too. 'He's marvellous company, just what I needed, but I don't think it was me he was playing to at supper. I'd say it's Robert he has in his sights.'

'Maybe.' Changing the subject, Liz asked, 'Did you really enjoy the evening?'

'I didn't want to come up but now I'm so glad I did. I feel better for the change. More able to think about the future. Granny suggested I move in with them. They'd make a terrific fuss of me. But it's going back. Too many old memories, poor Peter, poor Pa. I want my own home and my own friends. I think tonight has made me realise how much I have changed since we left Worthing.'

The taxi swung into Piccadilly Circus.

Electric advertisements flashed out names and slogans. Green and red, yellow and blue lines darting, writing words.

'Golly! I didn't realise, not from the black and white pictures in the papers.'

The taxi slowed, stopped in the stationary traffic. The flickering display cast intermittent lurid lights on the faces of the crowd as people paused, stared up. A couple, arm in arm on the pavement, turned to kiss. She swallowed, blinked to stop the tears that threatened suddenly.

The cab was speeding along now, free of the traffic as it went north towards Liz's rooms.

'I got another unhelpful letter from Ma, saying I need to get married again.'

'Oh, heavens!' Slowly, unusually quietly, Liz spoke. 'I wasn't going to say. She wrote to me. I didn't reply. I tore the letter up. You can guess. About Christopher not having married. How she was right about Nigel.'

'Oh, hell!'

'Sorry. I shouldn't have said.'

'I'm glad you did. Makes me realise I'm not imagining things with her. It's nothing new. She has said, and written, it all before. Except about Christopher.'

'I think she wants to want the best for you.'

'She was always manipulative, it's just got worse. Or perhaps I see it more clearly. I'm sorry for her, but the only thing is to keep her at arm's length so she can't make too much trouble.'

'I'd like to help, but I don't see how.'

'I shan't come to live in London. I like the countryside too much. I liked starting the farm with Nigel – not only because it was something we did together, but for its own sake. The pigs were lovely, intelligent, almost like dogs, and clean. Not at all what you expect.' She fell silent again, aware Liz wasn't on the same wavelength.

'Dear, you could put all your things in store at Pickfords, and go to Worthing for a little while, couldn't you?'

'Maybe. Don't worry, I'll sort something out.'

'Have you heard from Emma? Could you go to see her?'

'She wrote a long letter. How she and Jean-Pierre may move from the Channel Islands, go to France. She says they can't have children. It's not her, it's Jean-Pierre. And she loves him so much.'

'Promise you'll come up to stay here again.'

'It's been wonderful. So long as Barney's safe, and hasn't blotted his copybook at the farm, I'd love to.'

Apparently, Barney had excelled himself. At the farm next day, as soon as she got out of the car, the little dog tore down the track from the house.

The farmer, looking rather tidy in corduroys and navy Guernsey sweater, stood at the open back door, waving a welcome.

'Come on in, there's coffee on the range.' He looked down at the dog, stumpy tail and muscular little body shaking from side to side in excitement. 'A case of the tail wagging the dog, I think. He's a pukka little chap, behaved perfectly. Yesterday he got a couple of rats.'

He led the way into the kitchen. 'How was London? I like going up in the winter months, dark evenings and the lights suit towns, I think.'

'It was fun, thank you. Much more so than I expected. It was the first time I'd done anything like that since Nigel died.'

The man didn't look up, wiped at the already spotless scrubbed wooden table before setting down cups and saucers and a jug of milk. Was he embarrassed, unsure how to react?

'Nigel wouldn't want me to keep being sad. He'd want me to enjoy life. He didn't believe in heaven or hell. He thought it all happens here, on earth.' The coffee was good, strong and aromatic. The farmer was quiet so she went on. 'My friend's mother took us out to supper after the play. The food was wonderful, though the restaurant looked a bit primitive – no linen, just oilcloth covering the table. It was fun talking to the actors – stagey people seem superficial, but they are good company, and we laughed a lot. Guy Rodgers is the leading man. He's rather gorgeous.'

'No wonder you look so well.'

She caught his expression, and decided to put him right.

'Oh, no, not like that. He likes being seen with women, but his interests lie elsewhere I think.'

'Well, each to his own. Have you time to walk over to see Flossie, and the others? I bought a new sow last week. Uncle Harry found this gilt via one of his farming friends. He misses having his own farm, and his prizewinning Red Polls. When he turned eighty it got too much for him.'

They walked across the wooden bridge which led from the house to the farmyard. The air held a damp smell, of wet clay and the moat water, mixed with rotting leaves. Her feet crunched on the fallen acorns.

'That's old railway sleepers.' He was pointing down to the bridge. 'I got them for half of nothing, but it was a dreadful pantomime to fix them – they weigh a ton, almost literally.'

The sun came out, and the water in the moat sparkled.

'In Sussex it's only manor houses that have moats. Was this place much bigger once?'

'I think your south-country moats were built as defences, against invaders or the local peasants. Up here, they were ponds to keep the water for farming. The soil is heavy clay.' He scuffed at the dark yellow ground. 'Hard as nails in summer and clinging wet in winter.'

Flossie whinnied with pleasure, flicking her ears back and forth as Kitty scratched behind them. The new gilt was indeed handsome – long straight back, solid muscular withers.

They walked back to Speedy, where Barney was standing guard, waiting by the driver's door.

'Not risking my going without him, I see.' She smiled, hesitated, and said, 'Iain, thanks so much for having him.'

'It's been my pleasure.' He patted the dog's head. 'Useful, too. Thank you, Barney.'

She held out her hand – a bit formal, somehow inadequate – and added, 'Do come in for a drink when you're passing Flimstour.'

Back home she took Barney out round the fields. The dog scampered ahead, sniffing around in the damp grass.

He stopped, one paw lifted, pointer-like. A squirrel, its tail fluffed in alarm, was on the ground below the horse chestnut tree. The squirrel moved a fraction and Barney yapped his high-pitched quarry-sighted bark, and darted forward. He stopped at the base of the trunk and then leaped into the air, scrabbling to get a foothold. He fell back onto the ground. Shook himself, raced round the trunk as the squirrel made its escape along the branches.

She laughed aloud, turned, and ran back to the house, lighter-hearted and hungry.

Barney settled himself in his chair.

She unwrapped the slices of cold roast beef that she'd stopped to buy in the village on the way home. Laid the slices on a plate. Buttered the fresh white bread. Laid a knife and fork.

She'd taken to sitting at one end of the table, not as she and Nigel had eaten, siting opposite each other. He'd want mustard with ham. Mustard. Taste-deadening stuff. Always a bit dried out in the pot when she put it on the table.

No need any longer for a last-minute mixing up of fresh, the powder tending to lumpiness.

Not now. Not ever again. Not sit at the table here.

Gone away. Left her. Left the house. Left the pigs.

Just like Peter – but he couldn't help it.

Like Pa. Pa could have helped it – some of it. He didn't have to leave. Would he still have died if he had stayed in Dereham, with her there, to care for him?

She turned, swept the cutlery onto the floor. 'Don't want this. They all went away, left us alone!'

Alarmed, the dog sat up.

'God forgive me!' She perched beside Barney in his chair. 'I'm sorry. I'm so sorry. Nigel – you didn't choose to go.' She buried her face in the dog's rough coat, the tears flowing fast. Barney turned his little nose and licked at her face.

It was raining. Again. She watched the puddles growing on the lawn. Barney lay curled in his chair. Recently she had made a deliberate effort to look forward to the next trip to London by reading the theatre reviews, and cutting out the ones that sounded the sort of thing Liz might enjoy.

This morning she had gone round the empty fields, braving the rain, insisting Barney did too. The river was high, lapping at the banks. The locals had warned them about the road flooding, but so far it hadn't happened.

She put the kettle on the range to make a hot drink for something to do. Anything.

The rain kept pouring down. The house felt damp, the salt and sugar clogging into clusters.

The road flooded. The river lapped higher on the lawn. At teatime she retreated to bed.

The next day the sky lightened as the clouds began to clear. The rain stopped and the water level in the river dropped rapidly. By late morning, the sun was shining from a cloudless sky.

'Let's walk to the pub, Barney. Buy ourselves a drink. Spring is on the way.'

The dog was happy enough. They sat outside at a table in the sun.

The half-pint of shandy she'd asked for didn't taste of anything.

She got up from the table, left the most of it undrunk.

They walked back, passing the church. The noticeboard was newly painted with large gold letters proclaiming *Eternal Life – Christ is Risen.*

Eternal life?

At home, she went straight into the kitchen to feed the dog. Make someone happy at least.

She put the dog's bowl on the table. Got the ox cheek, bought for a few pence at the butcher's, out of the larder. Sharpened the carving knife, laid the raw meat on the chopping board, and began to cut through the tough outer skin.

The church bell tolled. The westerly wind was blowing the sound across the fields from the village.

Single mournful tolls. Maundy Thursday. Then Good Friday. The day Christ died. Then Sunday. Easter Sunday.

Risen from the dead.

She savaged at the lump of flesh on the board. The sharpened blade made bloody incisions.

No.

The church cheats people, pretending dead people live again. That the living and the dead all meet up in heaven. People can't come back. Nigel's not coming back. Peter won't. Pa won't.

'The babies I killed won't.'

She drove the knife into the board.

'Bloody hypocrites, all of them.'

She flung the meat across the kitchen.

It landed on the side of the draining board. Fell onto the floor, leaving a dribble of blood running down the sink, an untidy rivulet of red against the white.

'Bugger! Bugger! Bugger!'

Not loud enough.

'Bugger them all!' She roared out the words, and again, 'Bugger all of them!'

Barney, instinct getting the better of his surprise, darted to pick up the floppy mess, and began to drag it across the floor tiles.

The front doorbell pealed through the house.

The dog hesitated, abandoned his trophy and set off into the hall, barking furiously. The barking stopped, was replaced by whining.

Oh God, now what?

Someone he knows. Not Mason – he always comes to the back door. Jo?

She wiped her hands on the front of her apron, pushed them through her hair. Barney was jumping up against the window by the front door, his tail whirling around.

'Hello.'

Sports jacket. Cavalry twill trousers. Red silk cravat. 'As it's Easter I thought you might be able to use a bit of pork.' The farmer, Iain Chester, smiling. Bending down to pat Barney.

He looked at her apron, then at her face. 'I hope you're not busy.'

Oh Lord. She caught a whiff of the irony smell of fresh blood. On her hands? On the apron? Where she'd pushed back her hair?

'No, well, not really. I was doing Barney's food.'

'Look, I don't want to intrude.' Shy, stepping back away from the door.

'No, no, you're not. Come in, have a drink.' She pushed open the drawing room door for him. 'I'll just put this in the kitchen.'

She took the packet, scurried out to the kitchen, stepped around the debris on the floor, untied the apron, went to the sink and had started to wash her hands when, 'It looks as if that rascal's stolen his supper,' came from the kitchen doorway.

'Yes.' Blame dumb animals. She dropped the apron, letting it drape over the side of the sink. 'I'm going to close the door on this shambles. Leave him in here. Find that drink.'

She poured two huge gins, added tonic, carried the glasses through to the drawing room. She sank into the sofa, felt the spirit hit her gut. He was sitting on the edge of the fireside chair, not relaxed back into it.

'How's Flossie – and her piglets?'

'Growing fast still. Don't worry, I've a chap who comes in to feed and check on the stock if I'm away. As I develop the farm I'll need him all the time.'

He straightened up, his confidence returning as he talked, explaining about costs of new buildings, the increase in pork from better-housed stock. Or perhaps the gin had worked on him, too.

'It isn't true there's no future in farming, it's just that the old ways have to go, proper housing to keep the pigs in tip-top condition. The Danes know how to do it. It's a big investment.

Teak wood, you know, the units will last for generations.' He stopped. 'God, I'm sorry, boring on like that. But you can see Flossie will live in style.' He smiled. 'Talking of London, I drove Simon up there a couple of weeks ago.'

Which they hadn't been. Simon. A friend? His brother?

'Simon?'

'Look, sorry, Simon's the son of Mother's friends, the vicar and his wife, at Brimsworth. He's more or less a younger brother to me. We went to see *The Pirates of Penzance*. He'd have preferred something a bit more racy but I promised Mother I'd be responsible. Anyway, he enjoyed the drive back. The road was clear so we raced along. We go on treasure hunts sometimes – he navigates, and works out the clues, while I drive. The parents would be horrified if they knew the speeds we get up to, and the corners we cut. Last time I drove straight across a ploughed field.'

'Goodness, did you win?'

'Of course!'

'One of my childhood dreams was to be a rally driver – do the Monte Carlo rally, you know.'

'Really?'

The conversation moved to the river, visible through the French windows, glinting in the late sunshine. Her glass was empty, and glancing across she saw his was as well. He must have noticed her look. He stood up.

'Thank you for the drink, Kitty. Have a happy Easter.'

'I'll enjoy the pork. Thank you.'

After April, the weather settled into a spell of soft May sunshine, hotter and higher in the sky than she remembered in previous years. She established a mini routine for her day: first thing, as soon as she was dressed, she and Barney walked into the village to buy a *Daily Mail* and then at mid-morning she sat on the back doorstep, with a milky coffee and a slice of toast, to read the newspaper.

Then she would try to find some housework to do, though really the house remained forlornly clean and tidy.

In the afternoons she knitted, choosing increasingly complicated patterns as a challenge. She knitted half a dozen white matinée jackets for Jo's next baby, and a rather snazzy jumper for Tavish, with a Rupert Bear motif; a very devil to knit but the little boy's face was reward enough. She'd got him a Rupert annual to go with the woolly.

Jo made a point of joint shopping trips or asking her for the weekend. One hot July evening Alistair took her to the pub for a drink while Jo put the children to bed.

'You are looking better, Kitty. More part of the real world. But you're not cut out for celibacy. Jo would kill me for saying this, won't countenance inviting any unattached man to dinner while you are with us, but you mustn't let being alone become a habit. Too much of a loss to mankind, my dear.'

It was said in a brotherly way, typically Alistair – frank and practical. Unthreateningly honest.

She did tell Jo. 'I know,' Jo said. 'Let off the lead he'd line up every man he thinks suitable in some sort of identity parade and insist you choose one.'

Laughter bubbled up. 'What would I do without you two? He's right in a way. I rattle around, try to make a purpose to my days. Some of the awfulness has gone, only comes back once in a while. And I've learned to manage that a bit – read a happy book, play with Barney, try to teach him some tricks.'

They insisted she spend her birthday with them, was made to feel special and managed not to cry when Tavish appeared with a disorderly collection of garden and wild flowers.

In September, as the days began to shorten, blackberries in the hedgerows, the sun lower in the sky shining through the trees onto the river so it glistened in the late afternoons, she lost interest in eating, struggled to enjoy the dog, and couldn't face writing to Liz or going over to see Mary and Bernard. Her old horror of autumn came back.

She horrified herself by bursting into tears on the phone to Liz.

'But darling, I'm not surprised. Jo and I were talking… '

'About me? Behind my back?'

After a silence, 'We're only trying to be kind.' Liz's voice dropped several octaves, lost its sparkle. 'We want to help.'

'I'm sorry. You do, both of you – and Alistair. Elma, too, though William has got a sort of promotion, if that's what you have in the church, going to the diocese in Norwich, so they are moving. Even the farmer who took the pigs brings me a bit of bacon or pork sometimes. Everyone is nicely kind. Granny's invited me and Barney to Worthing for Christmas. It's nearly a year since Nigel died.'

There, she'd said it. And heard a quickly smothered intake of breath down the phone.

'I have to sort myself out. Being feeble can become a habit!'

But how does one stop getting feeble? By making decisions. Now. Do something different.

'Barney and I are planning an adventure. We are going… '

Where? The newspaper lay open, as she had left it. Rosemullion Hotel. In Devon. Red earth. Cliffs. The advertisement showed a three-storey building, established-looking, promoted its 'central heating', 'hard tennis court', 'sea views' and 'a motor park'!

'We are going to stay somewhere quite different, away from the flat lands here.'

To Budleigh Salterton. The spontaneous idea drilled out of her by Liz's well-meant interference worked. On the actual anniversary she sat, dry eyed, on the pebbly beach and watched as the sun rose above the River Otter, while Barney barked at the waves. Later, they walked miles over the gorse on Woodbury Common and then disgraced themselves by sharing two doughnuts filled with jam and Devon cream.

Home again at Mill House they settled into the dark evenings, Barney asleep in his chair while she busied herself making Christmas presents. She knitted a Fair Isle-patterned jumper for Uncle Bertie and a shawl in silvery grey angora for Granny.

. . .

Christmas at Granny's was unexpectedly enjoyable – safe, warm, familiar. Even the decorations were the same ones from those childhood Christmases. Tarnished, no longer fashionable, but a link to happier times.

At the staid sherry party on Christmas Eve, people who remembered her in a gymslip charmed and were charmed. A well-rounded country doctor, with twinkling eyes, once a tennis partner of Pa's, wanted to share tales of their youthful exploits.

As the housemaid topped up their glasses, he said, 'I need to sit down, my dear. Make it socially acceptable by joining me on the sofa here.' He patted the cushion beside him. 'Despite everything you don't look as if you have lost your humour or your humanity.'

CHAPTER 18

JANUARY 1936

She started the New Year by buying a diary.

'1936, Barney. My twenty-sixth year! We have to move on, away from here. I have to do something with my life.'

So she wrote to the landlords, gave notice to end her tenancy at Mill House at the end of June, which left five months to find somewhere else to live. And rather less than that to decide what to do to make enough money to live on and to be doing something useful.

'Oh, dog dear, nowadays women go to university, become scientists, lawyers – like Pa, or doctors or even politicians. Could I go to university – too old, not the right exams. Learn to fly, like Amy Johnson?' She pushed the diary to the edge of the table. 'And I sit here like a ruddy cabbage.'

The telephone bell tinkled, then rang its jangling summons properly. Liz? Jo? In the hallway, she lifted the receiver.

'Iain Chester here.'

Not Liz then, or Jo.

'Look, I hope you don't mind me phoning, but I'm in a bit of a fix. I remember you said the treasure hunts sounded fun. The thing is Simon was due to navigate for me tomorrow. He's ill, got 'flu or something. I can't go without a navigator.' There was a pause, and then he went on, 'Look, I wondered, would you step into the breach? If you're free.'

Decipher the clues, meet other drivers. Why not?

Do something different. In the evening.

'Well, yes, if it would help. What should I bring?'

'Just yourself.'

Slacks and the soft-shouldered camel-hair coat – the one bought at enormous expense from Bonds. A lifetime away. Stop thinking backwards. Be practical. Shoes?

She gave Barney a titbit of stale cheese and pulled the front door shut behind her.

As she slipped into the passenger seat, she said, 'I brought a torch.'

'Splendid. We start at The King's Head, in Dunmow. The route'll be convoluted, clues sending us up dead ends, doubling back on ourselves.'

They set off at considerable speed from the village with the first clue: '*No black cars here*'.

'That has to be Ford End.' Iain Chester drove confidently and fast, in full control of the car.

He was right. They drew up behind another car at the checkpoint in Ford End, collected the next clue and were off again.

The speedometer touched thirty. In second gear! Another lurch as he swung to the left. 'Sorry, nearly didn't see the pothole!'

She shone the torch on the clue. *Eggs but no hens here*. 'I hope we're right: High Easter?'

'Damn well hope so, this track's murdering the suspension.' He changed down, slowing, as lights appeared. The track became a farmyard.

Shafts of light burst out as the barn doors opened. A man appeared waving a pitchfork, followed by two black and white shapes, barking bundles of angry fur – Border Collies.

'See 'em off, dogs.' The man came up to the car. 'Bloody treasure hunters. I told 'em last time, I'd set the dogs on them.'

Iain wound down his window. 'Sorry about this, sir.'

The man waved the fork around, poking it towards the bonnet.

The dogs had lost interest, wandering away to sniff in the hedgerow.

'Discretion being the better part of valour, we're off.' He reversed sharply, the Lynx's wheels spun momentarily, and then the car was heading back down the track. He chuckled. 'Obviously we're not the first to make that mistake.'

They were the third car to reach the finish at The Harrow in Little Brook. They stayed for a couple of rounds in the pub, long enough to see the winners, an older couple, the man with a vast handlebar moustache, collect their prize of a cigarette holder and matching lighter.

Iain negotiated the lanes back to Flimstour at a gentler pace. Pulling up by the front of the house, he left the engine ticking over.

She gathered up the torch and her bag. 'Thanks, Iain, that was fun.'

'We did okay – third. Would you like to have another go, try for first next time?'

Another go? A bit of a challenge, company, cars, and chatting after in the pub with the others. Casual chatting, to other human beings. Why not?

'So long as your friend Simon doesn't mind.'

'I'll see what we can do. Good night, Kitty.'

She let Barney into the garden, then ran a hot bath, shovelled down under the water level so her shoulders kept warm. Woke up with a jolt, feeling wet hair, cold on her neck. Chilly, she got into bed, snuggled up against Barney and slept the clock round.

Ten days later Iain telephoned. Simon was away, at some army cadet camp, could she help out again?

They set off from Braintree and found the first clue easily enough, but then it started to rain and she struggled to read the signposts. She tried to work it out from the map but the torch flickered before the battery died. Then they spotted one of the other competitors ahead, and followed until both cars ended up back in Braintree.

Iain pulled the car up. 'Blind leading the blind! Never mind. Better call it a day for tonight.' He turned back towards Flimstour.

He turned into the drive at Mill House. Switched off the engine.

It seemed a let-down. She'd looked forward to their doing well, winning even, and to the bonhomie in the pub afterwards, the sense of a joint success.

'Sorry – stupid of me not to have put a new battery in the torch.'

'I'd like to thank my navigator – not her fault we misread the clue.' He leaned across, close. Hardly a kiss, the briefest social touch of his lips on her cheek.

'Give my love to Flossie.'

'Will you come over to the farm, see her for yourself, soon?'

She woke late, rested and dreamless. The sun was already high in the cloudless sky. She spent the morning turning out her wardrobe, putting summer clothes together in casual, smart and wet-day groups.

Folded away her winter woollies. The skirt and twinset worn to Fakenham market, and to see *The Scarlet Pimpernel*. Worn for Nigel. With him. Touched by his hands.

She lifted the cardigan out of the drawer, held it to her lips. 'Oh, my love. But you're not here now. If it were me who'd gone, died, I'd want you to be happy. To have someone to love, babies, a busy houseful of young life. I think you'd like Iain – he likes cars, the countryside, he does things. Barney loves him and his farm.' She sniffed, swallowed back the tears. 'Thank you for loving me. Sleep tight, Nigel.' Refolded the woolly, put it back.

'Walk, Barney. Fresh air, exercise. Help me count the daisies, see if summer is on its way.'

The sharp sunny weather of spring held for the rest of the week so it was warm enough to sit in the garden with the newspaper after lunch. The grass in the fields turned greener, grew in the warmth. And needed caring for, cultivating – hay or grazing.

On Saturday morning Iain telephoned.

'Will you drive over on Friday, say hello to Flossie and then we'll go across to lunch with Uncle Harry. I'm sure you'll like him.'

The roads were clear, dry and bright in the sunshine. Flossie whinnied with pleasure. Barney settled himself in the Lynx. Uncle Harry's house, three storeys of Georgian style, was in Towne Place, quite the most fashionable street in Norwich.

'Come in, my dear.' Uncle Harry, upright and slim, malacca cane in hand, opened the door himself. The old man's blue eyes twinkled. 'Iain told me he was bringing a young lady to lunch, but he didn't warn me to expect Greta Garbo.'

He led them into a room lined with books, wall to ceiling. Two spaniels lay against a club fender enjoying the warmth of a coal fire crackling in the grate. 'It's still chilly, despite the sun, so we'll have cocktails in here. What will you have?'

'A gin and French, please.'

'Good girl – proper drink, none of this sherry nonsense. I expect Iain told you about my young days in the Yukon. Hard spirits there, to keep the cold out. Doesn't seem to have done me any harm. Work hard, play hard, that's my motto.' Iain winked. He'd warned that Harry enjoyed life, despite his ninety-five years.

'Forgive me if I stay standing, my dear. My bones don't like getting up once I sit them down.'

With the two men standing it seemed natural to do so too. She moved towards the fire, bent to stroke the dogs. 'It's nice here, with the warmth of the fire. We've been sitting in the car.'

Harry raised his glass. 'Here's to fun! Now, Iain, how are you getting on with these plans of yours to outdo the Danes at pork production?'

For a full half-hour, until the neatly aproned housemaid came to say lunch was served, Iain talked. A crash course in pork and bacon production.

'That's enough about pigs for today, I think.' Harry lowered himself into the Chippendale carver at the top of the table. Iain eased the old man's chair forward for him.

'Greta my dear, you're far too pretty to be so interested in farming.' Harry smiled. 'Tell me about your home in Sussex.'

'I loved the hills of the South Downs, and the sea.' Too bland to hold this sophisticated old roué's interest. 'We used to climb up to Chanctonbury Ring, that's a Celtic holy place high on the Downs, and slide down on old brass trays until… '

She stopped. Hadn't thought about that day for years. Became aware she had both men's attention. Not now, too difficult. Think of something else to say.

'A poet, Edward Thomas, who was killed in the war, he heard voices on Chanctonbury Ring. He thought it was the Celts.'

'I met North American Indians who did that, heard their ancestors. In elemental places, where the past hadn't been driven out by the present.' Harry levered himself out of his chair. 'Now, my dear, if we've all finished, I'm going to show you my garden. Iain, you've seen it all before, so make yourself comfortable with the newspapers.'

Harry, free hand cupping her elbow, steered her out into the garden. Like a sheep being separated from the rest of the flock by an efficient sheepdog.

'We'll go this way, and finish by the pond, under the almond blossom tree.' He pointed to a large shrub. 'That's my Cornelian cherry, a blaze of yellow in February, and brassy red in the autumn.'

He moved on, using the end of his cane to poke a solitary weed out from the rose bed.

'I'm glad to meet you, my dear.' But there was a purpose to the old man's charm. 'I feel responsible for Iain. He didn't have a happy childhood. Funny business – with his mother and that vicar and his wife. When his father was dying, I promised to keep an eye on the boy, help him to make good use of his inheritance. When Iain told me he had met a pretty young widow, I thought about our young Edward the Eighth and this siren he seems to have got himself tied up with. I used to shoot with the old king. I remember once we'd been out all day, and went back in through the nursery, where little David was playing with his toy soldiers, hundreds of them, lined up on the floor. He said they were practising for his coronation. After we left the room his father said, 'That boy will never be king.' I didn't like to ask what he meant. He may have been a good monarch but he never struck me as a perceptive sort of man. Don't know, maybe he was wiser than he seemed.'

Harry fell silent. She chose not to break into it.

'Forgive my christening you Greta, my dear, but you are very lovely. Iain's a good boy, a bit wilful of course. Help me up the steps, will you, and we'll find him. I expect you want to be on your way home.'

Uncle Harry, and the spaniels, stood sentinel, watching, as Iain opened up the Lynx's coupé roof. The old man, one hand holding onto the iron railing, waved the cane in farewell as the car revved off, disturbing the well-mannered calm of the street.

'I think he's a grand old man. He's charming. Full of life, and shrewd.'

'He's an appalling flirt. I dread to think what he was like when he was younger. I knew Harry'd like you. If he was twenty years younger I wouldn't have let you near him.'

'Iain, if I were twenty years older you wouldn't keep me away from him.' She put her hand on his arm as it rested on the gear lever between them, and then smiled to take any sting out of her remark.

'Is that so?' He glanced at her and changed the subject back to the merits of teak wood for housing pigs.

The sun was still strong, slanting above the farmhouse roof and shadowing the colour-wash into yellow ochre, as they turned into the drive at Five Oaks. The moat was full after all the rain in March, the banks lit by splurges of buttery primroses poking above the grass. A pair of mallards, disturbed by the car as it rattled over the sleepers, swished off the water.

Iain pulled the Lynx off the driveway, nudging it alongside the old cart-shed, and switched off the engine. He pulled off his leather driving gloves, laying them neatly on the dashboard.

Swivelled round and put a hand on her shoulder, twisting her towards him. She saw the coloured flecks in his eyes grow, sharpening the hazel to green. She wondered if her eyes did the same at moments like this.

'Kitty, come inside the house.'

Go into the house? Go to bed, make love, because that's what he was asking. With Nigel love came first, making love, sex, followed. Gloriously. Now, here, friendship, attraction, first. Love might follow.

Into her silence he asked, 'Do you mind?'

Mind? No, nor would Nigel.

As she leaned forwards, his hand found its way through the opening of her coat, and settled on her breast. Her nipple hardened. She knew he'd felt it as he pressed it between his forefinger and thumb. She put her hands on his waist, let them slide down towards his hips.

Upstairs, temporarily sated, cocooned by the rafters of the old house, they lay together on his unmade bed. Bodies laid bare to each other, no places left private, they began to talk. She told him about Peter, and Pa, and then her longed-for-love with Nigel.

His head lay on her shoulder. He told her about his father, a remote figure who he remembered mostly in a darkened room as he lay dying.

'I was eight when he died.' Iain pulled himself up on one elbow, pushed his hair back from his face, frowned, touched her eyes.

'The first time you turned up here, after you'd left, for some reason the horror of Father's funeral came back. I think I'd buried it for years, but that night I had a nightmare. I was back in the church, the side of the coffin opened, I laughed, and Father, magically beside me in the pew, hit me with his cane. I thought I'd forgotten about his death, the smell in his room, and what happened afterwards. Nanny was kind, but she was sacked. Then we left the house, I had a model farm, a sort of boy's doll's house, which Uncle Harry gave me, it was huge. I used to play with it all the time. Mother said it was too big to take with us.' He dropped back onto the pillows, and said, 'Sounds daft talking about it now. We've lived with Uncle James and Maud ever since. Maud's kind, good to me, though she worries I'll lead her

Simon astray. Mother's so fixated with the church sometimes I think she should be the vicar's wife. She goes three times every Sunday.'

Kitty turned, pulled him towards her, wrapped him in her arms.

'Perhaps I've been lucky. Honestly. Peter and I had fun. We were friends. I told him everything. Pa was intelligent and sharp-witted, I loved listening to him, talking with him. With them both gone, home wasn't much fun, and then I found Nigel.' Her voice tailed off.

Iain's hand found her right one, tucked amongst the tumble of clothes and sheets. He squeezed it tightly, kept hold of it.

'Look, you don't want to drive home now, it's almost dark out there. Stay the night. No one will know.'

She hesitated only a moment. It was too late to turn the clock back. A night in this old house, with this man.

'Yes. Please.'

'It's got ruddy cold up here. I'll go down, kick the fire into life and we'll find something to eat and drink. Here's my dressing gown.'

She negotiated the narrow, circular stairs and found him, dressed in old corduroys and leather jerkin, on his knees, pumping the bellows into the embers of the log fire.

'It never goes out, the ashes stay hot all winter. I gave Barney something to eat, he was sulking by the range. I'll go out to turn the generator on, get some light in here. Sorry, I must do the evening feeds, the stock will be ravenous by now. And check the sows.'

She heard him call Barney, and pull the back door shut.

Flames licked up around the big branches of oak that filled the wide fireplace. The lights flickered, went off, came back and then stayed on. She padded out to the kitchen in search of something to put together as a supper. The larder offered bacon, ham, eggs, a pitcher of golden milk, and what was this? Gingerly she lifted the lid off a large earthenware pot. Tongue – a whole one, neatly pressed into its glossy jelly.

She ferreted around in the kitchen, finding eating irons, plates and pickle. She carried the loaded tray back into the drawing room and settled back to watch the fire, roaring away now.

The latch lifted on the door.

'That's a picture to warm a man's heart.' He came over, stood by her chair. 'Ah, you found the tongue – payment from the butcher in return for a couple of hams. I've left Barney in the kitchen, he's covered in mud.' He reached down, pulled her upright against him.

'You, too!' She picked stray straw from his hair, fair, tousled, and brushed at the mud on his jerkin.

They picnicked on the rug in front of the fire, chatting between mouthfuls. He explained the merits of oak over ash for logs, how the farm had enough timber for years of log fires.

She leaned back, resting against the sofa. 'Tell me about the pigs, the new Danish way. Where will you put the buildings?'

He stretched up, pulled his pen and a pad of paper down from the window table. Began to sketch.

'Look, like this: one long shed facing south to catch the sun, for the fattening house, and another here, at right angles, facing west for the farrowing units. The stuff there now will go. Most of it, not the newish boxes, over in the corner, good solid brickwork, ideal for the boars. Bosun's gentle, a good-natured old devil, but we'll need another, two perhaps.'

'Do the Danes use different breeds?'

He explained it was the living conditions, keeping them so they didn't lose condition, which mattered. How surprised he'd been, when he visited Denmark, at the contrast with the conditions on the farms there, compared to places at home.

She yawned, 'Sorry, it's the warmth and the food. Go on.'

'No, that's enough for now.'

He stood up, put the pad back on the table, screwed the top back onto his pen.

Knelt down beside her on the rug, and took hold of both of her hands.

'Kitty, come and live here with me. Help me turn the dream into reality.'

She watched the hazel eyes, so earnest, so direct. A

175

straightforward, uncomplicated sort of man. Live here, with him? A home for her. Barney would love it.

Then she saw a flash of comprehension in his eyes.

'I mean, marry me.' He dropped her hands, ran his hand through his hair. 'Look, Kitty, surely you realised I was serious about you? I mean, I know you've been married but you can't think I'd have bedded you unless I wanted to marry you. Say yes, please.'

The confident man was slipping away. Marry him? Have a farm, a homeful of children? She smiled, reached for his hands back.

'Yes. Please.'

Later, back upstairs but now snuggled between the sheets, Iain broached the practicalities. He was taken aback when she told him about Ma's opposition to Nigel, the furtive planning and deception of the marriage, not a wedding at all.

'Do you think she'll object to me? I'm sure my mother will like you. Anyhow, you have Uncle Harry's approval – in spades!'

'Ma will be fine about us. You have prospects, you see, and anyway since then, with me being independent and keeping her at a distance, she's less of a troublemaker. I expect she'd like me to have a proper wedding. But I wouldn't want it in Dereham.'

'Nor Flimstour, I'm sure. Shall we ask mother's friend, Uncle James, about Brimsworth? It's a nice church, very old.'

'I don't... ' Much mind where, or how, was what she was going to say.

Stopped.

A proper wedding? In a church. In a dress. Off-white, cream silk, perhaps. Flowers. Presents. A party.

Be a bride!

'Is it a pretty church?'

'Hang on.' He was out of bed, rifling through a stack of papers.

He turned on the light, climbed back into bed and passed her a photograph.

'Look, that's it.'

A proper country church, with a curved porch, set amongst trees.

'We should get on with it, so you move your stuff straight here.'

'What a practical soul you are.'

Setting out from home that morning, during the cosy lunch, even as they drove back to Five Oaks, she hadn't given a thought to going to bed with him. It just seemed to have happened.

'Iain, there might be another good reason for getting on with it. If enthusiasm has any bearing on conception I'll be having quadruplets. You wouldn't mind, would you?'

'No, woman, I'd love babies. Though four at once might be a bit much.'

Then, as his hands began to explore her some more, he asked, 'Will this make it five?'

'Five? I wasn't counting.'

He chuckled. 'Don't be indelicate. I meant babies.'

She woke alone in the bed. Felt across the sheet to the hollow of where he had lain. The light was strong outside.

Footsteps on the stairs.

'Breakfast, m'lady.' He was fully dressed, more straw in his hair. 'For both of us. I've done the outside feeds.'

'Whatever time did you get up?'

'Usual time. I'm coming back to bed now.' Catching her expression, 'Don't raise your eyebrows like that. To talk. Organise things.'

It was early afternoon. Iain had gone out to work in the barns, disgracefully late, he said, with the farm chores.

She pushed Barney into Speedy, pulled out the choke and pressed the self-starter. She moved the gear lever into first, let the car pull away, rumbling over the sleeper-bridge.

They had written up long lists, drawn lots for who did what, and by when. She swung the car left, taking the road to Saxted Green.

Speedy was bundling along. They rounded a wide sweeping bend on the edge of the green with its great windmill, gleaming white in the sun.

In front of her, taking up most of the road, stood two shire horses, their big leather-harnessed heads held high: the ploughman must have heard the car and pulled them to a standstill. She changed down sharply, braked and pulled onto the verge.

The horses' heads, two matching white blazes, dropped a little as the ploughman started to manoeuvre them, and what looked like a harrow, wide lines of rattling metal, passed the car. Barney sparked a bit as the horses went by, placid tons of power, dwarfing the car.

'Thank ye, ma'am.'

The hoofs, great hairy dinner-plates, clip-clopped away.

To wherever they were going.

Away. Somewhere. Unknown.

This time yesterday – well, never mind, this time the day before yesterday.

The windmill stood unmoving. Solid. Placid. Like the horses.

'Hello, friend. You've looked down on us, ants scurrying about our lives, for hundreds of years. Another of your kind welcomed me to Dereham. Nigel and Cervantes. It's not goodbye, Nigel. You'll be here, part of me, until I die.'

Barney was restless, looking to see who was there, whom she was talking to.

'No one there, Barns. Just me, thinking aloud.' She ruffled the wiry fur, tickled behind his ears. 'Are we doing the right thing? Well, you'll be in your element. Me, too, I think.' The ploughman and his horses disappeared from sight, down the track. 'Come on. My list is as long as my arm. No time to dawdle.'

CHAPTER 19

JUNE 1936

THE HARSH ILLUMINATED hands of the clock glowed, dragging slowly through the long night. Despite Liz, safely asleep no doubt, in the room next door, and Uncle Bertie along the corridor, a sense of isolation wound up her stomach muscles. There was nothing wrong exactly with the bed, except it was a big double and there was no Barney. The hotel room was hot and she tossed off the blankets.

Once they had arranged a date – with the church, with Iain's vicar friend and with Uncle Bertie who was to give her away – Iain had broached the subject of Ma. 'Look, let me drive us over, take her out to lunch on neutral territory. I can call the shots about when we leave.' In fact, it had been a surprisingly easy social occasion. At the end Iain had said, 'I'll be spending the night before the wedding in the vicarage with Mother and her friends. We've arranged for Kitty to stay in an old coaching inn, The Bugle Hotel, next to the church.' He'd paused. She hadn't expected the next bit. 'Dorothy, I've organised a decent chauffeur-driven car to pick you up in good time on the morning and wait until you want to leave the reception.'

Thank God, thank you Iain. And he had arranged for Barney to stay at the farm with Frank and Mrs Frank, actually Winnie, who'd be looking after the pigs, too.

Barney – he wouldn't run off would he? Get stuck in a rabbit hole?

Until, eventually, she got out of bed, opened the window and breathed in fresh clean air, let it blow over her bare arms.

Her clothes for tomorrow hung against the big wardrobe – for the service she'd chosen ivory silk, a knee-length dress and elegantly loose three-quarter length coat. Her suitcase and going-away garment, plain navy silk suit, lay ready.

Chilly, she went back to bed.

Was woken by the chambermaid bringing in a tray of breakfast.

She was up, washed, made up and ready to dress when Liz appeared.

'It's a perfect day, sunny and still. I'm thrilled for you. You and Iain have so much in common – plans for the farm, and to fill that old house with children. I couldn't say you are lucky, after everything that's happened, but you won't want for anything, ever again.'

'Thanks for being here.' She pushed the hairbrush away. 'Now, use your Fortnum skills, help me into the dress.'

'You do look well. So feminine – blooming, in fact.'

Standing up, she caught sight of herself in the long mirror. Looking good? Yes, she was, could see that for herself. In the three months since the first time at the farm, there had been other times. She'd felt it disingenuous, and not very fair on Iain, to pretend sudden virtuousness which didn't appeal much to her either. They'd been careful though, and she had not stayed overnight again.

Used to men showing interest in her, recently she'd recognised that her superficial confidence in social situations went much deeper now. Jo had quizzed her, quoting Alistair, always frank, who described her as looking well-bedded. It was deeper than that, she knew. Physical confidence, yes, but importantly too the shared interests, the frank friendship, the challenge of making a go of the farm together.

'Let me do those buttons, darling. Bertie's waiting, looking tremendously proper in tailcoat and dress trousers.'

'That turquoise suits you, better than mimicking my dress. Remember, the best man kisses the bridesmaid!'

'Maid of honour, and Simon's too young for me. He says he wants to be a fighter pilot.'

'His mother's upset, doesn't like the idea. All this talk of rearmament.'

Cooling Eau de Cologne onto her wrists. Touched the double string of pearls – she'd put them on as soon as she'd washed so the heat of her body had a chance to make them live. Picked up the posy of pink musk roses, held them to her face for a moment, inhaled the heady perfume.

'I'm ready.'

Out of the room, along the carpeted corridor lined with its numbered doors. Down the staircase. Onto the wide flagstones of the old hallway.

'Delightful, Kitty dear. Perfect taste.' Bertie held out his hands. 'Granny's pearls look lovely on you.'

'You will remember to tell her, won't you? I wish she were here.'

'She does too, but she's better at home. Has lost energy and weight recently.' He squeezed her arm. 'Ready, dear?'

They walked the short distance to the lychgate. The church path, swept clean and dry in the midsummer sun, wound through the sloping churchyard up to the porch.

It took a second to adjust to the dark of the church after the sun outside. The organ burst forth with the opening bars of a trumpet voluntary and the scent of roses wafted around her.

The church was a sea of faces. Beyond them all at the altar Iain stood square-shouldered, ramrod-still, flanked by Simon who turned, winked.

Reaching the foot of the altar she felt, rather than saw, Iain move closer to her.

She hardly heard the hymns, the ones they had chosen with such care, but they both managed the responses clearly, and then, the register signed, she was leaning on Iain's arm and heading back down the aisle.

The mist of faces fell into focus now: Uncle Harry, upright, top hat and silk gloves resting on the front pew, leaned towards them, whispered congratulations. Behind him Iain's mother and some of his friends and Matthew, whom he'd been to school with, and who lived in Woodbridge now.

Jo, expecting again, in an orange outfit topped with a huge hat of the same material, with Alistair.

Christopher Brownlow with his mother.

Then, alongside the aisle, Mary Gifford and Bernard.

She stopped, disentangled herself from Iain's arm

'Thank you for being here in the church.' She hesitated, not knowing what else to say, or indeed what she felt. She bent towards them.

Mary kissed her on the cheek. 'Bless you! We're here for Nigel, you know. He's wishing you all the happiness in the world. On you go now, my dear.'

She swallowed, blinked, leaned back into Iain, and they stepped on, down the aisle and out into the sunlight.

'Barney!' The dog was whirling around the black skirts of the verger who was struggling to keep control of him.

'You said you'd left him at the farm!'

The dog's high-pitched barking rose to a frenzied crescendo as he spun round, twisting on the lead, until he slipped out of his collar.

Iain grabbed the dog, and held him tight. 'Better my clothes than your dress, I think. Barney, what a devil you are, that poor man looks mortified. If you don't behave I'll change my mind about you coming with us.'

'With us? He's coming too?'

'Certainly. He pretty much introduced us!'

After the speeches and the toasts, her sleepless night caught up and a wave of fatigue hit her. She moved across the room to Iain, and whispered, 'Is it time we made a move? Shall I go and change?'

'God, yes. It's very wearing.'

They left the reception in a shower of confetti, holding hands as they turned to wave goodbye. Iain steered her firmly towards the Lynx, parked ready for their departure.

Tucking her skirt into the seat, he whispered, 'I've no doubt that there's half a ton of ironmongery attached to this car. Don't worry, I've got a penknife – we'll get round the corner and then sort ourselves out.'

Iain turned the key in the ignition, revved up the engine, moved the gear lever into first, and put his foot on the accelerator.

A shattering explosion came from the boot. She ducked, put her hands over her head.

'Firecrackers.' Iain grinned. 'I fear Simon's been borrowing things from his cadet force. I'm sure we won't be blown up, I'm going to put my foot down.'

They set off down the gravel at enormous speed, a series of mini-explosions leaving a strong smell of cordite to mingle with dust from the driveway.

'My God, that made me jump. Poor Barney looks terrified. I'm glad you've got strong nerves. I wonder what the matriarchs made of it.' She pushed Barney, calmer now, back into the footwell. 'I think Simon's going to find it hard without you around to leaven the atmosphere at the vicarage.'

She hadn't wanted any sort of honeymoon. What she wanted was to move into the security of Five Oaks, to be getting on with making the place the hub of their existence, somewhere to enjoy for itself, entertaining friends, helping with the farm, walking the fields with Barney.

But Iain had persuaded her. 'Look, they'll all expect us to go away. It is convention after all. We'll go to the Grand at Cromer. Enjoy luxury for a couple of nights. Dance in the evenings.'

She had smiled, given way gladly. He danced well: he'd taken her to London to celebrate the formal announcement of their engagement. Dinner and dancing at The Berkeley. Discovering that this workmanlike man could also dance, with a style and verve to match her own, had been an unexpected bonus. 'I do believe you're managing me! Dining and dancing, how could I refuse?'

They ate Cromer crab, drank champagne with their strawberries, walked along miles of pristine sand and demolished vast breakfasts served in their room, looking out over the North Sea.

Three whole days. Until the opulence began to cloy. On the last morning, she woke to see Iain studying the ceiling.

'Home today. Once I've done the feeds I'm going to sit down with that sketch pad, scale off the site, get an estimate for the concrete.'

She propped herself up, used her fingers to order his hair. 'I can't wait to be back, get on with things. This has been fun, wonderfully indulgent, but I couldn't... '

He finished for her. 'Live like this all the time. Nor me, be bored rigid. Both of us. Don't worry. That's not a problem we're ever likely to face. Come here.'

'We could be dressed, ready to go before our breakfast arrives.'

'Yes, woman, we could. But we won't.'

From that first day she had come to the farm, waited in the kitchen, she'd felt at home in the house. The other time, lying under its oak beams, the sound of its timbers creaking in the night-time silence, drowsy, she'd whispered that all the people before them were here, keeping them company, making her welcome.

Now, as they got out of their Cromer clothes, she sat on the edge of the bed, carefully rolling down the precious silk stockings, and said, 'There's a safe comfort about this old house.'

'It's the wood, all this oak.' He scuffed at the floor. 'I'm going to check on the farm, catch up with Frank.'

She climbed to the top floor, unlatched the window, leant out, felt the walls, lath and plaster, ran her hands along the beams, took her shoes off so her bare feet touched the wide wooden boards.

Held the door, ran her fingers up its slatted timbers, and edged the thick wooden arm back into its slot to close the door.

Stepped across the landing into the east-facing room, looked out over the moat towards Tuppers Field. The tip of the church spire showed above the trees – the village, pub, people, surprisingly close.

Down the stairs, twisting, narrow, the handrail worn shiny by generations of hands, rough, hard-worked hands. She worked her way through every room, savouring the atmosphere, finishing by the hearth in the drawing room.

'Introducing myself to you, House,' she said. 'I think you'll keep us safe. In return, House, I will tend you, nurture you, make you a little bit my own.'

The farm dictated the pattern of their lives, the routine of husbandry. The early starts came as an unexpected pleasure.

But it was summer, light long before even Iain had to be up.

What about the dark winter mornings? Wait and see. Log fires, hot chocolate for breakfast, long evenings together with a Bach concert, card games, or just talking. Winter would be fun, too.

Iain's practical confidence ate up the routine jobs on the farm. Those done, he started on some new project. He'd set off, loaded with tools, Barney racing ahead.

In the mornings, she tidied round in the house, sorted out food for the day's meals and took coffee out to Iain. Twice a week she got things ready for Winnie, Frank's wife, who came in to clean. Then she drove Speedy into the village to get the shopping. Shopping was a social event, so she always came back with snippets of local knowledge and farming gossip.

On the days she went with Iain to the markets, sometimes to buy or sell animals, sometimes just to get a feel for prices, they drove back into Woodbridge, had a beer and something to eat at The Crown.

They were invited to cocktails at neighbouring houses and farms. Superficial dos, Iain called them. He was right, of course, she replied, adding that they were a risk-free, useful way of meeting new people.

A couple of times they tried one of the local car treasure hunts, but the appeal seemed to have gone.

'We've grown out of them,' Iain said.

'Are we getting old before our time?'

'No, just changing. I'm happy enough with dinners with friends, or drinking in the pub.'

The house was furnished, bachelor fashion, with the essentials, good solid workmanlike pieces of furniture, and a smattering of Persian rugs, intricately worked pieces of art, about the only thing inherited from Iain's childhood home.

Kitty searched the auctions in Woodbridge and Ipswich hunting for a dining table, chairs, smaller finishing touches. One afternoon as she browsed along the side streets of Ipswich, she found a Jacobean tallboy, carved and glossy with centuries of loving polish.

The day the tallboy was delivered her excitement turned to frustration and then embarrassment. The delivery men looked at the old wooden spiral staircase, shook their heads, muttered together, and told her they'd have to take the staircase out to get the chest of drawers up to the bedroom.

Iain, coming across from the yard to inspect her purchase, laughed and told them to go ahead.

After the staircase had been replaced and the men had left, she polished the already spotless wood, and put a photo of Iain's mother, together with her favourite one of Peter, on the shining surface. She filled Pa's vase with roses from the garden and stood it on a glass mat. She transferred Iain's belts, cuff links, bow tie and cravats to one half-width drawer, before colonising the other with her hankies, belts and headscarves.

As they sat in the warmth of the evening sun drinking gin and tonic, Iain said, 'Frank and I agreed today. He'll start on clearing the site next week. I'm getting quotes for the cement. Tons and tons of it.'

'Tucked beyond the orchard, with that conglomeration of shacky sheds, it's difficult to picture neat buildings. How long before they arrive?'

'A couple of months. It'll be hell keeping things going out there once we've cleared the old buildings. We're going to re-erect some of them across the road in the big field as temporary housing. The pigs'll be happy, rooting around for the acorns under those oaks, but the new units have got to be finished by September. The fatteners will lose condition if they're out once the days shorten.'

'I can help with the paperwork and with the feeding. At least you won't have to dismantle the house to accommodate your purchases!'

The detritus from last night's party littered the kitchen. Cocktails, six till eight pm. It had gone on much longer, and new friends, Philip the local solicitor and his wife Nancy, had stayed on long after everyone else. Kitty stood, slightly fuzzy-headed, surveying the mess.

Breakfast. Any minute Iain would be in. He'd overslept and thumped out of bed, muttering that staying up till two am was a damn silly idea.

Put the bacon rashers in the hot oven. Give a sense of breakfast on its way.

She cleared a space on the table, put the coffee percolator on the hob.

Barney pushed through the back door, followed by Iain.

'That smells good.' The fresh air seemed to have improved his temper. 'I hate it when I start late. It's chaotic, temporary sties here, there and everywhere. No Frank, today, either. It was a good party, thank you.'

'Yes – fun, but the house looks a bit of a mess, despite Winnie's efforts. I'll have to rattle round before Simon comes tomorrow.'

'Probably not the best idea having him so soon after the party. Or while we're in the midst of the building out there. Never mind. He won't notice the house, don't worry.'

By afternoon the sun, low in the September sky, shone through the oak trees on the lawn outside. A wave of contentment swept through Kitty as she leaned against the range. The pigeons for tomorrow night's dinner were ready, casseroled to rich succulence. The house looked a good deal better. Iain was still outside, feeding the pigs.

What was that on the lawn?

A piglet. Two piglets.

'Iain!'

No answer. She shouted again, 'Iain! Wherever are you?'

She ran through the belt of trees and across the bridge to the farm buildings. The door to Flossie's sty was wide open, swinging in the breeze. No sign of Flossie, or any of her piglets.

Across the yard, Iain was calmly mixing meal into hot mash in the feed shed.

'Flossie's out. You've left her door open.'

'Rubbish.'

'The piglets are on the lawn. Heading for the moat.'

There was no funny side to two people chasing a dozen remarkably agile little lumps around an acre of lawn and orchard.

It was nearly dark before they managed to reunite Flossie with all but one of her offspring, and shepherd her back into the sty.

Then they found the last little pig, floating dead in the moat.

'How could you be so damn stupid? If I hadn't noticed we'd have lost them all. And Flossie, too.'

'Don't be hysterical. She's only a pig.'

The leanness of his face set into cold lines of dislike. She hadn't seen him angry before, not even irritated, with her.

'There's no need to look at me like that. It wasn't me who left the sty open.'

He flung his farm coat onto the kitchen floor.

'You're irrational about that ruddy sow.' He turned, kicked the coat into the corner, snatching at the back door.

'Supper's ready.'

'Sod that.' And shouting, added, 'And you'd better cancel Simon, or entertain him on your own.'

'Good riddance to bad rubbish.' She flung the wet dishcloth at the closing door. 'Barney!'

The dog was jumping into the Lynx with Iain.

Traitor!

The car disappeared, turning left, away from the village.

She sat down. In Barney's chair. It smelt of the little dog. Horrid little thing, choosing to go with Iain. Barney prefers him.

Her anger faded. Alone in the silence of the house it turned to sick fear in her tummy.

He's gone away.

Oh, God. Is there another woman? No, not that. Not yet. But there'd be plenty of takers. Had he been swept along with the ease of things between them? Is he regretting it?

Why hadn't she held her temper, silly to have a row. Nigel was never bad- tempered. They had never had a row.

But he's gone.

The dusk had deepened into proper night-time, the bare glass of the kitchen window shiny black. No moon tonight. What about Flossie? Was she safe?

She took the torch from beside the back door, and went over the moat, into the yard to check.

She peeped over the half-door of the sow's sty, inhaled the animal warmth. Flossie was stretched out with a line of piglets firmly attached to her, suckling, greedy, contented.

She counted them. Twice. They were all there. None the worse for their escapade. The sow's ears flicked, but her eyes stayed closed. She was asleep, all her world close to her, as nature intended.

Once back inside the house, she pushed the door shut. They never locked it unless they left the farm.

The rich, stewy smell of the pigeons, strong and so seductive earlier, made her queasy. No one was going to eat them anyway. She lifted the lid off the enamel rubbish bucket, and upended the casserole, tipping the contents away.

The house was deadly quiet. She went upstairs to bed. The room was cold. She was shivering. She got a hot-water bottle from the airing cupboard, and went down to the kitchen, boiled up the kettle.

The silence in the house was louder than ever. Standing at the range, she held the bottle round its narrow neck, balancing the kettle to steady the stream of hot water.

At a noise she spun round. The latch on the back door clanked and the door swung open. Boiling water slurped onto the floor.

'Sorry. I didn't mean to make you jump.'

Relief made her burst into tears. He took the bottle from her and dropped it into the sink. 'I knew the catch on Flossie's door was loose. I'm sorry for what I said. Barney told me off.'

'Oh, Iain. I'm sorry too. I should have helped you do the feeding.' She was gulping back tears and sniffing. 'I thought I might never see you again. That it was all over.'

'For an intelligent lady you can be a very stupid woman. I went over to see Matthew, dragged him out to the pub.' He pulled a handkerchief from his pocket, wiped her cheeks dry. 'You still look pretty, even with red eyes and a runny nose. It was only a squabble. Things don't end as quickly as that.' He wrapped his arms around her. Smoothed her hair. 'Shh, come on, shh.'

She was gulping back tears, of relief now, yet still she felt dark fingers of fear inside.

'Look at me!'

She obeyed. Met the amber pools of liquid, frank affection. Surprise, too.

CHAPTER 20

OCTOBER 1936

SIMON STOOD BY THE MANTELPIECE, poking at the logs with his foot. 'Splendid meal, your pork was delicious. If there is a war you'll live pretty well off the farm.'

'I don't reckon it's as much if, as when.' Iain passed three glasses of brandy round. 'Let's drink to the future, whatever that holds.'

'I wish I didn't think you were right.' She took a sip of the fiery liquid. 'About the war, I mean. Less than twenty years since the last one and look what that did to a whole generation. We were lucky, just too young.'

'Churchill's right.' Iain swirled the brandy round in the glass making the liquid reflect the firelight. 'Hitler and Germany must be stopped.'

'Things will be different this time.' Simon put his empty glass on the mantelpiece, thrust both hands into his trouser pockets. 'The generals learned their lesson about trench warfare. Mother hates me saying this, but the next war will be fought in the air. The Germans are building squadrons of aircraft.'

Simon and Iain talked on, discussing the wonders of German engineering and modern fighter aircraft. Simon regarded aeroplanes as giant sports cars, only without the constraints of roads or other traffic. Poor lad, champing at the bit to cut the apron strings, the prospect of war offering only opportunities, no threats, to his young male mind.

Drowsy, in the soft firelight Kitty daydreamed: sitting in this room, while upstairs a little boy is asleep, tired after a day running round the farm, his favourite teddy snuggled in with him; beside his bed, a baby girl in the cot about to wake crying for her midnight feed. Iain will be good with the boy, patient and happy to let the child help. The baby cried.

'Kitty, you've dozed off.' Iain's voice broke into her dream. 'Let's pack it in for tonight.'

Upstairs, as she sat at the dressing table, brushing her hair to a soft gloss, he rested a hand on her shoulder. 'Another lovely evening, thank you. Good to have Simon here, in the house. Shall we have lots of children? So they've got each other?'

'Lots. Two isn't enough – look what happened to my parents. They were destroyed by poor Peter and the years of his illness. For more than ten years they knew there was no hope, and had to watch him getting worse, more and more feeble and wizened. Ma should have had another baby; I've never asked why she didn't.'

'It was ten years of your childhood – almost all of it. Maybe I didn't have much family life, but Simon's always been there, like a brother.'

She pulled the hair from the brush, laid it blue- enamel side up on the dressing table beside the comb and mirror, reached across to turn off the light.

She slipped in between the sheets. 'We won't let history repeat itself, Iain.'

The November sun had an unexpected warmth as she sat on the wooden bench by the back door. In the still air a handful of late bees were making the most of the heat, working their way through the last of the Michaelmas daisies.

The steady rhythm of the yard broom, bristle on concrete, sounded from across the yard as Iain mucked out.

Forty finished fatteners had been loaded into the carrier's truck and driven off to slaughter that morning. Usually when the big lorry trundled away down the lanes, there was a pit of regret, guilt even, in her stomach. This morning she had put her hands on her stomach, and bustled on with her chores.

How to tell Iain? Ridiculous to feel bashful. She practised, 'I'm having a baby.' No, that's not right. 'Iain, you're going to be a father.' Better.

The brushing stopped. Silence. Then, 'Barney, lunchtime, dog.'

Iain and the dog arrived at the same moment, from different directions.

'You look comfy. This Indian summer's set to last.' He sat down alongside her. 'Bosun's a damn good boar – those two young sows are in pig.'

'Me too.' It just came out. So much for the carefully planned words.

A split second, then, 'You?'

He was up, on his feet reaching for her hands. 'Are you saying we're going to have a baby? When?' He held her at arm's length. 'We must take care of you, but you don't look any different.'

She laughed, and moved into his arms.

'It's not an illness, you know. You don't need to wrap me in cotton wool. I can do everything. Play tennis, drive, feed the animals, muck out, even dance.'

'Dance? Well, let's dance then.'

'Here? Now?'

'Of course! On the lawn. With music.'

Solemnly he carried the gramophone outside, balanced it on a chair in the middle of the lawn. Turned the handle round and round, stopping when the tightness told him it was fully wound. He dropped the needle onto the record.

'May I have this dance?' He held out his arms, swept her in a wide circle around the grass. As the November sun slanted across the moat, they waltzed on.

They didn't hear the van as it pulled up the drive, and were slightly taken aback to see old Bert Walsh the fishmonger shaking his head as he watched them whirling around the lawn.

'Shall we tell him?'

'No, he's a strange, sour man. He'd spoil it. Let him think we do this all the time. I'll buy something.'

She went across the lawn to the driveway, made an attempt at conversation with the man. 'What a wonderful day for this time of year.'

The spell was broken. She took her purchases into the kitchen, and put their lunchtime soup onto the range to heat.

'Kitty, let's celebrate with a trip to London. Do our dancing in style! Take in a show, and some serious shopping for you. Frank can manage here for a couple of days.'

She put the steaming bowls onto the table, and wrapped her arms around him.

They left the farm, pigs and Barney in Frank's capable hands, and drove to London. There were two almost empty suitcases in the car. She had carefully packed a case for each of them, and later had gone upstairs to find Iain unpacking, taking all the clothes out and putting them on the floor.

'Whatever are you doing? I pack well, pride myself on it.'

'You pack well. Very well.' He stood up, his face in shadow, the light from behind giving his hair a blond halo. 'Dear wife, you and I are going to town. In every sense. We are going to walk the length of Bond Street to choose silk and cashmere things for you. Italian shoes for us both.'

'But, Iain, I've got—'

'All you need.' He finished for her. 'We are, both of us, going to have the best. I can afford it. I don't trust the world, war is in the air.' He sensed her uncertainty. 'Look, I can't house my pigs in exotic teak, and my wife in rags!'

They stayed at the Hyde Park Hotel, shopped in Nichols and Bond Street, went to the theatre, dined and danced till dawn at the Four Hundred Club. She didn't tell Liz that they were in London, buried her sense of selfishness, and avoided Fortnum's.

. . .

Once started, the site cleared and the concrete laid, the construction of the teak housing had sped along, until now most of the stock had been re-housed in their new quarters.

Iain, clearly relieved but also distinctly proud, set out to bring Uncle Harry to inspect.

The old man, immaculate in tweed jacket, green velvet waistcoat and rakish red-spotted cravat, eased himself upright on his cane as Iain helped him out of the Lynx. 'This car of yours is the very devil on my old bones.'

She leaned forward, touched cheeks.

'My dear, you look more beautiful than ever. Iain shared your news with me. Congratulations. New life, hope.'

Harry had aged, shrunk somehow, and his skin was papery. She kept hold of one bony hand. 'Come in – have a gin and French after the journey.'

'No. I want to see this pigs' palace. Iain tells me the Danish people want to look over the farm. Quite a compliment. Lend me your arm, old boy.'

Iain set off at a gentle, ambling pace.

'Don't dawdle, man.'

An excited Barney led Cassius, Harry's better-mannered spaniel, off towards the orchard.

The men paused, allowing Kitty to step ahead. She watched for the old man's reaction as they emerged from the belt of trees.

Harry stopped, nearly lost his footing as he waved his cane towards the neat line of wooden buildings, new and gleaming in the sunlight.

'Good. Excellent. Take me round. Show me how it will all be managed.' He was in his element, frail certainly, but absorbed. He whistled through his teeth, walked across the newly concreted yard, leaned forward to inspect the slatted teak planks. He stepped back to look up at the sloping roofs and the big vents. He studied them for a minute, then looked searchingly at Iain and said, 'Now, explain the economics of all that investment.'

'We should go back inside, talk in the warm. I'll show you the figures when we've had lunch.'

She'd made a steak and kidney pudding, followed by cheese.

'Thank you, Kitty.' Harry pushed his cheese plate to one side. 'I'm proud of what you're doing with the farm, Iain.' He puffed on his cigar. 'If the old king were alive I'd want to show him.'

She caught Iain's eye and read her own thought in it – let the old man talk.

Harry coughed, cleared his throat. 'Shame about the new king's decision. Well, not his – Baldwin and that sanctimonious churchman, Lang.'

'Listening to the abdication broadcast, I remembered your story about him as a little boy.' She went on, 'I don't think he should have gone, he'd have been a good king, modern, and interested in ordinary people.'

'Perhaps. His father saw something amiss with the boy all those years ago. Either way, the monarchy is irreparably damaged. I don't like it. Not at all. Now, let's talk about you and this family that's on the way.'

They chatted on, but Harry was obviously flagging so Iain organised him into the Lynx. She waved goodbye and feared for the old man.

Her body ached, felt tired, drained. Winnie was tidying up in the kitchen, would leave the place immaculate. The round trip to Norwich would take Iain at least two hours. She sank down on the sofa by the fire. Rested her head on the big cushion. Dozed in the warmth.

Jerked awake.

Doubled over as the pain tore between her hips. She retched as the pain came again, crying out as it ripped through her guts.

'Ma'am, whatever is it?'

'The baby's coming! Oh, God! Winnie, help me.'

'It can't be. You've months to go yet.'

Winnie's hands, wet from the sink, pressed on her shoulders.

'It is. It's the same pain. In the same place. Telephone the doctor. Quick, please!'

The room started to shift round, and, giddy, she slipped out of the chair onto the floor, tasting the bile rising in her throat as warm wetness soaked into her skirt.

. . .

A man's voice floated into her consciousness. 'She'd passed out by the time I got here. I gave her a shot to ease the pain. Frank helped me get her up those stairs of yours. Winnie has been wonderful, tidied her up and packed hot-water bottles round her.'

Iain's voice. 'I'm so sorry I wasn't here. She seemed fine at lunch. We've been busy with the farm buildings.'

'Shouldn't matter, normally. She's coming round. I'll be off now, and be back tomorrow on my way to surgery.'

The bedroom door latched shut, wood meeting wood. Her head and eyes were leaden. Iain's hand closing over hers on the eiderdown.

'I am so sorry.'

'Don't be daft. It's not your fault. Chin up – it happens to the best sows! Quick kiss and back to sleep for you.'

It was morning when she opened her eyes and was astonished as much by the broad daylight outside as by the sight of Iain, not normally domesticated, setting the tray on the bed: tea steamed out of one of the wedding-present set of Royal Worcester porcelain cups, and a brown egg perched uneasily in one of the after-dinner coffee cups.

'I made you a cup of tea. And a boiled egg. You were fast asleep when I got up. How are you feeling?'

'I slept right through. I don't feel too bad. I'm not hurting down there.' This surprised her – not like the agony and long-drawn-out recovery last time.

'Good. Old Doctor Foster'll be here soon.'

'Don't call him that, you'll make me laugh. Anyhow, it'll slip out, and he'll be offended.'

'It's those spats he wears. I saw him in the village, tiptoeing around the puddle, the damn big one outside the basket-maker's shop the other day.' He perched on the edge of the bed. 'Do I detect the glimmer of a smile? Brave girl.'

Within a couple of days she was up and about. Her tummy felt tender, nothing worse. The doctor had told her, when they were alone, that the miscarriage was certainly the result of the botched-up abortion and that she must give her body time to heal – no pregnancy for at least two years.

Somehow, she managed to conceal the inner turmoil, shameful, angry guilt – three new lives destroyed. And now, the deception, as if she'd been unfaithful to Iain. The secret locked in her, no Nigel to hold her hand, to understand. It was only after Iain was fast asleep beside her in the bed that she sobbed, silently, night after night.

Iain and Frank were off the farm on a round trip to buy supplies, so she collected the piles of her soiled towels and took them over to the smouldering bonfire beyond the yard. Most of the mucked-out bedding from the sties went onto the manure heap in the field, but the dryish straw, hedge cuttings, old feed bags and general waste got burned on the bonfire.

She poked at the smouldering pile, pushing the used towels in their newspaper wrapping into the hot heart of the bonfire. Sat back on her haunches. Two years before a baby. Of abstinence, which was unthinkable, or of one or other of them fumbling around. She'd try the sponge and vinegar method. Jo swore it worked.

The bundles caught, and flamed up. She watched the smoke swirling away over the fields. Stared into the flames. Cleaning up, animal-like. Since man invented fire, women must have done this. Generations of women, every month, in this primeval way. And when they'd miscarried.

But not self-inflicted – yes, done it to themselves. For better reasons. Without medicine or doctors and nurses to help. And died. Not lived on with their past.

She might have died. Would it have been easier?

Don't be feeble, self-pitying. Like Ma.

She eased herself upright, and reached for the pitchfork to heap the remnants back together.

Glanced behind her. No one to hear.

Spoke out loud. Firmly, 'Pull yourself together! You didn't die. Something, someone, gave you another chance. You're young, living in comfort and safety. Iain needs you to build up the farm. To wait a year or two won't be so dreadful. In ten years the farm will be running itself, Iain managing the farmhands and the marketing, spending time with the children. A baby every two years. Four children and you'll still be young.'

She waited while the unburned detritus blazed up until all that remained was a neat circle of ash. All traces of the last week burned, and blown away. She turned, walked towards the house.

By Christmas normality was restored. Vinegar and sponge, two small ones cut to size, safely stored in the bathroom. Holly tacked into the beams. They went to the pub on Christmas Eve, then to Midnight Mass. Spent Christmas Day working on the farm, ate roast goose in the evening and lay longer than normal in bed the next morning.

The snow started in the middle of January. The air was cold and crisp. Kitty glanced out of the window of the farm office, really a large alcove off the drawing room. The post van crawled down the driveway, its wheels spinning despite the chains on the front wheels.

'Poor Postie's little wheels are struggling.'

'So is everything else. If it doesn't warm up soon we'll be in trouble. The heating in the farrowing sheds is working well, but the generator's eating paraffin.'

She brought in the pile of envelopes, began opening them. 'There's a hefty cheque here from the sausage factory.'

She picked out a thick parchment envelope, untucked the flap, studied the embossed card.

'We're invited to Christopher Brownlow's wedding – to that girl, Davinia. Ages ahead – in May. In London, all very smart, at St James's in Piccadilly and afterwards at The In and Out.'

'*That girl* – don't be waspish, Mrs Chester. We'll have to get through this Siberian winter before then or the cheques won't be so big, if at all.'

'The days will start to get longer, and there'll be more warmth in the sun too. Emptying the drinking troughs overnight makes it easier in the mornings. None of that knocking out the ice before you start. Come on, let's get back out there.'

Kitty was right. The longer daylight hours helped and then the biting easterly wind dropped. The snow started to thaw at the edges as the drifts sank into themselves. Dirty wet earth showed and then tuffs of grass stood up through the mucky snow.

She woke one morning, opened the window and smelt a change in the air. They had got the farm, and Iain's huge investment, through the winter. A blackbird trilled. Spring was on its way.

The night before the Brownlow wedding they stayed at the Great Eastern Hotel. The dining room, which they didn't use, looked better than it had for that dismal lunch with Pa. A new carpet, modern curtain fabric.

'Lucky they chose this week, rather than last. We'd never have got a room with the coronation on,' Iain said.

'I'd have liked to see the procession – horse guards, the state coach. It must be hard on the queen – she never expected all that.'

'Harry was right – it doesn't feel right. Duke and Duchess of Windsor! A discarded spare hanging around.' Iain didn't normally sound negative.

She glanced across, tried to read him.

'Cab's here. Come on.' He shepherded her down the steps.

The taxi drew into the kerb. Alongside them in Green Park, the plane trees were fully out, the leaves fresh, not yet darkened by London grime. Iain paid the cabbie, then stood back onto the wide pavement.

'What a glamorous wife I have. I trust you're not being uncharitable, trying to outshine the prospective Mrs Brownlow.'

'You look rather smart yourself, Mr Chester.' She had taken considerable trouble with her outfit, but it seemed wise to turn the attention back to her husband who had been uncharacteristically sharp about Christopher and his wedding; had even been reluctant to accept the invitation.

A genteel line of top hats and flowery creations was making its way from the pavement through the tall iron gates towards the church door.

'I suppose you know these people, all your old friends from Dereham days?' Iain said.

'You know Jo and Alistair, and Liz, she's coming. Come on, let's go on in.'

It was a conventionally pretty service: magnificent, towering pillars of hothouse flowers surrounding the altar; the bride, blonde beneath her veil, in yards of organza; Christopher, hair very much under control, in an impeccably cut morning suit. Traditional hymns, the twenty-third psalm, a pause for the signing of the register and then man and wife walked back down the aisle as the organist thundered out a trumpet voluntary.

Iain, seeming mollified, whispered, 'All very proper. Not as nice as ours. I prefer roses.'

The congregation moved, chatting. From across the aisle Liz called out to them, and then they saw Jo, with Alistair.

'Well met, friends.' Alistair raised his hat. 'Fine service, lots of singable hymns. Jo and I haven't met the bride. Don't think many of his friends have.'

The five of them strolled on, out into the stone courtyard. Alistair waved a neatly furled umbrella towards Piccadilly. 'The club's just there – let's walk along through the park a bit, then cross over.'

'Iain suggested we go dancing after the reception.'

Jo linked arms with Kitty and Liz. 'Let's – it isn't often we girls get together.'

As they went up the wide staircase towards the reception line on the first floor, Liz said, 'Darlings, this is going to be fun. The champagne will be good. Go on Kitty, be the first to congratulate Christopher.'

He looked distant, almost surprised to see her. And older, too. His hair was receding a bit, making his face look rounder. Formally, politely, but with no small talk, he introduced his bride, Davinia, who had a fixed smile that didn't reach her green eyes.

Christopher's mother, next in the line, gave a suppressed whoop of pleasure, and insisted on chatting for longer than was quite polite.

The champagne was indeed excellent. It was surprising how

many people she knew, and what fun reliving the tennis parties, point to points, and Elma's impromptu parties. She kept an eye out for Iain – he looked happy enough, chattering with Christopher's farming friends.

A hand touched her shoulder. 'It's Kitty, isn't it?'

Guy Rodgers, wickedly good looking, was beside her. Lord, what a loss to womankind!

'How clever of you to remember me.'

'Ah, a thing of beauty is a joy never forgotten, to misquote, darling girl.'

She wondered whether Iain was within earshot, and what he would make of this.

'You're wondering why I'm here. Christopher and I were at school together. Now, tell me, which is the lucky man who put that gold ring on your finger?'

Iain appeared.

Guy tempered his style, coming across more as the public schoolboy and less the star of stage and screen as she made the introductions, which was a relief.

Somewhat to her surprise, Iain said, 'We were thinking of going on to the Ritz to the tea dance, once we've seen the bride and groom on their way. Will you join us?'

Solving the problem of what to do about Liz without a partner if they were all to go dancing.

Even more to her surprise, Guy accepted and, duty done at the reception, they all walked across Piccadilly to the hotel.

'The fresh air made me a bit squiffy,' said Kitty.

'Easy to consume quite a bit when it's that good, and the glass is refilled before it's empty. We'll dance ourselves sober in no time.' Iain whirled her onto the floor.

As the band changed the tempo to a slow waltz, he looked over to where Liz and Guy were sailing decorously round the little floor.

'What exotic company we're keeping. Will those two get on? Liz doesn't strike me as his normal style.'

'She's a good dancer. And she'll chatter away about nothing I expect. I think he's lonely – he seemed out of character, unsure of himself, at the reception. Shy, almost.'

Back at the table, Alistair had ordered scrambled eggs, on the basis that they all needed a bit of blotting paper.

The pianist played the first few notes of 'A Nightingale Sang in Berkeley Square'.

'There are nightingales in the wood at home,' Kitty said. 'I love listening to them in the spring.'

Guy stood up. 'Kitty, have this dance with me. Tell me about your home and the Suffolk countryside.'

As they moved onto the floor the tempo of the other couples faltered. Women sitting at the tables close by shifted in their chairs, turning towards the dancing. Guy danced exquisitely, of course, and held her rather closer than necessary.

She told him about Barney, the moat, the old house and the farm, and then noticed a faraway look in the cornflower-blue eyes and said, 'I'm boring you.'

'No. It sounds settled and beautiful.' Guy was talking quietly, without the usual affectation. 'I'm envious. People think I lead such a glamorous life, money and fame. It's not like that.'

He steered her round, keeping their distance from other couples.

'East Anglia's not my stamping ground,' he said. 'I'm West Country born and bred. Hardy country. Exmoor. Wild, primitive landscapes.'

Two more steps, then he quoted, '*I have a love, I love too well, when Dunkery frowns on Exon Moor.* Hardy at his best. What would we do without the bards?'

Clearly a rhetorical question. What was coming next and where had this new Guy come from?

Another couple waltzed close, too close, the woman brushing into Guy.

The blue eyes seemed to shut off from inside. He leaned away. The theatrical voice, trained to carry, returned. 'Delicious girl. Dancing! Why is everyone in the vertical when they'd rather be in the horizontal?'

Back at Five Oaks the next day they were greeted by Frank with the news that one of the sows had farrowed. She hung their London clothes away before following Iain out to see the new arrivals. Contentment oozed through her as she went into the spotless yard and leaned against the sturdy hardwood unit. The piglets, just a few hours old, suckled happily.

They celebrated their first wedding anniversary sitting late into the evening, watching as the light faded on the moat. And thereafter this became a habit – so long as it was dry they ended their summer days sitting out until the light faded.

Until September, when the evenings grew too cold, so they went inside, lit the fire.

'Don't turn the wireless on, Iain. I don't want to hear the news – that awful German Himmler, setting up concentration camps for "enemies of the state" – what does that mean?'

'Anyone who doesn't fit in with Hitler's Nazi ideal. Things in the Far East are pretty sinister, too. God knows what the next year or so will bring.'

CHAPTER 21

MARCH 1939

'*DIG FOR VICTORY!*' Iain pushed the newspaper across the table. 'Two pounds an acre to plough up grazing land. Less than a third of our food is produced at home. The government's set up a Ministry of Supply.'

'The Italians invading Albania, Hitler in Poland, conscription here. It will be war any day now. Simon will be in his element.'

'I'm afraid so. Still, he's doing what he wanted, seems happier than for ages, enjoying being young, male and a bit wild.' Iain stood up, stretching. 'I've stashed away a fair bit of feed stuff, but we'll have our work cut out to keep the output at current levels.'

He went outside, sorted out the truck, climbed in, started the engine, and then reappeared in the kitchen doorway.

His face looked leaner, tensed up. 'When I telephoned Uncle Harry he sounded frail, not at all himself. I can't go over today. Would you pop across? Talk to the housekeeper, make sure he's okay?'

Popping over wasn't quite how she'd describe the fifty-mile round trip. Speedy would have been her choice to negotiate the traffic in Norwich, but the beloved little car was showing its age now, whereas the Lynx ate up the long straight miles across the flat countryside. They were thinking of getting rid of both cars, buying one new one, something a bit bigger – but still fun, she'd insisted.

Iain had grinned, said he didn't see either of them driving some staid saloon.

She turned her mind away from the cars back to old Uncle Harry. Over the last year, his age seemed to have caught up with him.

He'd begun to look frail, although his charm and wit remained as good as ever, and an hour or two in his company always left her seeing the world in brighter colours. At ninety-nine Harry was keenly anticipating his centenary party, and to receiving the telegram from, in his words, that most unlikely king of ours.

In Norwich she parked in the road, looked at the windows. The curtains on the first floor, Harry's bedroom, were half-closed. The housekeeper greeted her with relief, saying old Mr Chester was not himself, not at all.

Harry was propped up in bed, looking feeble and tired.

'Dear Kitty. Now, you hold my hand and listen to me. You and Iain are to have everything you want from this house.'

She sniffed, blinked back the wetness in her eyes.

'Don't you dare do that, woman. I can't say I mind going now. I don't have the stomach for another war. Just give Cassius here a home with Barney, and me a good funeral, and have a party yourselves.'

The old man sank back into the pillows, his blue eyes watery and glazing over.

'Go back to Iain. Tell him I'm proud of him. Of you and the farm he's built up. Goodbye kiss, Greta. I don't want to see either of you again. I want you to remember me as I was, walking round the farm, or in the garden. Not here, not like this.'

She stepped away from the house blinded by tears. She sat in the car, wondering how to break the news to Iain, to tell him Harry had signed off, that they would not, either of them, see him alive again. That she was sure he would die soon, very soon, before the month was out.

Only ten days later Iain took the telephone call from Harry's housekeeper to say the old man had died, peacefully in his sleep. They buried him on a blustery spring morning.

She held the newspaper so Iain could see it too. 'The report is here, on the first page. *The funeral service was held yesterday of Harry Chester. In his ninety-ninth year. Some one hundred mourners gathered to remember his well-led life. Those present included Lady Smithson, Mary, Dowager Countess...* and, gosh, the list goes on. I never got the names of half of them.'

'You said he asked for a good funeral. We managed that. All those lovely old ladies, claiming to have been his bridge partners.'

Iain leant down, patting the spaniel beside him. 'Barney and this chap seem all right together.'

Kitty didn't reply. Her eyes had moved left from the report of Harry's funeral to the births column.

'I see the lovely Davinia has given birth. It says here, to Christopher and Davinia Brownlow, a daughter.'

'Good Lord. Another? They haven't been married two years.'

'She's a brassy piece. Christopher's worth better than that.' Kitty piled up the crockery, swept away the crumbs.

A daughter – Christopher's child. Damn it all. Time to get their own babies. Throw that ruddy sponge away.

On the anniversary of Peter's death she sent Ma a double bunch of yellow roses. Iain frowned as he looked at the florist's bill. Kitty started to justify the cost, explaining the two lots of flowers, but he tossed the slip of paper to one side.

'No, it's not that. She should send you flowers – he was your brother. What strange mothers we have. I'm going into Woodbridge – do the rounds to pick up as many spares and reserves as I can.'

During the past year, as the inevitability of war had loomed, they'd started to invest in stockpiles of supplies so that by now the upper storey of the brick barn was comfortingly stacked with wire, nails, wheelbarrows, spare parts for the tractor and all manner of bits and pieces for running the farm. Stocking-up trips were a weekly event.

When Iain got back, she watched as he began to unload trophies including two brand new tyres for the tractor, and half a dozen rubber buckets.

She grinned, breathed a sigh of relief. Rubber buckets were vital for Bosun, who was a faultless boar, efficient, fertile, and unusually soft-natured. She could go into his sty and he'd lower his great head and flick his ears. If she didn't start to tickle behind the nearest ear, he'd push his snout against her, keep on rubbing at her leg with the occasional peer up at her from under his ears until she gave in. But the gentle giant had one fault: he beat up his feed dish. Metal ones, galvanised or enamel, would be picked up and bashed against the walls of his sty and then stamped upon, his great hoofs reducing the bowls to twisted lumps. Rubber buckets were the only solution, although the remains of a metal one was left in the sty for the boar to rattle at feeding time.

Reluctantly she turned back to the sink, put her hands in the cold water to scrub the mud off the leeks.

Cassius sat up in his basket as Iain opened the back door.

Heavens!

He was clutching a bunch of flowers. Blue amid drifts of white.

'For you. I remembered you picked scabious off the Downs for Peter. The woman in the shop insisted on adding that white stuff.'

He held out the flowers, almost a field of blue scabious and white gypsophila.

Her throat tightened, and so as not to cry she put her hands on his shoulders and kissed him.

May became June. Together they whiled away the long evenings. Often they were content just to sit in the garden, watching the sun sink below the belt of trees alongside the moat.

'More than twelve hours of high noon is about all I can cope with,' Iain said as the blue and silver hues of the sky darkened.

How brown he looked in the gathering dusk. The sun suited them both. Despite the hours outside they rarely went red, just a deep tan. She reached across, laying one brown hand, the gold of her wedding ring shining brighter, on his arm, the hairs burnished fair.

'Thanks for all this.' She moved her fingers, felt his hand tighten around them. 'It feels precious, tonight. Fragile somehow.'

Practical, just-get-on-with-it Iain turned her hand over, clasped it between both of his.

'Because we both know it can't go on like this. Like the last waltz at a party.' He paused, went on, 'Talking of which... '

'Let's have a party!' She finished for him.

And they did. Pimm's and dinner for Philip and Nancy. Long and late.

Days later, they accepted a return invitation. A round of gentle, long evenings developed. Their lives were in a state of suspension – war was coming, they all knew it. Half the time they tried to pretend it wasn't and the other half they crammed in as much fun as possible.

Spurred on by the talk of shortages and requisitioning, they traded in Speedy, dear Speedy, and the Lynx, for a smart new Riley. Black, this time. Sophisticated, Iain called it. The engine purred.

In July they made celebrating both their birthdays the excuse for a London party with Liz, Simon, Jo, Alistair, Nancy and Philip.

They ate dinner at the Savoy Grill, and afterwards they danced until dawn. She'd missed one period, wondered whether the dancing and excitement might bring one on. It didn't.

She went to see the doctor who told her to expect to have a normal pregnancy, just to be careful not to lift heavy weights, and otherwise she shouldn't worry. That evening she waited until they were in bed before telling Iain.

'We must waltz. Every time you're pregnant we shall dance.'

She said, 'Tomorrow, before lunch again.'

'No, no. Now!' He was out of bed, pulling her towards him.

She felt the summer grass dry under her feet, slipped easily into his rhythm, and sang out, her contralto voice carrying clear in the dark air. She stopped when the barn owl swooped out of the wood low across the lawn, and pulled Iain down onto the grass where they lay counting the stars sparkling above, until the midges from the moat drove them back into the house.

They woke early to another cloudless morning. Simon motored over for lunch. He stayed all day, told them about the fighter squadron he was joining stationed at Tangmere, near the South Downs.

'My last chance to see you for a while. They've warned us all leave will be cancelled.'

He left late, jauntily waving goodbye, and calling out that he couldn't wait to be some sort of an uncle.

Iain's face was expressionless. She touched his shoulder.

'He's brave and capable, I'm sure he'll be okay. I'll help you with the feeds and then let's go down to The Queen's Head.'

The pub was crowded, anticipation of the unknown making everyone, even normally solitary individuals, gregarious. While Iain set up the drinks, she gravitated to their usual corner of the bar. Nancy and Philip were already there, empty bottles littering the table.

'Forgive the dead men, Kitty.' Nancy looked mildly tipsy. 'We didn't bother with supper, came straight down here tonight. I've got the heebie-jeebies. It's war, I know it.'

The crowd hardly thinned as closing time approached.

Iain nudged Kitty, pointed to where the village bobby now stood looking pointedly at the clock above the bar.

The landlord, Rob, rang the bell for drinking-up time.

'Evening, constable,' he called out. 'Closing time, ladies and gents, but it just happens today is my birthday, constable. Landlord's birthday so the next round is on the house.'

Someone started to sing 'Happy Birthday', and everyone joined in.

Favourite tunes reverberated across the Suffolk countryside. The police constable, having made up for lost time, was now leading the choruses. Eventually, as the church clock struck one, he stood up. Sat down. Slowly, both hands on the bar, he stood up again.

'Now, vicar, help me find my bicycle. Landlord, your birthday was yesterday. I wouldn't want to have to report you to the justices. Goodnight.'

Iain was engrossed in a conversation with Philip. Kitty touched him on the shoulder, said, 'Let's all go home, have more there.' As Philip began to demur, she added, 'Nancy's all right with it, she says she'd love to.'

Philip insisted on buying a bottle of Gordon's from the bar to bring along.

In the languid heat of the night, they settled at the kitchen table, which the men had manoeuvred onto the lawn at the back of the house. Handing round glasses Iain said, 'Let's all help ourselves. Philip's gin should keep us going. There's whisky and brandy here too.'

'This is something we won't be able to do once war's declared,' he said, putting the tilly lamp on the table. 'God knows where we'll all be this time next year.'

Philip offered cigarettes around. 'Nor light cigarettes in the open, I gather. Nancy did the blackout curtains yesterday but I had a devil of a job painting whatever that stuff is to stop the glass shattering on our windows this afternoon.'

'I'm hungry,' Kitty said. 'I'll get us some blotting paper.'

She went back into the kitchen, starting to put together cold meats and pickles. Stood for a moment looking out of the window. The lantern flickered as the circle of light grew, showing up the features of the faces round the table: vibrant, determined faces. Philip, a territorial army officer, would be among the first to be called up; Nancy, round and kindly, had produced three bouncing babies in quick succession.

Quieter now, they talked about how this war would be fought. No one imagined that the pointless slaughter of the four years of trench warfare of the 1914–1918 war would be repeated. The government was issuing gas masks; little air raid shelters were being built in the towns. Would the Germans invade? Concrete pillboxes had sprung up all along the coast and great triangular lumps of concrete, dragon's teeth, were clustered in lines along the beaches to trap invading tanks.

They talked through the dark hours, and watched the sky

lighten over the moat to the east until the sun pushed long beams of light through the trees.

Philip took Kitty on one side. 'Will you keep an eye out for Nancy? Most of the TA has been mobilised. I'll have to go the moment war is declared. Twenty-four hours' notice. I've tried to leave things ready in the office, and at home, but I'd be happier if I knew she had a friend nearby.'

'Of course.' She kissed him on one cheek, then the other. 'Good luck.'

Philip, with Nancy tucked beside him, drove away over the sleeper bridge.

She reached for Iain's hand. 'Let's not bother with bed, do the morning feeds straightaway.'

At eleven o'clock that morning, Neville Chamberlain announced that Britain was at war with Germany.

Two weeks later Kitty went over to see Nancy. Philip had gone, been mobilised, a few days before.

'I'm pretty sure they've left, are on their way to France, even there already. I don't know when I'll hear from him,' Nancy said.

'I know we knew it was coming, yet it's still a shock. All those evacuees at the station when I went into Woodbridge yesterday brought it home a bit. Poor little mites, they looked utterly lost. I suppose we'll get used to it all, even no weather forecasts.'

Iain, back from the monthly farmers' evening at the pub, came into the kitchen. He lifted Barney out of his chair, sank into it himself, and pulled the little dog up onto his lap.

'The chap from this new-fangled War Agricultural Committee came tonight. He took a bit of ribbing from the old blokes round the bar – you know how they react to officialdom. He wanted to meet everyone before he starts formal visits, and before they carry out this survey thing, the Agricultural Census. It's all part of the drive to get food production up.'

'Shame I missed that. But we were busy – word about these

Emergency Nurse Sessions is getting around. I only just got back myself.'

'You'll meet the War Ag man soon enough. He was mighty impressed that we sent two hundred fatteners off last year. He's going to come to see how we're doing it, and set up rations for petrol, paraffin, feed and the rest of the stuff we need to keep going. He kept on about how important our farm is to the war effort. To me it feels like a damn poor substitute for being a soldier. Philip's been gone for weeks, proud to be fighting those Nazi buggers.'

Even before the outbreak of the war, the government had added farming to the list of reserved occupations, a measure of the importance it attached to developing the supply of food at home. It was only occasionally that Iain bridled at the enforced passivity, unsettled by his exclusion from the comradeship of his friends.

Best not to mention just now that Jo had telephoned earlier with the news that Alistair was gone too, joined up as an officer in his father's old regiment. Jo sounded sanguine, not surprised. Like Nancy she had taken it for granted that she'd be left alone with the children. Like everyone else, Kitty, she'd said.

Not everyone else – not her and Iain.

'The war doesn't seem as phoney as they say. All those poor children packaged up like luggage and sent away.'

'It's real enough – Nazis trampling all over Poland, U-boats sinking passenger ships. It will come here, Kitty.'

'Let's have a nightcap. I'll make us a snack – scrambled eggs with a bit of that cold ham.' She sliced the bread, passed the crusts to Barney, and one to Cassius, sleepy in his basket.

Three days later, as the October mist was clearing, the sun lifting it off the moat, the War Ag man, a Mr Mumley, arrived. Neat in new gumboots, he shook hands with Kitty, then Iain. A very indecisive sort of handshake. Not limp like old Trott, just, well, indecisive.

Mr Mumley spent the whole morning with them, meticulous, courteous, noting everything down in a pristine hard-backed notebook. 'There's not often a hard surface to lean on, so I find this best,' he explained.

When he had finished she offered him coffee. He settled at the kitchen table and talked about his wife and their three sons. How he'd been pleased to get this job, something simple he could do, his eyesight being too bad to enlist. How he grew sweet peas. Only the scented ones, he said. By the time Mr Mumley left to do his next visit they were on first-name terms. Mine's Alan, he had said when she suggested they do away with the formalities.

CHAPTER 22

JANUARY 1940

IT WAS at New Year that Iain grumbled he no longer could get his hands round her waist, and let them rest on her hips instead. His hands wandered downwards. 'Bed, Mrs Chester. Pregnancy suits you – you look blooming.'

'I feel it. And lucky.' Luckier than was fair. 'We're safe, you here, what we do, producing food, a vital part of the war effort, the days getting longer. I noticed the buds on the oaks, all the old leaves blown away.'

Then the weather turned icy, north winds bringing feet of snow. They struggled to keep the pig units warm on the rationed kerosene. The timbers of the little brick barn, which housed the generator, shook as it rattled away. Barney, affected by the cold, joined Cassius and spent most of the day curled up by the range in the kitchen.

During the worst of the weather, Ma sent a long letter saying that she'd decided to move back to Sussex because it would be safer there.

Iain raised his eyebrows. 'I doubt that, but if the Germans invade it won't make much odds where any of us are.'

'Don't! I can't bear to think about it.' Storm troopers stomping up the Mall. What would they do with the king? Get him away to

215

safety, to Australia? 'I'd like to go over to Ma's, collect my stuff that's left there before she goes.' As soon as the main roads were passable, and the sun was warm enough to keep the windscreen clear, she drove north through the still frozen countryside to Dereham.

The house was familiar. The windows, the front door, the paintwork, the curtains even, were unchanged. Yet, nothing, nothing at all, to do with her – someone else had lived here, not her.

Inside was a turmoil of packing cases. From a large heap of what Ma identified as rubbish she rescued two photos of Pa. She took the books, which had stood untouched in her old room since the morning she ran off to marry Nigel.

Ma was horrified when she told her they wouldn't be having a nanny.

'Katherine, that's a mistake. You must not neglect Iain's male needs.'

Male needs? God almighty, where had that come from suddenly? Kettles and pots came to mind. Ignore it. 'We've got lots of help on the farm.' Not quite true, never mind.

Outside the dark, icy cold of the late afternoon was setting in again. 'Ma, I must be getting back. Help me put this stuff in the Riley.'

Once everything was packed in the car, she went back into the house to say goodbye.

Ma was hovering in the hallway.

'I hope there's room for this.' She pointed to a sizeable box, the sort Harrods used for a ball gown, glossed cardboard, with rope handles. The box was open, its lid resting beside the telephone. 'I made these for you.'

The box was full – a collection of crocheted layette in the softest white wool. She lifted up a matinée jacket, worked in a pattern of roses, three satin ribbon bows down the front. It was about the size of both her hands, held close together.

She swallowed as tears prickled at the backs of her eyes. Dropped the jacket back into the box, and hugged Ma.

Friends at last.

'Enjoy Sussex again, Mummy.' She bent down, hugged the tubbier shoulders. Kissed the still softly powdered cheeks.

'Keep safe, Kitty dear.'

She wound down the car window, put out her arm to wave goodbye, but she didn't look back. The old windmill stood stolid and still. The sturdy structure had been a beacon of familiarity in this flat alien countryside in those early, happy days, parties and masses of friends; what would they all be doing now? Christopher, whose brassy little wife had none the less presented him with two babies in as many years, might be in the army, in France even, by now. And Jo. Poor Jo. The four children to care for, and Alistair already stationed in Scotland with his regiment.

Iain, summoned from the yard by Winnie, stood in the bedroom doorway.

'Not again. Only last week you went for a check-up. You said everything was fine. For God's sake, we waited long enough before trying again. I'm going to talk to that old fogey of a doctor.'

'Don't! It's not his fault. I was fine. Something has happened, that's all.' The tears trickled down. 'I didn't want this to happen either.'

'We must find another doctor to look after you. Don't cry. It isn't like you to make a fuss. I'll ring Nancy, get you some female company. It's cold up here, Winnie should get that fire going.'

Nancy, wrapped up against the cold in slacks and two of Philip's pullovers, crept into the room.

'I'm not asleep – just watching the pattern of the flames. You are good to come over in this weather. Iain shouldn't have bothered you.'

'Rubbish! I brought you this, it's only a quarter-bottle I'm afraid, from Philip's secret cache.' She put the gin on the floor. 'And these harbingers of spring, poking their heads above the snow under the old fig tree. How are you feeling?'

A log crackled and sparked up again.

The old doctor, kindly as always, had said she should see a specialist before trying for another baby. He also said that he'd been cross-examined by Iain about the cause of yet another miscarriage.

Nancy, homely, untidy, the mother of thriving boys whom she was managing happily in Philip's absence, sat down on the bedside chair.

'In pieces, Nancy.'

During that long-ago night when she and Iain had first made love, she told him that she'd had a miscarriage. She'd made light of it, not said how it happened, or that she did it.

'Iain's getting fed up. I cried so much this afternoon. I feel selfish, shabby, ashamed.'

'Don't be daft. He's a man, out of his depth with this. You can't help it.'

'I can. I must talk.' She started. About Nigel, that other doctor's fateful words, what she had done, what happened.

Forgot Nancy sitting, still and silent, beside the bed. 'So you see it is my fault. Sorry, so sorry about this.' Another gush of catarrhy tears dribbled out.

'We need some of that gin.' Nancy reached down for the bottle.

Alone she dozed off as the gin combined with the painkillers. It was quite dark when she woke. Someone had been in to shut the curtains and stoke up the fire. She turned over. Dozed again.

Iain came up to bed late. She kept her eyes closed while he put coals on the fire, and got into bed. He turned on his side, away from her.

It was light when she woke. The bed empty. She lay looking at the rafters. Then footsteps coming up the stairs.

He knelt down by the side of the bed. 'I'm so sorry. I don't know how to tell you.'

He held her face in his hands, looked very directly into her eyes. His face was very lined, drawn and grey.

'It's Barney. He never moved when I went downstairs. He was curled up, quite cold. He must have died in his sleep.'

She howled. Great gulping howls as the tears coursed down her face: the little dog, her constant companion, her last link with Nigel. Nigel.

The little dog gone. She never saw him, never even thought of him yesterday, his last day on earth.

Iain hadn't moved, still held her face. He had loved him too. His face was streaked with tears. She eased herself onto the edge of the bed, and their arms reached around each other.

'Come on, old girl. This won't do. There's a war on, somewhere out there.' He blew his nose, offered her the handkerchief. She wiped her face with it.

He stood up, used the poker to lift air into the coals on the fire. 'If the limp thing called our government thinks it is fooling anyone by stopping reports of the weather, they're worse than I thought. Several feet of frozen snow is pretty difficult to miss. I suppose this bloody awful winter can't go on for ever.'

He was right. The longer days, and the warmth of the sun, higher in the sky as spring approached, began to wear away at the frozen heaps of dirty snow. It took a couple of weeks before she had enough energy to do much, until one day she sat outside the back door, allowed the sun, surprisingly warm now, to soak through her body.

That evening while they waited for the nine o'clock news to come on the wireless, she said, 'Jo's been snowed in for weeks. I'd like to drive over to see her for a couple of days, before our land girl arrives – heaven knows what she'll be like.'

'Luck of the draw, I suppose. I think they're mostly pretty keen; how able is another matter,' Iain replied. The wireless was crackling. He fiddled with the tuning knob.

'Damn this thing. It's obvious they think the Germans will invade along the coast here. Flat landscape, easy for landing craft. Poor old Cassius, he's fitted in well, coming here must've been a culture shock, but we need another dog, one big enough to deter troublemakers. The two-legged sort. We're facing rough times,' Iain said.

'We'll manage, between us.'

'Your Mr Mumley is coming tomorrow, again. I'm damned if I can see how to increase production here. We're still waiting for our results from the Ag Census. Every sty is full, and four gilts in pig. We'll lose Frank. They expect us to replace him with a land girl.'

They fell silent as the BBC newsreader, in impassive tones, announced: 'Today the German government has declared that it will regard all North Sea fishing vessels as military targets in response to our own government's decision to arm the fishing fleet.'

'Things are going to get worse quickly.' Iain turned off the wireless. 'You'd be wise to go over to Jo as soon as possible.'

'Now bacon's rationed, I'd like to take some.'

'Take a hock, we won't miss it. When you're back let's have a couple of nights away, in London. May be our last chance.'

Kitty gathered gloves, overnight case. She opened the back door, slipping into her coat. Iain, beside the car, was struggling with the old wheelbarrow, the broken one that had been at the back of the barn for months.

'What are you doing?' He was using pliers to undo the rusty screws that held the wheel in place. 'That tyre's flat, the barrow's broken anyhow.'

'Shh.' He glanced round, un-Iain like, shiftily. 'They're checking traffic, stopping cars. If you get stopped just quote the War Ag reference, say you've got to get this repaired because we can't feed the stock otherwise.'

'Oh, my God! I hadn't thought of that.'

'Don't worry, you'll get away with it. Smile sweetly.' He tugged at the wheel, hit the nut with pliers. 'There, keep it on the back seat, nicely visible.'

She wasn't stopped, and saw only one roadblock. She arrived to find Jo looking well. Her mother had been widowed soon after the outbreak of war, and was sharing the house which exuded a happy atmosphere. New projects, little or big, one every day, that's the secret, the old lady confided.

During the afternoon Kitty taught all four children to play racing demon, encouraging Tavish to build on his baby sister's runs, and then helping the little girl to get her own back on him. She calmed them down before bedtime, Tavish sitting in his father's chair, the girls beside her on the sofa, with stories, only slightly gilded, of school, finishing with one about how she saved mending the holes in the dreadful thick stockings by inking in the bare patches on her legs.

Jo, coming to take them up to bed, laughed. 'I never heard that one before! Bedtime, you lot, the grown-ups want their supper.'

The three women settled at the kitchen table, drank each other's health. Then, without a shadow of mawkish sentimentality, Jo's mother raised her glass to absent friends. They stood up, clinked glasses, and obeyed Jo's command of down-in-one.

'Things are worse than we realise. There's a lot they're keeping from us all.' Jo stood up, started clearing the table. 'Let's organise a joint trip to London to coincide with Alistair's leave. I want to see *Gone With the Wind* – the American Civil War always fascinated me.'

Eventually the weather improved, longer days and more sun easing work on the farm and the stress of keeping the stock warm and nourished lessened.

'We've earned the trip to London. Jo is so looking forward to it. Liz will meet us at the cinema.'

'Just as well Frank hasn't been called up yet, nor one of these land girls foisted on us. We seem to be letting the Nazis make all the running. Pray God, Churchill becomes prime minister. Chamberlain's a disgrace.'

One week later Churchill took over, heading the coalition government. Iain cheered as the news came through on the BBC. The next day he shushed her to silence as Anthony Eden broadcast. The government was setting up a force of Local Defence Volunteers. 'I'll do that! Find out where to sign on. Woodbridge I suppose.'

They stayed at the Great Eastern Hotel for the trip to see *Gone with the Wind* and met the others, Jo and Alistair, and Simon, at the Empire cinema.

After the film as the five of them emerged into Leicester

Square, they hesitated in the dark, then turned inwards to each other on the pavement edge.

'London's horrid without the lights. Spooky!' Jo said and reached out for Alistair's hand.

On the farm, amid the East Anglian flatlands, there was always light – almost daylight with a full moon and cloudless sky, just less than pitch black on cloudy, moonless nights.

'Let's get a cab, safer I think. Can't have these chaps run over or they'd be absent without leave!' Iain strode into the darkened road.

Safely in the cab, bound for The Berkeley, Simon and Iain, perched on the bucket seats, talked about the new fighter station at Tangmere, and the acres of concrete being spread around East Anglia for runways. Alistair, unusually silent, sat with his arm round Jo.

The taxi edged its way along Shaftesbury Avenue, and then came to a complete stop.

'Sorry, guv.' The driver turned his head. 'It's this show with Guy Rodgers. The town's gone crazy for him – look at the crowds. Waiting to catch sight of him as he comes out of the stage door.'

People were spilling out from the pavement, shoals of them in the unlit street.

Familiar set of shoulders, trilby hat and British Warm overcoat.

'Good God! That's Christopher. Look Jo, over there.' Winding down the window, she called out. 'Christopher.'

The figure turned. Christopher's face.

The face spun away, the hat and coat melting into the crowd.

'He must have seen us.' Kitty looked at Alistair. 'He did, didn't he?'

'We don't see him much, nowadays,' Jo said. 'The marriage isn't working. Davinia spends most of her time at their pad in Belgravia. Leaves Christopher alone at the farm with the children. He's managing his neighbour's thousand acres, too.'

Poor Christopher. So gently organised. Too sensible to have made a silly marriage. The first man she'd got half-entangled with.

The Berkeley was crowded, so they shuffled, rather than danced, round the floor. Simon, definitely the worse for wear, was draped round a petite brunette in WAAF uniform. He came across,

222

winked at Iain, said he must make tracks, kissed Kitty goodbye, and disappeared with his arm round the WAAF's waist.

Jo pleaded tiredness, though she looked bouncy enough, leaving the two of them alone.

'Let's find somewhere to have a meal,' Iain said. 'I can't stand this scrum.'

The meal was no more successful than the dancing, and they both slept badly in the muggy London air. With Simon and his WAAF gone, Iain had become subdued, almost silent, and she couldn't get the image of Christopher, hiding, she was sure, in the crowd, out of her mind.

They left early the next morning, keen to get back to the farm, and found Frank uncharacteristically in such a panic that he forgot to take his cap off.

He greeted them with the news that one of the gilts had rejected her dozen piglets and squashed two of them before he'd managed to rescue the others which were now in an old trunk by the generator, and, without drawing breath, he said his call-up papers had arrived that morning.

In unison, they told him to go home, and take Winnie too. Iain went into the house, got cash out of the safe, gave Frank two months' wages.

They wished him luck, shook his hand, and went into the barn to look at the piglets.

Staring down at the heaving heap of pink flesh, she reached out for Iain's hand.

'God help us. It's here, on our doorstep, now.'

He squeezed her hand. 'Chin up, old girl. Let's get these mites sorted.'

He climbed the ladder up to their squirrels-lair. He reappeared with planks and nails and soon there was a wooden partition beside the kitchen range. The ten remaining piglets were relocated into her care for hand-rearing.

In the morning, she didn't stop to wash, just pulled slacks and a jumper on over her nightie, and went straight out to the piggeries to work alongside Iain mixing the bran mash into the swill, which they'd collected the previous day from the school kitchen in Framlingham. She fed the hens, left Iain to finish off the pigs and went in to get dressed while the breakfast cooked.

Three eggs, one for her, two for Iain, trembled in the frying pan. She eased the eggs and bacon onto plates and carried them through to the farm office, so they could listen to the BBC.

The news was dreadful, all about the humiliation of the British forces' retreat to the French coast. The cream of the British army, marooned on the beaches, a sitting-duck target for the Luftwaffe.

Tyres crunched over the sleeper-bridge. Bert Walsh was walking round to the kitchen door. Sighing, she got up, went through to open it.

'Help yourself.' No smile, the usual grim set to his face. He wasn't wearing his mucky white coat. Just ordinary clothes. 'I'm going out on the high tide, to Dunkirk, to fetch soldiers. Some.'

God almighty! His boat was a twelve-foot ketch, used to fish the inshore waters of Hellersea Bay and the river mouth. She had never dared to call him by his first name. 'But Bert, however will you manage?'

'No choice, missus. Can't abandon them.' He turned away, opened out the door of the van, stood, silent.

She took a couple of dabs. 'Wait, Bert.' She ran back into the house, and brought a handful of rashers from the larder.

'For your breakfast when you get home. Good luck.'

A wave of guilt swept over her as she tucked the fish onto an enamel plate in the larder. Safe, secure, husband and home intact, her only contribution to the war effort a bit of first aid training and helping with the farm.

She rested against the warmth of the range, thoughtful, worrying a little about Iain. The level-headed solidity, leavened by his sense of humour and ability to party, had gone. Not all the time, at odd moments it resurfaced, unexpectedly, reassuringly. Maybe he'd enjoy this new local defence force.

She sighed, looked at the clock. Time to do the trip to

Woodbridge, collect supplies of dowsing for the pigs, Jeyes Fluid, matches, any other essentials she could find in the shops.

The road into the town was empty – no lorries leaving the docks. She pulled up by the quay.

Realised she was looking at a reality she hadn't guessed at.

The quay was deserted. The normal bustle gone. No fishermen working on their boats. No seagulls hovering, wheeling, swooping down in raucous swirls as they scavenged off the boats. No boats. Not one boat. Not just Bert Walsh then. All of them. Fishing smacks, old tubs used to potter around the river mouth, the smarter boats, pleasure craft, those too had gone.

She got out of the car, inhaled the salty air. God speed them all. Those brave ordinary men, like Bert Walsh, as they sail those tubs across the Channel, wait in the shallows while men climb on board, sitting ducks to be bombed and shelled.

She turned, walked away, started to shop at the seed merchants. No one said much; there wasn't the usual chatter. The shopping finished, she got back into the car. She had little sense of achievement. It was a chore done, no pleasure.

Each morning she watched the lane, willing the fish van to trundle into the drive. After two weeks passed, she began to accept the fact that she wouldn't see Bert Walsh again. He wasn't coming back.

'It isn't just old sour-face,' Kitty said. They were cleaning down Flossie's sty, her last lot of weaners already moved, ready for her next visit to Bosun.

Iain stopped brushing. 'No, I know. It's Nancy too. Brings it all a bit close to home.'

'She's in a dreadful state. Still no news of Philip. She thinks she'd have heard if he was wounded, or dead.'

'I'm not so sure. Must be mayhem over there.'

'She asked me whether she'd hear if he'd been taken prisoner. I said it'd be ages, while they sort things out. I'll go over tonight, when her children are in bed, talk properly.'

. . .

225

Nancy, hands shaking, poured sherry into the glasses.

'It's awful English stuff. Shall I put a tot of gin in, perk it up?'

'That'll be lethal. Go on!'

'I sort of keep going during the day.' Nancy gulped at the alcohol. 'I can't sleep, just lie awake. Not crying, just thinking. Wondering what happened. Did he know what was happening? Did he think of us? Did he bleed? Oh, Kitty, I can't go on.'

She put her arms around the shaking woman, thanked God for the gin in the sherry. 'It's the uncertainty, isn't it?'

'I don't know what to tell the children.'

The next week Iain started as a Local Defence Volunteer. It was almost midnight when he got home from the first evening session. She poured him a whisky. He leaned against the mantelpiece, drained the glass.

'There was a lot of talk tonight about how badly the war's going. Damn sight worse than the papers say.'

He stood by the fire, poking at the great oak logs with his foot.

'That old colonel, the one with a wooden leg, is pretty well connected, and he told us the Germans are sweeping forwards into France, Paris bound to fall. Tonight we were working out our strategy to repel an invasion.'

'Invasion? Here?' She got the decanter, refilled his glass, and poured the last bit, the end of their stock, for herself. 'Well, they'd better give you the tools.'

Lost for words, they stood leaning into one another for comfort.

Aircraft hummed around, flying into the new air stations; lorries lumbered along the roads churning cement for the miles of landing strips.

Tank traps, great ugly lumps of concrete teeth, mushroomed across the countryside.

Bold daylight raids by the German bombers blasted away at ports around the country.

The wireless – listening to the news – became essential.

'The Jerries are using these long days to cut off our supply routes,' Iain said.

'Let's move this thing back into the office so we can listen while we work in there.' She pulled the Bakelite plug out of its socket, and wound the ropey wire into a ball. 'Heck, this thing's heavy. Don't look so stern, Iain.'

His face softened. 'I know it's really because you want to keep the sanctuary of the drawing room. Shut out the bad news.'

'Guernsey occupied by the Nazis. I can't get Emma out of my mind. What's happening to people there? Jean-Pierre's our age, where is he? Holed up in some cave, fighting a guerrilla war against them? In prison? Worse?'

'Don't know, Kitty. The real calamity is France surrendering; Jerries twenty miles from Dover.'

'What will you pitchfork soldiers do here, if they get across, invade?'

He shuffled the papers on the desk. 'Let's get on with this lot.'

She hesitated. Decided not to push him. Recently, he'd stopped talking about the Local Defence Volunteers, re-named by Churchill as the Home Guard, no more stories to make her laugh, had been tight-lipped, closing off any conversation.

To lift their spirits she organised a dinner party. Invited Nancy, and Jo who could leave her children with their willing and competent grandmother once more.

Too many females. Never mind, Iain should be so lucky.

She drove over to Saxted with a half-hock of gammon to exchange for an Aylesbury duckling, an unheard-of treat nowadays, from the old woman whose ducks lived on the village pond. There was a cluster of people on the green, heads bent back, squinting up at the bright sky. White vapour trails drew patterns against the blue, the metal of aircraft glinting in the sunlight.

There was a chatter of gunfire, and one white plume dropped down in a straight line, until there was a deep rumbling thud beneath the car as the plane hit the ground. Miles away. Friend or foe? Somebody's son.

Busying around, making the most of preparing for the party, she put the image of the crashing plane out of her mind. She foraged flowers, ox-eye daisies and feverfew, from the orchard, polished the silver, tried to decide how to finish the meal.

Soft-roes on toast? Fish – don't think about that, not poor lost Bert Walsh.

Instead, she used the pastry cutters, made circles of bread to toast into bite-sized Welsh rarebit.

She changed, put on the navy blue linen shirt-waister. Jo arrived with a whole bottle of blackberry wine, a lettuce and four fresh peaches from her garden – one for each of us, she said, laying the downy fruits on the kitchen table.

Iain was upstairs changing when Nancy drove across the bridge fast, her little car snapping up the gravel as she braked.

Normally placid Nancy jumped out, ran towards the house.

'Oh, God almighty, Jo, she's holding a letter or telegram.'

Nancy was red in the face, lines of dried tears streaking her make-up. She waved a buff-coloured scrap of paper in their faces.

'This came in the post. He's alive – it says he's a prisoner, in a POW camp.'

Iain came down, rubbing shaving soap off his chin. 'No champagne left, it'll have to be gin.'

Once more they drank to absent friends, to Philip, Alistair and Simon. Privately Kitty drank to Emma. Worried, too – once the initial euphoria wore off, would Nancy find it hard living with the reality that she mightn't see Philip, and must worry about him, for many years? Sufficient unto the day – worry about that later.

The blackberry wine went down well with the duck. They relaxed, even Iain, foreboding about the invasion, and what else they knew not, diminished by the alcohol and the companionship.

She had heard the scraping noise in the kitchen the evening of the dinner party. Now she made a conscious effort to listen. Iain, sipping at his coffee, didn't seem to have heard anything. Carrying her cup, she went over to sit down at the table. Cassius opened a sleepy eye, watching her.

No, not watching her.

'Look!' She pointed towards the dog.

'What? Hell's bells!' Iain grabbed at the poker but the rat, inches from the old dog's muzzle, was sharper on the uptake, and shot back under the skirting board. 'We'll have to do something. This chap's as thin as a rake under his coat. We need another dog. There's a litter of Bull Terriers for sale, over beyond Saxted.'

The puppies were tiny, just six weeks old. Iain chose a sturdy bitch, white except for a piratical black patch over her right eye.

She picked the puppy up. 'Patch!'

Iain said a rude word, vetoing such an insipid name, and pointed out that the dog was to protect them against invading Germans, and any other rats, two- or four-legged, that encroached onto the farm.

The puppy-with-no-name went home with them. By bedtime she had been christened Tigger and installed in Barney's old basket, alongside Cassius and the piglets by the range. In bed upstairs, Kitty closed her ears to the whimpers and scratching at the kitchen door.

First up in the morning, before Iain, she peered into the silent kitchen.

The piglets snoozed. Cassius's head was buried deep in his curled-up body.

The puppy. No sign of it. God, where had it gone? The back door was firmly shut.

'Damn dog, where are you?'

Down on her hands and knees she squinted under the dresser. Not there.

She sat back on her haunches, counted the piglets.

A white one.

The puppy lay tucked into the heap of warm pink flesh – white, smaller than the thriving piglets, and fast asleep.

'You little tyke!'

. . .

She was feeding the puppy in the kitchen at teatime. Iain was working in the office. The telephone jangled, the bell on the outside wall echoing into the kitchen. He answered, no conversation, put the phone down. He came out at once, pulled his gas mask from the coat hook.

'Our platoon's summoned.' He strode off, didn't even say goodbye.

Not a routine exercise, obviously. A frisson of anxiety turned at her tummy. Recently, new anti-aircraft gun emplacements and lookout posts had mushroomed until the countryside prickled with them.

Is this it? Already?

She got on with feeding and bedding down the stock. Tired out, she went to bed early.

She woke with the dawn. Her stomach lurched: no Iain. Had he come in late, slept downstairs?

The house was empty, no sign of him at all. He had not been home.

She boiled the kettle, made a cup of tea, warmed her shaking hands around the cup.

Fed the puppy, Cassius and the piglets. Her eyes wandered, constantly, to the lane.

She went out to the piggeries. Made up the mash, began the round of feeds. Bosun was banging away on his old dish. 'You'll have to wait, old chap, this lot is going to take me a long while.'

The sound of a jeep, slowing in the lane, made her drop the buckets. She ran into the driveway, watched as the jeep passed by, heading towards Tannington.

At lunchtime she was still washing down sties. Anyhow, she wasn't hungry. She worked on. When the last sty was mucked out, the brooms stood bristle-end up to dry, and barrows parked, she went into the kitchen, sat down. The clock, its ticking loud in the silence, said three o'clock.

He'd have telephoned. Or someone would, surely. Whatever was happening?

She went back outside, finished the round of afternoon feeds, and started to do something about supper.

It was nearly two hours later that she heard the car. The puppy heard it too, jumped up. Kitty picked her up, ran outside.

Iain, looking haggard and grubby, slammed the car door shut, almost walked past her.

'I've been worried stiff. Where've you been? What's happening?'

'There's a war on,' he snapped. 'Official secrets, so don't ask.' He flopped down in the dog-chair.

She made tea, put brandy in it. 'Have a bath.'

He fell asleep at the kitchen table. Barely awake, he climbed up to bed and was fast asleep before she got upstairs.

His screams awoke them both.

'Just a nightmare. Go back to sleep, Kitty.'

All next day he was distant, and short-tempered.

That night it happened again.

She lay still in the bed, her heart thumping after its rude awakening.

Iain, nightmares? He wasn't asleep, too quiet. Something to do with the other night? Damn official secrets, he needed to talk about whatever happened. She turned on her side, felt for his body with her fingers, moved them gently. He half-turned away. For a moment she thought he was going to reject her. She stopped, lifted her hand a fraction. He stayed still. The green light.

Afterwards, as he lay in her arms, she asked him to tell her.

He swore her to secrecy. In a whisper, he said his platoon and others had been shoved into lorries, driven down to the beach at Orford.

'When we got to the top of the dunes there was a moon, you'd have seen boats. Something had happened on the shingle, or maybe just out to sea. Someone said the sea had blazed, miles of flames.' The beach, the stones, the sand dunes, were littered with charred remains. 'Soft heaps, Kitty. Human bodies. The ones who'd made it to the dunes were less badly charred than those on the beach.'

She silenced her own intake of breath, tightened her arms around him.

'We had to bundle them up into heaps, for the truck. As I bent down to pick one up the eyes flickered, opened. I shouted to the army sergeant.'

She shivered. He began to shake again.

'He shot the man through the head, told me to get on with moving the bugger.'

Just before dawn, Iain fell silent.

She lay still until his breathing lengthened, and then she eased her arm from under his weight, and turned over.

She lay awake, wondering what other horrors were in store.

Neither of them spoke of the incident again. Nor did she hear any gossip, not the merest hint of anything. Whatever happened at Shingle Street that August night remained secret.

The morning was gently quiet outside, just the distant sound of aircraft engines that she hardly noticed nowadays. Sunshine shone into the warm kitchen. The pastry tended to stickiness. She sprinkled more flour onto her wooden rolling pin.

The heavy drone of a bomber, flying low, broke the stillness.

Closer, louder, lower, over towards Framlingham.

The dull thud of an explosion rumbled across the fields, shuddering through the ground so the china cups rattled on the dresser. She counted another four in quick succession.

Rooks swirled out of the oaks and the pheasants squawked alarm, flying low in all directions.

Bombs! Nearby – closer than the airbase at Martlesham, yet there had been no anti-aircraft fire.

Pastry forgotten, she stared across the grass, wondering what the target was, out here, in the middle of nowhere.

The first stage of the invasion?

What will happen to us, to all of this? Our pigs in their teak palace. This house. Peter's painted windmill. My books. Little Tigger. Poor old Cassius. Bosun. Will it all be destroyed, burned, killed?

She looked down at the solid roundness of the wooden rolling pin in her hand. Will things like this survive, be dug out of the rubble, to become a trophy for some strudel-making German frau?

Next day she drove into Framlingham to collect the swill for the pigs from the college. Iain had discovered that by removing the lid of the car's boot it was possible to transport the two outsize dustbins, upright. Eccentric, but practical.

She turned left into the street by the school. People were huddled in the roadway.

She gasped: the playground had disappeared – had become a deep crater, and the old school building was a great pile of rubble.

In the grocer's, the one where they sometimes still had ground coffee to sell, the man behind the counter said the Jerry bomber had flown low over the town, dropping its bombs.

'Mercy the school was empty, it being Sunday morning,' he said. 'The old lady, the headmistress, taught me my tables. A fine teacher. Killed by the blast, as she sat in the front parlour, darning her stockings.'

That evening Kitty and Iain took Tigger for a run round Top Field. The south-western sky burned an angry orange.

'Poor London. I suppose it's the docks again. Just five bombs in Framlingham and the place is a shambles.'

In the dark she reached for Iain's hand. 'Yesterday, when I heard the bombs landing, I got a funny feeling – as if it was all over. The Germans had invaded and we were all gone, dead I suppose. Our England, gone. I saw this house and the farm destroyed, burned, and some fat German frau rummaging through the rubble and finding my rolling pin.'

'Over my dead body. Not just mine, either,' he said. 'The blokes, some of us, in the Home Guard agree we'll go underground, live rough. We've got hideouts. And stuff, ammo, petrol, bottles. For Christ's sake, keep that to yourself.'

CHAPTER 23

JANUARY 1941

SHE BREATHED in the crisp cold air. 'Happy New Year. Hello 1941. What will you bring us?' She leaned against Iain. 'God, it's cold. Look at the stars. No burning glow from London, though.'

Iain put a firm arm around her waist, steadying her. They had spent the evening at The Queen's Head, amongst fellow farmers, and neighbours.

Somehow, against all the odds, England had survived the Nazi onslaught. At dreadful cost the Spitfires and Hurricanes had deterred Goebbels just sufficiently to keep the Huns on the other side of the Channel.

People looked askance at the craters and rubble that had been Coventry, Southampton, Bristol, and the East End. All around enemy bombs and crashed aircraft had gouged fissures out of the countryside.

'Tonight was fun,' she said. 'Comforting. Real people, being themselves.' Light years away from when Christopher, immaculate in tails, had escorted her to her first big Norfolk party. The sea of silk and satin, the heady scent of lilies mixing with women's perfume, champagne, cold goose, rare roast beef.

'Thank God you're still here.' She turned into his arms. 'Not like Alistair, or even poor Philip incarcerated.'

She felt the warmth of his body as he held his arms around her waist.

'I want babies, Iain. It's not just the gin talking, I'm getting old. Tomorrow I'll ask Gloucester-Foster to refer me to the specialist he suggested at the Royal Free.'

'Look, Mother was forty when she had me. Maybe that's a bad example but you're young still, and fit. Nubile, too. Come on, woman. Bedtime.'

He disentangled himself, led them back towards the house.

The obstetrician, grey, distinguished, and quite evidently well past the call-up age, displayed a well-practised bedside manner while he prodded around, talking all the time but saying little. Eventually he left her to get dressed.

Clothes back on, more in command of the situation, she settled in the wing chair on one side of the leather-topped desk and waited while he finished writing notes. He twisted the top back onto his fountain pen, laid it on the blotter, looked up, smiled.

'Everything looks in good working order to me.'

She sat straighter in the chair, the indignities of the last hour forgotten.

'I don't need to see you again until you've missed two periods. After that I'll see you regularly.'

She skipped down the steps into Harley Street. On the spur of the moment, she abandoned going straight home, hailed a cab to Fortnum & Mason.

She gave the elderly uniformed commissionaire an enormous smile as he ushered her through the door,

As she stepped inside, gentle wafts of expensive soap, leather and scents brought a pang – no Liz to meet her. Poor Liz was stationed miles away from a town, safe but not enjoying the remoteness, and struggling with the filing that was her contribution to the war effort.

Twenty feet into the shop, shoes sinking into the pile of the carpet, she gazed at the careful displays of tastefully expensive accessories. She bought, at sinful expense, a narrow black leather belt for herself, a cashmere sweater, in a subtle country-green to match his eyes, for Iain, and a packet of Marron Glacé.

The dark cold of February lessened, slightly, as the days grew longer, but it was bitter still. She had tried to wear gloves for farm work but the scoop kept slipping round in her gloved hand, spilling the precious feed onto the shed floor, so she used her bare hands for that job, and for when she doused the pigs. Then she'd work on, forgetting to put the gloves back until she tried to open the gate when the icy metal glued her flesh to the bolts. So she'd taken the advice proffered by old George in the pub one evening, and now whenever she could she wore mittens, two pairs.

She rubbed her chapped hands together as she waited outside the railway station for the long-promised land girl to arrive.

However was a girl from the East End of London going to cope?

'Margaret's a good worker,' the woman from the Land Army had promised Iain. He was unimpressed by the district commissioner, an earnest, middle-aged, grey-haired woman totally lacking in femininity. He'd watched the woman waddle away down the drive, and said he hoped that old battle-axe knew what she was talking about.

The steam engine tooted the train's arrival.

The passengers emerged from the ticket hall, milling around. A bird-like girl, humping a huge suitcase, headed towards the car, held out her right hand, gloved, and smiled up.

Oh Lord, this cannot, simply cannot, be her. Four foot ten. In her shoes. Whatever will Iain say? She won't be able to lift an empty bucket.

'Margaret?' Looking down, smiling, she took the girl's hand, a tiny, soft, well-cared-for hand. But the grasp was firm enough.

'Yes, ma'am. Where will I put my case, ma'am?'

'Here.' Kitty opened the boot, bent to lift the outsize case. No, it wasn't outsize, just out of proportion to Margaret.

The girl swung the case into the boot. Effortlessly.

She was quiet on the journey back to the farm, looking around.

'Ma'am, it's all so light.'

Which was exactly what had struck her, all those years ago as she and Ma drove to Dereham.

'Yes, I thought that when I first came to East Anglia.'

At the farm, Kitty showed Margaret her room, left her unpacking, and went to forewarn Iain.

'You'll have a fit. Don't say anything. What's left of her family live in Stepney still. She used to clean in the local pub, I think. Let's give her a chance. I'm not sure why, but I like her.'

The girl started work that afternoon, following what Kitty did. She was quick, practical and, despite her size, strong. She was interested in the animals, and not nervous of them. She copied Kitty, tickling Bosun behind his ears.

'You're right, she's good. Never been near a farm, let alone worked on one, but she is catching on,' Iain said. 'She's smart, a proper Cockney straight out of Dickens – Little Meg.'

The name stuck.

Iain was looking out of the window towards the orchard, the paperwork on the desk temporarily forgotten.

'Whatever has that dog caught now?' The puppy, its white coat smattered with mud, was struggling, carting a rope across the lawn. The rope twisted and spiralled about.

'It's alive. I bet the little devil's found an eel.' She ran outside, called the puppy. An eel it was, large, and very much alive. The dog dropped her trophy. Kitty tried to pick up the wet, squirming creature. It slithered out of her hands, wriggling off.

'Get it, Tigger. Fetch!' The puppy wagged her tail. Barked. Made no move to recapture the eel.

Kitty reached out, slipped and landed face down on the soft ground.

Guffaws of laughter from Iain, standing at the open window.

'Come and help.' She pulled herself upright. 'Catch it. It'll make a meal, several, it's big.'

'Slippery as an eel!' He strolled over, armed with a yard broom. 'Let's see if we can tangle you up in this.' Which worked. 'I'll dispatch it.'

'I'll cook it now, otherwise the sight of it'll put me off.'

It took ages to work out how to cope with the limp, slimy thing. She struggled to get the skin off, eventually resorting to pliers, holding the slippery body with a bit of towelling from the stock of cleaning cloths. She left the chunky joints simmering, surrounded by onions, and twigs of thyme and sage, in the preserving pan on the cooker and went to take the letters from Postie.

Iain slit open a bulky brown envelope.

'At long last! It's our Agricultural Census report.' He frowned. 'Damn cheek! *Due to personal failing. Lack of knowledge and implements to cultivate the land.* I'll give them personal failing.'

He pushed across several large sheets of paper.

'They've given us a B for management.' He stood up, stomped round the room. 'B! Sixteen sows in pig, and 180 weaners. I'll ruddy B them.'

'I shouldn't worry. The farmer beyond Tannington told me the War Ags gave him a C for his barley – too much mayweed in it. Whatever the form says, they're pleased with what we're doing. Last time Alan came he spent hours over his tea in the kitchen, extolling the virtues of our pigs.'

Iain glanced across.

'Alan? So long as it's the virtues of the pigs – funny how he always comes when I'm out.'

'He's quite harmless. He's upped our kerosene allowance again. Says the bacon I give him is the best he's tasted.'

'I'll bet it is!' Iain folded up the sheets. He leaned towards her, put a hand on her waist, and let it rest there. 'I can't think how you knew the way to cook the eel but it smells good.'

'I didn't. Just used my common sense.'

The telephone bell jangled.

'God, that thing's penetrating.' Iain reached across, lifted the receiver from its cradle.

'Mother! What a surprise.'

His mother never telephoned.

Iain became motionless. 'Yes, I see. No. Let me know.'

Her heart stopped, then pounded on, loud in her ears.

He put the handset back on its cradle, his face turned away.

'Simon. Missing, presumed dead. There's no doubt. His Spitfire was shot up. The squadron leader saw him go down.'

She went over, stood beside his chair circling her arms around him.

He was rigid. As if the life had gone out of him. A plaster-cast figure.

She stayed still, didn't move a muscle, waiting. He buried his face in her stomach and his body rocked hers with his silent sobbing.

She let several minutes pass and then put her hand to rest on the crown of his head and began to smooth his hair. She saw the tension ease a little from his shoulders. He moved his head backwards, looked up at her, exposing the streaks of tears.

'How perfectly bloody,' she said. 'Dearest Iain, he... '

He interrupted. 'I know, he was happy, fearfully, foolishly happy, and thank God for that.'

'Where did he go down?' she asked. A convention of not having a funeral in the old-fashioned sense had developed. There were too many, of course, and too often no one was quite sure what they were burying. All of it so unnecessarily depressing. But Simon's father was a vicar, his mother a devout churchgoer. How would they feel about no funeral?

'Into the drink – the English Channel. Not even the shell of his body to wish farewell to.' He stood up. 'I'll go for a walk. Back in a while.' The even keel of their lives was broken. When poor old Cassius died in his sleep three days later they buried him under the biggest, oldest of the oaks. There were tears in Iain's eyes as he turned away. She pulled him back, let her own tears flow.

'Too many of them gone, Kitty.'

CHAPTER 24

SPRING 1942

RELUCTANTLY, in a fractious mood, Iain went off to yet another Home Guard exercise. He came home early while she was sitting in the warmth of the kitchen.

'Another wasted evening.' He slung his coat down. 'I lost my temper with Pettiman tonight. Told him the Germans are too busy elsewhere to invade.'

Which was probably true. The Germans marching into Russia and hanging on in Tobruk had lessened the fear of invasion. And Little Meg had altered the dynamics of their life on the farm. It was no longer just the two of them.

Iain had become like a coiled spring, irritable, lacking his usual practical optimism. The weather was wrong, too: pouring rain, day after day. It was the wettest spring she could remember, and that wasn't helping his temper.

Removing mud from the kitchen floor yet again, Kitty turned over ideas in her head. Iain saw less and less point in what they were doing, because despite the vast investment of time, money and energy which they had put into creating the pig farm, and the massive output of pigs, they were in fact making less money than in previous years. She understood, too, that Iain was cut adrift now that the anchors of Uncle Harry and Simon were gone. At last she was sure she could produce babies but Iain seemed to have got used to a childless existence. The nursery, once so carefully decorated, was now home to Little Meg.

Outside dismal rain beat down. The door opened and the girl, dripping wet, struggled in.

'Meg! You poor thing. Dry your hair with this, you're soaked, and then go up and change out of those wet things.'

'Mr Chester's wetter than me. He sent me in. The rain hasn't stopped all day. It's puddling in the runs.'

'Awful weather. We should get some ducks. You can have the kitchen to yourself tonight. I'm going to take Mr Chester to The Queen's Head.'

Iain's mood lifted when they got to the pub. Old George, whose family farmed near Nancy's over at Bruisyard, insisted on buying a round.

'Mind, beer up by tuppence a pint. Landlord says it's this Budget For Victory.'

'Cheers, George.' Iain lifted his glass. 'Will it ever stop raining, or do we have to build an ark?'

'Be fine by next week, you see!' Old George drank through the head on his beer. 'Anyways, I doubt there's any wood left to build a boat, let alone an ark. Look what those Yanks have put up. Airfield, they call it. More like a town.'

The conversation rambled on, slow and mostly inconsequential. Kitty pulled gently on her cigarette. Those were up, too. Two shillings a packet now. She'd started smoking last winter, sitting here at the bar; it was soothing and companionable.

The door pushed open, and half a dozen grey uniforms filled the low-ceilinged room. Laughing, fresh-faced, gum-chewing American airmen.

It wasn't that they did anything wrong, just that they seemed out of place – big, well dressed, well fed and loudly calling for the landlord.

'Hi, guys. We just arrived. Off to bomb the Jerries for you.'

''Evening, then.' Old George and Iain edged into the corner of the bar.

Iain's mood changed, the tension returning to his face. She eased herself off the stool. 'Time to go, I think. I'm all in.'

Home and upstairs, she sat on the side of the bed, fully dressed, and waited for Iain.

'Come and sit here.' She patted the bed beside her.

A flicker of irritation passed over his face, the frown deepened. She patted the bed again. 'Please.'

Gingerly he perched on the edge of the mattress.

'This isn't easy to say.' She took a deep breath. 'I know you want to join up. Well, I think you should.'

She had his full attention now.

'Little Meg and I can manage the farm. We'll persuade the War Ag people that I'll keep it all going, keep up the pork output.'

The hazel eyes sparked open, the face lightened, and then the hesitation came.

'Look, I'd be deserting you and the farm.'

'No, you'd be fighting so we can keep it. So all of us can keep England. You should go. With my blessing.' She held out her arms to him. 'You won't desert me, you'll be back and I'll enjoy keeping it all here for you to come back to.'

'Christ, woman, I love you for this.'

Persuading the diligently unimaginative officials to release Iain from the reserved occupation lists proved a challenge.

Iain filled in form after form. Kitty was cross-examined by a series of faceless, middle-aged men who knew little about the countryside and less about farming, and who tried her patience until one made the mistake of saying she was only a woman.

'Like all the other land girls, the ones you're so proud of. If you don't let my husband go, I'll join the WAAFs myself.'

'That did it,' Iain grinned as they watched the round-shouldered figure trudge away over the sleeper-bridge. 'You've forced him to look outside his paper kingdom.'

Once the forms had been completed, signed and posted off, the pace altered. His travel warrant arrived within days.

'With indecent haste, now they've agreed,' Iain said.

. . .

On his last evening, she saw him leaning over Bosun's door, tickling the old boar behind his ears. And after supper, she found him with Tigger on his lap, his face buried in the young dog.

He stacked the documents to take in a neat pile on the kitchen table, warrant for his train journey to Nottingham: ten past eleven tomorrow from Woodbridge station.

They slept through the night encased in each other's arms.

She sneaked a glance at the familiar shape of him beside her as he swung the car out on to the lane. It was best, probably, that there'd been so little notice of his departure, nor time to drag out the arrangements.

The train was alongside the platform, puffing great billows of smutty smoke.

They hugged goodbye and then he was pulling the carriage door closed.

She blew him a final kiss and turned away. She left the platform and walked out through the barrier without looking back.

She ran her fingers over the silky fur on the dog's forehead. 'Only you and me now.'

On impulse, she took the road towards Saxted Green. The mill's great blades swished through the humid May morning.

She sat with her arm around the dog.

The steady drone of aircraft brought her back to the present.

Losing patience with herself, she heaved a huge sigh.

The dog fixed two dark eyes on her.

'I knew, in my mind I knew. But it's real now, Tigs. No good sitting here, stewing. Get home, get on.'

The engines droned, above now, as another squadron of Flying Fortresses thundered overhead, dropping down towards the airbase.

The chores took much longer than she expected despite all Iain's preparations. He'd left the yard spotless, the feed bins full, the afternoon feeds already prepared. She didn't finish working outside until her rumbling tummy told her it was long past supper time.

Little Meg, who had her tea, high tea, earlier was already upstairs in her room.

No one to share a drink, or supper. Say cheers to the newsreader on the wireless?

Don't bother. Go straight to bed.

The sheets were cold against her body. She got up and took a nightie from the drawer, climbed back into the bed. Pretend he is at the pub.

She tried to read.

She gave up and padded downstairs, the boards of the staircase hard on her bare feet.

In the kitchen, she picked up the dog's basket and then coaxed Tigger upstairs to the bedroom. She put the basket on Iain's side of the bed.

'Basket, Tigs!' The animal stood on the bedside rug. 'Come on, up girl.'

All four feet remained firmly planted on the floor.

'You are a disappointing dog.' Kitty shrugged her shoulders and started to get in between the sheets. Immediately the muscular white body launched itself on the mattress, burrowing down in the bed.

The work on the farm was unrelenting. She had loved the idle moments, watching the weaners learning to forage, sitting in the sun on a bale of straw with their mid-morning drink. Those days were gone. One less person to do the work and of course they lacked the muscle power of a man.

Inside the house she had the paperwork, more and more it seemed, demanded by the War Ag people, and there was still the basic stuff like meals and washing to keep on top of. She cut corners wherever she could, wore clothes which in the past would have been washed and ironed, and gave very little time to the cooking. At the end of each day she fell into bed, exhausted.

Soon after Iain had left she missed a period, but it must have been a bodily reaction to the disruption of his going because next month she had one, heavier than usual; lugging the buckets made her back ache so much she took Veganin at night.

Little Meg worked on, tough as ever and twice as determined, yet still the outside chores built up.

'The wire on the fence along Top Field is sagging, ma'am.'

'I'll check it. You finish your Bovril.'

The wire was loose, easy to push down. She found where a broken post had fallen into the moat.

Together she and Little Meg struggled to get new posts in the ground. The long-handled mallet was too heavy to wield with any force. Eventually she stood in the wheelbarrow, which gave her just enough purchase to drive in the posts. Little Meg clapped with glee as the last post stood firm.

'It's a good thing you're so slim, ma'am, or else the barrow would've tipped over.'

'I don't suppose we weigh twelve stone between us. You should call me Kitty.'

'Oh, I couldn't do that, ma'am.'

'Well try. Not ma'am. Mrs Chester if you must. Help me get the boot cover off the car. I'm late fetching the swill from Framlingham.'

Propping the curved black metal up against the side of the brick barn, the girl began to giggle.

'It looks that funny seeing you, hair pretty enough to go to a dance, in this smart car, with those filthy old metal bins sticking out.'

'I do get odd looks from strangers in the town. The locals don't notice any longer.'

She parked in the market square, intending to do the shopping before going on to get the swill. The queue stretched ten deep outside the baker's, and there was one outside the grocer's. The tussle with the fence had made her much later than usual.

With Iain, if they were late, they went into The Crown to have a beer and a sandwich.

There was only the old vet, Brian, leaning against the bar. He stood up and offered her a drink. For half an hour, she listened to his trials and tribulations trying to get around on a cupful of petrol and struggling to get medicines for the animals.

Lunchtime had diminished the queues and she found half-decent spring greens left in the greengrocer's and a couple of vast, probably woody, leeks. Iain loathed Scotch broth, too much like pig-swill he said, so she hadn't made it for years. She bought pearl barley from the grocer's and walked over to the butcher's shop in search of a bit of stewing lamb, or even mutton.

As she drove away from the town, a convoy of GIs, heading towards Martlesham, wolf-whistled their way past her. The smartly painted jeeps swept on, a line of shiny confidence.

If only they didn't seem so bumptious, maybe the local people would be a bit more welcoming. But it wasn't just that setting the stolid East Anglians against the Yanks: the presence of the American air force, in such huge numbers, was increasing the bombing attacks. Martlesham, christened the Fiftieth State by the locals, was a tempting target for the Germans.

She was unloading the swill when Tigger started to bark.

A bicycle – the telegraph boy's bike.

Nowadays telegrams meant one thing only. Who? Iain was at training camp. Wasn't he?

The boy, probably not more than fifteen, tried not to look at her as he handed her the flimsy envelope, and pedalled away.

'*Lt Chester seriously wounded. Come at once. Nottingham General Hospital.*'

Come at once. Not a broken leg. Not dead but dying. That's why it said come at once.

'Mrs Chester, ma'am – sit down.' Little Meg pushed her down onto the running board.

'No, that swill's making me feel sick. I'll get some clothes, ask Nancy to take me to the train. Can you manage here?'

'Yes, ma'am. Just go, ma'am.'

Nancy arrived within the hour. 'I called in on Old George, he'll come over. And here's a quarter-bottle of gin.'

'You are an angel!' She pushed the bottle into her suitcase. 'I'm ready.'

'Don't forget the gin – you'll need something whatever you find. Give Iain my love if… ' Nancy stopped. 'Good luck, Kitty.'

The train shuffled along, stopping and starting for no apparent reason in the middle of nowhere. She was cold and shivery and alone in the compartment. It was dark now, and rain thrashed against the window. In the damp, the carriage smelt of stale cigarette smoke. She dozed off, dreamed Little Meg had let all the piglets escape and fall into the moat. She woke, shaking, as the train jolted into another nameless station.

Two boys in RAF blue serge climbed in. They looked about ten years old. Chattering, they said they were on leave, and insisted she have a cigarette with them. They didn't ask what she was doing, and she found it easier not to say. When she had to change trains the younger boy heaved her case off the rack and dropped it onto the platform.

At Peterborough, there was a two-hour wait for her next train. The waiting room was full, standing room only, smelly and horrid, so she chose to stay on the platform. The rain, beating down on the roof, dripped onto the platform. The damp cold ate into her until she ached all over, tense and miserable.

Nancy's gin. Gypsy-like, she squatted on the filthy platform and unlatched the suitcase. A strong junipery smell wafted out. Her fingers touched wet silk, and then they felt a sharp edge of broken glass.

She buried her face in her hands and wept.

'You there, move along.'

She looked up at the porter, and snapped herself back together.

'Thank you, I will when your ruddy train comes. To see my husband, in hospital, if he's still alive.' Oh, God. Not his fault. She must stink of gin. 'I'm sorry. You weren't to know… '

When the train came in the old porter appeared at her side. 'I'll put this in for you, ma'am. Good luck.'

It was half-past four in the morning when her final train heaved its way into Nottingham. She shared a cab to the hospital with two nurses returning to duty. They worked on the obstetrics unit and knew nothing of Iain, but took her to the front desk.

The orderly looked at his lists. Flat-toned, expressionless, he said, 'Go up the main staircase. To the second floor.'

The whole place, all sharp walls and cold colours, reeked of the dreaded hospital smell. The grim reaper of antiseptic.

Why the second floor, why nothing about visiting times?

She stepped off the stairway and read the signs on the landing wall: Burns Unit, Mortuary, Chapel.

The floor started to come up towards her. She reached the line of wooden chairs by the double doors.

A grey-haired woman, spotless in navy cotton uniform, white apron, silver- buckled belt at the waist, came up the stairs.

'Can I help you?'

'I'm Iain Chester's wife. The man at the desk sent me up here.'

'Ah, my dear. He was very badly burned. Shall I take you to see him?'

Unable to make any words, throat and tongue gagging, Kitty gestured to the sign.

The ward sister followed her gaze, and put an arm around her.

'No, not that. However, he is very ill, and you must be prepared not to show how shocked you are. The plastic blew up in his face.'

She followed the sister into the ward. Scanned the lines of beds for someone who looked remotely like Iain. They came to a cubicle.

'He may be asleep. We are keeping him sedated. You mustn't tire him, stay just a few minutes and then find me in my office.'

There was something in the bed. It was propped up on pillows, and an arm was suspended above the bed.

Every bit of him was covered in bandages, a mask of them over his face.

'Iain.' She crept forward. 'It's me.'

Close to, she saw his lips and his left eye just visible. The lips moved.

'Kitty!'

She talked a little, told him the farm was fine, Tigger in charge of Little Meg, that he must rest now. She kissed her own fingers, touched his lips with them. 'I'll be back later, Iain.'

Ward sister was in her office, a pot of tea waiting.

'We feared for his life when he was admitted, but he's fit and a fighter. One of those new plastic grenades blew up in his hand.' She topped up the cups. 'He's badly burned, chest and back as well as his face. He will be here for several weeks. There's a hotel across the road if you can stay for a few days.'

In her room at the hotel, she opened the suitcase. The silk shirt was ruined. She put it in the waste bin. The rest she laid round the room to dry, and opened a window to lessen the smell. She lay on top of the counterpane and fell fast asleep.

Each day she spent long hours just sitting beside Iain. If he was awake, she read bits from the newspaper.

One afternoon when he was bright, perky, almost recognisably Iain inside the bandages, she told him how frightened she had been when she'd seen the other signs outside the ward, believing he was dead.

'I'm indestructible, old girl.' Self-pity was not one of his faults.

'Maybe,' the doctor said when she repeated this. 'He's a long way to go. Somehow, we have to get the plastic fragments out of his face and body. With grenades we use magnets to get the bits out – won't work with this new plastic stuff, so I'm afraid we're going to have to dig around a bit. We'll do as much as we can, then send him home to your tender care.'

She stayed for five days. The morning she left to go back to the farm she kissed him firmly on the lips, told him to get home soon, and managed to arrive at the station just as her train pulled in.

She slipped off her coat; the carriage didn't feel cold. Not yet, anyhow. It was daylight, and the horror of the marathon six days earlier was gone. As the train pulled away from the platform, she let her back relax into the seat, her head resting on the little white linen cloth. The rhythm of the wheels, faster now, but calming – tiddly-pom, tiddly-pom. She gazed out of the window, and stopped thinking.

Fell asleep. Didn't notice the train stop. The sound of the compartment door must have roused her. The Yankee uniform was smart, well cut. Tailored. Not off the peg. Four stars on the epaulettes.

He removed his beret, acknowledged her with a nod, and turned to settle himself in the corner seat away from the window.

Unexpectedly, self-effacingly, he apologised. 'I'm afraid I'm disturbing you.'

'Don't be sorry. Some company will be nice. I'm less than halfway through a horribly long journey all the way to Woodbridge, in Suffolk.'

He half-rose to his feet. 'Well, well. Me too. I'm Franklin. Not Roosevelt. Just ordinary Franklin.'

Not so ordinary. Even in wartime, no four-star general could be ordinary. His voice was soft, the accent less penetrating than usual, and educated. Always she found it impossible to differentiate between the varieties of accents the Americans had brought with them, unable to guess whether they came from the deep South or cosmopolitan New York.

'I'm Kitty. Katherine really, once upon a time.'

She found herself talking to this unknown general as if he were an old friend, one she'd known for years, and told him about Pa, and then about Peter. The wetness behind her eyes went away with the shared laughter when she told the story of Conker's ears.

She turned the easy conversation back to Franklin, and asked how he found England. He said his men, and the officers, found England, and the English, strangely foreign: warm beer, no ice, and cold, inhibited people, in dull clothes. He didn't find it so bad, though; and she said, no, she could imagine: people here didn't like to be rushed into false friendship, she could see that his quiet ways would go down better.

She told him about Iain's wounds. He was intelligent. 'Do you think he'd rather have died?'

'No. He's a get-on-with-it sort of man. Determined.'

This time the journey was soothing her, even when they had to change trains. He would take her case, find an empty compartment. They sat in the two corner seats by the window. It occurred to her that an apparently endless journey, a train compartment and her own emotional upheaval were cloistering them from the usual conventions of social contact. She told him about meeting Iain. About Nigel.

He told her about his family back home in Utah, the alcoholic wife he had left behind whom he hoped, but doubted, was caring for his five children. 'I knew, right at the start, it wasn't going to work. She said she was pregnant, threatened to kill herself if I didn't marry her. I shouldn't have gone ahead, should have pulled out.'

'Hindsight. The nun who taught me Latin, bits of it anyhow, said that *if only I had*, with the pluperfect I think it is, is the saddest phrase of all. *If only I hadn't* drummed round in my head after Nigel died.'

It came quite naturally then to tell him about aborting herself, killing not one child but two. Only Nigel, Nancy and now, unexpectedly, this unknown man. He didn't look shocked, as dear Nancy had. Wasn't complicit, partially responsible, as Nigel had been. He asked matter-of-fact questions, why hadn't she gone to another doctor, got a second opinion about the TB? Was it possible in England to have a pregnancy aborted medically, so as not to harm the mother? Was she all right now, could she have a baby? Answering, she understood herself more clearly, saw her actions in the perspective of time and context.

'I'm sorry.' Tears continued to run down her face.

'My staff car will be at Woodbridge, with plenty of gas. Let me give you a lift home,' he said.

Tigger barked at the strange jeep, white star and all, as it crossed the sleepers.

The general helped her out, shook her firmly by the hand, wished her luck, and climbed back in beside his driver.

The dog was jumping up, leaving paw marks on her coat.

Little Meg took hold of the dog's collar, dragging her inside.

'Don't worry, it's already been covered in smuts. My God, Meg, I'm exhausted.'

'I'll make you tea, ma'am.'

They sat at the kitchen table, Tigger pushing all the while at her knee, wanting the comfort of stroking.

'Ma'am, Mrs Chester, I couldn't sleep for worrying about you.

Do you think Mr Chester might get better quicker than they think?' Then she asked, 'Was the journey awful?'

She managed to make the nightmare journey up into a joke, so they both laughed.

'Gin! Ma'am, Mrs Chester, what a waste!'

CHAPTER 25
SEPTEMBER 1942

Flocks of gulls, harsh-voiced, swirled around the station platform at Woodbridge. The fishing boats, those that had made it home two years ago, were working again. The September sun was lower in the sky but hot on her back.

It was four weeks since she'd gone up to Nottingham for a second visit to the hospital, just a fortnight after the first. She'd stayed only one night. He had been in obvious pain and edgy. 'He'll be better when he gets home,' the sister had said.

She squinted into the sun, watching for the signal to move. It was a long journey; even fully fit she'd found it dreadfully tiring – how would Iain cope, straight out of hospital? At home, the house and bedroom were spotless, the wireless set up on his side of the bed, which had a hot-water bottle in it despite the sun.

The crowd of people on the platform shifted, moved forward, as the engine passed the signal, slowing as it moved to the far end of the platform and stopped.

Passengers emerged from the carriages. No sign of Iain.

A young naval rating was helping one man, in uniform, onto the platform.

'How did you know which carriage I was in?'

He looked a cruel caricature of the man she had waved off on this platform, just months ago. Wasted, unsteadily leaning on the rating's outstretched hand, a patch over his right eye, and his face blotched and marked where the bits of plastic had been.

'Iain.' To cover her confusion, to avoid the embarrassment of kissing or not, she became effusive. 'Darling. Tigger's in the car.'

She nursed him in bed for two days, invalid-sized portions of his favourite meals, and then brought him down to sit in the afternoon sun near the back door.

Upstairs he had been very quiet, not asking about the farm, but now as they sat sharing a packet of cigarettes in the shade of the old fig tree, wasps working above them, he called out to Little Meg as she wheeled a barrow across the bridge.

'Forgive me not getting up.'

She left Little Meg sitting beside him, and slipped away to make a start on the sadly neglected farm paperwork.

Gradually colour came back to his face as his strength and energies improved. One day when she got back with the swill from Framlingham, she found him no longer sitting in the house as she'd left him, but in the food shed, preparing the afternoon feeds.

He rested the scoop on the bin. 'Let's go for a pint this evening. I'm not going to spend the rest of my life in purdah.'

Purdah? Because of his distorted face? Where the red scars were paling into pallid lifeless parchment? Go to the pub? Meet old friends?

'Goody – yes.'

In The Queen's Head, he chatted farming with old George, and lit the cigarette of a young airman both of whose arms were swaddled in bandages.

That night he turned to her in bed. They slept, always, with the curtains wide open. The huge harvest moon shone into the room. Months of abstinence, awareness of something special nearly lost and now regained, gave an urgency to her passion. She forgot to be careful of his wounded body, kissed the scars, followed them down the side of his neck and shoulder. Waist down there were no scars – the blast had hit his face and chest only.

'No one would recognise us as the couple who walked out of the church six years ago.' God, she hadn't meant to say that. 'I don't mean physically, I mean we're different inside.'

'I'm not sure you meant that, either.' He touched her cheek, grinned, then, 'Sorry – cheap joke. You're right. Whatever would the nuns at your proper school make of you driving around with swill in the car boot? Nothing about our lives will ever be the same again, whatever happens in this ruddy war.'

'But… ' She bit her bottom lip, looked away, out at the moon. 'Do you still want us to have children?'

'Of course! They'll be our future. The first years of the war, I couldn't bear being here, like a conchie, but it wasn't you that was wrong. Come here, woman.'

Afterwards he said nursing wasn't the only thing she was good at, lit them both a cigarette, and they lay side by side, talking longer and deeper than for years.

They began to enjoy his sick leave, turning the time together, finite and hence the more precious, into a gentle sort of holiday at home. His help around the farm made things a lot easier and she was touched that he saw it like that, him helping her.

Nancy invited them to supper. The driveway up to her house was long and increasingly unkempt nowadays.

Away from the gravel turning-circle a US jeep was parked, tucked back in the shrubbery.

'I thought it was just us.'

Iain asked, 'Who do you think she's roped in?'

Nancy, looking relaxed, and rather smart, led them through to the drawing room. 'Come and meet a friend who is joining us for supper.'

Not in uniform, yet unmistakably Franklin.

The flash of recognition on his face.

He said, 'Pleased to meet you, ma'am,' and held out a hand for her to shake. She took the outstretched hand, deliberately blanking expression from her own face.

It was a happy evening. Franklin was gently, unembarrassedly, attentive to Nancy and seemed to know his way around the house. He was good value, as easy a conversationalist at the dinner table as he had been on the train, and he provided Iain with the sort of company he lacked at home.

'Thoroughly good dinner,' Iain said. 'Nancy's looking well.'

'Yes.' She tried to put the sad wife in Utah from her mind.

Iain was much better, his eyesight nearly back to normal, and he was physically fit again. Fit. But not fighting fit. He was barrowing muck across to the heap behind the fatteners' unit. Together they were scrubbing down two farrowing units, ready for the new sows. Large Whites. Ordinary sort of pigs. Not like poor old long-gone Flossie.

'I'll be transferred into a support unit, supplies, that sort of thing – not front line stuff.'

How would he cope dropped back into harsh army life? The army was desperate, of course, for every sort of recruit.

'I'm a fully trained officer. Needed, Kitty.'

She stopped brushing. Stood still.

Nothing to be done to stop him going back. Not now. Her suggestion, her encouragement, to join up in the first place.

What if she hadn't stepped in? But he'd wanted it, then and now.

Damn this ruddy war.

She hid her reluctance at his going. Made light of not having his help around the place. Packed his kitbag, and smiled as she handed it to him.

The sense of foreboding grew, deep in her guts. When they got to the station, her eyes moistened, her throat tightened. Quickly she kissed him lightly on the lips. 'Off you go. I'll get on, get home. See you at Christmas.'

She turned away at once, not able to bear watching as he

walked away to join the cluster of khaki-clad figures waiting for the train.

Late on Christmas Eve, she drove again to Woodbridge station. Iain was at training camp, this time learning about the practicalities of transporting tanks and ammunition, and home for only four days.

'I'm desperate for a pint,' he said. So she drove directly to The Queen's Head. Both bars were packed. He was waylaid, welcomed back, as he struggled to reach the bar. Afterwards they all trooped across to the church for Midnight Mass. She found his hand, squeezed it, as the choir sang out the first notes of 'It Came Upon the Midnight Clear'.

He left again the day after Boxing Day.

CHAPTER 26

JANUARY 1943

ANOTHER CHRISTMAS GONE. The fourth of the war, and it had been especially fun because their time together was so short.

She spent New Year's Eve at home with Little Meg for company. Exhausted from the extra winter work, they struggled to keep awake till midnight, raised their glasses to 1943 as the chimes of Big Ben rang out from the wireless, and went straight to their beds.

Snuggling down, the warmth of Tigger's body tucked by her feet, Kitty tossed, restless in the bed. Thirty-three years old. Definitely time to have a baby. Difficult though. She'd be lucky to see Iain more than a couple of times before he got sent to some front line.

The East Anglian winter, the rigid, dry cold, brought new challenges. The drinking troughs needed unfreezing two or three times a day. One day the newly farrowed sow, the one who was an inadequate sort of mother, suffocated one of her little tribe, so Kitty got up in the middle of the night, pulled on slacks, socks, boots, and went out to check on her. Tigs came, of course, and chased off into the dark of the wood. The sow and remaining piglets looked fine. Kitty ran back to the kitchen, and had to stand, getting increasingly cold and cross, whistling for the dog. Who came, wagging her stumpy tail, snow on her snout. Kitty grinned, forgave the dog, and together they retreated to bed.

More snow fell during the night. Iain's winter ritual of listening to the weather forecast at five to six used to irritate her. Now she saw the sense of it.

The round of feeds and clearing out the sties took the two women three hours on a normal day. This morning the snow – and then she slipped over and spilled a full bucket of precious hot mash – delayed them. It was not until lunchtime that she started to put the chains on the tyres. Her hands were already icy, the snow was freezing and she was going to be late to collect the swill.

She would be lucky to get home before dark. Iain, forewarned by the forecast, would have put the chains on the night before.

Damn. Her hand slipped, tearing a nail back from her finger.

He would also have come in to a neatly laid supper table, a casserole of hot rabbit awaiting him when he had changed into the newly ironed shirt already laid out on the bed.

Finally she got the car going, and drove into Framlingham rather faster than was wise given the state of the roads.

She collected the swill from a disgruntled school porter, who had hoped to leave earlier, it being so cold, and arrived back at the farm to start the afternoon round of feeds, which took longer than ever, the water troughs all frozen again. Even Bosun, drumming away, failed to lighten her mood.

Afterwards, thoroughly fed up, she ran a bath, and nearly dozed off in the increasingly tepid water until her tummy started to rumble, stirred into activity by the smell of frying onions wafting up the stairs.

Little Meg was busy at the range, turning sausage and onions in the pan. The table set for two.

'I found the sausages in the larder. You looked so tired I thought we needed something hot and tasty.'

'Oh, Meg. What a dear you are. I was, but it was my fault – I shan't make that mistake again.'

The sausages tasted spicy, were perfectly browned, much better than when she cooked them, the onions were golden, crisp on the edges, sweet and soft in the middle.

'You should think about cooking for a living.'

The girl blushed. 'I cooked at home, while my mam looked after the littler ones.'

They cleared the table, and washed up together. Thereafter they took it in turns to cook supper.

In April Iain was back for ten days' leave. He tackled a great list of jobs, those that were beyond her, so that the daylight hours were filled with the sound of hammering and sawing as he mended gates and fences, and split logs for the drawing room fire, its voracious appetite never satisfied.

'Listen.' It was Easter Sunday. She had made their mid-morning drink, Bovril nowadays in the absence of coffee. 'The church bells are ringing – the first time since the war started.'

The three of them went outside onto the lawn and listened as bells from the local church rang out, and then in the still air the sound of bells from further afield rolled across the flat landscape.

'The tide has turned,' Iain said. 'We'll be invading them next, no threat of invasion here now. Our training is about protecting troops as they advance. It'll be a long, bloody fight because Hitler's got nothing to lose, he'll fight on to the bitter end, but we will beat the Germans... I'm not so sure about the Japanese, and war in the Far East.'

Next day she drove him to the station once more. She'd learned to adjust to his comings and goings. Until the moment they said goodbye. That was when the reality got to her, that this time she might not see him again before he was pitched off into the front line to play his part in the invasion of northern Europe, whenever that was launched.

The longer, warmer summer days eased the work on the farm. She went to see Nancy, who seemed a little down. There had been no more news of Philip and no mention of Franklin, so she suggested a treat in London for the two of them. She got tickets for a matinée of *This Happy Breed* at the Haymarket Theatre.

'Let's have a decent lunch first. They say the play is Noël Coward's tribute to the ordinary Englishman.'

'A bit ironic, isn't it? I mean, I can't imagine anyone less like an ordinary Englishman.'

'Oh, I know, Nancy, but that's part of it. He's so polished, and, I don't know, so very funny without making a joke. Makes that dreadful Arthur Askey look primitive.'

When they got home, Nancy insisted they have a nightcap.

'A quick one for the road, Kitty. I don't know how I'd have coped all these years without you nearby.'

'Nor I you. I suppose things haven't worked out for either of us the way we expected.'

They settled at the kitchen table. Nancy tipped more gin into their glasses. Sat down opposite, fiddled with the cigarette packet.

'I've got to talk about this. Will you be my mother-confessor? You met Franklin, that evening you came to supper.'

Don't interrupt – let her tell it her own way.

'I met him in The Crown. I'd gone in on my own. We got talking.' She pulled on her cigarette. 'He was kind, friendly. A man. God, having him here, around the house, after the children were asleep, of course. I'd forgotten what I was missing.'

'I guessed, that night we came round to supper,' Kitty said. 'He was very discreet, didn't let on he and I had met. Did he tell you?'

'No!' Ash fell from Nancy's cigarette.

'Nothing happened, not like that.'

Nancy continued to gaze, her cigarette forgotten.

'Cerebral, though,' Kitty said. 'We talked. On a train. You and he are the only people I've ever told about my abortion apart from Nigel. I'm glad it was him you found.'

'Good God.' Nancy noticed her cigarette. Relit it. 'He's lovely, an intellectual mind in a soldier's body. He's married, but didn't talk about his wife, or whether they had children. I didn't ask, didn't feel I wanted to know. He saved my sanity, made me human again.'

Discreet, or secretive? A man who could compartmentalise his two lives.

'He's gone now, hasn't he?' Kitty asked. 'Probably leading his troops into Italy.'

'I think so. He said goodbye, thanked me, said he was happy. If Philip ever comes back, I'll need to be dreadfully careful.'

Little Meg was away for a night, had gone to her one remaining aunt's funeral. Through the kitchen window, the evening star was bright in the clear sky. Dark already, with the silence of dusk as the wildlife hunkered down for the night.

The range was being temperamental, once again. Sod's law, she muttered, marvelling at the stove's capacity to play up, always, without fail, when she was late or in a hurry.

It had been grey all day, never really got light. She must finish feeding the fatteners while there was enough light to see the troughs.

Boil, kettle, boil, damn you.

The drone of the plane was loud in the stillness. It was late for the fighters to be coming back in.

She shuffled the kettle round the hotplate in a vain attempt to get it to boil.

The engine noise came closer, reverberated through the house, shaking its foundations. An aircraft thundered low over the oaks, going towards Riddetts Field.

Seconds later the impact of the crashing plane brought plates tumbling off the dresser, made the lights flicker. The floor quaked beneath her feet.

She grabbed the torch and her first aid bag and ran across the lane. Through the gate, towards the oaks.

Seconds later the explosions began. Poor devils. One of ours, or one of them? But still a dreadful way to die. Combusted alive.

She held back, under one of the oaks. The fireball was beyond the trees, in the next field.

Tigger started to bay, head in the air. She followed the dog's gaze. A parachute, light in the dusk, weighted by a body, was caught in the tree. The feet dangled just above her head.

The figure moved, it wasn't just the parachute swinging.

Her eyes began to adjust, but it was too dark to make out any sort of uniform.

The man was pulling something from inside his flying jacket.

Oh, God, how many times had Iain told her to take the gun with her? She shone the torch up. His face was a featureless blob. His hand was waving around. Her torch picked out the solid black lump of the revolver. The snub-nosed barrel swung directly at her face.

Fear turned to anger.

'Drop that gun, or I'll set my dog on you.'

It was true. The dog, sensing her fear, was growling, teeth bared and hackles like a porcupine.

The parachute was shifting around in the wind; the man's face swung away from her, back again.

'If you shoot my dog, I'll ring your bloody neck with my bare hands.' English wouldn't do. She shouted the only German words she could remember. *'Verboten. Nein, nein. Da fest Verboten.'*

She kept shining the torch up at the man. Look him in the eyes. But she couldn't see his eyes, just the gun and round white blob of face.

'Drop that fucking gun!'

The gun landed at her feet. She bent to pick it up. Jerked her head upwards as, in a shaky drawl, the man said, 'Gee, lady, steady on. We're on the same side.'

She recovered herself.

'Thank God. Well, jump down then.' She took the belt off her trousers as a makeshift lead for Tigger, calmer now but not to be trusted. 'Come on, the dog'll be all right.'

She hoped so, was glad to have it close to her.

The man hit the ground suddenly, his legs buckling under him, and lay unmoving.

'Are you all right?'

'Yeah, lady, I think so.'

Keeping the dog tight on the other side of her, she put out a hand and helped to pull him upright.

She took him back to the house, sat his shuddering body in the chair by the range. She poured them both a large brandy.

'Get this inside you.'

He was a boy still. Soft, downy hair where his beard would be. His face the colour of his parachute, which was left still hanging in the tree.

Her hands, clammy after the shock, were shaking. She got a blanket, filled a hot-water bottle, wrapped him up in an attempt to deal with the shock. It wasn't the burns, which were slight, to his hands. Stutteringly, he said his rear gunner had gone down with the plane. She saw the spectres behind his eyes.

She wrapped the blanket tighter, gave him hot Bovril, in the willow pattern cup, and then went to telephone his base at Martlesham.

She told him to stay by the range while she went to finish feeding the pigs.

'They'll be here for me soon,' he said when she got back inside. 'I'm sorry to have scared you, but I'm mighty glad I'm not a German. Keep my 'chute. They don't know it's here. It's silk. Make you some nice petticoats.'

Silk. Cream silk. Yards and yards of it. Unheard of luxury nowadays, when the best they could buy was utility cloth, not even rayon now.

'What a treat. I shall have underwear for life. Thank you.'

Tigger, hackles up and head on one side, announced the arrival of the jeep from the base. As she accepted a box of goodies from the sergeant, the pilot, recovering some colour, winked, so she said nothing about her silk undies hanging in the oak tree.

At first light the next morning, it took a good deal of determined ingenuity to retrieve the parachute. The ladder was steady, resting firm against a limb of the great oak, but the wind was blustery, and the silk kept whipping around her, flapping against her face; the cords were tangled in the branches, and the scissors wouldn't cut the tightly woven silk. She went back to the yard, looked at the line of tools suspended on pairs of six-inch nails, and selected a pitchfork and the scythe, the one Frank used.

The pitchfork was no use at all. But hooking the scythe over the cords, and jerking downwards, she managed to release the 'chute. Yards of silk billowed around, smothering her.

'Stop it, Tigs.' The dog was bouncing on the material, snapping at it.

At last, she got the better of the slippery stuff, and managed to suppress it all into the emptied USAF supplies box. How, she wondered, do the WAAFs repack the things?

She consulted Nancy about how best to convert fifty yards of parachute into nightdresses and cami-knickers. Nancy offered to do the stitching. 'Bring it over here, Kitty. I'll enjoy doing it. It may be as well to be careful who else we tell about this.'

With the box carefully stowed on the back seat, Kitty drove across to Bruisyard.

The entrance gate, broken since Philip left, remained propped in the bushes. She was forced to brake sharply as she swung through the gateway to avoid the telegraph boy, free-wheeling down the steep drive.

Silly lad.

And then, oh, my God, a telegram. Philip.

Up the drive, round the last bend. The front door was open.

Nancy, waving her arms, tears streaming down her face, was beside the car in a trice.

'Come here.' Kitty put her arms round the hysterical woman. How to cope with normally placid Nancy? Shock and grief affected people differently. 'Come inside, and sit down.'

'No, no… ' The tears flowed faster.

Nancy began to laugh.

'Is it Philip?'

'Yes, no,' Nancy gulped, gagged silent.

Kitty slapped her face.

'Don't do that! He's coming home.'

Oh, God. Is she unhinged?

'It says, *Have been exchanged, landed in Leith. Meet me Woodbridge three o'clock.* This afternoon! My hair, the house!'

'You look fine. He hasn't seen you for years, all he's going to want is a big kiss, a hot bath and a proper meal. I'll see what I can find in the shops. You have time to yourself here. If you've gone when I get back I'll put the stuff in the larder.'

She managed to wheedle lamb chops from the butcher, four ounces of butter from the grocer's and then bought, at ridiculous cost, three stems of chrysanthemums, which she put in a jug on Nancy's kitchen table with 'Welcome Home' written on a new packet of cigarettes.

She let three weeks elapse before going over to see Philip, to give them time on their own to adjust, and was glad she had done so. Nancy looked tense, not at all her usual comfortable self, and Philip struggled to observe the basic courtesies.

She left after an uncomfortable half-hour. That evening Nancy telephoned to apologise. 'Come over next Friday and stay to eat, please, we need to learn to be social.'

Philip, thin, pale, and somehow still dishevelled despite nearly a month of Nancy's tender care, stood up as Kitty entered the warm room. 'Good to see you again, my dear. I'm afraid I wasn't very good company last week.'

'You were. Just a bit quiet. It can't be easy, years shut away, and then dropped back here and expected to be normal.'

'Nancy's been wonderful. I find it difficult with the children. I know they want me to tell them about it. Can't do that. And my leg hurts like hell. The Boche medics weren't so bad, did their best in the circumstances but it set crooked. Now tell me about Iain.'

Kitty spent Christmas Day with Jo and her family. Iain had volunteered to postpone taking his seventy-two hour Christmas leave: 'Hardly any time at home and the journey will be ghastly, crowded and unreliable. There's a chap here who'd like to swop, he's got two toddlers. I'll take mine in the spring. We can have the time in London together.'

It made sense – three proper days and nights in London was much more appealing.

'I envy you both.' Jo, attacking the vast pile of dirty crockery, looked frazzled. Her mother, increasingly frail and confused, was trying, unsuccessfully, to help. The two youngest children were squabbling. 'A glamorous reunion. Just the two of you, free as air, in London.'

'Much more fun than less than two days at the farm, I know.' Kitty stood the last of the plates on the dresser and reached for the saucepans. 'Things seem to be going better. Everyone is whispering about the invasion of Europe.'

'I don't know where Alistair is. I haven't heard from him for ages.'

Uncharacteristic tears trickled down Jo's face into the washing-up water.

'Jo, dear Jo, you're brave. I've had an easy time.'

'Not how I'd describe your life.' Jo lifted her face, smiled and said, 'This won't do – not our style, Kitty: let's round up this disparate lot for one last game of charades before you have to go.'

CHAPTER 27

JANUARY 1944

THE AFTERNOON SUN hung low in the winter sky, shining directly into the farm office. Kitty pinned last year's accounts papers together. This used to be Iain's job. She picked up the thick wad of papers and checked through them all. A whole year on the farm finished, packed into an envelope. That was 1943 gone. She addressed the envelope, sealed it up.

The water lapped at the edge of the moat. The garden birds were active, swooping in and out of the bushes. A female blackbird, all feminine bustle, was pulling a worm from the softening ground while two males, yellow beaks catching the shafts of sunlight, were vying, territorial, around each other – sensing spring. The weather had been gentle, kinder than in previous years, and the grass was already greening up.

She leaned back into the chair.

1944 stretched ahead. News of the Allied air raids on Germany, especially the devastating ones on Berlin, dominated the papers. Locally, though, the rumours were of huge losses at the airbases, and people had begun to doubt what they read and heard on the wireless. Some time, this year perhaps, the Allies would try to invade Europe. Iain would go, be part of that. Yet, the routine of life on the farm stayed the same, shaped by the seasons, cold, and wet, and then the summer sunshine.

Thirty-four years old this year. And no babies, no little people to nurture, to help makes lives for themselves.

Tigger barked, jumped at the window. A moment later, the hatted and coated figure of Winnie turned into the driveway.

Oh, God, what now? Frank?

Winnie looked composed but then her stoic face never displayed much emotion.

'Ma'am, I won't stop. I just wanted to tell you I heard about Frank. I'm going to use my coupons to stock up on things. Frank's coming back. He's wounded, being invalided home.'

'Good God. When? How badly hurt is he?' She hugged Winnie.

'Sounds bad, ma'am, but I'll have him home, we'll manage.'

'Here's a bit to help.' Kitty reached up to the top shelf of the dresser and drew out four ten shilling notes from the Toby jug.

Kitty wasn't entirely surprised when Iain's leave was postponed. The news in March had been miserable, culminating in the awful business at Monte Cassino, and Germany taking over Hungary.

It was late one evening when Iain telephoned. He sounded terse, tense she supposed.

'So sorry but my leave's been put off – no chance of fixing another date just now. I can't talk and scores of other blokes are waiting to use this thing.'

After the line went dead she kept hold of the receiver as if it were still connected to Iain. Rumours were rife that the invasion of Europe was about to be launched despite, or maybe because of, some mess-up during an exercise at Slapton Sands. There had been nothing official on the news or in the papers but people were talking and noticing things like the ships being massed at Harwich. General Eisenhower's visit to inspect the airfields in East Anglia had fuelled rumours too. A successful invasion to drive the Nazis to surrender, the longed-for and inevitable step towards the end of this ruddy war.

She shivered and in a conscious effort to put the grim reality out of her mind she boiled the kettle for a hot-water bottle despite the mild April air, took the old favourite *Berry and Co.* from the bookshelf, in the hope its soft, safe humour might alter her mood.

Frank had been home for two weeks. He had lost his left arm, amputated at the shoulder, and his left leg was broken in two places. Winnie insisted he was well enough to have visitors, so Kitty walked across to their cottage, which was surrounded by fields of sugar beet, rows of spinachy leaves showing now.

The kettle was humming on the stove and there was a plate of warmly fragrant oat biscuits on the table.

Frank tried to get up out of his chair, using his one remaining arm on the walking stick. 'Don't get up, please.' She put a hand on his shoulder, pressing gently to ease him down again. 'We're just so pleased to have you home.'

Hovering, Winnie said, 'He's in a lot of pain, but doctor says if he rests the leg, it will get better.'

'Fresh air is what I need,' Frank said. 'The beet is growing up well. They'll need to be hoeing between the rows any day.'

'Don't even think about it, Frank! The weather's been kind this year, a bit dry that's all. When you feel up to it come across and tell Little Meg and me what we're doing wrong.'

On her way home, she looked more closely at the sugar beet fields and saw that Frank's countryman's eye was right: the weeds were establishing and needed hoeing off.

She pulled the bedroom window shut. The kind winter had become an unpleasant June, despite the hours of daylight. Not winter cold, just wet and miserable. But she left the curtains open as usual and fell asleep quickly.

She woke suddenly. Aircraft. She climbed out of bed and opened the window.

It was massed fighter planes that had woken her, she could see those. And something else. Not as high in the sky as the fighters.

Little Meg's window opened.

'Strings of gliders,' Kitty called out. 'Fighters flying above them.'

They watched as rank upon rank of planes passed high above, heading south. Towards mainland Europe. This is it, she thought. The invasion is happening.

Her feet were cold so she got back into bed. The noise of the aircraft droned on. The gliders must be full of soldiers about to be parachuted into enemy territory; every one of them somebody's son, most someone's husband. Iain. Was he there, among them? No good thinking about that, letting imagination take over.

She decided to get up, to pull herself together and do something useful with the time. No chance now of Iain's leave, no time together in London. She pushed the chosen silk dresses to the back of the wardrobe.

Downstairs she made tea, and toast for a treat, and walked around the yard checking on the pigs. She disciplined herself not to wonder where he was or what was happening to him because she knew she couldn't know and so the only thing was to put it all right out of her mind.

She suggested to Little Meg that they keep the wireless on all that day and tried to make sure that one or other of them was near enough to hear it. At midday, Little Meg shouted for her and together they listened to the announcer: 'Allied naval forces, supported by strong air forces, began landing Allied armies this morning on the northern coast of France.'

Frank started to make a gentle return to helping on the farm. His leg improved daily so that he now moved around easily, appearing unexpectedly, but there were few tasks that he could attempt.

He devised a method of mixing the feeds with one hand and they thanked him and tried not to notice the time it took or the fact that he looked tired and drawn at the end of each afternoon. But Winnie said although he did get tired he slept better, more calmly, after tiring himself out in the fresh air.

CHAPTER 28

JUNE 1944

SHE WAS ONLY JUST UP, not quite awake. The telephone jangled. She snatched up the receiver.

Early, much too early, to be an ordinary call.

'It's me.'

'Iain!'

'I've got dates for my leave. It'll be my last for a while. The unit here's pretty much ready for embarkation.'

She dropped the receiver back onto its cradle. Her hands were shaking. What a see-saw of emotion. Momentarily, she wished he had already gone, that her efforts at distancing herself from worry and heartache wouldn't be undone by his company and the shared nights.

Iain was waiting in the faded, once-baroque splendour of the hotel foyer at the Great Eastern. He looked well, better than for years. The tan was hiding the scars on his face, his chin dimpled again, his features etched sharper, making him look more determined than ever. Crisp and polished in his uniform, but then he'd always been a tidy dresser; clothes fitted him somehow.

'Good afternoon, Mrs Chester. Nothing up-from-the-country about you.' He bowed low and then kissed her hard, directly on the mouth. 'The word is that we're about to be mobilised. Told to make the most of this leave. I've got the key to the room.'

Re-dressed in his uniform, Iain began to fidget, flicking over the pages of the newspaper. 'Come on, we've got forty-eight hours to paint this town red.'

'Just a tick, while I do my face.' Her hair looked okay, not too messed up, and the red silk of the cocktail dress she'd got into gave her face colour. The gentle days of summer seemed to have given back her high cheekbones and lifted her brown hair so the odd blond streak shone through.

She got up from the little stool, held out her hand to him. 'Ready.'

They took a cab across to The Ivy where he'd booked a table.

'Just as well,' he said, surveying the crowd of diners: the grey RAF, the khaki, and the black dinner jackets mingling with bare-shouldered dresses. 'Plenty of people here out to enjoy themselves.'

She chose carefully, fish rather than meat to avoid the pitfalls of horsemeat. The Dover sole was good and enhanced by Iain's choice of wine, a very expensive Vouvray. The service was impeccable.

As they left the restaurant, she said, 'It's heavenly to be spoiled, waited on.' She stood up on tiptoe, kissed him lightly on the lips. 'Let's walk, get a breath of air.'

Crowds bustled along the pavements. London was alive again, released after the darkened years. They turned into Charing Cross Road, heading for the Savoy, and paused to look at a crowd clustered by a newspaper vendor. 'Read all about it! Star's death. Tragic accident.'

'I'll get a *Standard*.' Iain felt in his pocket for the coins, came back with the paper. 'Good God. It's that bloke, the actor, Guy Rodgers.'

She gasped and screwed up her eyes trying to read in the dim light.

'Says he was out shooting on his farm. Didn't realise he had one.' Iain read on. 'He tripped, the gun went off. Killed outright.'

'How dreadful. He was such fun.'

'Hmm, and famous. Let's get dancing.'

The waiter found them the last table tucked into a tiny alcove. Iain ordered a bottle of champagne. She sipped at it, fiddled with her glass, remembering the meal at J. Sheekey when Guy's gentle charm had lifted her morale.

Iain eased her onto the crowded dance floor.

What a waste. Not killed by a bomb, just a stupid accident.

'Sorry.' She realised she'd been silent, in a world of her own, and that Iain was watching her. 'It's ironic, I know, but Guy was the first man to make me feel like a woman again after Nigel died.'

'He seemed good company the only time I met him.'

'At Christopher's wedding.' She felt her face puckering up. 'A silly accident and he's gone. God almighty, isn't the war destroying enough lives?'

The music stopped. He rested his hands on her shoulders, smiled down at her.

'Chin up.' Exaggeratedly he cocked his head on one side as the band struck up again. 'Waltz on, Kitty.' He swirled her away at a tremendous pace using the very edge of the floor until she was breathless and the exhilaration had chased the shadows away.

Despite the hours of dancing, they woke surprisingly early next morning. They explored the shops, walked along the Embankment, lunched at his club, and spent the afternoon back in the hotel bedroom.

That evening they went to The Berkeley to dine, and stayed dancing until her feet ached.

In the cool of the night, they walked along Piccadilly, down Haymarket, and into Trafalgar Square.

'My feet… ' she started to say.

'Are killing you, I know.' He flagged down a cab.

Waiting while she brushed her hair, he stood behind her.

'Thanks for my leave, and things.'

She met his eyes in the mirror. 'I shan't know when you go, or where. Poor Jo doesn't know where Alistair is, so she worries whatever the news is.'

'How about we have a code? If I write *Moriarty is dead* it will mean I'm with the fighting units in Europe; *Jehosophat is dead* will mean I'm going to the Far East.'

The next morning she insisted on going with him to Paddington Station. At the kiosk, he bought *The Times* and an *Illustrated London News* for her, and checked the platform number for his train.

'Time to go, Kitty. Don't come to the platform.'

The dimpled chin, the same old direct gaze, two hazel eyes. She moved her hand up towards his face. He caught it, held it, bent down towards her, kissed her on the lips, while soldiers heading for the train swirled around them.

'So long. Got to scoot.'

He was gone, striding off, not looking back. She watched until he was swallowed up into the surging mass of uniforms. She bit her bottom lip, looked at the magazine in her hand, turned and walked quickly to the cab rank.

She settled back into the seat, flexed her ankles, glad of the anonymity of the cab that was winding its way east, through Trafalgar Square towards Liverpool Street Station and the hotel. Plenty of time to collect her things from the room and walk down onto the station concourse for the afternoon train home.

She felt tired now, the anti-climax setting in, the intensity of the last two days and very little sleep catching up with her.

The cabbie leaned round, and pulled down the glass partition.

'Which way through the City, love?'

She was opening her mouth to reply when the world exploded.

Her chest hurt, and her wrist was caught under the weight of her body. The floor of the cab was on top of her.

She tried to open her eyes and closed them again as she felt the gritty dust. She coughed, and inhaled a mouthful of it. The smoke was choking her.

'Out of here, lady.' A hand was dragging at her coat, pulling her up out of the cab. Shrieks, shouting.

'Get on with it.' Harsh, rough tones in her ear. 'Down the shelter.'

She felt herself pushed towards a cluster of people. 'Move it, there's more like that on the way.'

She was jostled down the stairway. The stale hot air, the smell of fetid fear, hit her nostrils.

People crowded behind her, pressing her downwards. A little boy in front of her looked up, his face made old by fright.

To give him space she held her ground, smiled, and said, 'Chin up, young man,' and winked. She was rewarded by a softening of the tense creases.

Another explosion. Someone behind shoved. She lost her footing and swore loudly. The woman, the one with the little boy, steadied her.

Feeling her feet together, both on the same level, she realised they had reached the bottom of the stairs. The floor was cold and damp. She had no shoes on. Had got here in stocking-feet. Her wrist hurt. Warm human flesh pressed up against her.

In the gloom of the Tilley lamps she saw the lines of people crowded together on the makeshift benches. People pushed around her, more coming down. Her eyes adjusted to the dark.

All these people. Silent. No one talking. Shock. She felt her own body sway.

A hand on her arm, fingers touching her body.

A bloody groper! Surely not here. Not now. Shivers ran down her spine.

The grip tightened, twisting her around. Her heart was thudding. She pulled her arms closer into her body and tried to move sideways. The man was still slightly behind her in the crush.

'Kitty.'

On reflex, she reacted to her name, turned to look, peering in the dark. British Warm overcoat. Not buttoned-up, unfinished-looking. The round face, the mousey hair flopping over the forehead. She gasped.

'Christopher!'

'You're shaking like a leaf. Let's find a corner, sit us both down.'

She realised he was right, her whole body was shuddering, her knees started to buckle. She felt his arm round her shoulders.

He found them eighteen inches of bench, waited while she sat down and then squeezed down beside her. He kept hold of her arm. 'Where were you?'

'On my way back to the hotel in a cab. Oh, Christ, the cabbie!' She started to shudder again, took several deep breaths, and said, 'Sorry. Perhaps he was lucky like me.'

'Just you in the cab?'

'What? Oh, yes. What about you?'

She looked at him properly, and was shocked. Even in the gloom she could see his face was lined, he looked years older, and unkempt.

'Never mind where I was.'

A rumbling thud overhead shook the walls and silenced the tentative gentle chatter in the shelter.

'However have they coped with this for years? Tell me where you were.'

'Not the sort of thing you need to know.'

'I've done first aid at bomb sites, heard about things.' She reached for his hand, felt him grasp it, tight. 'Iain and I were in London. Not a bomb to be heard.'

Not a word from beside her. Not the urbane Christopher she remembered.

'Christopher, I think we're going to be here a long while. How's the family?'

'Mother's not well, she's almost blind. Not happy, either.'

'I'm sorry, she was always so sweet. And Davinia?'

No comment.

'What has happened?'

'Can't. Too bad.'

Tears started to trickle down his face. Placid, competent, Christo crying? Dear God.

She put her hand on his arm. Noticed the little boy and his mother sitting opposite and saw the woman watching Christopher.

'Don't be nice to me. It makes it worse.'

'All right. I shall tell you all about the farm, the pigs, my Bull Terrier, about my... ' She searched for something, anything else to say. 'About my parachute silk underwear. And when we're let out of here I am going to buy you a large gin and French. In the Savoy.'

She talked about anything that came into her head, keeping hold of his arm. When she thought he had gathered himself together she tried again.

'Christo, tell me where you were? Is it the children? Or Davinia? Are they, were they, with you?'

He pulled away from her.

'No, no, they're all safe. Well, sort of.'

'Sort of?'

He was trying not to let his body touch hers. She saw him clench his fist, bite his bottom lip. Under his breath, not looking at her, he said, 'It's sordid. Something I did. No, what I didn't do.'

Carefully, aware now she was on unknown ground, she offered him an opening.

'Once I told a stranger, a man, about something I'd done, something I've paid for ever since. He didn't judge. Told me about his own dark places. Is it Davinia?'

'No. She left me and the children. All but, anyway. Stayed in London, at the flat. I expect you heard from Jo. Sometimes she came home, spent a bit of time playing at being my wife. Mother warned me but I didn't want to know.'

'Are you divorcing her? What about the children?'

'She wanted the money. Not the children. She counter-sued.'

He was shaking, sobbing beside her.

'God almighty, this is hideous, telling you.'

Not everything. Not yet.

'Christo, you have to get whatever this is off your chest. You have to share it.' She waited. Moved her arm around his waist.

He fished in a pocket, blew his nose.

'He killed himself. He was my friend, ever since I was thirteen. I couldn't have coped then, at school, without him. I walked away. It wasn't an accident, like they say. He shot himself.'

Whatever was he talking about?

He? One of Davinia's lovers?

She forgot the claustrophobia of the shelter, the whispering rows of people, the woman watching them.

'I'd warned Davinia, told her I'd divorce if she kept on, she'd had a string of lovers. She knew I was going to the London flat and deliberately she let me find her. She wanted me to sue for divorce.'

Not really surprised about Davinia, she wondered – if the brassy piece so wanted a divorce and he gave it to her, where was the problem?

'I hadn't guessed. She wanted me to sue so she could blackmail me. Force me to buy her off. She wanted the lot, even the farm and the house. My home. Mother's home.'

'Bitch!' Then she realised what he'd said. 'Blackmail you? Not literally?'

He didn't reply. Literally? Perhaps he did mean literally. About what, for heaven's sake? Decent Christopher. Well-mannered, law-abiding, unexciting Christopher. She couldn't imagine him doing anything blackmailable.

'Christopher?'

He hardly breathed the words. 'I don't know how, but she'd found out about Guy.'

What about Guy?

'She signed an affidavit, swore our marriage was a sham. She…
' He turned to face her. His hair was hanging straight and brown, he was unshaven, several days' dark brown growth on his face. The whites of his eyes, which used to look so white contrasting with the brown irises, were bloodshot red.

'She cited Guy Rodgers as the co-respondent.'

She clamped her lips together, hoped that in the gloom he wouldn't see the shock on her face. Guy. Applauded star of stage and screen. At Christopher's wedding. That night in the blackout when she called to him. It *had* been Christopher. How to react? How to handle this?

'Kitty, that wasn't true.' He reached for her hand, clutched it. 'He was a bit older, looked after me at school. Well, made me feel safe there. In his strange promiscuous way he was faithful, never stopped loving me. Just occasionally he'd ask to meet for dinner, *to see you, Christopher, hear how you are.* It wasn't the same for me. Before I left school even, I had girlfriends – proper ones, I mean. Women. I wanted to marry.'

The face beside her broke into what might have been a smile, lifted and for a moment she recognised the old Christopher.

'But the girl I chose found someone else.'

Her eyes were watering. She leaned across, put her lips against the bristly face. 'Tell me the rest, Christopher.'

'It wasn't just the money, I'd have let that go. I wasn't going to lose the children, whether I fathered them or not, they are my children, to them I'm their father, and it was their home. And Mother's home. So I went to see Guy and told him, intending to ask for his help, but he offered before I had the chance. He went to his solicitor to sign an affidavit to put the record straight, for my lawyers to use. It was brave. He knew, we both knew, there'd be a scandal. It would finish his career. He said he'd do it for me, because, well, of the past. I believed him, took it all at face value.

'The day before divorce was due the lawyers told me she'd withdrawn her counter-action. I was about to ring Guy, thank him, tell him no one need ever know. Then I heard it on the wireless. The news, that he was dead.'

The same evening Iain had bought the paper. 'It was an accident, wasn't it?'

'No. He'd bought her off. Gave her his fortune. Before. Before he shot himself. Finished it all, to save my home, my children.'

She stood up and pulled the shuddering man close to her, held him in her arms while he buried his face in her coat.

She had no idea how long she held him. God almighty, what a bloody waste. And let her head drop down onto Christopher's unruly thatch.

'Sorry, Kitty. I'm all right now. Sit down again.'

She did, but kept an arm around his waist. He admitted to getting himself drunk, deliberately totally senseless, and that he had not been home since. Better not to ask where he'd been. They remained, silent, amid the mixture of humanity around them.

Timeless hours after, when the all clear sounded, they were ejected by the pushing crowd of people, and emerged, blinking, into the daylight. She noticed the little boy, clutching the woman's hand, bouncing away, stopping to pick up some debris, his fear forgotten. She felt the dried streaks of tears on her own face.

'Christopher, come on, time to find that drink.'

'Not the Savoy, Kitty. Look at me.'

Her eyes adjusted to the daylight. By now she too must look a mess and she wondered at the sight of him.

'No, all right. But you are to come with me, back to the hotel, have a proper drink there.'

The commissionaire at the Great Eastern opened the cab door, averting his glance from Christopher as he spoke to Kitty. 'I am told the rockets have done a lot of damage this morning, ma'am. Dreadful business, when we thought it was all over.'

'You saw what he thought. You can't be seen with me.'

'Nonsense, of course I can.'

'No, Kitty, you look lovely, but a mess too. We can't be seen like this, neither of us. You've been crying. Hell almighty, I'm a self-centred pig. You started to tell me something earlier. I didn't listen. Tell me now.'

'All right. Come up to the room. We'll order drinks, have something to eat.'

She strode off, did not glance behind her. His innate good manners would ensure he followed.

With seconds to go before the last train left she rushed through the barrier onto the platform. She called to the guard, who was leaning out of his van blowing the whistle, as she ran towards the carriages; her coat was open, flapping, she clutched her headscarf and handbag in one hand and her weekend case in the other. As the train jolted away from the platform she stood in the corridor, her breath coming fast from her scurry through the crowds onto the platform.

The guard, mellower now his train was on its way, smiled a rather toothless old man's smile and told her she would find a seat in the next carriage. She said thank you, but she was better here.

Better because the banality of other passengers would be an affront. Steadying herself with one hand on the window bar, she struggled to hang onto the strings of her emotions which were pulling at her, balloon-like, up and away.

Iain away, facing God knew what, alone. Not to be seen again for months. Or ever. The horror of the cab upside down. The smell of the shelter. Christo.

The cleansing of sharing her own guilt: not with kind but never-to-be-seen-again Franklin; not with Nancy, who had never known the girl who was married to Nigel; not with Nigel, who had gone before she found out the consequences of her all-consuming love for him. No, with a man she might have married, a pillar of proper county society. With his own dark past.

He hadn't judged. Hadn't looked shocked. Had told her, 'But you did it for the best of reasons.'

He had sat in the apology for an armchair, the one meant really for clothes to rest on. He pushed back the locks of hair, grinned at her and said, 'Look at us! Two derelicts, straight out of William Locke. Do you mind if I use your bathroom to wash away the last few days?'

The train jolted as it got up speed, rattling over a set of points. She clutched the rail along the corridor window. She lit a cigarette, looked out at the moonlit suburbs. Why had she followed him?

There was no sense of shame, none whatever, about walking through the open bathroom door and shedding her blooded clothes, tainted by emotion and fear. It had simply seemed the natural thing to do, born of friendship and compassion.

All those.

And then, unexpectedly, pure passion as she traced the carmine line that outlined his lips until she was lost in the great brown pools that were his eyes. Christo was a very accomplished lover.

They tidied up, and were dressed, ready to go, when he put his hands on her shoulders. 'Safe journey, Kitty. Enjoy your home and Iain. We were two ships who berthed one afternoon. Thank you.'

He made no move to kiss her, smiled down into her eyes, proprietorially tightened the belt on her coat and turned her towards the door.

It was past midnight when she drove over the sleeper bridge. Little Meg and Tigger burst out of the back door.

'I was that worried, ma'am – Mrs Chester.' Streaks of tears marked Little Meg's face. 'I heard on the wireless about the V1 attacks. When you didn't come back I started to worry. But I lit the fire and made a rabbit stew to fill the time. Since it got dark I gave up hope. I didn't know what to do, how to find out.'

'You poor thing.' She hugged the girl, and the ecstatic dog. She said how there was no warning, about the weight of the taxi on top of her, and the hours in the shelter. 'It was horrible. But I'm home safe.'

No more. No mention of meeting anyone. The pact of silence between them.

CHAPTER 29
AUGUST 1944

THE AUGUST SUN WAS HOT, and the pigs were short of water. Kitty's shoulders ached as she carried the buckets, water slopping onto her bare legs, from the pond across to the sties.

Tired suddenly, she let the buckets down. The lawn around the house looked neater, mown yesterday achingly slowly by Frank, learning ways to manage one-handed. He was desperate to work but so limited in what he was able to achieve.

Tigger emerged from the bushes, a rabbit hanging from her mouth. 'Dog, you and I shall enjoy my thirty-fourth birthday by reading in the sun this afternoon.'

The figs were ripe, richly aromatic in the heat of the afternoon. Mindful of the wasps, she lifted the big leaves with care. Found three more purple fruits, let them fall into her outstretched palm. Yesterday she'd eaten too many and made herself queasy.

Every year she ate them, all the best things about summer captured in the soft, sweet flesh.

Queasy, from eating figs? August. July. June. Three months since London.

No, it couldn't be.

Getting undressed that night she felt her breasts. Fuller, yes, and tender if she pressed them.

. . .

In the morning, she went to see old Dr Foster on her way to collect the swill from Framlingham.

'Yes, Mrs Chester. Definitely pregnant, my dear lady. Your body's had a good long break, try not to worry. I am sure all will be well this time.'

She sat in the car. He had thought she was worrying but it wasn't that. Without realising, she had come to accept she would be childless. She hadn't bothered with precautions since the old obstetrician in Harley Street gave her the all clear, and her periods were often a bit erratic. She hadn't got pregnant despite Iain's leaves, or when he was home recovering, with stored up passion aplenty.

But, oh God. What about Christo? What if it were his? Could it be?

No, absolutely not. For the forty-eight hours before Christo, she and Iain had been locked into each other a dozen times, she'd been pumped full of him.

The baby was Iain's. After all, finally, their first child.

A new life.

She did a little shopping in the town and set about feeding the pigs when she got home. All automatic jobs.

Observant Little Meg was wiser than her years. Next morning, the girl spoke.

'My Mam said mashed potato was best for morning sickness. Funny thing to have for breakfast but she said it worked for her.'

'How did you know?'

'Your face is rounder, has been for a few weeks now. You'll need my room, for the nursery.'

'I hadn't thought. It's a shock after all these years. No, the baby can have the room next to my bedroom.'

'It'll be nice for Mr Chester, something to look forward to after the war.'

'Oh, Little Meg, you're right. We both used so much to want babies.'

. . .

285

The discarded sheets of her best, and scarce, Basildon Bond filled the waste paper basket, as testament to her struggle. '*Dear Iain…* ' No chance to see his face light up as she told him. He must have embarked within days of London, he might be anywhere. No time to write, and post would take ages from the Far East if he were there. '*I wish you were here so we could dance because I am expecting a baby.*'

She wrote to Ma, and expected a telephone call. Instead, she received a telegram. '*Congratulations, letter follows.*' When the letter came it was full of advice on what she should and should not do, on how she must leave the farm and move into a proper house in the town. She shoved the letter away.

August had become September and still no reply from Iain. She reached across the table for her teacup and felt swamped in a sense of aloneness. Pull yourself together, woman. Iain can't help being away, he doesn't even know, and Ma's response is par for the course.

Nancy was reassuringly excited. She came round with her own brood's outgrown nursery things because, as she said, there's nothing worth having in the shops nowadays. Together they carried it all up the staircase, edging the cot round the bend.

Kitty waved goodbye and climbed back up the stairs.

The cot looked cold because it had no bedding, just the shallow little mattress. Where were all the things Ma had given her before? Buried out of sight at the back of her cupboard. She delved into the cardboard box, placed the doll-sized things at one end of the cot, made it look snug, welcoming, and safe against the old plaster wall. She shifted the high chair and playpen back into a corner.

She hugged herself and sped down the stairs to hunt out her old knitting pattern book, needles and a ball of white wool left over from making rompers for one of Jo's babies.

As the sun set, she was knitting under the fig tree.

'The pigs are all fed. There's nothing more that needs doing, Mrs Chester.'

．　．　．

Nowadays it was Little Meg and Frank who kept things on the farm going, shooing her back to the house where she made nursery curtains, turned out cupboards and enlarged the waistbands on her slacks and skirts.

Sometimes she woke in the night, restless and unreasonably hot. Unable to get back to sleep, she lay worrying. Was the baby all right? Where was Iain?

She tried to put the debacle of Arnhem out of her mind – men dropped down through the night sky into German soldiers. Was he there? Why hadn't he replied to her letter? But what about the Far East – God forbid he was out there.

She took to waiting around the house at the time that the post arrived. This morning the sun had broken through the clouds. A cart loaded with sugar beet trundled along the lane. The harvest was poor this year, but the carts kept passing. Yet another one went by, leaving great lumps of wet clay in its wake. Postie bicycled behind the cart, wheeling around the worst of the clods.

He handed her half a dozen letters. Among the bills and stuff for the farm was a murky-brown standard-issue envelope.

Iain's spidery script!

Carefully, mustn't tear the tissue-thin paper, she used the sharp-ended carving knife to slit the envelope and drew out a single sheet.

'*Splendid news. Take care of both yourselves.*' Then the answer to her unwritten question: '*Moriarty is dead, four weeks ago.*'

She propped the letter on the dresser and walked down the driveway, onto the sleeper bridge. The surface of the moat shivered as a water vole, sensing her presence, swam off, leaving a v-shaped wake on the mirror of the still water.

She turned, walked back over the lawn where they had waltzed that bright morning.

Iain's Acre. His place. Created by his determination.

Please let him come back and find it here waiting for him.

She held her hands against the base of her rounding belly.

．　．　．

Although both Dr Foster and the midwife said her pregnancy was going normally, that she did not need to worry, she couldn't, wouldn't take any chances. Now, at six months, she made an appointment with the obstetrician in London.

The blackout restrictions lifted, lights lit the streets again, and there might, she hoped, be proper Christmassy displays in the shop windows.

She dressed in slacks, smart ones, and flat shoes, determined to make the most of the day, including lunch with Liz who, released early from the hateful paper-pushing in darkest Dorset, was back in London.

The consultant, who looked precisely the same, no older and in the same spotless black tailcoat, could see no problem with the pregnancy but insisted she book into his hospital for the confinement.

No problems then. She hadn't expected any but the man's verdict was a relief. She skipped down the wide steps from his consulting rooms in Harley Street. The sun was shining as she stopped on the pavement enjoying the elegance of the terraces on either side of the street. Down the road a gaping hole in the row of buildings dented her euphoria. Bombed. A set of teeth with the centre ones knocked out.

Liz had suggested a little place she'd found in Marylebone High Street for lunch.

'It's too wonderful to be back.' Her face heavily made up, she displayed bright red fingernails. 'I had my nails done. Now, darling, does the doctor think you are all right? Where will you have the baby?'

'The baby's growing well, everything is quite normal. I need to ask you a favour. He wants me to be in London, a taxi-ride away from the hospital, for the last couple of weeks. Could I sleep on your sofa, or something?'

'I'd love to help.'

'If you're sure. I can't risk anything going wrong, not now, not after all this time.'

'But you will sleep in my bed, and I'll be on the sofa. It'll be fun. What about Iain?'

'I wrote to tell him about the baby. He's in Europe, we had a sort of code, but I don't know any more than that. The newspapers are full of the Allied advance, all the good news, but they don't tell us the bad news. I try not to think about him out there, just picture him back home, at the farm, when the war's all over.'

After her lunch hour Liz went back to work. She had found a different job, working for Dubels, interior designers for the rich and famous. She loved it, said it was much more interesting than being a shop girl.

Kitty walked down to the shops in Oxford Street and along to Selfridges She made herself buy presents for other people before going up to the maternity department where she bought nightdresses for the baby, in the softest cotton, with pearl buttons, blankets for the pram, and a maternity dress, in midnight-blue silk, to wear on Christmas Day. Like last year she was going to spend it with Jo and her tribe.

On the day before Christmas Eve, she packed presents and her case into the car and left Little Meg, with Frank to help, in charge of the farm. It was dry and cold, easy driving weather.

Jo was looking out for her. 'My word, you look blooming. Leave your case and things, my truculent children can bring them in later. Come in out of this wind – straight off the Russian steppe – and have a drink.'

'Thanks for having me, once again.'

'I love it. Takes me back to when we were barely out of gymslips. I'm sorry if the children are ratty.'

'I expect it's a combination of over-excitement and young male hormones. Young Tavish is the spitting image of Alistair. I'll get him to help me do the Christmas Eve shopping round for you tomorrow. Give you time with the younger ones, and he can feel useful. I'll let him drive to the road.'

'I'm finding things hard here. I suppose you're right, they are growing up, the boys missing their father.'

Tavish proved an apt pupil, enjoying driving the car so much that when they reached the main road Kitty suggested they go back and start the journey all over again.

In the town, he directed Kitty round the back roads to avoid the bottleneck by the market, carried the shopping bags for her and then touched her deeply by asking if she would help him choose some flowers for his mother, like Dad always did on Christmas Eve.

It was dark when they got back. Something was wrong about the house, all the lights shining out of the windows, the curtains not closed.

Jo was sitting on the wooden hall settle, surrounded by the other children. Tears poured down all their faces.

Tavish froze. 'Mummy!'

The boy went over to his mother, helped her to stand up and put both his arms around her.

Kitty hugged them one by one. She read the telegram which Jo thrust at her, saw the empty agony on the face of the younger girl, took her by the hand and said, 'Come on, let's go and make Mummy a cup of tea.'

Alistair dead, lost fighting the Japanese, so far away from home, now, when the war was almost won. Cruel fate.

Why was it so often that the best people went? Peter, Pa, Simon.

Alistair.

Not the Trotts of this world. Not Ma. Not ruddy Davinia.

Jo came into the kitchen, her children following, like mother duck and her flotilla of ducklings. Her face was newly washed, hair combed, lipstick applied.

Tavish stepped forward. 'We've been talking. We've agreed to carry on with Christmas, that's what Daddy would want, what he'd do if, well, would have done… ' His voice tailed off.

'But we thought we'd do it the French way,' Jo said. 'Have our presents tonight, after supper, all stay up and sing songs at midnight.'

'What a good idea. I haven't wrapped all my presents. You girls come and help me.'

It was a good idea to keep them all together, busy until they were dropping with tiredness. She stayed up with Jo long after the children were asleep, letting her talk, or be silent, as she chose.

'Kitty, you are a dear. You must be exhausted. I shall be all right. We were so happy, Alistair always made life such fun, I shall do the same. Now, off to bed and get that rest you should be having.'

At the end of March, her body became unwieldy and cumbersome. She felt sick if she slept on her back, but the doctor said this was normal, the baby pressing on something inside.

Two weeks before her due date she packed her suitcase for London. Tigger became watchful, following her around.

The dog, her ears very flat, slunk into her basket and lay down with a deep sigh. She remained there despite the sound of Nancy's car coming up the driveway.

'Don't sulk, Tigs.' She stroked the dog. 'I'll be back soon with a new young friend for you to look after.'

'Come on – you've a train to catch,' Nancy said. 'I'll put this case in the car.'

Her tension, her sense of anticipation heightened. She didn't want to close the door on life as she'd known it for so long. She wished it was all over and that she was already home with the baby asleep in its cot.

Once she was on her way, the train rattling along towards London, her spirits lifted. Liz, waiting for her at the flat, had the kettle on. Some of the strangeness left her in the warmth of Liz's welcome.

Next morning Liz brought a tray of breakfast before she went off to work. 'What luxury. Thank you!' And so it was, to potter around, no responsibilities, all the time in the world to get up and dressed.

Later she walked along the scruffy pavements to the local shops. Liz's little flat was part of a fine early Victorian house and the two rooms were large and square with high ceilings, though the area was run down and definitely not a fashionable part of town, and several of the houses she walked past were obviously slums. In one garden, someone was making a valiant attempt to grow vegetables, and a couple of hens clucked away.

At the shops, she enjoyed the small compensations of town living, and bought a bunch of violets for the table from a woman street seller on the corner by the bus stop.

The gas cooker terrified her with the ferocity of its flame when she held the match to the burner. Then she was surprised at how quickly the liquid in the pan came to the boil. Supper was simmering to keep warm when Liz arrived home.

'You can't imagine how wonderful it is to find someone here and supper waiting.'

'Oh, but I can!' She told Liz about Little Meg's cooking.

A week later, soon after Liz had left for work, a band of pain tightened low in her tummy.

Easy to recognise, all too familiar.

Pains in the right place, and this time at the right time.

Time for a quick bath – to last for several days no doubt, call a cab, ask him to go via a bank, get some cash. She left a note for Liz, picked up her little case and pulled the door shut. Was waiting at the bottom of the steps when the cab arrived.

At the hospital, they got her on a trolley with smiling, unhurried speed. The smell was the same, of course, the rest oozed optimism. She squirmed, gripped the metal rail as another contraction came.

A youthful lad, white-coated, appeared. 'The boss is on his way. Till then I'm in charge.'

Her whole body contracted again. Sweat poured down her face.

'She's fully dilated. Gas and air please sister, and get her into the labour room.'

As the knives cut into her tummy again a rubbery mask was put over her face. She floated away.

'A boy, my dear.' A bundle, warm, soft, alive, was nestled between her breasts.

Mewing.

The midwife peered round the door. 'Wants his drink. We'll get you two sorted out.'

Propped against the pillows feeling the warmth of the sun shining through the open window onto her bed, she let her fingers run over the baby's face. The eyes, blue and clear, opened.

'Hello, you… ' She gazed at him. 'What would you like to be called?' The baby nuzzled against her chest. 'That's right, food first. What fun we're going to have.'

Her entire world was here. All seven pounds of it.

She dozed off. Was woken by the arrival of Liz, who dropped a vast bunch of roses and her handbag, always the size of a small suitcase, on the bed.

'Darling, well done. Was it awfully horrid? Painful?'

Painful?

'Not really. So soon over that I don't remember.'

Liz was hovering over the cot. 'Isn't he just divine? May I kiss him?'

Which was noble of undomesticated Liz.

'Such a lucky baby. What's his name?'

'Guzzler, at the moment, but I'll find something better. When Iain writes we'll think about proper names.'

Liz was most uncharacteristically silent. Then she said, 'I'm so happy for you. After all these years, and everything. I prayed for you, prayed the baby would be well.'

She squeezed Liz's hand. 'That's sweet.'

Very sweet – not so superficial Liz.

'Could you get a few days off, come home with me and my friend here? Help me to manage the train journey home with this chap. Be company for us for our first days at home. Tell me how to redecorate. I want Iain to find the house, everything, looking smart.'

'I'd adore to.' Liz's face lit up. 'You're tired, I'm going now.' She said goodnight and pulled the door closed behind her.

The baby nuzzled at Kitty's nightie. 'All right, little man.' She put him to her breast where he sucked gently, a bit half-heartedly.

'Come on, let's settle us down.' She put the baby down onto the bed, and wincing a little, trying not to twist her sore tummy, slowly and carefully climbed out of bed. She picked him up and put him on the changing trolley to check his nappy. It seemed dry and clean, so she just pinned it back on. She wrapped the flannel blanket loosely around the tiny body and bent over the cot. 'Goodnight.'

She let her head drop onto her pillow and knew she would be fast asleep within seconds.

She awoke with a start. The night light from the corridor was casting shadows into the room. The cot. Her baby... Heaving herself up on one elbow, she looked into the cot, which someone, the night nurse no doubt, had pushed right up against her bed. In the soft light she saw one perfect, minute set of fingers had found their way outside the bedding. The fingers moved, and then the entire nine inches of small person began to shift around. The mouth opened and even in the half-light she could see the face turning red as her little boy began to voice his demand for food. Penetratingly and surprisingly loudly. She lifted him onto her chest.

She could feel the suction of his lips. 'Strong chap, aren't you, Buster?'

Buster. Well, why not? But what would Iain like? After they'd danced on the lawn, before she'd lost the baby, Iain had suggested Harry if the baby were a boy – Uncle Harry would like that, and she'd added Edward, saying Ted sounds nice, cuddly but strong.

'Buster, I think you'll have to put up with Harry Edward.' The baby was dozing off, the eyelashes closed together. She traced her fingers round the face.

The first thing she'd done after the nurses had tidied her up, got her and the baby settled, had been to telegraph Iain. She had no idea where he might be, what he might be doing. Safe behind the front line, and not being shot at? Sitting in some army vehicle, ordering equipment? Or on the front line while the Nazi shells landed all around him blasting them all to perdition?

Shut up. Don't think about it.

She kissed each of the eyelids. 'Before, I couldn't understand anyone naming a child Hope. I can now. Back to sleep, my lad.'

It was not until the day before she was due to be discharged that one of the nurses handed her the telegram from Iain.

Smiling the girl said, 'These days it's nice to be handing out happy telegrams.'

The stencilled letters read '*Well done, will write*'. Okay, it was a telegram. But it was brief to the point of... No love, not even a couple of kisses. Wherever was he? Injured, not wanting to tell her? Too badly shot up by German guns to find the right words?

She folded the flimsy sheet up, put it in her purse. Bent down, touched the tiny sleeping mite. Waited for her touch to wake him. Held the stirring child close, comforting herself as much as the baby.

Liz got a week off work. Her boss, charming and thoughtful, had given her yards of curtain material, old stock he called it. They got a cab from the hospital, and a porter at Liverpool Street Station. They seemed to have a great deal of baggage, what with Buster's things, and their own two cases as well as the material and Liz's sewing equipment. But they managed, and Nancy was waiting on the platform at Woodbridge.

Clumps of primroses lined the banks of the moat though the oaks stood bare-branched against the sky. Little Meg was waiting, came out to help them all from Nancy's car.

When they were all settled in and Buster was fed and tucked, tiny, into the cot that looked huge around him, Kitty changed into comfy, country clothes and took Tigger to walk around the farm. She walked the perimeter of the fields, inhaled the countryside, warm, and fresh. Clean after the heavy air in London.

Every morning Kitty put Buster in his pram and pushed him across to the pigsties so she could work and keep an eye on him. Her arms ached when she finished mucking out. She upturned the buckets, tidied the tools away. Stretched, relishing the physical exertion of farming denied for the past few months. Liz had insisted she should be supper-cook for the week, and started on making the curtains.

In the evenings, they sat down to eat at a prettily laid dining table.

'I didn't realise how much more food, variety I suppose, there was out in the country,' Liz said. 'Such a joy to cook with proper onions.'

'Stuffed onions. Little Meg and I never had time for that sort of cooking! We were lucky out here, I suppose. A good deal of swopping went on. It was sugar, flour and then silly little things like baking powder that we struggled with mostly.'

They washed up, sat down to listen to the news.

'It can't go on for much longer, the Allies are over the Rhine, thundering towards Berlin.'

After Little Meg went up to bed, Kitty made up the fire, and poured a finger of brandy for them both.

'What's happened to Emma?' Liz asked.

'I wish I knew. Nothing, not even a card, since the war began.'

'How ghastly, living under German occupation,' Liz said, and then added, 'Or like Jo, worrying, hoping and then half a dozen words finishing everything.'

'Unthinkable – even if only half of the rumours of rape and pillage after France fell are true. Why didn't the German people stop Hitler before the war? The poor Jews. And the Poles. But us too – Iain's school friend, Matthew, was killed at Arnhem – I don't think Iain will know yet – I'll have to tell him. Simon, Alistair, Matthew – all because of vile Nazism.'

Liz concentrated on her glass. 'It's going to be like last time, after the war, isn't it? Not enough men to go round. I shall never find someone now.'

'Don't say that. You might. Things will be different, not the same social limits.'

'I don't mind too much. I love the new job – next week I'm taking swathes of French curtain swatches up to Chatsworth. I can share other people's children, be an aunt. Will you let me be godmother to Buster?'

The spring days lengthened towards summer. Kitty took to spending the afternoon in the sun with Buster next to her in his pram, Tigger stretched out beside it. Buster was an easy baby, a self-contained little person. He woke when it was time for food, gurgled happily for a while and then dropped off to sleep.

The farm was running well, and Frank was managing the everyday maintenance jobs that had built up.

Life was almost perfect. Almost, because it was three weeks since the monosyllabic telegram and still there was no letter. Where was Iain? Wounded? Kept it secret when he sent the telegram? Was he…? Best not to think about it. Okay, don't then.

Buff, BFPO, Iain's handwriting. She seized the envelope from Postie, hardly said thank you. Slit it open with the bread knife.

'Well done. I hope it will not be long before I see you and the baby. There is a lot of fighting here. The places we have advanced through are destroyed. Iain.'

The longed-for letter. So formal, no love, nothing.

Did someone else write it for him? No – his writing. Something is wrong. Has he cracked up?

Damn. Don't read too much into it. A few words written as the Luftwaffe shoot at him – a hell-hole of cordite and carnage.

Dear God, please let him come back. She put the letter in her pocket, kept it there as a sort of talisman for his safe return.

But then one day she washed the trousers, forgetting it, and a lump of papier mâché fell out as she hung them on the line.

Little Meg was waiting to greet her as she drove back across the bridge from the swill run to Framlingham. 'A big parcel's come for you. From Harrods.'

Who would send something from there? She went upstairs to open the parcel.

She undid the string on the expensive packaging, lifted off the lid. Opened the miniature envelope inside. '*With love from Iain.*'

Pale blue satin! Underwear? She lifted up the slippery material and the tissue sheets fell to the floor.

A nightdress.

It was a handsome present, so why wasn't she thrilled? Why this sense of let-down?

And the answer came, unbidden, spoken aloud. 'Because I have nighties already, which you know I don't wear, and I wanted a proper letter.' She fingered the sleekly smooth fabric. You, my girl, are an ungrateful, spoilt child. This must have been sent, organised, weeks ago. A lovely present any other woman would die for, from a man who had to use initiative to send it when he's halfway across a battle-strewn Europe. Who may never come back, already killed by a Hun's bayonet, so shut up.

And then she cried because this was not how she had expected life to be.

She put on the nightdress that night, slept in it. In the morning she stayed on in bed to write a newsy letter, thanking him for the glorious present, enclosing another snapshot of Buster (not very different from the first one she'd sent), wrote how Frank's one-armed help on the farm was making such a difference, how they all longed to have him back.

CHAPTER 30

MAY 1945

IT WAS OVER, officially.

She stood beside Little Meg to listen as Churchill's familiar jowly tones broadcast the news. 'The German war is at an end. Long live the cause of freedom.'

Despite the steady May drizzle she insisted they went outside. She stood on the lawn with Little Meg gently rocking Buster in his pram as the church bells sang out across the flat landscape.

She felt no sense of excitement, nor even relief, which might come if the war in the Far East ever ended. Just now a sort of emptiness. 'Well, that's that. Back to normal for us here.'

'Being here is normal for me. The pigs, the fields, living with you. And Buster. My old home's flattened along with the rest of the East End.'

'Dear Little Meg. This is your home, until you want to leave.' She put her arm round the bird-like shoulders. 'You're right, of course. Things won't be normal, not normal as they were. Those bloody Germans have seen to that. Come on now, no tears. Things will get better: more food, more clothes, more jobs, everyone home, safe. Let's push Buster into the village, see what's happening there.'

. . .

Six weeks after that May morning an envelope came – Iain's writing. She ran upstairs with it, sat on the bed.

'*I expect to be demobbed shortly. The country here is flattened. I feel sorry for the ordinary people.*' Ordinary people? Sorry for the Germans? '*The fighting was very hard. The CO is recommending me for a gallantry award. Don't bother to reply to this – there is no knowing where I will be. I will let you know when I will be back. With love, Iain.*'

Another monosyllabic letter. But then, they had never written to each other – and now she thought about it, Iain hadn't kept in touch by letter with friends like Simon or Matthew, nor even his mother. He always telephoned.

Nothing to be done then, except wait. Keep things going, ready for him to come back.

She smoothed at her skirt, eased the belt round to centre it. Iain used to like this duck-egg-green linen shirt-waister dress. To greet him she'd spruced it up with a new red belt and red sandals. She had considered taking Buster to the station but decided against the idea on the basis that a baby cosy in his cot would be less of a culture shock than a bundle, woken and possibly fractious, vying with him for his wife's attention.

She left Tigger sat in the passenger seat, scratching at the red, white and blue bow round her neck.

The signal at the end of the platform clanked. Three blasts on the whistle as the engine driver brought the train to a halt.

Khaki figures poured from the carriages.

The shoes and Sam Brown gleamed with polish, the uniform was crisply ironed. Every inch the officer.

'Hello Kitty. Where's the car?'

'Round on the road I'm afraid, so many people here meeting you all off that train. I left Tigger in charge. Buster's waiting at home with Little Meg.'

They rounded the corner into the road. The dog turned. Its ears pointed upwards. Then a muscular white bombshell leapt out of the car, hurling itself at Iain.

'Gently, dog! I see you dressed up for my return.' He knelt on the pavement, tried to cuddle the animal, but the dog, ecstatically excited, ran round and round them both, barking.

'Come on, Tigs, in the back. You drive, Iain.'

'It'll make a change from the jeeps.'

He swung his legs under the steering wheel and swore loudly, stringing several, not normally related, expletives together. She had forgotten to adjust the driver's seat.

'Sorry.'

'I'd rather you didn't castrate me.'

Pulling onto the road, he crashed the gears and swore again.

'This car feels effete.'

The car roared onwards, pretty much in the middle of the road. She made an effort to keep her eyes from looking at the quivering needle on the speedometer and suppressed spectres of tractors, wagons of hay, or a horse and cart pottering along the narrow road. Best to make impersonal conversation.

'Things are getting easier here, supplies and stuff. I don't like the sound of the Labour government's plans. Poor Churchill, whatever got into people?'

'It was the Forces' votes. You could tell from what the men were saying, and even some in the officers' mess. Desperate not to go back to the thirties.'

He drove, smoothly now, up the lane from Saxted Green and turned right into the farm. He pulled up, alongside the cart shed.

'It'll be good to be home. Take a bit of getting used to, though.'

He put an arm round her shoulders. 'Give me my welcome home kiss and then introduce me to the little person.'

Buster lay blissfully asleep and looking angelic with his newly developed wispy curls blond against the white of the pram sheet.

'You can pick him up, or I will.'

'No, don't disturb it. Let's go round the outside. I want to smell English soil.'

He led the way, heading towards the farrowing units.

He moved on, inspecting each unit, finishing at Bosun's sty. The old boar, lying asleep on the straw, flicked an ear and opened an eye. He lifted his head, studying the two of them as they leant over the door.

In an instant the half-ton was onto its feet and flinging itself against the door, using its tusks to bang against the wood.

'You're pleased to see me!' Iain leaned over, rubbing between the pig's ears. 'I'm going to walk the fields.'

'Take Tigs. I'll be in the house with Buster. Little Meg will do the feeds, bed this lot down for the night.'

The drawing room fire caught quickly as she stoked it up. It wasn't cold outside, just autumnally grey. Thank God, not a sulking fire, which would not do at all. Buster stirred, making the pram, well sprung, quiver on its bicycle-sized wheels. He yawned, a huge and adult opening of the mouth. She tickled him under the chin and lifted him up, pre-empting wails of hunger, and carried him into the kitchen, where she settled into the dog-chair and undid the top three buttons on her blouse. He suckled, first one side, changed to the other, and then back again to the first. Buster's enthusiasm waned, his jaws slackened and the eyelids slipped down. She shifted him up onto her shoulder and put her blouse back together.

Tigger nosed open the back door. Iain followed the dog in and stopped short in the doorway.

'Let me introduce you to each other.' She moved the baby around in her arms so he was facing Iain.

'Hello, Buster. I'm your father.' He reached out to touch the baby, put his hand on the tiny body and looked taken aback as his finger was grasped in the child's fist.

She laid a cot blanket on the rug in front of the drawing room fire. The baby's hands pushed at the rough tweed of Iain's jacket. The small face turned upwards to study this new person in the house.

'Weighing me up, is he?' Iain said. 'Can I put him down on this thing?'

She left them together, the baby chuckling with delight when Iain tickled his tummy, and went back into the kitchen to cook the supper.

The hall door latched open. Iain stood in the doorway, Buster held firmly, rigidly, in his arms.

'He's real. More than I expected. Shall I put him up to bed?'

'Let's do it together. I'll need to change him before we sit down to eat.' She smiled at the expression on his face. 'Not into a dinner jacket – a clean nappy.'

After supper, he poured a brandy, kicked the logs into flames and settled into his chair.

'Liz made the curtains in here.'

'You said. It looks nice. The whole place, inside and out, is in good shape. You've managed well.'

His face had relaxed slightly. Looked less taut.

'I enjoyed it. Mostly it was easy. Safe, except the once.' Everyone here knew she'd been caught in the rocket attack. 'Not like you – days on end of fighting. What about your bravery award, what happened?'

He stood up, turned his back on her, staring into the flames in the fireplace. 'I don't want to talk about it. Not anything about it. It's over. I have to forget it.' He turned the dial on the wireless. 'We should hear the nine o'clock news.'

Routine returned, though she needed to do more in the house, less time to herself, no more slumbering in the quiet of the afternoon. She said as much to Nancy, who commiserated, saying it was only after Philip came home that she'd realised just how much mess one man could make. 'It's the bathroom, Kitty, I think he baths on the floor.'

Generally, Iain was quiet, not wanting to go out. Not the same old gregarious Iain. She blessed the necessity of work that the farm generated.

He worked outside from early morning until dusk. He had always been organised, efficiently tidy, but there was a new sharpness to his actions, no more leaning on the broom, chatting. Once in a while she glimpsed him standing still, staring out over the fields, Tigger loyally at his side.

His grasp on the reality of no longer being in the army, part of a victorious military machine, was erratic. One moment he seemed relaxed, aware that stuff was in short supply, that people were free to make choices, to talk, but the next he exploded with impatience, exhibiting utter intolerance of the constraints of civilian life. Each week he set off to market seemingly not minding, not even noticing, that she did not go, and arrived home mid-afternoon having had a snack lunch in the pub. At these times, he was chatty, almost the old Iain, which she put down to the change of scene and the male company. One week he came back with a duck and drake, and a hutch, which he erected on the bank of the moat. The next week he returned with two wooden beehives.

Reluctantly he agreed to accept Nancy's pressing invitation to supper. After they had eaten, while Philip and Iain sat smoking in the drawing room, Kitty helped Nancy tidy up. 'He seems so distant. I don't feel it's the man I married inside him. When he got back with the beehives I made a silly joke, something about will the bees know it is for them, and he looked daggers at me. In the old days, he'd have laughed. Was it as difficult between you and Philip?'

'I don't think so. It wasn't easy and Philip got very tired, slept during the day, and for hours at night. We went to bed at nine o'clock for ages. Well, he did. After a while I gave up, I just couldn't sleep, so I left him to it. But Philip had been a POW for years.'

'Iain says nothing about what he did, not even about other people, the ones he was fighting alongside. I haven't probed. Do you think I should?'

'Probably not. He looks very well, you know. I'll ask Philip what he thinks.'

Nancy came back with the not altogether reassuring news that Philip, too, found it strange that Iain didn't open up much. Give him time, Nancy said.

How much time does he need? She grated the carrot, scraping it into the mixing bowl. Apple, spices, brandy. A Christmassy smell. She moved the heavy mixture around in the bowl, cutting through it with the big metal spoon, lifting up, folding it back into itself. She spooned it all into the white bowl, scrubbed clean from the last steak and kidney, and knotted a belt of string around the greaseproof paper lid. Put the old boiling pan on the range.

They'd gone to The Queen's Head for a strangely muted celebration the night after the Japanese finally surrendered. So much horror, too many lost for it to be a party.

The first Christmas for six years with no war. A proper family one. Buster's first, Iain here. And Little Meg. Jo, dear Jo, had brought over a box of presents for Buster. 'Not really presents, Kitty, just toys my crew have outgrown. They did all the wrapping. The paper is pretty dreadful, but it's all I could find.' Kitty had ordered a goose from Frank who was fattening a dozen birds.

Now she glanced up at the clock. Any moment Buster would wake, want to crawl around the floor, making his rompers grubby yet again. Iain was good with the boy. Not snappy with him. Nor with Little Meg and never with Tigger. Only snappy with her.

She sat down. In Barney's old chair.

What was wrong? Even bed was different – mechanical, not unsatisfying, but what? Soulless. He wasn't talking afterwards. That was the difference.

On Christmas Eve Iain drove them down to the pub, leaving Buster tight asleep in his cot with Little Meg in charge. She perched on the bar stool in their old corner as he went to the bar to set up their round of drinks. He was facing away from her, talking to Rob behind the bar. Rob laughed at some shared joke as he placed Iain's pewter mug, the froth visible above its rim, on the counter.

Normality, like a warm blanket of security, enveloped her.

At a quarter to midnight, they walked over the village green, frozen crisp under their feet, to the candlelit service. Going home, cosy in the car, the headlights picked up the telegraph wires, frosted with hoar.

'Christmas weather.' She reached across to put her hand over his resting on the gear lever. 'It's wonderful to have you home, here, for a proper family Christmas.'

Inside, the house was silent, just the hall light left on. Tigger, deeply asleep, opened her eyes, twitched the end of her tail in greeting, and went back to sleep.

'Nightcap, Kitty?'

She put a log on the fire, pumped the bellows, watched patterns in the flames. Rearranged the presents around the tree.

'Happy Christmas.' She took a deep breath, crossed the fingers on her left hand, the one without the glass. 'I'm sorry if Buster takes up too much of my time. Coming home, after all the horrors, must be difficult. And then to find another little person in the house.'

She gave a little laugh.

His head snapped up, facing her. She couldn't read the emotion on his face.

'The boy's no trouble. Things here run very well, you manage it all perfectly. Always have done.'

'But something's wrong. I know it is.'

'Not wrong. Different.'

She put her glass on the mantelpiece and moved across to stand close by him.

'I'm sorry. I suppose I wanted, expected, things to be like they were. Once. Years ago. Before… well, before the war. They won't be, can't be.'

'No.' But he put his arm around her. 'Never mind. Happy Christmas.'

Disturbed by the postman, the heron heaved off the moat, the broad wings beating in deep movements to lift him to safety.

'It's always about February time when we see him. I suppose the fish are too deep in the river for him to catch so he comes here.'

The great bird flapped away, flying low over the fields. 'The moat's dreadfully silted up. I'll get the post.'

Little Meg, sitting at the kitchen table, was reading the daily paper aloud to Buster, who looked blissfully unaware of the problems facing England in the aftermath of war.

'I think he enjoys hearing me talk. You don't mind?'

Kitty grinned. 'He'd probably make more sense of it than we can. What a muddle it all is. In a strange way we knew where we were back then.'

She glanced at the envelopes as she walked back into the office, sorting the ones addressed to Iain. Brown, all bills surely, just one on more substantial brown paper with On His Majesty's Service printed instead of a stamp, and another handwritten white envelope.

'Bills, I'm afraid. Here's one from the army, probably something to do with your demob.'

Iain reached for the paper knife, slit the envelope open. His eyes skimmed over the letter, his fingers starting to drum on the desk.

'What is it? What's happened?'

'Nothing has happened. They've given me a DSO. For helping to kill Germans. Read it yourself, I'm going to douse the pigs.'

The door banged behind him. She looked at the scrappy official letter: the impersonal typewritten words at odds with the significance of the words *awarded for extreme bravery*.

More of the shutting everyone out?

Just moody and distant. Again.

She sorted through the rest of the envelopes on the desk. Tucked in amongst them was a pale blue one. It was oddly addressed – not to Mrs Chester, not even Kitty Chester, but just Kitty.

Whoever? She squinted at the postmark, which was fudged, quite indecipherable. The writing was unfamiliar, a shaky script. The postage stamp had the king's head, certainly, but the colour and pattern were odd.

'Oh, good God.'

From Guernsey, from someone in Guernsey who wasn't Emma. She tore at the envelope and pulled out two sheets of writing paper, tightly covered with spidery words.

I am so sorry I don't know your married name. Sorry not to have written before. I hoped for so long that she would reappear, come back and that the last years were just a bad dream. Then, after they told me, I was in pieces. I couldn't bear to think. I was too selfish to write to you. Last week I found the courage to sort through her old room. The last time I saw her she brought a big cardboard box round. Just a few bits and pieces. 'Mummy,' she said, 'for you to keep safe.' I opened the box. Amongst the stuff was a bundle of cards from you – she'd scribbled on top of them, 'Please tell Kitty'.

She never told me a thing, of course. Just that she and Jean-Pierre were going away. They don't know how Jean-Pierre died or when. They told me she was brave, didn't break down despite the torture. That she knew a lot which was why the Gestapo kept her alive for so long. I asked what had happened but I don't think they told me everything.

The tears stung the back of her eyes. Blurred the letters. Dripped onto the page so the ink ran into tears of its own.

Bouncy. Happy.

Making love in French.

Brave. She spoke fluent French, she had no children to keep safe and then there had been that sudden, so un-Emma-like, silence and the disappearance.

Fingering the letter, Kitty folded it back into the envelope, propped it on the desk. One more of our friends gone, wiped away by the Nazis. Should she ring Liz, or write perhaps? Ask Iain.

Absently, automatically, she shuffled up the brown envelopes into a neat heap.

Where had Iain gone?

Outside was unusually quiet. No squealing from the pigs. Not a sound from the yard – not even the sound of the broom bristles scratching away at the concrete.

Two great thudding crashes, the sound of wood splintering.

Iain's shout came from the cart shed. 'Bloody war! Sodding silly rules.'

For a second she stood still.

Thud, thud. She raced towards the shed, her feet slipping under her on the clay.

She stopped in the open doorway, gasping for breath.

He was slouched on the brick floor, with his head in his hands.

'Iain, what in God's name…?'

The axe stuck out of a heap of the shattered wood. What wood? Clean wood. The beehives. The shattered remains of the new beehives.

Fear, anger and foreboding made her reckless.

'What the hell's the matter? Look at me! You should be proud.'

The white of an envelope stood out against the dirt on the floor.

'And what's this about?' She reached down for it.

'Don't touch! That's private.' He snatched it up.

'Private! Well, it's bloody well not staying private. You've shut me out, not just me either, all of us ever since you got back.'

He looked up at her, his face streaked with tears.

Her tummy twisted. 'Christ almighty, man! Everyone knows it was hell for you – all of you. You're not the only one. You weren't specially picked on by fate. Thousands of other men went through the same. I don't want you to relive the thing, just try to treat the rest of us as normal human beings. We've not had it exactly easy either. I just found out the Gestapo tortured Emma. Killed her.'

He didn't react and his inert passivity drove her on.

'Stop snivelling in the corner! You're not a coward!'

'No, Kitty. Just a traitor.'

She steadied herself on the stack of straw bales.

The un-mended tap dripped into the puddle outside.

'What?'

He levered himself up, pulled down a bale and sat on it.

She stood over him, pity and anger struggling inside until pity got the upper hand.

'Your CO recommended you for this. Did you go too far, kill the wrong people?' She knelt on the straw beside him. 'Normal mores go out of the window in war. We've all done things unthinkable before. Tell me about it. It helps to talk.'

It struck her that she had been here before, all that time ago after Shingle Street. But he didn't look broken – distraught and distant, but not broken.

'Iain, we can't live the rest of our lives like this. Tell me.'

'You won't like this.'

'Go on, better we both know.'

'It was mayhem and carnage as we fought forward to cross the Rhine. Everywhere was deserted, mostly burned or bombed to the ground. If we came across a starving dog or some cadaverous farm animal we shot it, kinder that way. On the edge of what had been a village a woman was scraping away at one of the piles of rubble, on her knees, using her bare hands to shift the debris. The sergeant took aim, in German he told her to put her hands up. She replied in English that her father was under the rubble. We marched on, left her. When we halted a few miles on, I broke away, went back.'

It wasn't cold but her shaking body turned rigid. 'Ruddy stupid orders – no consorting with the enemy. Monty's dictat, easy for a general, safe in his HQ. That's what camp followers were for – no need to consort with the enemy in Wellington's army. We found her father, what remained of him. They had a hunting lodge in the woods nearby. We made a shallow grave and buried him. Later we made love in the lodge. In May, after the surrender, I went back, spent time with her. She says I am going to be a father. She is having my baby. We needed each other. She's not well. She needs me now.'

Be a father? Have his baby? A German woman is having Iain's baby. He fucked with a Hun – more than once – a woman whose husband may have killed Simon, shot up Matthew, been friends with the Gestapo who tortured Emma.

Automaton-like she stepped out of the cart shed. Forced herself to walk normally back to the house, past Buster, averting her eyes from Little Meg and got to the bathroom as the vomit rose up her throat.

She went to sit on the edge of the bed. There was ice instead of blood flowing through her veins and she was shaking uncontrollably, so much so that the bed was rattling on the floorboards.

The stairs outside creaked.

'I came to see if you were all right.'

'All right? To see if I am all right?'

She clenched her teeth together, then bit at her lip until she tasted the blood.

'I was wrong, wasn't I? You are a bloody traitor. A traitor to all of us. We've stayed here and worked at keeping your farm, Iain's Acre, safe for five years while those bloody Huns did their best to destroy it and everyone else here.'

'She knew I wanted a child.'

She knew I wanted a child. I wanted a child. You didn't give me a child. He touched her like he touches me. I touched Christo. Once. Just once. And not a disloyal word about Iain spoken between us. He talked about us, told her I lost his babies, couldn't give him babies.

All she had had was an afternoon, half an afternoon with Christo – almost one of the family. Alone, needing her too. Neither of them had considered, even dreamed of, breaking up her marriage,

'You bloody bastard!' The ice was melting and turning to a burning liquid. 'Don't demean yourself by lying, Iain. Don't try to justify your rutting, pretending high morals. You know that I, we, you and I, always wanted babies.'

'She needed me.'

'And I don't? What about Buster?'

'You've managed very well without me. It's not the same between us.'

'I wonder why?' Her shock was fading. Defensive anger was kicking in as she recognised the threat to Buster's security and everything she had hoped for and worked towards. 'Because you chose to go effing around with a Nazi wench.'

A Nazi. The Enemy. Treason. He'd be court-martialled. Yes, labelled a traitor.

'You didn't have the decency to fuck a few WAAFs or some sex-starved FANNY.'

He didn't move, just stood there with his arms hanging by his sides.

'You bastard traitor.' She picked up Pa's Worcester vase from the bedside table and aimed it directly at his head.

He ducked. The porcelain shattered. He turned and left without a word.

One letter, a bit of a morning, and all the certainties of her world were gone. It wasn't cold outside but she was shaking like a leaf. Queasy too. She got a thick woollen cardigan from the drawer, pulled it right around her.

Buster started to cry. Hungry for his lunch.

Lunch?

Oh, God, up it came again. In the bathroom, she pulled the plug, rinsed out her mouth from the tap, went back down to the kitchen.

The door from the hallway, which she had closed firmly, opened. Iain came across towards her carrying an old biscuit tin.

She pushed the pan to one side and turned to face him. Her raw anger returned. Fierce physical revulsion at the sight of him pulsed through her.

'I'm sorry this has happened, Kitty, please believe me.' He held out the tin. 'I collected the pieces of your vase.'

'Sorry! You should be ashamed.' She held out her hand to take the tin from him. 'You should have stayed away! Never come back. Better if you'd been killed.' She hadn't meant to say that but now the words were out she fed off her own anger. 'So bloody brave that you want to run back to your German whore!'

She threw the tin and the pieces of the vase back onto the floor.

'I won't desert her, won't be a Judas, Kitty.'

He knelt down on the floor, began to pick up the scattered remains of the vase.

'Judas, Judas! What the hell do you think Alistair or Jo would call you? Or Philip?' A head of blonde curls, a once smiling face battered and streaked with blood. 'And Emma! Do you know what your bitch's friends did to Emma?'

She saw him register the name. 'And what about Matthew and Simon? Your Simon is dead. Killed by a German.'

A spasm crossed his face.

Buster wailed.

'Go to your strumpet, become a Hun. I don't care, I won't be here, waiting for you to come back. This time it's me who is going away!'

She picked up the saucepan, didn't bother with a bowl, pushed past him, lifted Buster from the pram. The little face was puckered, red with angry tears.

'My little man!' Upstairs in his room he calmed in her arms as she used her hankie to wipe his face. 'Not your fault, none of this. We'll be all right. I won't let you suffer. How could he do it?'

Hungry, Buster started to cry again, shushed as she put the spoon to his lips. 'We'll go away, just the two of us. I'll keep you safe.'

Keep this bundle of innocent warmth safe. Safe from the shame of treachery. Get away quickly. Before she met Nancy, before Jo telephoned, before Winnie found out, told Frank, before anyone found out that Iain was a collaborator, told the army. Or the police.

London. Easy to fade into the background there, be anonymous. Find a job as a mother's help, a home for her and Buster.

She went to telephone Liz. She wasn't crying but her voice must have been cracking up because Liz went very quiet.

'I can't explain now.' She begged sanctuary for Buster and herself. 'Tomorrow. Only for a day or two until I find a place for us.'

She dragged down the biggest suitcase, put in all of Buster's things, filled it up with some of her clothes, took down *The Windmill* and wrapped it in two winter skirts, and added her jewellery.

She spent the night, sleepless, on the floor beside Buster's cot.

In the morning, she telephoned for a taxi. Iain was out in the piggeries, she could hear that. She had no idea where, or whether, he had slept.

The taxi horn sounded.

Holding Buster tight to her chest, she said goodbye to the house. Goodbye to the drawing room, its hearth, the beams.

Little Meg, stoic and silent, stood by the range in the kitchen.

'Goodbye, Little Meg. Thank you for your friendship and help.'

The girl began to cry, her own security thrown out of the window. In her distress she reverted and became monosyllabic, repeating, 'Oh, ma'am! Oh, ma'am!'

The taxi tooted again. Kitty tightened her hold on Buster.

CHAPTER 31

MARCH 1947

THE LIVING ROOM of the flat, always bereft of style, looked frankly squalid in the presence of Liz, smartly dressed and make-up still perfect at the end of a day helping titled ladies redecorate their homes.

'Thanks for coming round, Liz, and for the sherry.'

She should have moved the nappies, not left them drying in front of the gas fire. She twisted the top out of the bottle and poured liquor into the glasses. 'I'm sorry about the state of this place. Little Tess seems to soil many more nappies than Buster ever did.'

'I don't suppose you noticed them so much when they hung on the line to blow dry in the fresh air,' Liz said and added, 'You look done in.'

'Poor little Tess never settles. You remember how Buster at that age was solidly content all the time. She hardly slept at all last night. And that woke Buster. The room gets icy cold as soon as the gas fire is off.'

Liz reached for the bottle. 'Have some more, Kitty. I want to talk to you. Like a Dutch uncle.' Liz reached out. The feel of a soft, cared-for hand. 'You can't go on like this, whatever happened between you and Iain. For months now, you've hidden yourself away. It is wrong for the children. In any case Iain has a right to know about Tess, that he has another child.'

Not go on like this… So much for her plan to make a safe life for Buster. The sickness hadn't stopped when they got to London. Expecting again. Iain's baby. She hadn't told Liz, had not tried to find a live-in job, settled for this flat.

Now, on her empty stomach, the sherry had gone straight to her head. Iain has a right to know? Another child?

'Don't meddle, Liz. You don't understand.'

There was a sharp silence before Liz replied. 'Because you've shut me out. Not just me. All your friends are worried about you.'

Friends? Which friends?

She shrivelled down into the chair.

Liz took an audibly deep breath. 'I've broken your confidence. Last week I rang Jo. I promise I didn't say where you are. And Nancy last night. They both send their love. Want to hear from you. They don't understand, Kitty. They are hurt by your silence and absolutely horrified, both of them, to hear about Tess. That you were alone all through the pregnancy, trying to care for a toddler and a baby during this ghastly winter.' Liz spoke gently, the theatrical cadences quietened. 'They both said the same thing. That it isn't like you, not the you they knew, to be selfish like this.'

Selfish? I'm not being selfish, I'm doing everything for the children. Iain's a traitor. He broke all the rules. He's fathered a Hun. They don't know that. They must not ever know that.

Liz kept on talking. 'I told Nancy you said Iain was having an affair. Nancy replied that it happens in war and that she was surprised you couldn't handle it, because you had a friend who had an affair while her husband was away and that you had understood how it happened.'

'That's different. Nancy was sleeping with… '

One of us. An ally. A man on our side. Oh, God, with poor Franklin. What does it matter if Liz knows now? What does any of it matter? Buster matters. Little Tess, too. But she's such hard work.

Liz's face, so firm-looking just before, looked uncertain now, downcast even. Poor Liz, always missing out on the men.

'Forget I said that. Maybe you're right, I'm getting selfish. How was Jo?'

'Don't be upset.' Liz rubbed at her perfectly polished

fingernails, studied them a moment. 'Jo's very well. A little embarrassed to tell me, I think.'

'Tell you what?'

'She… ' Liz gulped. 'She is living with Christopher. She's very happy. And they've got Tigger, too.'

Christo and Jo? Tigger with them. Christo safe, loved. Loving. Lucky Jo!

'Good for Jo. And Christo, after that other cow.' And all the rest. 'I'm glad they'll have each other. Thank you for being here, always when I've needed you. Ever since school.'

She put her arms around the ample shoulders. 'Sorry.'

Loyal Liz for whom things never worked out.

'Give Nancy my address if you want.'

After Liz left, she slid the bolt on the door, pushed the rolled-up blanket against it to keep the worst of the cold draughts out. For once both children were asleep, less cold now perhaps that the temperature outside had lifted. The ice had gone from the pavements leaving them dirty and wet.

She filled a hot-water bottle and crept into her bed. Looked at the newspaper pictures of the floods as the tons of snow melted. London might be cold, damp and dirty with smog threatening but she supposed it was relatively safe, and there was still food in the shops, limited and rationed but just about enough, and just about affordable. The new Family Allowance for Tess helped a little, and the extra money from poor Granny who had died not knowing that she had another grandchild.

She answered the telephone expecting it to be a wrong number – nobody rang except Liz who never phoned from work, always waited till the evening.

'Kitty, dear, Liz gave me your telephone number.'

Nancy! So soon. Liz must have rung her last night as soon as she got home.

'Please can we meet – just you and me – for lunch? Bring the children to Lyons' Corner House at Marble Arch.'

. . .

The catch on Buster's reins was stiff. As she struggled to snap it together her hands shook. Buster tried to wriggle away to pick up Heffalump, his faded cuddly, previously a maroon velvet curtain.

'We'll be horribly late to meet Nancy. Come here!'

Tess was restless in the pram. Perhaps the walk would send the tense little soul off to sleep.

Nancy was waiting on the pavement outside. She knelt down. 'Buster, how you've grown! Have you been looking after Mummy?' In reply, he waved Heffalump in the air.

Tess was mercifully quiet while they ate lunch, a scalding hot macaroni cheese. Nancy did the talking. 'Philip's well, pretty much back to how I remember before the war. It's taken a long time.'

The waitress cleared the plates, put cups of coffee, no doubt Camp, on the table.

'I'm not asking you to tell me what happened between you and Iain, but do remember that both of you had gone to hell and back, one way or another. Philip always thought what a good couple you were, ad idem, he said.'

The lawyer's mind! Had she and Iain been like that, as one? Heading in the same direction, enjoying the same things – the dancing, the trips to London, loving poor old Barney, choosing Tigger, wanting lots of children. If she hadn't encouraged him to join up none of the rest, his injuries, going away, finding that other woman, becoming a social pariah, none of that would have happened. She would have had Buster, and then Tess and maybe more babies.

She put sugar into her coffee. If... *If ifs and buts were pots and pans there'd be no work for tinkers' hands.* A silly little rhyme with a grain of truth – if only. The spoon spun circles in the liquid.

Nancy went on. 'We could see Iain was a different person. I knew things were edgy between you but I never dreamed you'd break up. I lost touch with Iain after you left that morning. A client of Philip's rented Five Oaks, took over the pigs, the whole thing as a going concern. Little Meg, too, she stayed on, is still there.'

The pigs. Grand old Bosun. Little Meg. Loyal, capable, staying with the pigs. Her home now, she had said, as they listened to the bells marking peace in Europe.

'I don't want to talk about it. I couldn't bear what Iain had become.'

'Don't judge too harshly. Remember me: things happen in a war.'

'It's too late, no going back. I'll work something out.'

'I'm not going to let you disappear again – we'll lunch next time I'm in London.'

They kissed goodbye.

She pushed the pram back towards the flat, along the grime-sodden pavement, tightening Buster's reins as a bus trundled past close up against the pavement edge.

What Nancy had said was pretty much the same as Liz. And it had been lovely to be with a friend, to laugh about the coffee, to eat in a restaurant, even Lyons'.

It was another overcast London day. Dank and cold. Because of Buster's chesty cough she had decided against their usual apology for a walk – along dirty fume-ridden streets, past craters where houses, homes, had once stood, and to the baker's where she bought half a loaf of bread and Buster chose one of the iced finger buns.

The gas fire was on, consuming shilling pieces at a fearsome rate, to dry the nappies. The windows had steamed up again. Both children were asleep, but it was too early for her to go to bed. She picked up her knitting, reworked wool from one of her old cardigans to make Buster a jumper.

The telephone rang.

'Nancy!'

'We want you to come and stay for a few days.'

It was one thing to have lunch, but to go and stay? Too much.

'Buster isn't well. I think I'm going down with it too.'

'I shall ring tomorrow, see how you all are.'

She picked up the knitting, but the wool caught on her fingers.

Away in the fresh East Anglian air, Nancy and Philip would be settling in for their companionable pre-dinner drink.

The flat looked sordid. Her hair clung, greasy as it had never been. Her hands rougher than when they lugged buckets.

The telephone rang again.

Philip!

'I was just talking to Nancy,' she said.

'I know. I'm not taking no for an answer. I shall drive up tomorrow and collect you. We'll be back here in time for the evening.'

'Philip, it's kind—'

He interrupted her. 'No, it's settled. I shall be there at midday. You had better be ready.'

The line went dead as he put the receiver down without waiting for her reply. She stood for a moment, hearing the click as the call disconnected and the dialling tone came on.

They, Liz, Nancy and now Philip, were managing her. Well-meaningly. They wouldn't criticise, judge, not like Ma whom she had mercifully managed not to see, kept at arm's length with letters. They were kind, broad-minded people, her own age.

Philip would come, be on time. She would have to go.

A few days in a warm bedroom, in a proper house. Meals, nice meals that she hadn't struggled to put together.

Buster started to cough, woke up, rubbing his eyes, hardly awake.

'Sip this.' The lemon and honey was cold now but it helped. 'Nancy, who we had lunch with, has asked us to stay in the country. We're going tomorrow morning. Back to sleep now.'

She slept lightly and was up early washing, tidying, feeding, changing. Energy and interest seeped back. When Buster and Tess were as organised as they would ever be she washed her hair, found decent nylons, put on a skirt, which hung loose round her now.

On the very dot of midday Philip arrived, helped her get the children and her stuff into the car.

'Some country air will do you all good. You've lost weight, Kitty. Nancy's been cooking most of the night – she said you needed feeding up.'

. . .

Nancy lifted Tess's Moses basket up the stairs. 'We're a houseful, I'm afraid. Don't hurry, make yourself comfy after you've sorted these two little mites out. Drinks in the drawing room.'

The bedroom, Nancy's best spare room, was warm, the curtains closed already, shutting out the last of the daylight. Tess settled at once, her little lids closing before the nappy-pin was clipped shut.

Kitty knelt on the floor and pulled Buster's night things from the case. She ran warm water into the basin.

'Quick lick and a promise tonight, young man.' She rubbed the flannel over his face and hands. She tucked him in on one side of the double bed, showed him her nightie on the pillow beside him.

'I'll be here when you wake up.' She kissed him. 'Now – Heffalump's turn.' She kissed the cuddly.

Using the mirror over the basin, she re-did her make-up.

Downstairs, she opened the door into the drawing room and looked across towards the sofas around the roaring log fire.

At the sight of him, the room spun away from her.

Philip was there in an instant, held out his arms, kissed her on both cheeks. 'You look exhausted. I'll get you a gin.'

She clutched at the back of the sofa, heard the door close behind Philip.

Iain!

'Don't blame them. I was sure you wouldn't come if you knew I was here.'

He was right. She would not have come.

Philip appeared with a huge gin. 'Nancy and I'll be in the kitchen.'

She let the sofa provide stability, resting her right arm on the back in an effort to disguise how much her hand was shaking. Gingerly she lowered her head towards the glass and lifted her arm so that she met the glass halfway. Like a horse at a trough, she sucked in the drink: very little tonic, it was almost neat gin.

He stood still, hands hanging by his side. The scar around his eye showing raw red against the pallor of the furrowed, drawn skin of his face.

Her heart pounded against her ribs.

'I think we should sit down.' He perched on the edge of an upright chair.

She remained standing, unbending, immobile. Until the lunch with Nancy she'd managed not to think about him and the farm after she'd run away. Run away? Well, yes, that was what she had done. Gone away. Because it was easier?

The sound of the splintering wood, the sight of the shattered beehives. The crumpled heap of him. A strong man, broken into bits.

She had taken her revenge after the scene that last day in the kitchen when she had stood above him and watched as, for the second time, he picked up the pieces of the vase.

God forgive me, it pleased me to see him grovelling around on the floor.

Iain moved, came towards her. 'It was only the other day that Nancy rang. Philip hadn't told her where I was because I'd sworn him to secrecy. Nancy told me about Tess. She said that she and Philip would be father confessors to us both. What did she mean, Kitty?'

Nancy doesn't know about Buster – that is, if there's anything to know.

'What Nancy meant isn't important. She said you left Five Oaks.'

'As soon as you'd gone. I didn't want you to go.'

'No, but you… '

He stopped her short. 'Listen to me. Please. I don't expect you to understand what happened with Inge. Nor that anyone else ever will – it has to be my secret. She was mature, a beautiful woman, who needed me. I never expected to get through the carnage of the Allied advance, or see you again. Then, well… it doesn't matter.'

She cut in. 'You mean it was nice?'

'Yes. It was. But I didn't expect it to follow me home. I thought you and I were going to be all right. I didn't know she was pregnant, although she talked about having a baby to please me.'

Iain coughed, cleared his throat, pulled out a handkerchief and blew his nose. His face was in shadow.

His words rolled around and grew in her mind: he enjoyed it because the woman was beautiful and mature; they had talked about things, about having children or actually, probably, about not having had children. Her mind, quite detached from emotion, sorted through the information.

This man had been her husband. In truth, pretty much all she had hoped for in a husband; not Nigel, her perfect soulmate, but a proper spouse nonetheless. Would they have found their level again if she hadn't found out?

He shifted in the chair. She glimpsed him as he had looked once in old Harry's drawing room, and coming back into the house that night after he'd done the feeds, and then she remembered the night after Shingle Street.

She said simply, 'Go on.'

'There's nothing left over there – no electricity, nothing. Don't imagine it's like London or Coventry. The whole country is wiped out. Hospitals are a mess. You had gone, left. She was alone, in that destroyed country. I had needed her as she needed me.' He took another gulp of the drink. 'I'm sorry Kitty, but the baby, her baby, came from our love. Lust if you like, but it became love. When I got back there, she wasn't well. She never recovered after having the child. I tried to make her flat warm and feed her properly.'

Beautiful. Needful. And needed, because she knew how much he must have needed the woman.

She didn't speak. Not because she was angry or trying to hurt him any more, but because she felt nothing – she was dead inside, all emotion exhausted.

In the silence he went on. 'I took her to hospital. She was very ill, the doctors said she wouldn't last through the night. I held her hand. Just before dawn she died.'

As he came closer, a warning current ran across to her.

He said, 'I promised to take care of our baby. I got false documents. Tess isn't the only baby visiting here, in this house.'

With her back towards him she asked, 'Where is this child? I want to see him.'

'Her.'

He led the way upstairs to the other spare room. In a child's bed, just like the one Nancy had set up for Tess, lay a flaxen-haired little mite, tucked up with a large pink cuddly, a sort of rabbit to tell by its ears.

A young life. Hadn't asked to be born. Unknowing of the muddle they had made of her world.

She avoided looking at Iain. Turned, left the room.

Walked back down the stairs.

She sat down on the sofa, drew a deep breath, pressed her lips together, and then said, 'I told Nancy something when I had the second miscarriage. I told her I had killed four of my children.'

He tensed and turned to stare.

'Nigel knew, forgave me. I got rid of his babies when the doctor said Nigel mustn't live with me and the babies. I didn't fall down the stairs, I bumped down, on my bottom, several times until I felt the bleeding start. After he died, I was eaten up with regret. Nigel was dead and by killing his babies I'd killed what should have been left of him. And I was ashamed. We never told anyone. The only way I coped was by pretending it hadn't happened, putting it right away. Old Dr Foster realised, of course, when I miscarried. That's how I killed our first two babies as well. I thought I'd never be able to have a baby. I told Nancy – that's what she meant.'

And two other people, men, but he doesn't need to know that.

'You should have told me. I would have understood.'

She rather doubted that he would have, then, at the time. 'I'm not so sure. We were young. Our sharp edges hadn't been knocked off by life.'

'By the war you mean. Christ, I need another gin.'

His hand was shaking, making him spill tonic onto the drinks tray. He handed back her glass, remained within arm's length of her.

'Look, Kitty. Can we start again – try to make some sense of this whole ruddy mess? Come back to share a home with me. Not to share my bed if you don't want but in the same house. We can go where no one knows us, won't ask questions. Will you be a mother to little Angela, and let Buster and Tess have their father around?'

He picked up some papers from the table.

'I sold Five Oaks. There is a farm for sale on the Sussex Weald, on one of your great hills of the South Country. Come to live with me there.' On a farm. In the fresh air of the country. Away from the flat lands. Make a home.

Compromise? Forgive? Mother his child. His daughters. And Buster.

EPILOGUE
CHRISTMAS EVE 1970

THE DOG, definitely deaf nowadays, had curled himself up in his basket, both eyes firmly closed.

A current of cold north wind blew across the back of her neck.

'My singing wife.' He lumbered through the door, pushed it closed with one foot and dropped several plastic shopping bags in a heap on the floor. In his other hand, he held a great armful of variegated holly and pillar-box-red tulips.

'Good God, Iain, you made me jump.' The strange mixture of emotions that had churned inside her all day finally erupted. Tears streamed down her face. 'Like that time Flossie got out – we'd had our first row and I was frightened you wouldn't come back.' But he had come back. Had always come back. The only one who had – apart from the children. 'I felt sad inside this afternoon in the empty house, thinking about the children. Silly me, they're all happy, healthy, enjoying their own lives.'

'Come on, Kitty.' His arm was firm around her shoulders as he shepherded her to the chair. He fished a handkerchief from his pocket.

She took it, blew her nose. 'Thank you for coming back.' After Flossie's escape, after Shingle Street, after he'd been blown up by the grenade, even after Germany. He had come back. Was here now. 'And for having me back after I went away.'

'Well, it was your turn.' He still held the bunch of tulips. 'Will these go in your vase, the mended one?'

Pa's vase. The one Iain had rescued, kept the broken pieces safe and painstakingly stuck them back together. She'd found it carefully placed on the table beside her bed in the spare room when she'd moved back with Buster and little Tess. Shamed, she had carried it into the other bedroom, the one where he slept. An olive branch. He hadn't been asleep. Had said, 'I mended it.' And tears had trickled out of his eyes when she replied, 'I think both it and I belong in this bedroom.'

Now, when she didn't reply, he glanced across at her, stood the flowers in the sink and said, 'Time for a gin, Kitty. As strong as the ones Philip poured us both so long ago.'

'I was just thinking about that evening – it was the first time the three children slept under the same roof!'

He pulled at the frosted-up front to the little freezer shelf in the fridge and fished out ice-cubes for their drinks, one for her, two for him.

She eased herself up from the chair and fingered the silky petals of the tulips. 'There's an awful lot here – more than two dozen.'

'One for each of our Christmases – thirty-four exactly, the florist counted them out for me.'

'That's one too many – every year since we were married. We didn't have one, the one when I'd gone off with Buster.'

'You've made our homogenised family work. You put the broken bits of our marriage back together – the pattern may be different but the pieces are all here.'

He reached into his pocket and pulled out a small plastic bag, with HMV in black letters. 'I saw this when I was shopping.' He held the oblong box in his hand, turned it so she could read the title. *Great Tunes of the 1930s.*

He pulled at the cellophane wrapping, let it drop to the floor and slotted the cassette into the cassette player on the radio, silencing the choirboys with one flick of the switch.

The dated notes tinkled, nostalgic and rhythmic.

'Let's dance, Kitty.'

The old dog, suddenly excited, tried to jump up at them.

She hummed the notes. After a moment, the words came back to her. *We can face the music together, dancing in the dark.*

They twirled away, out of the kitchen and into the frosted garden.

ACKNOWLEDGEMENTS

I am deeply indebted to the Romantic Novelists Association New Writers Scheme and the Society of Authors for so much invaluable advice.

The whole publication process has been made wonderfully easy by the team at Prepare to Publish. My especial thanks to Mary Chesshyre for her sensitive use of the editing pen.

My belated thanks to David and the many other kind people in Suffolk who helped as I researched the background to this story.

My 'writers group' met every Thursday morning in the gardens at Mottistone Manor. I thank co-volunteer Carol for her critical interest in this book; and to the double border for allowing us to muse as we hoed.

My love and thanks to Dudley, and Owen, James and Thomas who have been wonderfully supportive and have kept me going – once again.

ABOUT THE AUTHOR

Barbara, a country woman at heart, lives on the western edge of the Isle of Wight with Dudley, her husband. They share their home and garden with Nellie, a large black Labrador, but the place really belongs to Tigger, the cat. Their three sons are based in London.

After living and working in Winchester for more than twenty-five years Dudley and Barbara retired to the Island. Here she rambles the stunning landscape, gardens and writes – her window looks out over half a mile of countryside to the English Channel and the Needles.

Barbara's book, Twyford Down, Roads, Campaigning and Environmental Law, *her account of their campaign to preserve Winchester's ancient landscape backcloth, published by E&FN Spon in 1996, is available on Amazon.*